Enter Jeeves
15 Early Stories

P. G. WODEHOUSE

EDITED BY

DAVID A. JASEN

DOVER PUBLICATIONS, INC.
Mineola, New York

Bibliographical Note

This Dover edition, first published in 1997, is a new compilation of stories by P. G. Wodehouse. The sources of the texts are as follows: "Extricating Young Gussie" from *The Saturday Evening Post*, 1915; "Leave It to Jeeves," "The Aunt and the Sluggard," "Jeeves Takes Charge," "Jeeves and the Unbidden Guest" from *The Saturday Evening Post*, 1916; "Jeeves and the Hard-boiled Egg" from *The Saturday Evening Post*, 1917; "Jeeves and the Chump Cyril" from *The Saturday Evening Post*, 1918; "Jeeves in the Springtime" from *Cosmopolitan*, 1921; "Absent Treatment" from *Collier's Weekly*, 1911; "Lines and Business" from *Pictorial Review*, 1912; "Disentangling Old Duggie" from *Collier's Weekly*, 1912; "Brother Alfred" from *Collier's Weekly*, 1913; "Rallying Round Clarence" from *Pictorial Review*, 1914; "Concealed Art" from *The Strand*, 1915; "The Test Case" from *Illustrated Sunday Magazine*, 1915.

Library of Congress Cataloging-in-Publication Data

Wodehouse, P. G. (Pelham Grenville), 1881–1975.
Enter Jeeves : 15 early stories / P. G. Wodehouse ; edited by David A. Jasen.
p. cm.
ISBN 0-486-29717-9 (pbk.)
1. Jeeves (Fictitious character)—Fiction. 2. Humorous stories, English. 3. Butlers—England—Fiction. I. Jasen, David A. II. Title.
PR6045.053A6 1997
823′.912—dc21 97-1768
CIP

Manufactured in the United States of America
Dover Publications, Inc., 31 East 2nd Street, Mineola, N.Y. 11501

Contents

Introduction

THIS is the first time that the first eight Jeeves short stories have been published together with the complete Reggie Pepper series. P. G. Wodehouse had realized the need to create a series character to establish a following among the magazine-reading public. His first (he was eventually to create eight such series) was Reggie Pepper, a charter member of the Drones Club, who became the prototype for Bertram Wilberforce Wooster, his second series character, who was joined by Jeeves, his valet (or, as he put it, his gentleman's personal gentleman).

"Treatment is everything," Wodehouse used to say. During his long writing career, he rewrote two of the Pepper stories for Jeeves and Wooster. The first, "Lines and Business," he rewrote fifteen years later as "Fixing It for Freddie," and the second, forty-six years later, when he turned "Rallying Round Clarence" into "Jeeves Makes an Omelette."

For many years, Wodehouse used the popular general magazine as his major outlet, his stories appearing in the most prestigious of those periodicals—*The Saturday Evening Post* and *Cosmopolitan* in the United States; *The Strand* in England. Most of his writing consisted of short stories and serials, which would then be turned into books—the short stories in collections or disguised as episodic novels, and the serials as novels. When television killed the mass general magazine in the early 1950s, Wodehouse drastically cut down on writing short stories and made his novels shorter by eliminating the serious romance necessary for the magazine-reading public and highlighting the comic situations.

David A. Jasen

Extricating Young Gussie

SHE sprang it on me before breakfast. There in seven words you have a complete character sketch of my Aunt Agatha. I could go on indefinitely about brutality and lack of consideration. I merely say that she routed me out of bed to listen to her painful story somewhere in the small hours. It can't have been half-past eleven when Jeeves, my man, woke me out of the dreamless and broke the news:

"Mrs. Gregson to see you, sir."

I thought she must be walking in her sleep, but I crawled out of bed and got into a dressing-gown. I knew Aunt Agatha well enough to know that, if she had come to see me, she was going to see me. That's the sort of woman she is.

She was sitting bolt upright in a chair, staring into space. When I came in she looked at me in that darn critical way that always makes me feel as if I had gelatine where my spine ought to be. Aunt Agatha is one of those strong-minded women. I should think Queen Elizabeth must have been something like her. She bosses her husband, Spencer Gregson, a battered little chappie on the Stock Exchange. She bosses my cousin, Gussie Mannering-Phipps. She bosses her sister-in-law, Gussie's mother. And, worst of all, she bosses me. She has an eye like a man-eating fish, and she has got moral suasion down to a fine point.

I dare say there are fellows in the world—men of blood and iron, don't you know, and all that sort of thing—whom she couldn't intimidate; but if you're a chappie like me, fond of a quiet life, you simply curl into a ball when you see her coming, and hope for the best. My experience is that when Aunt Agatha wants you to do a thing you do it, or else you find yourself wondering why those fellows in the olden days made such a fuss when they had trouble with the Spanish Inquisition.

"Halloa, Aunt Agatha!" I said.

"Bertie," she said, "you look a sight. You look perfectly dissipated."

I was feeling like a badly wrapped brown-paper parcel. I'm never at my best in the early morning. I said so.

"Early morning! I had breakfast three hours ago, and have been walking in the park ever since, trying to compose my thoughts."

If I ever breakfasted at half-past eight I should walk on the Embankment, trying to end it all in a watery grave.

"I am extremely worried, Bertie. That is why I have come to you."

And then I saw she was going to start something, and I bleated weakly to Jeeves to bring me tea. But she had begun before I could get it.

"What are your immediate plans, Bertie?"

"Well, I rather thought of tottering out for a bite of lunch later on, and then possibly staggering round to the club, and after that, if I felt strong enough, I might trickle off to Walton Heath for a round of golf."

"I am not interested in your totterings and tricklings. I mean, have you any important engagements in the next week or so?"

I scented danger.

"Rather," I said. "Heaps! Millions! Booked solid!"

"What are they?"

"I—er—well, I don't quite know."

"I thought as much. You have no engagements. Very well, then, I want you to start immediately for America."

"America!"

Do not lose sight of the fact that all this was taking place on an empty stomach, shortly after the rising of the lark.

"Yes, America. I suppose even you have heard of America?"

"But why America?"

"Because that is where your Cousin Gussie is. He is in New York, and I can't get at him."

"What's Gussie been doing?"

"Gussie is making a perfect idiot of himself."

To one who knew young Gussie as well as I did, the words opened up a wide field for speculation.

"In what way?"

"He has lost his head over a creature."

On past performances this rang true. Ever since he arrived at man's estate Gussie had been losing his head over creatures. He's that sort of chap. But, as the creatures never seemed to lose their heads over him, it had never amounted to much.

"I imagine you know perfectly well why Gussie went to America, Bertie. You know how wickedly extravagant your Uncle Cuthbert was."

She alluded to Gussie's governor, the late head of the family, and I am bound to say she spoke the truth. Nobody was fonder of old Uncle Cuthbert than I was, but everybody knows that, where money was concerned, he was the most complete chump in the annals of the nation. He had an expensive thirst. He never backed a horse that didn't get housemaid's knee in the middle of the race. He had a system of beating the bank at Monte Carlo which used to make the administration hang out the bunting and ring the joy-bells when he was sighted in the offing. Take him for all in all, dear old Uncle Cuthbert was as willing a spender as ever called the family lawyer a bloodsucking vampire because he wouldn't let Uncle Cuthbert cut down the timber to raise another thousand.

"He left your Aunt Julia very little money for a woman in her position. Beechwood requires a great deal of keeping up, and poor dear Spencer, though he does his best to help, has not unlimited resources. It was clearly understood why Gussie went to America. He is not clever, but he is very good-looking, and, though he has no title, the Mannering-Phippses are one of the best and oldest families in England. He had some excellent letters of introduction, and when he wrote home to say that he had met the most charming and beautiful girl in the world I felt quite happy. He continued to rave about her for several mails, and then this morning a letter has come from him in which he says, quite casually as a sort of afterthought, that he knows we are broadminded enough not to think any the worse of her because she is on the vaudeville stage."

"Oh, I say!"

"It was like a thunderbolt. The girl's name, it seems, is Ray Denison, and according to Gussie she does something which he describes as a single on the big time. What this degraded performance may be I have not the least notion. As a further recommendation he states that she lifted them out of their seats at Mosenstein's last week. Who she may be, and how or why, and who or what Mr. Mosenstein may be, I cannot tell you."

"By Jove," I said, "it's like a sort of thingummy-bob, isn't it? A sort of fate, what?"

"I fail to understand you."

"Well, Aunt Julia, you know, don't you know? Heredity, and so forth. What's bred in the bone will come out in the wash, and all that kind of thing, you know."

"Don't be absurd, Bertie."

That was all very well, but it was a coincidence for all that. Nobody ever mentions it, and the family have been trying to forget it for twenty-five years, but it's a known fact that my Aunt Julia, Gussie's mother, was a vaudeville artist once, and a very good one, too, I'm told. She was playing in pantomime at Drury Lane when Uncle Cuthbert saw her first. It was before my time, of course, and long before I was old enough to take notice the family had made the best of it, and Aunt Agatha had pulled up her socks and put in a lot of educative work, and with a microscope you couldn't tell Aunt Julia from a genuine dyed-in-the-wool aristocrat. Women adapt themselves so quickly!

I have a pal who married Daisy Trimble of the Gaiety, and when I meet her now I feel like walking out of her presence backwards. But there the thing was, and you couldn't get away from it. Gussie had vaudeville blood in him, and it looked as if he were reverting to type, or whatever they call it.

"By Jove," I said, for I am interested in this heredity stuff, "perhaps the thing is going to be a regular family tradition, like you read about in books—a sort of Curse of the Mannering-Phippses, as it were. Perhaps each head of the family's going to marry into vaudeville for ever and ever. Unto the what-d'you-call-it generation, don't you know?"

"Please do not be quite idiotic, Bertie. There is one head of the family who is certainly not going to do it, and that is Gussie. And you are going to America to stop him."

"Yes, but why me?"

"Why you? You are too vexing, Bertie. Have you no sort of feeling for the family? You are too lazy to try to be a credit to yourself, but at least you can exert yourself to prevent Gussie's disgracing us. You are going to America because you are Gussie's cousin, because you have always been his closest friend, because you are the only one of the family who has absolutely nothing to occupy his time except golf and night clubs."

"I play a lot of auction."

"And, as you say, idiotic gambling in low dens. If you require another reason, you are going because I ask you as a personal favour."

What she meant was that, if I refused, she would exert the full bent of her natural genius to make life a Hades for me. She held me with her glittering eye. I have never met anyone who can give a better imitation of the Ancient Mariner.

"So you will start at once, won't you, Bertie?"

I didn't hesitate.

"Rather!" I said. "Of course I will."

Jeeves came in with the tea.

"Jeeves," I said, "we start for America on Saturday."

"Very good, sir," he said; "which suit will you wear?"

New York is a large city conveniently situated on the edge of America, so that you step off the liner right on to it without an effort. You can't lose your way. You go out of a barn and down some stairs, and there you are, right in among it. The only possible objection any reasonable chappie could find to the place is that they loose you into it from the boat at such an ungodly hour.

I left Jeeves to get my baggage safely past an aggregation of suspicious-minded pirates who were digging for buried treasures among my new shirts, and drove to Gussie's hotel, where I requested the squad of gentlemanly clerks behind the desk to produce him.

That's where I got my first shock. He wasn't there. I pleaded with them to think again, and they thought again, but it was no good. No Augustus Mannering-Phipps on the premises.

I admit I was hard hit. There I was alone in a strange city and no signs of Gussie. What was the next step? I am never one of the master minds in the early morning; the old bean doesn't somehow seem to get into its stride till pretty late in the p.m.'s, and I couldn't think what to do. However, some instinct took me through a door at the back of the lobby, and I found myself in a large room with an enormous picture stretching across the whole of one wall, and under the picture a counter, and behind the counter divers chappies in white, serving drinks. They have barmen, don't you know, in New York, not barmaids. Rum idea!

I put myself unreservedly into the hands of one of the white chappies. He was a friendly soul, and I told him the whole state of affairs. I asked him what he thought would meet the case.

He said that in a situation of that sort he usually prescribed a "lightning whizzer," an invention of his own. He said this was what rabbits trained on when they were matched against grizzly bears, and there was only one instance on record of the bear having lasted three rounds. So I tried a couple, and, by Jove! the man was perfectly right. As I drained the second a great load seemed to fall from my heart, and I went out in quite a braced way to have a look at the city.

I was surprised to find the streets quite full. People were bustling along as if it were some reasonable hour and not the grey dawn. In the tramcars they were absolutely standing on each other's necks. Going to business or something, I take it. Wonderful johnnies!

The odd part of it was that after the first shock of seeing all this frightful energy the thing didn't seem so strange. I've spoken to fellows since who have been to New York, and they tell me they found it just the same. Apparently there's something in the air, either the ozone or the phosphates or something, which makes you sit up and take notice. A kind of zip, as it were. A sort of bally freedom, if you know what I mean, that gets into your blood and bucks you up, and makes you feel that

God's in His Heaven:
All's right with the world,

and you don't care if you've got odd socks on. I can't express it better than by saying that the thought uppermost in my mind, as I walked about the place they call Times Square, was that there were three thousand miles of deep water between me and my Aunt Agatha.

It's a funny thing about looking for things. If you hunt for a needle in a haystack you don't find it. If you don't give a darn whether you ever see the needle or not it runs into you the first time you lean against the stack. By the time I had strolled up and down once or twice, seeing the sights and letting the white chappie's corrective permeate my system, I was feeling that I wouldn't care if Gussie and I never met again, and I'm dashed if I didn't suddenly catch sight of the old lad, as large as life, just turning in at a doorway down the street.

I called after him, but he didn't hear me, so I legged it in pursuit and caught him going into an office on the first floor. The name on the door was Abe Riesbitter, Vaudeville Agent, and from the other side of the door came the sound of many voices.

He turned and stared at me.

"Bertie! What on earth are you doing? Where have you sprung from? When did you arrive?"

"Landed this morning. I went round to your hotel, but they said you weren't there. They had never heard of you."

"I've changed my name. I call myself George Wilson."

"Why on earth?"

"Well, you try calling yourself Augustus Mannering-Phipps over here, and see how it strikes you. You feel a perfect ass. I don't know what it is about America, but the broad fact is that it's not a place where you can call yourself Augustus Mannering-Phipps. And there's another reason. I'll tell you later. Bertie, I've fallen in love with the dearest girl in the world."

The poor old nut looked at me in such a deuced cat-like way, standing with his mouth open, waiting to be congratulated, that I simply hadn't the heart to tell him that I knew all about that already, and had come over to the country for the express purpose of laying him a stymie.

So I congratulated him.

"Thanks awfully, old man," he said. "It's a bit premature, but I fancy it's going to be all right. Come along in here, and I'll tell you about it."

"What do you want in this place? It looks a rummy spot?"

"Oh, that's part of the story. I'll tell you the whole thing."

We opened the door marked "Waiting Room." I never saw such a crowded place in my life. The room was packed till the walls bulged.

Gussie explained.

"Pros," he said, "music-hall artistes, you know, waiting to see old Abe Riesbitter. This is September the first, vaudeville's opening day. The early fall," said Gussie, who is a bit of a poet in his way, "is vaudeville's springtime. All over the country, as August wanes, sparkling comediennes burst into bloom, the sap stirs in the veins of tramp cyclists, and last year's contortionists, waking from their summer sleep, tie themselves tentatively into knots. What I mean is, this is the beginning of the new season, and everybody's out hunting for bookings."

"But what do you want here?"

"Oh, I've just got to see Abe about something. If you see a fat man with about fifty-seven chins come out of that door there grab him, for that'll be Abe. He's one of those fellows who advertise each step up they take in the world by growing another chin. I'm told that way back in the nineties he only had two. If you do grab Abe, remember that he knows me as George Wilson."

"You said that you were going to explain that George Wilson business to me, Gussie, old man."

"Well, it's this way—"

At this juncture dear old Gussie broke off short, rose from his seat, and sprang with indescribable vim at an extraordinarily stout chappie who had suddenly appeared. There was the deuce of a rush for him but Gussie had got away to a good start, and the rest of the singers, dancers, jugglers, acrobats, and refined sketch teams seemed to recognize that he had won the trick, for they ebbed back into their places again, and Gussie and I went into the inner room.

Mr. Riesbitter lit a cigar, and looked at us solemnly over his zareba of chins.

"Now, let me tell ya something," he said to Gussie. "You lizzun t' me."

Gussie registered respectful attention. Mr. Riesbitter mused for a moment and shelled the cuspidor with indirect fire over the edge of the desk.

"Lizzun t' me," he said again. "I seen you rehearse, as I promised Miss Denison I would. You ain't bad for an amateur. You gotta lot to learn, but it's in you. What it comes to is that I can fix you up in the four-a-day, if you'll take thirty-five per. I can't do better than that, and I wouldn't have done that if the little lady hadn't of kep' after me. Take it or leave it. What do you say?"

"I'll take it," said Gussie, huskily. "Thank you."

In the passage outside, Gussie gurgled with joy and slapped me on the back. "Bertie, old man, it's all right. I'm the happiest man in New York."

"Now what?"

"Well, you see, as I was telling you when Abe came in, Ray's father used to be in the profession. He was before our time, but I remember hearing about him—Joe Danby. He used to be well known in London before he came over to America. Well, he's a fine old boy, but as obstinate as a mule, and he didn't like the idea of Ray marrying me because I wasn't in the profession. Wouldn't hear of it. Well, you remember at Oxford I could always sing a song pretty well; so Ray got hold of old Riesbitter and made him promise to come and hear me rehearse and get me bookings if he liked my work. She stands high with him. She coached me for weeks, the darling. And now, as you heard him say, he's booked me in the small time at thirty-five dollars a week."

I steadied myself against the wall. The effects of the restoratives supplied by my pal at the hotel bar were beginning to work off, and I felt a little weak. Through a sort of mist I seemed to have a vision of Aunt Agatha hearing that the head of the Mannering-Phippses was about to appear on the vaudeville stage. Aunt Agatha's worship of the family name amounts to an obsession. The Mannering-Phippses were an old-established clan when William the Conqueror was a small boy going round with bare legs and a catapult. For centuries they have called kings by their first names and helped dukes with their weekly rent; and there's practically nothing a Mannering-Phipps can do that doesn't blot his escutcheon. So what Aunt Agatha would say—beyond saying that it was all my fault—when she learned the horrid news, it was beyond me to imagine.

"Come back to the hotel, Gussie," I said. "There's a sportsman there who mixes things he calls 'lightning whizzers.' Something tells me I need one now. And excuse me for one minute, Gussie. I want to send a cable."

It was clear to me by now that Aunt Agatha had picked the wrong man for this job of disentangling Gussie from the clutches of the American vaudeville profession. What I needed was reinforcements. For a moment I thought of cabling Aunt Agatha to come over, but reason told me that this would be overdoing it. I wanted assistance, but not so badly as that. I hit what seemed to me the happy mean. I cabled to Gussie's mother and made it urgent.

"What were you cabling about?" asked Gussie, later.

"Oh, just to say I had arrived safely, and all that sort of tosh," I answered.

Gussie opened his vaudeville career on the following Monday at a rummy sort of place uptown where they had moving pictures some of the time and, in between, one or two vaudeville acts. It had taken a lot of careful handling to bring him up to scratch. He seemed to take my sympathy and assistance for granted, and I couldn't let him down. My only hope, which grew as I listened to him rehearsing, was that he would be such a frightful frost at his first appearance that he would never dare to perform again; and, as that would automatically squash the marriage, it seemed best to me to let the thing go on.

He wasn't taking any chances. On the Saturday and Sunday we practically lived in a beastly little music-room at the offices of the publishers whose songs he proposed to use. A little chappie with a hooked nose sucked a cigarette and played the piano all day. Nothing could tire that lad. He seemed to take a personal interest in the thing.

Gussie would clear his throat and begin:

"There's a great big choo-choo waiting at the deepo."

THE CHAPPIE (playing chords): "Is that so? What's it waiting for?"

GUSSIE (rather rattled at the interruption): "Waiting for me."

THE CHAPPIE (surprised): "For you?"

GUSSIE (sticking to it): "Waiting for me-e-ee!"

THE CHAPPIE (sceptically): "You don't say!"

GUSSIE: "For I'm off to Tennessee."

THE CHAPPIE (*conceding a point*): "Now, I live at Yonkers."

He did this all through the song. At first poor old Gussie asked him to stop, but the chappie said, No, it was always done. It helped to get pep into the thing. He appealed to me whether the thing didn't want a bit of pep, and I said it wanted all the pep it could get. And the chappie said to Gussie, "There you are!" So Gussie had to stand it.

The other song that he intended to sing was one of those moon songs. He told me in a hushed voice that he was using it because it was one of the songs that the girl Ray sang when lifting them out of their seats at Mosenstein's and elsewhere. The fact seemed to give it sacred associations for him.

You will scarcely believe me, but the management expected Gussie to show up and start performing at one o'clock in the afternoon. I told him they couldn't be serious, as they must know that he would be rolling out for a bit of lunch at that hour, but Gussie said this was the usual thing in the four-a-day, and he didn't suppose he would ever get any lunch again until he landed on the big time. I was just condoling with him, when I found that he was taking it for granted that I should be there at one o'clock, too. My idea had been that I should look in at night, when—if he survived—he would be coming up for the fourth time; but I've never deserted a pal in distress, so I said good-bye to the little lunch I'd been planning at a rather decent tavern I'd discovered on Fifth Avenue, and trailed along. They were showing pictures when I reached my seat. It was one of those Western films, where the cowboy jumps on his horse and rides across country at a hundred and fifty miles an hour to escape the sheriff, not knowing, poor chump! that he might just as well stay where he is, the sheriff having a horse of his own which can do three hundred miles an hour without coughing. I was just going to close my eyes and try to forget till they put Gussie's name up when I discovered that I was sitting next to a deucedly pretty girl.

No, let me be honest. When I went in I had seen that there was a deucedly pretty girl sitting in that particular seat, so I had taken the next one. What happened now was that I began, as it were, to drink her in. I wished they would turn the lights up so that I could see her better. She was rather small, with great big eyes and a ripping smile. It was a shame to let all that run to seed, so to speak, in semi-darkness.

Suddenly the lights did go up, and the orchestra began to play a tune which, though I haven't much of an ear for music, seemed somehow familiar. The next instant out pranced old Gussie from the wings in a purple frock-coat and a brown top-hat, grinned feebly at the audience, tripped over his feet, blushed, and began to sing the Tennessee song.

It was rotten. The poor nut had got stage fright so badly that it practically eliminated his voice. He sounded like some far-off echo of the past "yodeling" through a woollen blanket.

For the first time since I had heard that he was about to go into vaudeville I felt a faint hope creeping over me. I was sorry for the wretched chap, of course, but there was no denying that the thing had its bright side. No management on earth would go on paying thirty-five dollars a week for this sort of performance. This was going to be Gussie's first and only. He would have to leave the profession. The old boy would say, "Unhand my daughter." And, with decent luck, I saw myself leading Gussie on to the next England-bound liner and handing him over intact to Aunt Agatha.

He got through the song somehow and limped off amidst roars of silence from the audience. There was a brief respite, then out he came again.

He sang this time as if nobody loved him. As a song, it was not a very pathetic song, being all about coons spooning in June under the moon, and so on and so forth, but Gussie handled it in such a sad, crushed way that there was genuine anguish in every line. By the time he reached the refrain I was nearly in tears. It seemed such a rotten sort of world with all that kind of thing going on in it.

He started the refrain, and then the most frightful thing happened. The girl next me got up in her seat, chucked her head back, and began to sing too. I say "too," but it wasn't really too, because her first note stopped Gussie dead, as if he had been pole-axed.

I never felt so bally conspicuous in my life. I huddled down in my seat and wished I could turn my collar up. Everybody seemed to be looking at me.

In the midst of my agony I caught sight of Gussie. A complete change had taken place in the old lad. He was looking most frightfully bucked. I must say the girl was singing most awfully well, and it seemed to act on Gussie like a tonic. When she came to the end of the refrain, he took it up, and they sang it together, and the end of it was that he went off the popular hero. The audience yelled for more, and were only quieted when they turned down the lights and put on a film.

When I had recovered I tottered round to see Gussie. I found him sitting on a box behind the stage, looking like one who had seen visions.

"Isn't she a wonder, Bertie?" he said, devoutly. "I hadn't a notion she was going to be there. She's playing at the Auditorium this week, and she can only just have had time to get back to her *matinée*. She risked being late, just to come and see me through. She's my good angel, Bertie. She saved me. If she hadn't helped me out I don't know what would have happened. I was so nervous I didn't know what I was doing. Now that I've got through the first show I shall be all right."

I was glad I had sent that cable to his mother. I was going to need her. The thing had got beyond me.

During the next week I saw a lot of old Gussie, and was introduced to the girl. I also met her father, a formidable old boy with thick eyebrows and a sort of determined expression. On the following Wednesday Aunt Julia arrived. Mrs. Mannering-Phipps, my Aunt Julia, is, I think, the most dignified person I know. She lacks Aunt Agatha's punch, but in a quiet way she has always contrived to make me feel, from boyhood up, that I was a poor worm. Not that she harries me like Aunt Agatha. The difference between the two is that Aunt Agatha conveys the impression that she considers me personally responsible for all the sin and sorrow in the world, while Aunt Julia's manner seemed to suggest that I am more to be pitied then censured.

If it wasn't that the thing was a matter of historical fact, I should be inclined to believe that Aunt Julia had never been on the vaudeville stage. She is like a stage duchess.

She always seems to me to be in a perpetual state of being about to desire the butler to instruct the head footman to serve lunch in the blue room overlooking the west terrace. She exudes dignity. Yet, twenty-five years ago, so I've been told by old boys who were lads about town in those days, she was knocking them cold at the Tivoli in a double act called "Fun in a Tea-Shop," in which she wore tights and sang a song with a chorus that began "Rumpty-tiddley-umpty-ay."

There are some things a chappie's mind absolutely refuses to picture, and Aunt Julia singing "Rumpty-tiddley-umpty-ay" is one of them.

She got straight to the point within five minutes of our meeting.

"What is this about Gussie? Why did you cable for me, Bertie?"

"It's rather a long story," I said, "and complicated. If you don't mind, I'll let you have it in a series of motion pictures. Suppose we look in at the Auditorium for a few minutes."

The girl, Ray, had been re-engaged for a second week at the Auditorium, owing to the big success of her first week. Her act consisted of three songs. She did herself well in the matter of costume and scenery.

She had a ripping voice. She looked most awfully pretty; and altogether the act was, broadly speaking, a pippin.

Aunt Julia didn't speak till we were in our seats. Then she gave a sort of sigh.

"It's twenty-five years since I was in a music-hall!"

She didn't say any more, but sat there with her eyes glued on the stage.

After about half an hour the Johnnies who work the card-index system at the side of the stage put up the name of Ray Denison, and there was a good deal of applause.

"Watch this act, Aunt Julia," I said.

She didn't seem to hear me.

"Twenty-five years! What did you say, Bertie?"

"Watch this act and tell me what you think of it."

"Who is it? Ray. Oh!"

"Exhibit A," I said. "The girl Gussie's engaged to."

The girl did her act, and the house rose at her. They didn't want to let her go. She had to come back again and again. When she had finally disappeared I turned to Aunt Julia.

"Well?" I said.

"I like her work. She's an artist."

"We will now, if you don't mind, step a goodish way uptown."

And we took the subway to where Gussie, the human film, was earning his thirty-five per. As luck would have it, we hadn't been in the place ten minutes when out he came.

"Exhibit B," I said. "Gussie."

I don't quite know what I had expected her to do, but I certainly didn't expect her to sit there without a word. She did not move a muscle, but just stared at Gussie as he drooled on about the moon. I was sorry for the woman, for it must have been a shock to her to see her only son in a mauve frock-coat and a brown top-hat, but I thought it best to let her get a strangle-hold on the intricacies of the situation as quickly as possible. If I had tried to explain the affair without the aid of illustrations I should have talked all day and left her muddled up as to who was going to marry whom, and why.

I was astonished at the improvement in dear old Gussie. He had got back his voice and was putting the stuff over well. It reminded me of the night at Oxford when, then but a lad of eighteen, he sang "Let's All Go Down the Strand" after a bump supper, standing the while up to his knees in the college fountain. He was putting just the same zip into the thing now.

When he had gone off Aunt Julia sat perfectly still for a long time, and then she turned to me. Her eyes shone queerly.

"What does this mean, Bertie?"

She spoke quite quietly, but her voice shook a bit.

"Gussie went into the business," I said, "because the girl's father wouldn't let him marry her unless he did. If you feel up to it perhaps you wouldn't mind tottering round to One Hundred and Thirty-third Street and having a chat with him. He's an old boy with eyebrows, and he's Exhibit C on my list. When I've put you in touch with him I rather fancy my share of the business is concluded, and it's up to you."

The Danbys lived in one of those big apartments uptown which look as if they cost the earth and really cost about half as much as a hall room down in the forties. We were shown into the sitting room, and presently old Danby came in.

"Good afternoon, Mr. Danby," I began.

I had got as far as that when there was a kind of gasping cry at my elbow.

"Joe!" cried Aunt Julia, and staggered against the sofa.

For a moment old Danby stared at her, and then his mouth fell open and his eyebrows shot up like rockets.

"Julie!"

And then they had got hold of each other's hands and were shaking them till I wondered their arms didn't come unscrewed.

I'm not equal to this sort of thing at such short notice. The change in Aunt Julia made me feel quite dizzy. She had shed her *grande-dame* manner completely, and was blushing and smiling. I don't like to say such things of any aunt of mine, or I would go further and put it on record that she was giggling. And old Danby, who usually looked like a cross between a Roman emperor and Napoleon Bonaparte in a bad temper, was behaving like a small boy.

"Joe!"

"Julie!"

"Dear old Joe! Fancy meeting you again!"

"Wherever have you come from, Julie?"

Well, I didn't know what it was all about, but I felt a bit out of it. I butted in:

"Aunt Julia wants to have a talk with you, Mr. Danby."

"I knew you in a second, Joe!"

"It's twenty-five years since I saw you, kid, and you don't look a day older."

"Oh, Joe! I'm an old woman!"

"What are you doing over here? I suppose"—old Danby's cheerfulness waned a trifle—"I suppose your husband is with you?"

"My husband died a long, long while ago, Joe."

Old Danby shook his head.

"You never ought to have married out of the profession, Julie. I'm not saying a word against the late—I can't remember his name; never could—but you shouldn't have done it, an artist like you. Shall I ever forget the way you used to knock them with 'Rumpty-tiddley-umpty-ay'?"

"Ah! how wonderful you were in that act, Joe." Aunt Julia sighed. "Do you remember the back-fall you used to do down the steps? I always have said that you did the best back-fall in the profession."

"I couldn't do it now!"

"Do you remember how we put it across at the Canterbury, Joe? Think of it! The Canterbury's a moving-picture house now, and the old Mogul runs French revues."

"I'm glad I'm not there to see them."

"Joe, tell me, why did you leave England?"

"Well, I—I wanted a change. No, I'll tell you the truth, kid. I wanted you, Julie. You went off and married that—whatever that stage-door Johnny's name was—and it broke me all up."

Aunt Julia was staring at him. She is what they call a well-preserved woman. It's easy to see that, twenty-five years ago, she must have been something quite extraordinary to look at. Even now she's almost beautiful. She has very large brown eyes, a mass of soft grey hair, and the complexion of a girl of seventeen.

"Joe, you aren't going to tell me you were fond of me yourself!"

"Of course I was fond of you. Why did I let you have all the fat in 'Fun in a Tea-Shop'? Why did I hang about up-stage while you sang 'Rumpty-tiddley-umpty-ay'? Do you remember my giving you a bag of buns when we were on the road at Bristol?"

"Yes, but——"

"Do you remember my giving you the ham sandwiches at Portsmouth?"

"Joe!"

"Do you remember my giving you a seed-cake at Birmingham? What did you think all that meant, if not that I loved you? Why, I was working up by degrees to telling you straight out when you suddenly went off and married that cane-sucking dude. That's why I wouldn't let my daughter marry this young chap, Wilson, unless he went into the profession. She's an artist——"

"She certainly is, Joe."

"You've seen her? Where?"

"At the Auditorium just now. But, Joe, you mustn't stand in the way of her marrying the man she's in love with. He's an artist, too."

"In the small time."

"You were in the small time once, Joe. You mustn't look down on him because he's a beginner. I know you feel that your daughter is marrying beneath her, but——"

"How on earth do you know anything about young Wilson?"

"He's my son."

"Your son?"

"Yes, Joe. And I've just been watching him work. Oh, Joe, you can't think how proud I was of him! He's got it in him. It's fate. He's my son and he's in the profession! Joe, you don't know what I've been through for his sake. They made a lady of me. I never worked so hard in my life as I did to become a real lady. They kept telling me I had got to put it across, no matter what it cost, so that he wouldn't be ashamed of me. The study was something terrible. I had to watch myself every minute for years, and I never knew when I might fluff in my lines or fall down on some bit of business. But I did it, because I didn't want him to be ashamed of me, though all the time I was just aching to be back where I belonged."

Old Danby made a jump at her, and took her by the shoulders.

"Come back where you belong, Julie!" he cried. "Your husband's dead, your son's a pro. Come back! It's twenty-five years ago, but I haven't changed. I want you still. I've always wanted you. You've got to come back, kid, where you belong."

Aunt Julia gave a sort of gulp and looked at him.

"Joe!" she said in a kind of whisper.

"You're here, kid," said Old Danby, huskily. "You've come back. . . . Twenty-five years! . . . You've come back and you're going to stay!"

She pitched forward into his arms, and he caught her.

"Oh, Joe! Joe! Joe!" she said. "Hold me. Don't let me go. Take care of me."

And I edged for the door and slipped from the room. I felt weak. The old bean will stand a certain amount, but this was too much. I groped my way out into the street and wailed for a taxi.

Gussie called on me at the hotel that night. He curveted into the room as if he had bought it and the rest of the city.

"Bertie," he said, "I feel as if I were dreaming."

"I wish I could feel like that, old top," I said, and I took another glance at a cable that had arrived half an hour ago from Aunt Agatha. I had been looking at it at intervals ever since.

"Ray and I got back to her flat this evening. Who do you think was there? The mater! She was sitting hand in hand with old Danby."

"Yes?"

"He was sitting hand in hand with her."

"Really?"

"They are going to be married."

"Exactly."

"Ray and I are going to be married."

"I suppose so."

"Bertie, old man, I feel immense. I look round me, and everything seems to be absolutely corking. The change in the mater is marvellous. She is twenty-five years younger. She and old Danby are talking of reviving 'Fun in a Tea-Shop,' and going out on the road with it."

I got up.

"Gussie, old top," I said, "leave me for awhile. I would be alone. I think I've got brain fever or something."

"Sorry, old man; perhaps New York doesn't agree with you. When do you expect to go back to England?"

I looked again at Aunt Agatha's cable.

"With luck," I said, "in about ten years."

When he was gone I took up the cable and read it again.

"What is happening?" it read. "Shall I come over?"

I sucked a pencil for a while, and then I wrote the reply.

It was not an easy cable to word, but I managed it.

"No," I wrote, "stay where you are. Profession overcrowded."

Leave It to Jeeves

JEEVES — my man, you know — is really a most extraordinary chap. So capable. Honestly, I shouldn't know what to do without him. On broader lines he's like those chappies who sit peering sadly over the marble battlements at the Pennsylvania Station in the place marked "Inquiries." You know the Johnnies I mean. You go up to them and say: "When's the next train for Melonsquashville, Tennessee?" and they reply, without stopping to think, "Two-forty-three, track ten, change at San Francisco." And they're right every time. Well, Jeeves gives you just the same impression of omniscience.

As an instance of what I mean, I remember meeting Monty Byng in Bond Street one morning, looking the last word in a grey check suit, and I felt I should never be happy till I had one like it. I dug the address of the tailors out of him, and had them working on the thing inside the hour.

"Jeeves," I said that evening, "I'm getting a check suit like that one of Mr. Byng's."

"Injudicious, sir," he said, firmly. "It will not become you."

"What absolute rot! It's the soundest thing I've struck for years."

"Unsuitable for you, sir."

Well, the long and the short of it was that the confounded thing came home, and I put it on, and when I caught sight of myself in the glass I nearly swooned. Jeeves was perfectly right. I looked a cross between a music-hall comedian and a cheap bookie. Yet Monty had looked fine in absolutely the same stuff. These things are just Life's mysteries, and that's all there is to it.

But it isn't only that Jeeves's judgment about clothes is infallible, though, of course, that's really the main thing. The man knows everything. There was the matter of that tip on the "Lincolnshire." I forget now how I got it, but it had the aspect of being the real, red-hot tabasco.

"Jeeves," I said, for I'm fond of the man, and like to do him a good turn when I can, "if you want to make a bit of money, have something on Wonderchild for the Lincolnshire."

He shook his head.

"I'd rather not, sir."

"But it's the straight goods. I'm going to put my shirt on him."

"I do not recommend it, sir. The animal is not intended to win. Second place is what the stable is after."

Perfect piffle, I thought, of course. How the deuce could Jeeves know anything about it? Still, you know what happened. Wonderchild led till he was breathing on the wire, and then Banana Fritter came along and nosed him out. I went straight home and rang for Jeeves.

"After this," I said, "not another step for me without your advice. From now on consider yourself the brains of the establishment."

"Very good, sir. I shall endeavour to give satisfaction."

And he has, by Jove! I'm a bit short on brain myself: the old bean would appear to have been constructed more for ornament than for use, don't you know; but give me five minutes to talk the thing over with Jeeves, and I'm game to advise any one about anything. And that's why, when Bruce Corcoran came to me with his troubles, my first act was to ring the bell and put it up to the lad with the bulging forehead.

"Leave it to Jeeves," I said.

I first got to know Corky when I came to New York. He was a pal of my cousin Gussie, who was in with a lot of people down Washington Square way. I don't know if I ever told you about it, but the reason I left England was because I was sent over by my Aunt Agatha to try to stop young Gussie marrying a girl on the vaudeville stage, and I got the whole thing so mixed up that I decided that it would be a sound scheme for me to stop on in America for a bit instead of going back and having long cosy chats about the thing with aunt. So I sent Jeeves out to find a decent apartment, and settled down for a bit of exile. I'm bound to say that New York's a topping place to be exiled in. Everybody was awfully good to me, and there seemed to be plenty of things going on, and I'm a wealthy bird, so everything was fine. Chappies introduced me to other chappies, and so on and so forth, and it wasn't long before I knew squads of the right sort, some who rolled in dollars in houses up by the Park, and others who lived with the gas turned down mostly around Washington Square—artists and writers and so forth. Brainy coves.

Corky was one of the artists. A portrait-painter, he called himself, but he hadn't painted any portraits. He was sitting on the side-lines with a blanket over his shoulders, waiting for a chance to get into the game. You see, the catch about portrait-painting—I've looked into the thing a bit—is that you can't start painting portraits till people come along and ask you to, and they won't come and ask you to until you've painted a lot first. This makes it kind of difficult for a chappie. Corky managed to get along by drawing an occasional picture for the comic papers—he had rather a gift for funny stuff when he got a good idea—and doing bedsteads and chairs and things for the advertisements. His principal source of income, however, was derived from biting the ear of a rich uncle—one Alexander Worple, who was in the jute business. I'm a bit foggy as to what jute is, but it's apparently something the populace is pretty keen on, for Mr. Worple had made quite an indecently large stack out of it.

Now, a great many fellows think that having a rich uncle is a pretty soft snap; but, according to Corky, such is not the case. Corky's uncle was a robust sort of cove, who looked like living for ever. He was fifty-one, and it seemed as if he might go to par. It was not this, however, that distressed poor old Corky, for he was not bigoted and had no objection to the man going on living. What Corky kicked at was the way the above Worple used to harry him.

Corky's uncle, you see, didn't want him to be an artist. He didn't think he had any talent in that direction. He was always urging him to chuck Art and go into the jute business and start at the bottom and work his way up. Jute had apparently become a sort of obsession with him. He seemed to attach almost a spiritual importance to it. And what Corky said was that, while he didn't know what they did at the bottom of a jute business, instinct told him that it was something too beastly for words. Corky, moreover, believed in his future as an artist. Some day, he said, he was going to make a hit. Meanwhile, by using the utmost tact and persuasiveness, he was inducing his uncle to cough up very grudgingly a small quarterly allowance.

He wouldn't have got this if his uncle hadn't had a hobby. Mr. Worple was peculiar in this respect. As a rule, from what I've observed, the American captain of industry doesn't do anything out of business hours. When he has put the cat out and locked up the office for the night, he just relapses into a state of coma from which he emerges only to start being a captain of industry again. But Mr. Worple in his spare time was what is known as an ornithologist. He had written a book called *American Birds*, and was writing another, to be called *More American Birds*. When he had finished that, the presumption was that he would begin a third, and keep on till the supply of American birds gave out. Corky used to go to him about once every three months and let him talk about American birds. Apparently you could do what you liked with old

Worple if you gave him his head first on his pet subject, so these little chats used to make Corky's allowance all right for the time being. But it was pretty rotten for the poor chap. There was the frightful suspense, you see, and, apart from that, birds, except when broiled and in the society of a cold bottle, bored him stiff.

To complete the character-study of Mr. Worple, he was a man of extremely uncertain temper, and his general tendency was to think that Corky was a poor chump and that whatever step he took in any direction on his own account was just another proof of his innate idiocy. I should imagine Jeeves feels very much the same about me.

So when Corky trickled into my apartment one afternoon, shooing a girl in front of him, and said, "Bertie, I want you to meet my *fiancée*, Miss Singer," the aspect of the matter which hit me first was precisely the one which he had come to consult me about. The very first words I spoke were, "Corky, how about your uncle?"

The poor chap gave one of those mirthless laughs. He was looking anxious and worried, like a man who has done the murder all right but can't think what the deuce to do with the body.

"We're so scared, Mr. Wooster," said the girl. "We were hoping that you might suggest a way of breaking it to him."

Muriel Singer was one of those very quiet, appealing girls who have a way of looking at you with their big eyes as if they thought you were the greatest thing on earth and wondered that you hadn't got on to it yet yourself. She sat there in a sort of shrinking way, looking at me as if she were saying to herself, "Oh, I do hope this great strong man isn't going to hurt me." She gave a fellow a protective kind of feeling, made him want to stroke her hand and say, "There, there, little one!" or words to that effect. She made me feel that there was nothing I wouldn't do for her. She was rather like one of those innocent-tasting American drinks which creep imperceptibly into your system so that, before you know what you're doing, you're starting out to reform the world by force if necessary and pausing on your way to tell the large man in the corner that, if he looks at you like that, you will knock his head off. What I mean is, she made me feel alert and dashing, like a jolly old knight-errant or something of that kind. I felt that I was with her in this thing to the limit.

"I don't see why your uncle shouldn't be most awfully bucked," I said to Corky. "He will think Miss Singer the ideal wife for you."

Corky declined to cheer up.

"You don't know him. Even if he did like Muriel, he wouldn't admit it. That's the sort of pig-headed guy he is. It would be a matter of principle with him to kick. All he would consider would be that I had gone and taken an important step without asking his advice, and he would raise Cain automatically. He's always done it."

I strained the old bean to meet this emergency.

"You want to work it so that he makes Miss Singer's acquaintance without knowing that you know her. Then you come along——"

"But how can I work it that way?"

I saw his point. That was the catch.

"There's only one thing to do," I said.

"What's that?"

"Leave it to Jeeves."

And I rang the bell.

"Sir?" said Jeeves, kind of manifesting himself. One of the rummy things about Jeeves is that, unless you watch like a hawk, you very seldom see him come into a room. He's like one of those weird chappies in India who dissolve themselves into thin air and nip through space in a sort of disembodied way and assemble the parts again just where they want them. I've got a cousin who's what they call a Theosophist, and he says he's often nearly worked the thing himself, but couldn't quite bring it off, probably owing to having fed in his boyhood on the flesh of animals slain in anger and pie.

The moment I saw the man standing there, registering respectful attention, a weight seemed to roll off my mind. I felt like a lost child who spots his father in the offing. There was something about him that gave me absolute confidence.

Jeeves is a tallish man, with one of those dark, shrewd faces. His eye gleams with the light of pure intelligence.

"Jeeves, we want your advice."

"Very good, sir."

I boiled down Corky's painful case into a few well-chosen words.

"So you see what it amounts to, Jeeves. We want you to suggest some way by which Mr. Worple can make Miss Singer's acquaintance without getting on to the fact that Mr. Corcoran already knows her. Understand?"

"Perfectly, sir."

"Well, try to think of something."

"I have thought of something already, sir."

"You have!"

"The scheme I would suggest cannot fail of success, but it has what may seem to you a drawback, sir, in that it requires a certain financial outlay."

"He means," I translated to Corky, "that he has got a pippin of an idea, but it's going to cost a bit."

Naturally the poor chap's face dropped, for this seemed to dish the whole thing. But I was still under the influence of the girl's melting gaze, and I saw that this was where I started in as the knight-errant.

"You can count on me for all that sort of thing, Corky," I said. "Only too glad. Carry on, Jeeves."

"I would suggest, sir, that Mr. Corcoran take advantage of Mr. Worple's attachment to ornithology."

"How on earth did you know that he was fond of birds?"

"It is the way these New York apartments are constructed, sir. Quite unlike our London houses. The partitions between the rooms are of the flimsiest nature. With no wish to overhear, I have sometimes heard Mr. Corcoran expressing himself with a generous strength on the subject I have mentioned."

"Oh! Well?"

"Why should not the young lady write a small volume, to be entitled—let us say—*The Children's Book of American Birds*, and dedicate it to Mr. Worple? A limited edition could be published at your expense, sir, and a great deal of the book would, of course, be given over to eulogistic remarks concerning Mr. Worple's own larger treatise on the same subject. I should recommend the dispatching of a presentation copy to Mr. Worple, immediately on publication, accompanied by a letter in which the young lady asks to be allowed to make the acquaintance of one to whom she owes so much. This would, I fancy, produce the desired result, but as I say, the expense involved would be considerable."

I felt like the proprietor of a performing dog on the vaudeville stage when the tyke has just pulled off his trick without a hitch. I had betted on Jeeves all along, and I had known that he wouldn't let me down. It beats me sometimes why a man with his genius is satisfied to hang around pressing my clothes and what not. If I had half Jeeves's brain, I should have a stab at being Prime Minister or something.

"Jeeves," I said, "that is absolutely ripping! One of your very best efforts."

"Thank you, sir."

The girl made an objection.

"But I'm sure I couldn't write a book about anything. I can't even write good letters."

"Muriel's talents," said Corky, with a little cough, "lie more in the direction of the drama, Bertie. I didn't mention it before, but one of our reasons for being a trifle nervous as to how Uncle Alexander will receive the news is that Muriel is in the chorus of that show 'Choose your Exit' at the Manhattan. It's absurdly unreasonable, but we both feel that that fact might increase Uncle Alexander's natural tendency to kick like a steer."

I saw what he meant. Goodness knows there was fuss enough in our family when I tried to marry into musical comedy a few years ago. And the recollection of my Aunt Agatha's attitude in the matter of Gussie and the vaudeville girl was still fresh in my mind. I don't know why it is—one of these psychology sharps could explain it, I suppose—but uncles and aunts, as a class, are always dead against the drama, legitimate or otherwise. They don't seem able to stick it at any price.

But Jeeves had a solution, of course.

"I fancy it would be a simple matter, sir, to find some impecunious author who would be glad to do the actual composition of the volume for a small fee. It is only necessary that the young lady's name should appear on the title page."

"That's true," said Corky. "Sam Patterson would do it for a hundred dollars. He writes a novelette, three short stories, and ten thousand words of a serial for one of the all-fiction magazines under different names every month. A little thing like this would be nothing to him. I'll get after him right away."

"Fine!"

"Will that be all, sir?" said Jeeves. "Very good, sir. Thank you, sir."

I always used to think that publishers had to be devilish intelligent fellows, loaded down with the grey matter; but I've got their number now. All a publisher has to do is to write cheques at intervals, while a lot of deserving and industrious chappies rally round and do the real work. I know, because I've been one myself. I simply sat tight in the old apartment with a fountain-pen, and in due season a topping, shiny book came along.

I happened to be down at Corky's place when the first copies of *The Children's Book of American Birds* bobbed up. Muriel Singer was there, and we were talking of things in general when there was a bang at the door and the parcel was delivered.

It was certainly some book. It had a red cover with a fowl of some species on it, and underneath the girl's name in gold letters. I opened a copy at random.

"Often of a spring morning," it said at the top of page twenty-one, "as you wander through the fields, you will hear the sweet-toned, carelessly-flowing warble of the purple finch linnet. When you are older you must read all about him in Mr. Alexander Worple's wonderful book, *American Birds*."

You see. A boost for the uncle right away. And only a few pages later there he was in the limelight again in connexion with the yellow-billed cuckoo. It was great stuff. The more I read, the more I admired the chap who had written it and Jeeves's genius in putting us on to the wheeze. I didn't see how the uncle could fail to drop. You can't call a chap the world's greatest authority on the yellow-billed cuckoo without rousing a certain disposition towards chumminess in him.

"It's a cert!" I said.

"An absolute cinch!" said Corky.

And a day or two later he meandered up the Avenue to my apartment to tell me that all was well. The uncle had written Muriel a letter so dripping with the milk of human kindness that if he hadn't known Mr. Worple's handwriting Corky would have refused to believe him the author of it. Any time it suited Miss Singer to call, said the uncle, he would be delighted to make her acquaintance.

Shortly after this I had to go out of town. Divers sound sportsmen had invited me to pay visits to their country places, and it wasn't for several months that I settled down in the city again. I had been wondering a lot, of course, about Corky, whether it all turned out right, and so forth, and my first evening in New York, happening to pop into a quiet sort of little restaurant which I go to when I don't feel inclined for the bright lights, I found Muriel Singer there, sitting by herself at a table near the door. Corky, I took it, was out telephoning. I went up and passed the time of day.

"Well, well, well, what?" I said.

"Why, Mr. Wooster! How do you do?"

"Corky around?"

"I beg your pardon?"

"You're waiting for Corky, aren't you?"

"Oh, I didn't understand. No, I'm not waiting for him."

It seemed to me that there was a sort of something in her voice, a kind of thingummy, you know.

"I say, you haven't had a row with Corky, have you?"

"A row?"

"A spat, don't you know—little misunderstanding—faults on both sides—er—and all that sort of thing."

"Why, whatever makes you think that?"

"Oh, well, as it were, what? What I mean is—I thought you usually dined with him before you went to the theatre."

"I've left the stage now."

Suddenly the whole thing dawned on me. I had forgotten what a long time I had been away.

"Why, of course, I see now! You're married!"

"Yes."

"How perfectly topping! I wish you all kinds of happiness."

"Thank you so much. Oh, Alexander," she said, looking past me, "this is a friend of mine—Mr. Wooster."

I spun round. A chappie with a lot of stiff grey hair and a red sort of healthy face was standing there. Rather a formidable Johnnie, he looked, though quite peaceful at the moment.

"I want you to meet my husband, Mr. Wooster. Mr. Wooster is a friend of Bruce's, Alexander."

The old boy grasped my hand warmly, and that was all that kept me from hitting the floor in a heap. The place was rocking. Absolutely.

"So you know my nephew, Mr. Wooster," I heard him say. "I wish you would try to knock a little sense into him and make him quit this playing at painting. But I have an idea that he is steadying down. I noticed it first that night he came to dinner with us, my dear, to be introduced to you. He seemed altogether quieter and more serious. Something seemed to have sobered him. Perhaps you will give us the pleasure of your company at dinner to-night, Mr. Wooster? Or have you dined?"

I said I had. What I needed then was air, not dinner. I felt that I wanted to get into the open and think this thing out.

When I reached my apartment I heard Jeeves moving about in his lair. I called him.

"Jeeves," I said, "now is the time for all good men to come to the aid of the party. A stiff b.-and-s. first of all, and then I've a bit of news for you."

He came back with a tray and a long glass.

"Better have one yourself, Jeeves. You'll need it."

"Later on, perhaps, thank you, sir."

"All right. Please yourself. But you're going to get a shock. You remember my friend, Mr. Corcoran?"

"Yes, sir."

"And the girl who was to slide gracefully into his uncle's esteem by writing the book on birds?"

"Perfectly, sir."

"Well, she's slid. She's married the uncle."

He took it without blinking. You can't rattle Jeeves.

"That was always a development to be feared, sir."

"You don't mean to tell me that you were expecting it?"

"It crossed my mind as a possibility."

"Did it, by Jove! Well, I think you might have warned us!"

"I hardly liked to take the liberty, sir."

Of course, as I saw after I had had a bite to eat and was in a calmer frame of mind, what had happened wasn't my fault, if you came down to it. I couldn't be expected to foresee that the scheme, in itself a cracker-jack, would skid into the ditch as it had done; but all the same I'm bound to admit that I didn't relish the idea of meeting Corky again until time, the great healer, had been able to get in a bit of soothing work. I cut Washington Square out absolutely for the next few months. I gave it the complete miss-in-baulk. And then, just when I was beginning to think I might safely pop down in that direction and gather up the dropped threads, so to speak, time, instead of working the healing wheeze, went and pulled the most awful bone and put the lid on it. Opening the paper one morning, I read that Mrs. Alexander Worple had presented her husband with a son and heir.

I was so darned sorry for poor old Corky that I hadn't the heart to touch my breakfast. I told Jeeves to drink it himself. I was bowled over. Absolutely. It was the limit.

I hardly knew what to do. I wanted, of course, to rush down to Washington Square and grip the poor blighter silently by the hand; and then, thinking it over, I hadn't the nerve. Absent treatment seemed the touch. I gave it him in waves.

But after a month or so I began to hesitate again. It struck me that it was playing it a bit low-down on the poor chap, avoiding him like this just when he probably wanted his pals to surge round him most. I pictured him sitting in his lonely studio with no company but his bitter thoughts, and the pathos of it got me to such an extent that I bounded straight into a taxi and told the driver to go all out for the studio.

I rushed in, and there was Corky, hunched up at the easel, painting away, while on the model throne sat a severe-looking female of middle age, holding a baby.

A fellow has to be ready for that sort of thing.

"Oh, ah!" I said, and started to back out.

Corky looked over his shoulder.

"Halloa, Bertie. Don't go. We're just finishing for the day. That will be all this afternoon," he said to the nurse, who got up with the baby and decanted it into a perambulator which was standing in the fairway.

"At the same hour to-morrow, Mr. Corcoran?"

"Yes, please."

"Good afternoon."

"Good afternoon."

Corky stood there, looking at the door, and then he turned to me and began to get it off his chest. Fortunately, he seemed to take it for granted that I knew all about what had happened, so it wasn't as awkward as it might have been.

"It's my uncle's idea," he said. "Muriel doesn't know about it yet. The portrait's to be a surprise for her on her birthday. The nurse takes the kid out ostensibly to get a breather, and they beat it down here. If you want an instance of the irony of fate, Bertie, get acquainted with this. Here's the first commission I have ever had to paint a portrait, and the sitter is that human poached egg that has butted in and bounced me out of my inheritance. Can you beat it! I call it rubbing the thing in to expect me to spend my afternoons gazing into the ugly face of a little brat who to all intents and purposes has hit me behind the ear with a black-jack and swiped all I possess. I can't refuse to paint the portrait, because if I did my uncle would stop my allowance; yet every time I look up and catch that kid's vacant eye, I suffer agonies. I tell you, Bertie, sometimes when he gives me a patronizing glance and then turns away and is sick, as if it revolted him to look at me, I come within an ace of occupying the entire front page of the evening papers as the latest murder sensation. There are moments when I can almost see the headlines: 'Promising Young Artist Beans Baby With Axe.' "

I patted his shoulder silently. My sympathy for the poor old scout was too deep for words.

I kept away from the studio for some time after that, because it didn't seem right to me to intrude on the poor chappie's sorrow. Besides, I'm bound to say that nurse intimidated me. She reminded me so infernally of Aunt Agatha. She was the same gimlet-eyed type.

But one afternoon Corky called me on the 'phone.

"Bertie."

"Halloa?"

"Are you doing anything this afternoon?"

"Nothing special."

"You couldn't come down here, could you?"

"What's the trouble? Anything up?"

"I've finished the portrait."

"Good boy! Stout work!"

"Yes." His voice sounded rather doubtful. "The fact is, Bertie, it doesn't look quite right to me. There's something about it—— My uncle's coming in half an hour to inspect it, and—I don't know why it is, but I kind of feel I'd like your moral support!"

I began to see that I was letting myself in for something. The sympathetic co-operation of Jeeves seemed to me to be indicated.

"You think he'll cut up rough?"

"He may."

I threw my mind back to the red-faced chappie I had met at the restaurant, and tried to picture him cutting up rough. It was only too easy. I spoke to Corky firmly on the telephone.

"I'll come," I said.

"Good!"

"But only if I may bring Jeeves!"

"Why Jeeves? What's Jeeves got to do with it? Who wants Jeeves? Jeeves is the fool who suggested the scheme that has led——"

"Listen, Corky, old top! If you think I am going to face that uncle of yours without Jeeves's support, you're mistaken. I'd sooner go into a den of wild beasts and bite a lion on the back of the neck."

"Oh, all right," said Corky. Not cordially, but he said it; so I rang for Jeeves, and explained the situation.

"Very good, sir," said Jeeves.

That's the sort of chap he is. You can't rattle him.

We found Corky near the door, looking at the picture, with one hand up in a defensive sort of way, as if he thought it might swing on him.

"Stand right where you are, Bertie," he said, without moving. "Now, tell me honestly, how does it strike you?"

The light from the big window fell right on the picture. I took a good look at it. Then I shifted a bit nearer and took another look. Then I went back to where I had been at first, because it hadn't seemed quite so bad from there.

"Well?" said Corky, anxiously.

I hesitated a bit.

"Of course, old man, I only saw the kid once, and then only for a moment, but—but it *was* an ugly sort of kid, wasn't it, if I remember rightly?"

"As ugly as that?"

I looked again, and honesty compelled me to be frank.

"I don't see how it could have been, old chap."

Poor old Corky ran his fingers through his hair in a temperamental sort of way. He groaned.

"You're quite right, Bertie. Something's gone wrong with the darned thing. My private impression is that, without knowing it, I've worked that stunt that Sargent and those fellows pull—painting the soul of the sitter. I've got through the mere outward appearance, and have put the child's soul on canvas."

"But could a child of that age have a soul like that? I don't see how he could have managed it in the time. What do you think, Jeeves?"

"I doubt it, sir."

"It—it sort of leers at you, doesn't it?"

"You've noticed that, too?" said Corky.

"I don't see how one could help noticing."

"All I tried to do was to give the little brute a cheerful expression. But, as it has worked out, he looks positively dissipated."

"Just what I was going to suggest, old man. He looks as if he were in the middle of a colossal spree, and enjoying every minute of it. Don't you think so, Jeeves?"

"He has a decidedly inebriated air, sir."

Corky was starting to say something, when the door opened and the uncle came in.

For about three seconds all was joy, jollity, and good will. The old boy shook hands with me, slapped Corky on the back, said that he didn't think he had ever seen such a fine day, and whacked his leg with his stick. Jeeves had projected himself into the background, and he didn't notice him.

"Well, Bruce, my boy; so the portrait is really finished, is it—really finished? Well, bring it out. Let's have a look at it. This will be a wonderful surprise for your aunt. Where is it? Let's——"

And then he got it—suddenly, when he wasn't set for the punch; and he rocked back on his heels.

"Oosh!" he exclaimed. And for perhaps a minute there was one of the scaliest silences I've ever run up against.

"Is this a practical joke?" he said at last, in a way that set about sixteen draughts cutting through the room at once.

I thought it was up to me to rally round old Corky.

"You want to stand a bit farther away from it," I said.

"You're perfectly right!" he snorted. "I do! I want to stand so far away from it that I can't see the thing with a telescope!" He turned on Corky like an untamed tiger of the jungle who has just located a chunk of meat. "And this—this—is what you have been wasting your time and my money for all these years! A painter! I wouldn't let you paint a house of mine! I gave you this commission, thinking that you were a competent worker, and this—this—this extract from a comic coloured supplement is the result!" He swung towards the door, lashing his tail and growling to himself. "This ends it! If you wish to continue this foolery of pretending to be an artist because you want an excuse for idleness, please yourself. But let me tell you this. Unless you report at my office on Monday morning, prepared to abandon all this idiocy and start in at the bottom of the business to work your way up, as you should have done half a dozen years ago, not another cent—not another cent—not another—— Boosh!"

Then the door closed and he was no longer with us. And I crawled out of the bomb-proof shelter.

"Corky, old top!" I whispered, faintly.

Corky was standing staring at the picture. His face was set. There was a hunted look in his eye.

"Well, that finishes it!" he muttered, brokenly.

"What are you going to do?"

"Do? What can I do? I can't stick on here if he cuts off supplies. You heard what he said. I shall have to go to the office on Monday."

I couldn't think of a thing to say. I knew exactly how he felt about the office. I don't know when I've been so infernally uncomfortable. It was like hanging round trying to make conversation to a pal who's just been sentenced to twenty years in quod.

And then a soothing voice broke the silence.

"If I might make a suggestion, sir!"

It was Jeeves. He had slid from the shadows and was gazing gravely at the picture. Upon my word, I can't give you a better idea of the shattering effect of Corky's uncle Alexander when in action than by saying that he had absolutely made me forget for the moment that Jeeves was there.

"I wonder if I have ever happened to mention to you, sir, a Mr. Digby Thistleton, with whom I was once in service? Perhaps you have met him? He was a financier. He is now Lord Bridgnorth. It was a favourite saying of his that there is always a way. The first time I heard him use the expression was after the failure of a patent depilatory which he promoted."

"Jeeves," I said, "what on earth are you talking about?"

"I mentioned Mr. Thistleton, sir, because his was in some respects a parallel case to the present one. His depilatory failed, but he did not despair. He put it on the market again under the name of Hair-o, guaranteed to produce a full crop of hair in a few months. It was advertised, if you remember, sir, by a humorous picture of a billiard-ball, before and after taking, and made such a substantial fortune that Mr. Thistleton was soon afterwards elevated to the peerage for services to his Party. It seems to me that, if Mr. Corcoran looks into the matter, he will find, like Mr. Thistleton, that there is always a way. Mr. Worple himself suggested the solution of the difficulty. In the heat of the moment he compared the portrait to an extract from a coloured comic supplement. I consider the suggestion a very valuable one, sir. Mr. Corcoran's portrait may not have pleased Mr. Worple as a likeness of his only child, but I have no doubt that editors would gladly consider it as a foundation for a series of humorous drawings. If Mr. Corcoran will allow me to make the suggestion, his talent has always been for the humorous. There is something about this picture—something bold and vigorous, which arrests the attention. I feel sure it would be highly popular."

Corky was glaring at the picture, and making a sort of dry, sucking noise with his mouth. He seemed completely overwrought.

And then suddenly he began to laugh in a wild way.

"Corky, old man!" I said, massaging him tenderly. I feared the poor blighter was hysterical.

He began to stagger about all over the floor.

"He's right! The man's absolutely right! Jeeves, you're a life-saver! You've hit on the greatest idea of the age! Report at the office on Monday! Start at the bottom of the business! I'll buy the business if I feel like it. I know the man who runs the comic section of the *Sunday Star*. He'll eat this thing. He was telling me only the other day how hard it was to get a good new series. He'll give me anything I ask for a real winner like this. I've got a gold-mine. Where's my hat? I've got an income for life! Where's that confounded hat? Lend me a fiver, Bertie. I want to take a taxi down to Park Row!"

Jeeves smiled paternally. Or, rather, he had a kind of paternal muscular spasm about the mouth, which is the nearest he ever gets to smiling.

"If I might make the suggestion, Mr. Corcoran—for a title of the series which you have in mind—'The Adventures of Baby Blobbs.' "

Corky and I looked at the picture, then at each other in an awed way. Jeeves was right. There could be no other title.

"Jeeves," I said. It was a few weeks later, and I had just finished looking at the comic section of the *Sunday Star*. "I'm an optimist. I always have been. The older I get, the more I agree with Shakespeare and those poet Johnnies about it always being darkest before the dawn and there's a silver lining and what you lose on the swings you make up on the roundabouts. Look at Mr. Corcoran, for instance. There was a fellow, one would have said, clear up to the eyebrows in the soup. To all appearances he had got it right in the neck. Yet look at him now. Have you seen these pictures?"

"I took the liberty of glancing at them before bringing them to you, sir. Extremely diverting."

"They have made a big hit, you know."

"I anticipated it, sir."

I leaned back against the pillows.

"You know, Jeeves, you're a genius. You ought to be drawing a commission on these things."

"I have nothing to complain of in that respect, sir. Mr. Corcoran has been most generous. I am putting out the brown suit, sir."

"No, I think I'll wear the blue with the faint red stripe."

"Not the blue with the faint red stripe, sir."

"But I rather fancy myself in it."

"Not the blue with the faint red stripe, sir."

"Oh, all right, have it your own way."

"Very good, sir. Thank you, sir."

Of course, I know it's as bad as being hen-pecked; but then Jeeves is always right. You've got to consider that, you know. What?

The Aunt and the Sluggard

NOW that it's all over, I may as well admit that there was a time during the rather rummy affair of Rockmetteller Todd when I thought that Jeeves was going to let me down. The man had the appearance of being baffled.

Jeeves is my man, you know. Officially he pulls in his weekly wage for pressing my clothes, and all that sort of thing; but actually he's more like what the poet Johnnie called some bird of his acquaintance who was apt to rally round him in times of need—a guide, don't you know; philosopher, if I remember rightly, and—I rather fancy—friend. I rely on him at every turn.

So naturally, when Rocky Todd told me about his aunt, I didn't hesitate. Jeeves was in on the thing from the start.

The affair of Rocky Todd broke loose early one morning in spring. I was in bed, restoring the good old tissues with about nine hours of the dreamless, when the door flew open and somebody prodded me in the lower ribs and began to shake the bedclothes. After blinking a bit and generally pulling myself together, I located Rocky, and my first impression was that it was some horrid dream.

Rocky, you see, lived down on Long Island somewhere, miles away from New York; and not only that, but he had told me himself more than once that he never got up before twelve, and seldom earlier than one. Constitutionally the laziest young devil in America, he had hit on a walk in life which enabled him to go the limit in that direction. He was a poet. At least, he wrote poems when he did anything; but most of his time, as far as I could make out, he spent in a sort of trance. He told me once that he could sit on a fence, watching a worm and wondering what on earth it was up to, for hours at a stretch.

He had his scheme of life worked out to a fine point. About once a month he would take three days writing a few poems; the other three hundred and twenty-nine days of the year he rested. I didn't know there was enough money in poetry to support a chappie, even in the way in which Rocky lived; but it seems that, if you stick to exhortations to young men to lead the strenuous life and don't shove in any rhymes, American editors fight for the stuff. Rocky showed me one of his things once. It began:—

Be!
Be!
        The past is dead.
        To-morrow is not born.
                Be to-day!
To-day!
        Be with every nerve,
        With every muscle,
        With every drop of your red blood!
Be!

It was printed opposite the frontispiece of a magazine with a sort of scroll round it, and a picture in the middle of a fairly nude chappie, with bulging muscles, giving the rising sun the glad eye. Rocky said they gave him a hundred dollars for it, and he stayed in bed till four in the afternoon for over a month.

As regarded the future he was pretty solid, owing to the fact that he had a moneyed aunt tucked away somewhere in Illinois; and, as he had been named Rockmetteller after her, and was her only nephew, his position was pretty sound. He told me that when he did come into the money he meant to do no work at all, except perhaps an occasional poem recommending the young man with life opening out before him, with all its splendid possibilities, to light a pipe and shove his feet upon the mantelpiece.

And this was the man who was prodding me in the ribs in the grey dawn!

"Read this, Bertie!" I could just see that he was waving a letter or something equally foul in my face. "Wake up and read this!"

I can't read before I've had my morning tea and a cigarette. I groped for the bell.

Jeeves came in, looking as fresh as a dewy violet. It's a mystery to me how he does it.

"Tea, Jeeves."

"Very good, sir."

He flowed silently out of the room—he always gives you the impression of being some liquid substance when he moves; and I found that Rocky was surging round with his beastly letter again.

"What is it?" I said. "What on earth's the matter?"

"Read it!"

"I can't. I haven't had my tea."

"Well, listen then."

"Who's it from?"

"My aunt."

At this point I fell asleep again. I woke to hear him saying: —

"So what on earth am I to do?"

Jeeves trickled in with the tray, like some silent stream meandering over its mossy bed; and I saw daylight.

"Read it again, Rocky, old top," I said. "I want Jeeves to hear it. Mr. Todd's aunt has written him a rather rummy letter, Jeeves, and we want your advice."

"Very good, sir."

He stood in the middle of the room, registering devotion to the cause, and Rocky started again: —

> MY DEAR ROCKMETTELLER, —
> I have been thinking things over for a long while, and I have come to the conclusion that I have been very thoughtless to wait so long before doing what I have made up my mind to do now.

"What do you make of that, Jeeves?"

"It seems a little obscure at present, sir, but no doubt it becomes clearer at a later point in the communication."

"It becomes as clear as mud!" said Rocky.

"Proceed, old scout," I said, champing my bread and butter.

> You know how all my life I have longed to visit New York and see for myself the wonderful gay life of which I have read so much. I fear that now it will be impossible for me to fulfil my dream. I am old and worn out. I seem to have no strength left in me.

"Sad, Jeeves, what?"

"Extremely, sir."

"Sad nothing!" said Rocky. "It's sheer laziness. I went to see her last Christmas and she was bursting with health. Her doctor told me himself that there was nothing wrong with her whatever. But she will insist that she's a hopeless invalid, so he has to agree with her. She's got a fixed idea that the trip to New York would kill her; so, though it's been her ambition all her life to come here, she stays where she is."

"Rather like the chappie whose heart was 'in the Highlands a-chasing of the deer,' Jeeves?"

"The cases are in some respects parallel, sir."

"Carry on, Rocky, dear boy."

> So I have decided that, if I cannot enjoy all the marvels of the city myself, I can at least enjoy them through you. I suddenly thought of this yesterday after reading a beautiful poem in the Sunday paper about a young man who had longed all his life for a certain thing and won it in the end only when he was too old to enjoy it. It was very sad, and it touched me.

"A thing," interpolated Rocky, bitterly, "that I've not been able to do in ten years."

> As you know, you will have my money when I am gone; but until now I have never been able to see my way to giving you an allowance. I have now decided to do so—on one condition. I have written to a firm of lawyers in New York, giving them instructions to pay you quite a substantial sum each month. My one condition is that you live in New York and enjoy yourself as I have always wished to do. I want you to be my representative, to spend this money for me as I should do myself. I want you to plunge into the gay, prismatic life of New York. I want you to be the life and soul of brilliant supper parties.
>
> Above all, I want you—indeed, I insist on this—to write me letters at least once a week, giving me a full description of all you are doing and all that is going on in the city, so that I may enjoy at secondhand what my wretched health prevents my enjoying for myself. Remember that I shall expect full details, and that no detail is too trivial to interest
>
> Your affectionate Aunt,
> ISABEL ROCKMETTELLER.

"What about it?" said Rocky.

"What about it?" I said.

"Yes. What on earth am I going to do?"

It was only then that I really got on to the extremely rummy attitude of the chappie, in view of the fact that a quite unexpected mess of the right stuff had suddenly descended on him from a blue sky. To my mind it was an occasion for the beaming smile and the joyous whoop; yet here the man was, looking and talking as if Fate had swung on his solar plexus. It amazed me.

"Aren't you bucked?" I said.

"Bucked!"

"If I were in your place I should be frightfully braced. I consider this pretty soft for you."

He gave a kind of yelp, stared at me for a moment, and then began to talk of New York in a way that reminded me of Jimmy Mundy, the reformer chappie. Jimmy had just come to New York on a hit-the-trail campaign, and I had popped in at the Garden a couple of days before, for half an hour or so, to hear him. He had certainly told New York some pretty straight things about itself, having apparently taken a dislike to the place, but, by Jove, you know, dear old Rocky made him look like a publicity agent for the old metrop!

"Pretty soft!" he cried. "To have to come and live in New York! To have to leave my little cottage and take a stuffy, smelly, over-heated hole of an apartment in this Heaven-forsaken, festering Gehenna. To have to mix night after night with a mob who think that life is a sort of St. Vitus's dance, and imagine that they're having a good time because they're making enough noise for six and drinking too much for ten. I loathe New York, Bertie. I wouldn't come near the place if I hadn't got to see editors occasionally. There's a blight on it. It's got moral delirium tremens. It's the limit. The very thought of staying more than a day in it makes me sick. And you call this thing pretty soft for me!"

I felt rather like Lot's friends must have done when they dropped in for a quiet chat and their genial host began to criticize the Cities of the Plain. I had no idea old Rocky could be so eloquent.

"It would kill me to have to live in New York," he went on. "To have to share the air with six million people! To have to wear stiff collars and decent clothes all the time! To —" He started. "Good Lord! I suppose I should have to dress for dinner in the evenings. What a ghastly notion!"

I was shocked, absolutely shocked.

"My dear chap!" I said, reproachfully.

"Do you dress for dinner every night, Bertie?"

"Jeeves," I said, coldly. The man was still standing like a statue by the door. "How many suits of evening clothes have I?"

"We have three suits full of evening dress, sir; two dinner jackets —"

"Three."

"For practical purposes two only, sir. If you remember, we cannot wear the third. We have also seven white waistcoats."

"And shirts?"

"Four dozen, sir."

"And white ties?"

"The first two shallow shelves in the chest of drawers are completely filled with our white ties, sir."

I turned to Rocky.

"You see?"

The chappie writhed like an electric fan.

"I won't do it! I can't do it! I'll be hanged if I'll do it! How on earth can I dress up like that? Do you realize that most days I don't get out of my pyjamas till five in the afternoon, and then I just put on an old sweater?"

I saw Jeeves wince, poor chap! This sort of revelation shocked his finest feelings.

"Then, what are you going to do about it?" I said.

"That's what I want to know."

"You might write and explain to your aunt."

"I might—if I wanted her to get round to her lawyer's in two rapid leaps and cut me out of her will."

I saw his point.

"What do you suggest, Jeeves?" I said.

Jeeves cleared his throat respectfully.

"The crux of the matter would appear to be, sir, that Mr. Todd is obliged by the conditions under which the money is delivered into his possession to write Miss Rockmetteller long and detailed letters relating to his movements, and the only method by which this can be accomplished, if Mr. Todd adheres to his expressed intention of remaining in the country, is for Mr. Todd to induce some second party to gather the actual experiences which Miss Rockmetteller wishes reported to her, and to convey these to him in the shape of a careful report, on which it would be possible for him, with the aid of his imagination, to base the suggested correspondence."

Having got which off the old diaphragm, Jeeves was silent. Rocky looked at me in a helpless sort of way. He hasn't been brought up on Jeeves as I have, and he isn't on to his curves.

"Could he put it a little clearer, Bertie?" he said. "I thought at the start it was going to make sense, but it kind of flickered. What's the idea?"

"My dear old man, perfectly simple. I knew we could stand on Jeeves. All you've got to do is to get somebody to go round the town for you and take a few notes, and then you work the notes up into letters. That's it, isn't it, Jeeves?"

"Precisely, sir."

The light of hope gleamed in Rocky's eyes. He looked at Jeeves in a startled way, dazed by the man's vast intellect.

"But who would do it?" he said. "It would have to be a pretty smart sort of man, a man who would notice things."

"Jeeves!" I said. "Let Jeeves do it."

"But would he?"

"You would do it, wouldn't you, Jeeves?"

For the first time in our long connection I observed Jeeves almost smile. The corner of his mouth curved quite a quarter of an inch, and for a moment his eye ceased to look like a meditative fish's.

"I should be delighted to oblige, sir. As a matter of fact, I have already visited some of New York's places of interest on my evening out, and it would be most enjoyable to make a practice of the pursuit."

"Fine! I know exactly what your aunt wants to hear about, Rocky. She wants an earful of cabaret stuff. The place you ought to go to first, Jeeves, is Reigelheimer's. It's on Forty-second Street. Anybody will show you the way."

Jeeves shook his head.

"Pardon me, sir. People are no longer going to Reigelheimer's. The place at the moment is Frolics on the Roof."

"You see?" I said to Rocky. "Leave it to Jeeves. He knows."

It isn't often that you find an entire group of your fellow-humans happy in this world; but our little circle was certainly an example of the fact that it can be done. We were all full of beans. Everything went absolutely right from the start.

Jeeves was happy, partly because he loves to exercise his giant brain, and partly because he was having a corking time among the bright lights. I saw him one night at the Midnight Revels. He was sitting at a table on the edge of the dancing floor, doing himself remarkably well with a fat cigar and a bottle of the best. I'd never imagined he could look so nearly human. His face wore an expression of austere benevolence, and he was making notes in a small book.

As for the rest of us, I was feeling pretty good, because I was fond of old Rocky and glad to be able to do him a good turn. Rocky was perfectly contented, because he was still able to sit on fences in his pyjamas and watch worms. And, as for the aunt, she seemed tickled to death. She was getting Broadway at pretty long range, but it seemed to be hitting her just right. I read one of her letters to Rocky, and it was full of life.

But then Rocky's letters, based on Jeeves's notes, were enough to buck anybody up. It was rummy when you came to think of it. There was I, loving the life, while the mere mention of it gave Rocky a tired feeling; yet here is a letter I wrote home to a pal of mine in London:—

DEAR FREDDIE, —

"Well, here I am in New York. It's not a bad place. I'm not having a bad time. Everything's pretty all right. The cabarets aren't bad. Don't know when I shall be back. How's everybody? Cheer-o! —

Yours,
BERTIE.

P.S. — Seen old Ted lately?

Not that I cared about old Ted; but if I hadn't dragged him in I couldn't have got the confounded thing on to the second page.

Now here's old Rocky on exactly the same subject: —

DEAREST AUNT ISABEL, —

How can I ever thank you enough for giving me the opportunity to live in this astounding city! New York seems more wonderful every day.

Fifth Avenue is at its best, of course, just now. The dresses are magnificent!

Wads of stuff about the dresses. I didn't know Jeeves was such an authority.

I was out with some of the crowd at the Midnight Revels the other night. We took in a show first, after a little dinner at a new place on Forty-third Street. We were quite a gay party. Georgie Cohan looked in about midnight and got off a good one about Willie Collier. Fred Stone could only stay a minute, but Doug. Fairbanks did all sorts of stunts and made us roar. Diamond Jim Brady was there, as usual, and Laurette Taylor showed up with a party. The show at the Revels is quite good. I am enclosing a programme.

Last night a few of us went round to Frolics on the Roof——

And so on and so forth, yards of it. I suppose it's the artistic temperament or something. What I mean is, it's easier for a chappie who's used to writing poems and that sort of tosh to put a bit of a punch into a letter than it is for a chappie like me. Anyway, there's no doubt that Rocky's correspondence was hot stuff. I called Jeeves in and congratulated him.

"Jeeves, you're a wonder!"

"Thank you, sir."

"How you notice everything at these places beats me. I couldn't tell you a thing about them, except that I've had a good time."

"It's just a knack, sir."

"Well, Mr. Todd's letters ought to brace Miss Rockmetteller all right, what?"

"Undoubtedly, sir," agreed Jeeves.

And, by Jove, they did! They certainly did, by George! What I mean to say is, I was sitting in the apartment one afternoon, about a month after the thing had started, smoking a cigarette and resting the old bean, when the door opened and the voice of Jeeves burst the silence like a bomb.

It wasn't that he spoke loud. He has one of those soft, soothing voices that slide through the atmosphere like the note of a far-off sheep. It was what he said that made me leap like a young gazelle.

"Miss Rockmetteller!"

And in came a large, solid female.

The situation floored me. I'm not denying it. Hamlet must have felt much as I did when his father's ghost bobbed up in the fairway. I'd come to look on Rocky's aunt as such a permanency at her own home that it didn't seem possible that she could really be here in New York. I stared at her. Then I looked at Jeeves. He was standing there in an attitude of dignified detachment, the chump, when, if ever he should have been rallying round the young master, it was now.

Rocky's aunt looked less like an invalid than any one I've ever seen, except my Aunt Agatha. She had a good deal of Aunt Agatha about her, as a matter of fact. She looked as if she might be deucedly dangerous if put upon; and something seemed to tell me that she would certainly regard herself as put upon if she ever found out the game which poor old Rocky had been pulling on her.

"Good afternoon," I managed to say.

"How do you do?" she said. "Mr. Cohan?"

"Er—no."

"Mr. Fred Stone?"

"Not absolutely. As a matter of fact, my name's Wooster—Bertie Wooster."

She seemed disappointed. The fine old name of Wooster appeared to mean nothing in her life.

"Isn't Rockmetteller home?" she said. "Where is he?"

She had me with the first shot. I couldn't think of anything to say. I couldn't tell her that Rocky was down in the country, watching worms.

There was the faintest flutter of sound in the background. It was the respectful cough with which Jeeves announces that he is about to speak without having been spoken to.

"If you remember, sir, Mr. Todd went out in the automobile with a party earlier in the afternoon."

"So he did, Jeeves; so he did," I said, looking at my watch. "Did he say when he would be back?"

"He gave me to understand, sir, that he would be somewhat late in returning."

He vanished; and the aunt took the chair which I'd forgotten to offer her. She looked at me in rather a rummy way. It was a nasty look. It made me feel as if I were something the dog had brought in and intended to bury later on, when he had time. My own Aunt Agatha, back in England, has looked at me in exactly the same way many a time, and it never fails to make my spine curl.

"You seem very much at home here, young man. Are you a great friend of Rockmetteller's?"

"Oh, yes, rather!"

She frowned as if she had expected better things of old Rocky.

"Well, you need to be," she said, "the way you treat his flat as your own!"

I give you my word, this quite unforeseen slam simply robbed me of the power of speech. I'd been looking on myself in the light of the dashing host, and suddenly to be treated as an intruder jarred me. It wasn't, mark you, as if she had spoken in a way to suggest that she considered my presence in the place as an ordinary social call. She obviously looked on me as a cross between a burglar and the plumber's man come to fix the leak in the bathroom. It hurt her—my being there.

At this juncture, with the conversation showing every sign of being about to die in awful agonies, an idea came to me. Tea—the good old stand-by.

"Would you care for a cup of tea?" I said.

"Tea?"

She spoke as if she had never heard of the stuff.

"Nothing like a cup after a journey," I said. "Bucks you up! Puts a bit of zip into you. What I mean is, restores you, and so on, don't you know. I'll go and tell Jeeves."

I tottered down the passage to Jeeves's lair. The man was reading the evening paper as if he hadn't a care in the world.

"Jeeves," I said, "we want some tea."

"Very good, sir."

"I say, Jeeves, this is a bit thick, what?"

I wanted sympathy, don't you know—sympathy and kindness. The old nerve centres had had the deuce of a shock.

"She's got the idea this place belongs to Mr. Todd. What on earth put that into her head?"

Jeeves filled the kettle with a restrained dignity.

"No doubt because of Mr. Todd's letters, sir," he said. "It was my suggestion, sir, if you remember, that they should be addressed from this apartment in order that Mr. Todd should appear to possess a good central residence in the city."

I remembered. We had thought it a brainy scheme at the time.

"Well, it's bally awkward, you know, Jeeves. She looks on me as an intruder. By Jove! I suppose she thinks I'm some one who hangs about here, touching Mr. Todd for free meals and borrowing his shirts."

"Yes, sir."

"It's pretty rotten, you know."

"Most disturbing, sir."

"And there's another thing: What are we to do about Mr. Todd? We've got to get him up here as soon as ever we can. When you have brought the tea you had better go out and send him a telegram, telling him to come up by the next train."

"I have already done so, sir. I took the liberty of writing the message and dispatching it by the lift attendant."

"By Jove, you think of everything, Jeeves!"

"Thank you, sir. A little buttered toast with the tea? Just so, sir. Thank you."

I went back to the sitting-room. She hadn't moved an inch. She was still bolt upright on the edge of her chair, gripping her umbrella like a hammer-thrower. She gave me another of those looks as I came in. There was no doubt about it; for some reason she had taken a dislike to me. I suppose because I wasn't George M. Cohan. It was a bit hard on a chap.

"This is a surprise, what?" I said, after about five minutes' restful silence, trying to crank the conversation up again.

"What is a surprise?"

"Your coming here, don't you know, and so on."

She raised her eyebrows and drank me in a bit more through her glasses.

"Why is it surprising that I should visit my only nephew?" she said.

Put like that, of course, it did seem reasonable.

"Oh, rather," I said. "Of course! Certainly. What I mean is —"

Jeeves projected himself into the room with the tea. I was jolly glad to see him. There's nothing like having a bit of business arranged for one when one isn't certain of one's lines. With the teapot to fool about with I felt happier.

"Tea, tea, tea—what? What?" I said.

It wasn't what I had meant to say. My idea had been to be a good deal more formal, and so on. Still, it covered the situation. I poured her out a cup. She sipped it and put the cup down with a shudder.

"Do you mean to say, young man," she said, frostily, "that you expect me to drink this stuff?"

"Rather! Bucks you up, you know."

"What do you mean by the expression 'Bucks you up'?"

"Well, makes you full of beans, you know. Makes you fizz."

"I don't understand a word you say. You're English, aren't you?"

I admitted it. She didn't say a word. And somehow she did it in a way that made it worse than if she had spoken for hours. Somehow it was brought home to me that she didn't like Englishmen, and that if she had had to meet an Englishman I was the one she'd have chosen last.

Conversation languished again after that.

Then I tried again. I was becoming more convinced every moment that you can't make a real lively *salon* with a couple of people, especially if one of them lets it go a word at a time.

"Are you comfortable at your hotel?" I said.

"At which hotel?"

"The hotel you're staying at."

"I am not staying at an hotel."

"Stopping with friends—what?"

"I am naturally stopping with my nephew."

I didn't get it for the moment; then it hit me.

"What! Here?" I gurgled.

"Certainly! Where else should I go?"

The full horror of the situation rolled over me like a wave. I couldn't see what on earth I was to do. I couldn't explain that this wasn't Rocky's flat without giving the poor old chap away hopelessly, because she would then ask me where he did live, and then he would be right in the soup. I was trying to induce the old bean to recover from the shock and produce some results when she spoke again.

"Will you kindly tell my nephew's manservant to prepare my room? I wish to lie down."

"Your nephew's manservant?"

"The man you call Jeeves. If Rockmetteller has gone for an automobile ride there is no need for you to wait for him. He will naturally wish to be alone with me when he returns."

I found myself tottering out of the room. The thing was too much for me. I crept into Jeeves's den.

"Jeeves!" I whispered.

"Sir?"

"Mix me a b.-and-s., Jeeves. I feel weak."

"Very good, sir."

"This is getting thicker every minute, Jeeves."

"Sir?"

"She thinks you're Mr. Todd's man. She thinks the whole place is his, and everything in it. I don't see what you're to do, except stay on and keep it up. We can't say anything or she'll get on to the whole thing, and I don't want to let Mr. Todd down. By the way, Jeeves, she wants you to prepare her bed."

He looked wounded.

"It is hardly my place, sir——"

"I know—I know. But do it as a personal favour to me. If you come to that, it's hardly my place to be flung out of the flat like this and have to go to an hotel, what?"

"Is it your intention to go to an hotel, sir? What will you do for clothes?"

"Good Lord! I hadn't thought of that. Can you put a few things in a bag when she isn't looking, and sneak them down to me at the St. Aurea?"

"I will endeavour to do so, sir."

"Well, I don't think there's anything more, is there? Tell Mr. Todd where I am when he gets here."

"Very good, sir."

I looked round the place. The moment of parting had come. I felt sad. The whole thing reminded me of one of those melodramas where they drive chappies out of the old homestead into the snow.

"Good-bye, Jeeves," I said.

"Good-bye, sir."

And I staggered out.

You know, I rather think I agree with those poet-and-philosopher Johnnies who insist that a fellow ought to be devilish pleased if he has a bit of trouble. All that stuff about being refined by suffering, you know. Suffering does give a chap a sort of broader and more sympathetic outlook. It helps you to understand other people's misfortunes if you've been through the same thing yourself.

As I stood in my lonely bedroom at the hotel, trying to tie my white tie myself, it struck me for the first time that there must be whole squads of chappies in the world who had to get along without a man to look after them. I'd always thought of Jeeves as a kind of natural phenomenon; but, by Jove! of course, when you come to think of it, there must be quite a lot of fellows who have to press their own clothes themselves, and haven't got anybody to bring them tea in the morning, and so on. It was rather a solemn thought, don't you know. I mean to say, ever since then I've been able to appreciate the frightful privations the poor have to stick.

I got dressed somehow. Jeeves hadn't forgotten a thing in his packing. Everything was there, down to the final stud. I'm not sure this didn't make me feel worse. It kind of deepened the pathos. It was like what somebody or other wrote about the touch of a vanished hand.

I had a bit of dinner somewhere and went to a show of some kind; but nothing seemed to make any difference. I simply hadn't the heart to go on to supper anywhere. I just sucked down a whisky-and-soda in the hotel smoking-room and went straight up to bed. I don't know when I've felt so rotten. Somehow I found myself moving about the room softly, as if there had been a death in the family. If I had had anybody to talk to I should have talked in a whisper; in fact, when the telephone-bell rang I answered in such a sad, hushed voice that the fellow at the other end of the wire said "Halloa!" five times, thinking he hadn't got me.

It was Rocky. The poor old scout was deeply agitated.

"Bertie! Is that you, Bertie? Oh, gosh! I'm having a time!"

"Where are you speaking from?"

"The Midnight Revels. We've been here an hour, and I think we're a fixture for the night. I've told Aunt Isabel I've gone out to call up a friend to join us. She's glued to a chair, with this-is-the-life written all over her, taking it in through the pores. She loves it, and I'm nearly crazy."

"Tell me all, old top," I said.

"A little more of this," he said, "and I shall sneak quietly off to the river and end it all. Do you mean to say you go through this sort of thing every night, Bertie, and enjoy it? It's simply infernal! I was just snatching a wink of sleep behind the bill of fare just now when about a million yelling girls swooped down, with toy balloons. There are two orchestras here, each trying to see if it can't play louder than the other. I'm a mental and physical wreck. When your telegram arrived I was just lying down for a quiet pipe, with a sense of absolute peace stealing over me. I had to get dressed and sprint two miles to catch the train. It nearly gave me heart-failure; and on top of that I almost got brain fever inventing lies to tell Aunt Isabel. And then I had to cram myself into these confounded evening clothes of yours."

I gave a sharp wail of agony. It hadn't struck me till then that Rocky was depending on my wardrobe to see him through.

"You'll ruin them!"

"I hope so," said Rocky, in the most unpleasant way. His troubles seemed to have had the worst effect on his character. "I should like to get back at them somehow; they've given me a bad enough time. They're about three sizes too small, and something's apt to give at any moment. I wish to goodness it would, and give me a chance to breathe. I haven't breathed since half-past seven. Thank Heaven, Jeeves managed to get out and buy me a collar that fitted, or I should be a strangled corpse by now! It was touch and go till the stud broke. Bertie, this is pure Hades! Aunt Isabel keeps on urging me to dance. How on earth can I dance when I don't know a soul to dance with? And how the deuce could I, even if I knew every girl in the place? It's taking big chances even to move in these trousers. I had to tell her I've hurt my ankle. She keeps asking me when Cohan and Stone are going to turn up; and it's simply a question of time before she discovers that Stone is sitting two tables away. Something's got to be done, Bertie! You've got to think up some way of getting me out of this mess. It was you who got me into it."

"Me! What do you mean?"

"Well, Jeeves, then. It's all the same. It was you who suggested leaving it to Jeeves. It was those letters I wrote from his notes that did the mischief. I made them too good! My aunt's just been telling me about it. She says she had resigned herself to ending her life where she was, and then my letters began to arrive, describing the joys of New York; and they stimulated her to such an extent that she pulled herself together and made the trip. She seems to think she's had some miraculous kind of faith cure. I tell you I can't stand it, Bertie! It's got to end!"

"Can't Jeeves think of anything?"

"No. He just hangs round, saying: 'Most disturbing, sir!' A fat lot of help that is!"

"Well, old lad," I said, "after all, it's far worse for me than it is for you. You've got a comfortable home and Jeeves. And you're saving a lot of money."

"Saving money? What do you mean — saving money?"

"Why, the allowance your aunt was giving you. I suppose she's paying all the expenses now, isn't she?"

"Certainly she is; but she's stopped the allowance. She wrote the lawyers to-night. She says that, now she's in New York, there is no necessity for it to go on, as we shall always be together, and it's simpler for her to look after that end of it. I tell you, Bertie, I've examined the darned cloud with a microscope, and if it's got a silver lining it's some little dissembler!"

"But, Rocky, old top, it's too bally awful! You've no notion of what I'm going through in this beastly hotel, without Jeeves. I must get back to the flat."

"Don't come near the flat!"

"But it's my own flat."

"I can't help that. Aunt Isabel doesn't like you. She asked me what you did for a living. And when I told her you didn't do anything she said she thought as much, and that you were a typical specimen of a useless and decaying aristocracy. So if you think you have made a hit, forget it. Now I must be going back, or she'll be coming out here after me. Good-bye."

Next morning Jeeves came round. It was all so home-like when he floated noiselessly into the room that I nearly broke down.

"Good morning, sir," he said. "I have brought a few more of your personal belongings."

He began to unstrap the suit-case he was carrying.

"Did you have any trouble sneaking them away?"

"It was not easy, sir. I had to watch my chance. Miss Rockmetteller is a remarkably alert lady."

"You know, Jeeves, say what you like—this *is* a bit thick, isn't it?"

"The situation is certainly one that has never before come under my notice, sir. I have brought the heather-mixture suit, as the climatic conditions are congenial. To-morrow, if not prevented, I will endeavour to add the brown lounge with the faint green twill."

"It can't go on—this sort of thing—Jeeves."

"We must hope for the best, sir."

"Can't you think of anything to do?"

"I have been giving the matter considerable thought, sir, but so far without success. I am placing three silk shirts—the dove-coloured, the light blue, and the mauve—in the first long drawer, sir."

"You don't mean to say you can't think of anything, Jeeves?"

"For the moment, sir, no. You will find a dozen handkerchiefs and the tan socks in the upper drawer on the left." He strapped the suit-case and put it on a chair. "A curious lady, Miss Rockmetteller, sir."

"You understate it, Jeeves."

He gazed meditatively out of the window.

"In many ways, sir, Miss Rockmetteller reminds me of an aunt of mine who resides in the south-east portion of London. Their temperaments are much alike. My aunt has the same taste for the pleasures of the great city. It is a passion with her to ride in hansom cabs, sir. Whenever the family take their eyes off her she escapes from the house and spends the day riding about in cabs. On several occasions she has broken into the children's savings bank to secure the means to enable her to gratify this desire."

"I love to have these little chats with you about your female relatives, Jeeves," I said, coldly, for I felt that the man had let me down, and I was fed up with him. "But I don't see what all this has got to do with my trouble."

"I beg your pardon, sir. I am leaving a small assortment of your neckties on the mantelpiece, sir, for you to select according to your preference. I should recommend the blue with the red domino pattern, sir."

Then he streamed imperceptibly toward the door and flowed silently out.

I've often heard that chappies, after some great shock or loss, have a habit, after they've been on the floor for a while wondering what hit them, of picking themselves up and piecing themselves together, and sort of taking a whirl at beginning a new life. Time, the great healer, and Nature, adjusting itself, and so on and so forth. There's a lot in it. I know, because in my own case, after a day or two of what you might call prostration, I began to recover. The frightful loss of Jeeves made any thought of pleasure more or less a mockery, but at least I found that I was able to have a dash at enjoying life again. What I mean is, I braced up to the extent of going round the cabarets once more, so as to try to forget, if only for the moment.

New York's a small place when it comes to the part of it that wakes up just as the rest is going to bed, and it wasn't long before my tracks began to cross old Rocky's. I saw him once at Peale's, and again at Frolics on the Roof. There wasn't anybody with him either time except the aunt, and, though he was trying to look as if he had struck the ideal life, it wasn't difficult for me, knowing the circumstances, to see that beneath the mask the poor chap was suffering. My heart bled for the fellow. At least, what there was of it that wasn't bleeding for myself bled for him. He had the air of one who was about to crack under the strain.

It seemed to me that the aunt was looking slightly upset also. I took it that she was beginning to wonder when the celebrities were going to surge round, and what had suddenly become of all those wild, careless spirits Rocky used to mix with in his letters. I didn't blame her. I had only read a couple of his letters, but they certainly gave the impression that poor old Rocky was by way of being the hub of New York night life, and that, if by any chance he failed to show up at a cabaret, the management said, "What's the use?" and put up the shutters.

The next two nights I didn't come across them, but the night after that I was sitting by myself at the Maison Pierre when somebody tapped me on the shoulder-blade, and I found Rocky standing beside me, with a sort of mixed expression of wistfulness and apoplexy on his face. How the chappie had contrived to wear my evening clothes so many times without disaster was a mystery to me. He confided later that early in the proceedings he had slit the waistcoat up the back and that that had helped a bit.

For a moment I had the idea that he had managed to get away from his aunt for the evening; but, looking past him, I saw that she was in again. She was at a table over by the wall, looking at me as if I were something the management ought to be complained to about.

"Bertie, old scout," said Rocky, in a quiet, sort of crushed voice, "we've always been pals, haven't we? I mean, you know I'd do you a good turn if you asked me."

"My dear old lad," I said. The man had moved me.

"Then, for Heaven's sake, come over and sit at our table for the rest of the evening."

Well, you know, there are limits to the sacred claims of friendship.

"My dear chap," I said, "you know I'd do anything in reason; but——"

"You must come, Bertie. You've got to. Something's got to be done to divert her mind. She's brooding about something. She's been like that for the last two days. I think she's beginning to suspect. She can't understand why we never seem to meet any one I know at these joints. A few nights ago I happened to run into two newspaper men I used to know fairly well. That kept me going for a while. I introduced them to Aunt Isabel as David Belasco and Jim Corbett, and it went well. But the effect has worn off now, and she's beginning to wonder again. Something's got to be done, or she will find out everything, and if she does I'd take a nickel for my chance of getting a cent from her later on. So, for the love of Mike, come across to our table and help things along."

I went along. One has to rally round a pal in distress. Aunt Isabel was sitting bolt upright, as usual. It certainly did seem as if she had lost a bit of the zest with which she had started out to explore Broadway. She looked as if she had been thinking a good deal about rather unpleasant things.

"You've met Bertie Wooster, Aunt Isabel?" said Rocky.

"I have."

There was something in her eye that seemed to say: —

"Out of a city of six million people, why did you pick on me?"

"Take a seat, Bertie. What'll you have?" said Rocky.

And so the merry party began. It was one of those jolly, happy, bread-crumbling parties where you cough twice before you speak, and then decide not to say it after all. After we had had an hour of this wild dissipation, Aunt Isabel said she wanted to go home. In the light of what Rocky had been telling me, this struck me as sinister. I had gathered that at the beginning of her visit she had had to be dragged home with ropes.

It must have hit Rocky the same way, for he gave me a pleading look.

"You'll come along, won't you, Bertie, and have a drink at the flat?"

I had a feeling that this wasn't in the contract, but there wasn't anything to be done. It seemed brutal to leave the poor chap alone with the woman, so I went along.

Right from the start, from the moment we stepped into the taxi, the feeling began to grow that something was about to break loose. A massive silence prevailed in the corner where the aunt sat, and, though Rocky, balancing himself on the little seat in front, did his best to supply dialogue, we weren't a chatty party.

I had a glimpse of Jeeves as we went into the flat, sitting in his lair, and I wished I could have called to him to rally round. Something told me that I was about to need him.

The stuff was on the table in the sitting-room. Rocky took up the decanter.

"Say when, Bertie."

"Stop!" barked the aunt, and he dropped it.

I caught Rocky's eye as he stooped to pick up the ruins. It was the eye of one who sees it coming.

"Leave it there, Rockmetteller!" said Aunt Isabel; and Rocky left it there.

"The time has come to speak," she said. "I cannot stand idly by and see a young man going to perdition!"

Poor old Rocky gave a sort of gurgle, a kind of sound rather like the whisky had made running out of the decanter on to my carpet.

"Eh?" he said, blinking.

The aunt proceeded.

"The fault," she said, "was mine. I had not then seen the light. But now my eyes are open. I see the hideous mistake I have made. I shudder at the thought of the wrong I did you, Rockmetteller, by urging you into contact with this wicked city."

I saw Rocky grope feebly for the table. His fingers touched it, and a look of relief came into the poor chappie's face. I understood his feelings.

"But when I wrote you that letter, Rockmetteller, instructing you to go to the city and live its life, I had not had the privilege of hearing Mr. Mundy speak on the subject of New York."

"Jimmy Mundy!" I cried.

You know how it is sometimes when everything seems all mixed up and you suddenly get a clue. When she mentioned Jimmy Mundy I began to understand more or less what had happened. I'd seen it happen before. I remember, back in England, the man I had before Jeeves sneaked off to a meeting on his evening out and came back and denounced me in front of a crowd of chappies I was giving a bit of supper to as a moral leper.

The aunt gave me a withering up and down.

"Yes; Jimmy Mundy!" she said. "I am surprised at a man of your stamp having heard of him. There is no music, there are no drunken, dancing men, no shameless, flaunting women at his meetings; so for you they would have no attraction. But for others, less dead in sin, he has his message. He has come to save New York from itself; to force it—in his picturesque phrase—to hit the trail. It was three days ago, Rockmetteller, that I first heard him. It was an accident that took me to his meeting. How often in this life a mere accident may shape our whole future!

"You had been called away by that telephone message from Mr. Belasco; so you could not take me to the Hippodrome, as we had arranged. I asked your man-servant, Jeeves, to take me there. The man has very little intelligence. He seems to have misunderstood me. I am thankful that he did. He took me to what I subsequently learned was Madison Square Garden, where Mr. Mundy is holding his meetings. He escorted me to a seat and then left me. And it was not till the meeting had begun that I discovered the mistake which had been made. My seat was in the middle of a row. I could not leave without inconveniencing a great many people, so I remained."

She gulped.

"Rockmetteller, I have never been so thankful for anything else. Mr. Mundy was wonderful! He was like some prophet of old, scourging the sins of the people. He leaped about in a frenzy of inspiration till I feared he would do himself an injury. Sometimes he expressed himself in a somewhat odd manner, but every word carried conviction. He showed me New York in its true colours. He showed me the vanity and wickedness of sitting in gilded haunts of vice, eating lobster when decent people should be in bed.

"He said that the tango and the fox-trot were devices of the devil to drag people down into the Bottomless Pit. He said that there was more sin in ten minutes with a negro banjo orchestra than in all the ancient revels of Nineveh and Babylon. And when he stood on one leg and pointed right at where I was sitting and shouted 'This means you!' I could have sunk through the floor. I came away a changed woman. Surely you must have noticed the change in me, Rockmetteller? You must have seen that I was no longer the careless, thoughtless person who had urged you to dance in those places of wickedness?"

Rocky was holding on to the table as if it was his only friend.

"Y-yes," he stammered; "I—I thought something was wrong."

"Wrong? Something was right! Everything was right! Rockmetteller, it is not too late for you to be saved. You have only sipped of the evil cup. You have not drained it. It will be hard at first, but you will find that you can do it if you fight with a stout heart against the glamour and fascination of this dreadful city. Won't you, for my sake, try, Rockmetteller? Won't you go back to the country to-morrow and begin the struggle? Little by little, if you use your will——"

I can't help thinking it must have been that word "will" that roused dear old Rocky like a trumpet call. It must have brought home to him the realization that a miracle had come off and saved him from being cut out of Aunt Isabel's. At any rate, as she said it he perked up, let go of the table, and faced her with gleaming eyes.

"Do you want me to go back to the country, Aunt Isabel?"

"Yes."

"Not to live in the country?"

"Yes, Rockmetteller."

"Stay in the country all the time, do you mean? Never come to New York?"

"Yes, Rockmetteller; I mean just that. It is the only way. Only there can you be safe from temptation. Will you do it, Rockmetteller? Will you—for my sake?"

Rocky grabbed the table again. He seemed to draw a lot of encouragement from that table.

"I will!" he said.

"Jeeves," I said. It was next day, and I was back in the old flat, lying in the old arm-chair, with my feet upon the good old table. I had just come from seeing dear old Rocky off to his country cottage, and an hour before he had seen his aunt off to whatever hamlet it was that she was the curse of; so we were alone at last. "Jeeves, there's no place like home—what?"

"Very true, sir."

"The jolly old roof-tree, and all that sort of thing—what?"

"Precisely, sir."

I lit another cigarette.

"Jeeves."

"Sir?"

"Do you know, at one point in the business I really thought you were baffled."

"Indeed, sir?"

"When did you get the idea of taking Miss Rockmetteller to the meeting? It was pure genius!"

"Thank you, sir. It came to me a little suddenly, one morning when I was thinking of my aunt, sir."

"Your aunt? The hansom cab one?"

"Yes, sir. I recollected that, whenever we observed one of her attacks coming on, we used to send for the clergyman of the parish. We always found that if he talked to her a while of higher things it diverted her mind from hansom cabs. It occurred to me that the same treatment might prove efficacious in the case of Miss Rockmetteller."

I was stunned by the man's resource.

"It's brain," I said; "pure brain! What do you do to get like that, Jeeves? I believe you must eat a lot of fish, or something. Do you eat a lot of fish, Jeeves?"

"No, sir."

"Oh, well, then, it's just a gift, I take it; and if you aren't born that way there's no use worrying."

"Precisely, sir," said Jeeves. "If I might make the suggestion, sir, I should not continue to wear your present tie. The green shade gives you a slightly bilious air. I should strongly advocate the blue with the red domino pattern instead, sir."

"All right, Jeeves," I said, humbly. "You know!"

Jeeves Takes Charge

NOW, touching this business of old Jeeves—my man, you know—how do we stand? Lots of people think I'm much too dependent on him. My Aunt Agatha, in fact, has even gone so far as to call him my keeper. Well, what I say is: Why not? The man's a genius. From the collar upward he stands alone. I gave up trying to run my own affairs within a week of his coming to me. That was about half a dozen years ago, directly after the rather rummy business of Florence Craye, my Uncle Willoughby's book, and Edwin, the Boy Scout.

The thing really began when I got back to Easeby, my uncle's place in Shropshire. I was spending a week or so there, as I generally did in the summer; and I had had to break my visit to come back to London to get a new valet. I had found Meadowes, the fellow I had taken to Easeby with me, sneaking my silk socks, a thing no bloke of spirit could stick at any price. It transpiring, moreover, that he had looted a lot of other things here and there about the place, I was reluctantly compelled to hand the misguided blighter the mitten and go to London to ask the registry office to dig up another specimen for my approval. They sent me Jeeves.

I shall always remember the morning he came. It so happened that the night before I had been present at a rather cheery little supper, and I was feeling pretty rocky. On top of this I was trying to read a book Florence Craye had given me. She had been one of the house-party at Easeby, and two or three days before I left we had got engaged. I was due back at the end of the week, and I knew she would expect me to have finished the book by then. You see, she was particularly keen on boosting me up a bit nearer her own plane of intellect. She was a girl with a wonderful profile, but steeped to the gills in serious purpose. I can't give you a better idea of the way things stood than by telling you that the book she'd given me to read was called "Types of Ethical Theory," and that when I opened it at random I struck a page beginning:—

> *The postulate or common understanding involved in speech is certainly co-extensive, in the obligation it carries, with the social organism of which language is the instrument, and the ends of which it is an effort to subserve.*

All perfectly true, no doubt; but not the sort of thing to spring on a lad with a morning head.

I was doing my best to skim through this bright little volume when the bell rang. I crawled off the sofa and opened the door. A kind of darkish sort of respectful Johnnie stood without.

"I was sent by the agency, sir," he said. "I was given to understand that you required a valet."

I'd have preferred an undertaker; but I told him to stagger in, and he floated noiselessly through the doorway like a healing zephyr. That impressed me from the start. Meadowes had had flat feet and used to clump. This fellow didn't seem to have any feet at all. He just streamed in. He had a grave, sympathetic face, as if he, too, knew what it was to sup with the lads.

"Excuse me, sir," he said gently.

Then he seemed to flicker, and wasn't there any longer. I heard him moving about in the kitchen, and presently he came back with a glass on a tray.

"If you would drink this, sir," he said, with a kind of bedside manner, rather like the royal doctor shooting the bracer into the sick prince. "It is a little preparation of my own invention. It is the Worcester Sauce that gives it its colour. The raw egg makes it nutritious. The red pepper gives it its bite. Gentlemen have told me they have found it extremely invigorating after a late evening."

I would have clutched at anything that looked like a life-line that morning. I swallowed the stuff. For a moment I felt as if somebody had touched off a bomb inside the old bean and was strolling down my throat with a lighted torch, and then everything seemed suddenly to get all right. The sun shone in through the window; birds twittered in the tree-tops; and, generally speaking, hope dawned once more.

"You're engaged!" I said, as soon as I could say anything.

I perceived clearly that this cove was one of the world's wonders, the sort no home should be without.

"Thank you, sir. My name is Jeeves."

"You can start in at once?"

"Immediately, sir."

"Because I'm due down at Easeby, in Shropshire, the day after to-morrow."

"Very good, sir." He looked past me at the mantelpiece. "That is an excellent likeness of Lady Florence Craye, sir. It is two years since I saw her ladyship. I was at one time in Lord Worplesdon's employment. I tendered my resignation because I could not see eye to eye with his lordship in his desire to dine in dress trousers, a flannel shirt, and a shooting coat."

He couldn't tell me anything I didn't know about the old boy's eccentricity. This Lord Worplesdon was Florence's father. He was the old buster who, a few years later, came down to breakfast one morning, lifted the first cover he saw, said "Eggs! Eggs! Eggs! Damn all eggs!" in an overwrought sort of voice, and instantly legged it for France, never to return to the bosom of his family. This, mind you, being a bit of luck for the bosom of the family, for old Worplesdon had the worst temper in the county.

I had known the family ever since I was a kid, and from boyhood up this old boy had put the fear of death into me. Time, the great healer, could never remove from my memory the occasion when he found me — then a stripling of fifteen — smoking one of his special cigars in the stables. He got after me with a hunting-crop just at the moment when I was beginning to realise that what I wanted most on earth was solitude and repose, and chased me more than a mile across difficult country. If there was a flaw, so to speak, in the pure joy of being engaged to Florence, it was the fact that she rather took after her father, and one was never certain when she might erupt. She had a wonderful profile, though.

"Lady Florence and I are engaged, Jeeves," I said.

"Indeed, sir?"

You know, there was a kind of rummy something about his manner.

Perfectly all right and all that, but not what you'd call chirpy. It somehow gave me the impression that he wasn't keen on Florence. Well, of course, it wasn't my business. I supposed that while he had been valeting old Worplesdon she must have trodden on his toes in some way. Florence was a dear girl, and, seen sideways, most awfully good-looking; but if she had a fault it was a tendency to be a bit imperious with the domestic staff.

At this point in the proceedings there was another ring at the front door. Jeeves shimmered out and came back with a telegram. I opened it. It ran:

Return immediately. Extremely urgent. Catch first train. Florence.

"Rum!" I said.

"Sir?"

"Oh, nothing!"

It shows how little I knew Jeeves in those days that I didn't go a bit deeper into the matter with him. Nowadays I would never dream of reading a rummy communication without asking him what he thought of it. And this one was devilish odd. What I mean is, Florence knew I was going back to Easeby the day after to-morrow, anyway; so why the hurry call? Something must have happened, of course; but I couldn't see what on earth it could be.

"Jeeves," I said, "we shall be going down to Easeby this afternoon. Can you manage it?"

"Certainly, sir."

"You can get your packing done and all that?"

"Without any difficulty, sir. Which suit will you wear for the journey?"

"This one."

I had on a rather sprightly young check that morning, to which I was a good deal attached; I fancied it, in fact, more than a little. It was perhaps rather sudden till you got used to it, but, nevertheless, an extremely sound effort, which many lads at the club and elsewhere had admired unrestrainedly.

"Very good, sir."

Again there was that kind of rummy something in his manner. It was the way he said it, don't you know. He didn't like the suit. I pulled myself together to assert myself. Something seemed to tell me that, unless I was jolly careful and nipped this lad in the bud, he would be starting to boss me. He had the aspect of a distinctly resolute blighter.

Well, I wasn't going to have any of that sort of thing, by Jove! I'd seen so many cases of fellows who had become perfect slaves to their valets. I remember poor old Aubrey Fothergill telling me—with absolute tears in his eyes, poor chap!—one night at the club, that he had been compelled to give up a favourite pair of brown shoes simply because Meekyn, his man, disapproved of them. You have to keep these fellows in their place, don't you know. You have to work the good old iron-hand-in-the-velvet-glove wheeze. If you give them a what's-its-name, they take a thingummy.

"Don't you like this suit, Jeeves?" I said coldly.

"Oh, yes, sir."

"Well, what don't you like about it?"

"It is a very nice suit, sir."

"Well, what's wrong with it? Out with it, dash it!"

"If I might make the suggestion, sir, a simple brown or blue, with a hint of some quiet twill——"

"What absolute rot!"

"Very good, sir."

"Perfectly blithering, my dear man!"

"As you say, sir."

I felt as if I had stepped on the place where the last stair ought to have been, but wasn't. I felt defiant, if you know what I mean, and there didn't seem anything to defy.

"All right, then," I said.

"Yes, sir."

And then he went away to collect his kit, while I started in again on "Types of Ethical Theory" and took a stab at a chapter headed "Idio-psychological Ethics."

Most of the way down in the train that afternoon, I was wondering what could be up at the other end. I simply couldn't see what could have happened. Easeby wasn't one of those country houses you read about in the society novels, where young girls are lured on to play baccarat and then skinned to the bone of their jewellery, and so on. The house-party I had left had consisted entirely of law-abiding birds like myself.

Besides, my uncle wouldn't have let anything of that kind go on in his house. He was a rather stiff, precise sort of old boy, who liked a quiet life. He was just finishing a history of the family or something, which he had been working on for the last year, and didn't stir much from the library. He was rather a good instance of what they say about its being a good scheme for a fellow to sow his wild oats. I'd been told that in his youth Uncle Willoughby had been a bit of a rounder. You would never have thought it to look at him now.

When I got to the house, Oakshott, the butler, told me that Florence was in her room, watching her maid pack. Apparently there was a dance on at a house about twenty miles away that night, and she was motoring over with some of the Easeby lot and would be away some nights. Oakshott said she had told him to tell her the moment I arrived; so I trickled into the smoking-room and waited, and presently in she came. A glance showed me that she was perturbed, and even peeved. Her eyes had a goggly look, and altogether she appeared considerably pipped.

"Darling!" I said, and attempted the good old embrace; but she side-stepped like a bantam weight.

"Don't!"

"What's the matter?"

"Everything's the matter! Bertie, you remember asking me, when you left, to make myself pleasant to your uncle?"

"Yes."

The idea being, of course, that as at that time I was more or less dependent on Uncle Willoughby I couldn't very well marry without his approval. And though I knew he wouldn't have any objection to Florence, having known her father since they were at Oxford together, I hadn't wanted to take any chances; so I had told her to make an effort to fascinate the old boy.

"You told me it would please him particularly if I asked him to read me some of his history of the family."

"Wasn't he pleased?"

"He was delighted. He finished writing the thing yesterday afternoon, and read me nearly all of it last night. I have never had such a shock in my life. The book is an outrage. It is impossible. It is horrible!"

"But, dash it, the family weren't so bad as all that."

"It is not a history of the family at all. Your uncle has written his reminiscences! He calls them 'Recollections of a Long Life'!"

I began to understand. As I say, Uncle Willoughby had been somewhat on the tabasco side as a young man, and it began to look as if he might have turned out something pretty fruity if he had started recollecting his long life.

"If half of what he has written is true," said Florence, "your uncle's youth must have been perfectly appalling. The moment we began to read he plunged straight into a most scandalous story of how he and my father were thrown out of a music-hall in 1887!"

"Why?"

"I decline to tell you why."

It must have been something pretty bad. It took a lot to make them chuck people out of music-halls in 1887.

"Your uncle specifically states that father had drunk a quart and a half of champagne before beginning the evening," she went on. "The book is full of stories like that. There is a dreadful one about Lord Emsworth."

"Lord Emsworth? Not the one we know? Not the one at Blandings?"

A most respectable old Johnnie, don't you know. Doesn't do a thing nowadays but dig in the garden with a spud.

"The very same. That is what makes the book so unspeakable. It is full of stories about people one knows who are the essence of propriety to-day, but who seem to have behaved, when they were in London in the 'eighties, in a manner that would not have been tolerated in the fo'c'sle of a whaler. Your uncle seems to remember everything disgraceful that happened to anybody when he was in his early twenties. There is a story about Sir Stanley Gervase-Gervase at Rosherville Gardens which is ghastly in its perfection of detail. It seems that Sir Stanley—but I can't tell you!"

"Have a dash!"

"No!"

"Oh, well, I shouldn't worry. No publisher will print the book if it's as bad as all that."

"On the contrary, your uncle told me that all negotiations are settled with Riggs and Ballinger, and he's sending off the manuscript to-morrow for immediate publication. They make a special thing of that sort of book. They published Lady Carnaby's 'Memories of Eighty Interesting Years.' "

"I read 'em!"

"Well, then, when I tell you that Lady Carnaby's Memories are simply not to be compared with your uncle's Recollections, you will understand my state of mind. And father appears in nearly every story in the book! I am horrified at the things he did when he was a young man!"

"What's to be done?"

"The manuscript must be intercepted before it reaches Riggs and Ballinger, and destroyed!"

I sat up.

This sounded rather sporting.

"How are you going to do it?" I enquired.

"How can I do it? Didn't I tell you the parcel goes off to-morrow? I am going to the Murgatroyds' dance to-night and shall not be back till Monday. You must do it. That is why I telegraphed to you."

"What!"

She gave me a look.

"Do you mean to say you refuse to help me, Bertie?"

"No; but—I say!"

"It's quite simple."

"But even if I—— What I mean is—— Of course, anything I can do—but—if you know what I mean——"

"You say you want to marry me, Bertie?"

"Yes, of course; but still——"

For a moment she looked exactly like her old father.

"I will never marry you if those Recollections are published."

"But, Florence, old thing!"

"I mean it. You may look on it as a test, Bertie. If you have the resource and courage to carry this thing through, I will take it as evidence that you are not the vapid and shiftless person most people think you. If you fail, I shall know that your Aunt Agatha was right when she called you a spineless invertebrate and advised me strongly not to marry you. It will be perfectly simple for you to intercept the manuscript, Bertie. It only requires a little resolution."

"But suppose Uncle Willoughby catches me at it? He'd cut me off with a bob."

"If you care more for your uncle's money than for me——"

"No, no! Rather not!"

"Very well, then. The parcel containing the manuscript will, of course, be placed on the hall table to-morrow for Oakshott to take to the village with the letters. All you have to do is to take it away and destroy it. Then your uncle will think it has been lost in the post."

It sounded thin to me.

"Hasn't he got a copy of it?"

"No; it has not been typed. He is sending the manuscript just as he wrote it."

"But he could write it over again."

"As if he would have the energy!"

"But——"

"If you are going to do nothing but make absurd objections, Bertie——"

"I was only pointing things out."

"Well, don't! Once and for all, will you do me this quite simple act of kindness?"

The way she put it gave me an idea.

"Why not get Edwin to do it? Keep it in the family, kind of, don't you know. Besides, it would be a boon to the kid."

A jolly bright idea it seemed to me. Edwin was her young brother, who was spending his holidays at Easeby. He was a ferret-faced kid, whom I had disliked since birth. As a matter of fact, talking of Recollections and Memories, it was young blighted Edwin who, nine years before, had led his father to where I was smoking his cigar and caused all of the unpleasantness. He was fourteen now and had just joined the Boy Scouts. He was one of those thorough kids, and took his responsibilities pretty seriously. He was always in a sort of fever because he was dropping behind schedule with his daily acts of kindness. However hard he tried, he'd fall behind; and then you would find him prowling about the house, setting such a clip to try and catch up with himself that Easeby was rapidly becoming a perfect hell for man and beast.

The idea didn't seem to strike Florence.

"I shall do nothing of the kind, Bertie. I wonder you can't appreciate the compliment I am paying you—trusting you like this."

"Oh, I see that all right, but what I mean is, Edwin would do it so much better than I would. These Boy Scouts are up to all sorts of dodges. They spoor, don't you know, and take cover and creep about, and what not."

"Bertie, will you or will you not do this perfectly trivial thing for me? If not, say so now, and let us end this farce of pretending that you care a snap of the fingers for me."

"Dear old soul, I love you devotedly!"

"Then will you or will you not——"

"Oh, all right," I said. "All right! All right! All right!"

And then I tottered forth to think it over. I met Jeeves in the passage just outside.

"I beg your pardon, sir. I was endeavouring to find you."

"What's the matter?"

"I felt that I should tell you, sir, that somebody has been putting black polish on our brown walking shoes."

"What! Who? Why?"

"I could not say, sir."

"Can anything be done with them?"

"Nothing, sir."

"Damn!"

"Very good, sir."

I've often wondered since then how these murderer fellows manage to keep in shape while they're contemplating their next effort. I had a much simpler sort of job on hand, and the thought of it rattled me to such an extent in the night watches that I was a perfect wreck next day. Dark circles under the eyes — I give you my word! I had to call on Jeeves to rally round with one of those life-savers of his.

From breakfast on I felt like a bag-snatcher at a railway station. I had to hang about waiting for the parcel to be put on the hall table, and it wasn't put. Uncle Willoughby was a fixture in the library, adding the finishing touches to the great work, I supposed, and the more I thought the thing over the less I liked it. The chances against my pulling it off seemed about three to two, and the thought of what would happen if I didn't gave me cold shivers down the spine. Uncle Willoughby was a pretty mild sort of old boy, as a rule, but I've known him to cut up rough, and, by Jove, he was scheduled to extend himself if he caught me trying to get away with his life work.

It wasn't till nearly four that he toddled out of the library with the parcel under his arm, put it on the table, and toddled off again. I was hiding a bit to the south-east at the moment, behind a suit of armour. I bounded out and legged it for the table. Then I nipped upstairs to hide the swag. I charged in like a mustang and nearly stubbed my toe on young blighted Edwin, the Boy Scout. He was standing at the chest of drawers, confound him, messing about with my ties.

"Hallo!" he said.

"What are you doing here?"

"I'm tidying your room. It's my last Saturday's act of kindness."

"Last Saturday's?"

"I'm five days behind. I was six till last night, but I polished your shoes."

"Was it you —— "

"Yes. Did you see them? I just happened to think of it. I was in here, looking round. Mr. Berkeley had this room while you were away. He left this morning. I thought perhaps he might have left something in it that I could have sent on. I've often done acts of kindness that way."

"You must be a comfort to one and all!"

It became more and more apparent to me that this infernal kid must somehow be turned out eftsoons or right speedily. I had hidden the parcel behind my back, and I didn't think he had seen it; but I wanted to get at that chest of drawers quick, before anyone else came along.

"I shouldn't bother about tidying the room," I said.

"I like tidying it. It's not a bit of trouble—really."

"But it's quite tidy now."

"Not so tidy as I shall make it."

This was getting perfectly rotten. I didn't want to murder the kid, and yet there didn't seem any other way of shifting him. I pressed down the mental accelerator. The old lemon throbbed fiercely. I got an idea.

"There's something much kinder than that which you could do," I said. "You see that box of cigars? Take it down to the smoking-room and snip off the ends for me. That would save me no end of trouble. Stagger along, laddie."

He seemed a bit doubtful; but he staggered. I shoved the parcel into a drawer, locked it, trousered the key, and felt better. I might be a chump, but, dash it, I could out-general a mere kid with a face like a ferret. I went downstairs again. Just as I was passing the smoking-room door, out curveted Edwin. It seemed to me that if he wanted to do a real act of kindness he would commit suicide.

"I'm snipping them," he said.

"Snip on! Snip on!"

"Do you like them snipped much, or only a bit?"

"Medium."

"All right. I'll be getting on, then."

"I should."

And we parted.

Fellows who know all about that sort of thing—detectives, and so on—will tell you that the most difficult thing in the world is to get rid of the body. I remember, as a kid, having to learn by heart a poem about a bird by the name of Eugene Aram, who had the deuce of a job in this respect. All I can recall of the actual poetry is the bit that goes:

Tum-tum, tum-tum, tum-tumty-tum,
I slew him, tum-tum-tum!

But I recollect that the poor blighter spent much of his valuable time dumping the corpse into ponds and burying it, and what not, only to have it pop out at him again. It was about an hour after I had shoved the parcel into the drawer when I realised that I had let myself in for just the same sort of thing.

Florence had talked in an airy sort of way about destroying the manuscript; but when one came down to it, how the deuce can a chap destroy a great chunky mass of paper in somebody else's house in the middle of summer? I couldn't ask to have a fire in my bedroom, with the thermometer in the eighties. And if I didn't burn the thing, how else could I get rid of it? Fellows on the battle-field eat dispatches to keep them from falling into the hands of the enemy, but it would have taken me a year to eat Uncle Willoughby's Recollections.

I'm bound to say the problem absolutely baffled me. The only thing seemed to be to leave the parcel in the drawer and hope for the best.

I don't know whether you have ever experienced it, but it's a dashed unpleasant thing having a crime on one's conscience. Towards the end of the day the mere sight of the drawer began to depress me. I found myself getting all on edge; and once when Uncle Willoughby trickled silently into the smoking-room when I was alone there and spoke to me before I knew he was there, I broke the record for the sitting high jump.

I was wondering all the time when Uncle Willoughby would sit up and take notice. I didn't think he would have time to suspect that anything had gone wrong till Saturday morning, when he would be expecting, of course, to get the acknowledgment of the manuscript from the publishers. But early on Friday evening he came out of the library as I was passing and asked me to step in. He was looking considerably rattled.

"Bertie," he said—he always spoke in a precise sort of pompous kind of way—"an exceedingly disturbing thing has happened. As you know, I dispatched the manuscript of my book to Messrs. Riggs and Ballinger, the publishers, yesterday afternoon. It should have reached them by the first post this morning. Why I should have been uneasy I cannot say, but my mind was not altogether at rest respecting the safety of the parcel. I therefore telephoned to Messrs. Riggs and Ballinger a few moments back to make enquiries. To my consternation they informed me that they were not yet in receipt of my manuscript."

"Very rum!"

"I recollect distinctly placing it myself on the hall table in good time to be taken to the village. But here is a sinister thing. I have spoken to Oakshott, who took the rest of the letters to the post office, and he cannot recall seeing it there. He is, indeed, unswerving in his assertions that when he went to the hall to collect the letters there was no parcel among them."

"Sounds funny!"

"Bertie, shall I tell you what I suspect?"

"What's that?"

"The suspicion will no doubt sound to you incredible, but it alone seems to fit the facts as we know them. I incline to the belief that the parcel has been stolen."

"Oh, I say! Surely not!"

"Wait! Hear me out. Though I have said nothing to you before, or to anyone else, concerning the matter, the fact remains that during the past few weeks a number of objects—some valuable, others not—have disappeared in this house. The conclusion to which one is irresistibly impelled is that we have a kleptomaniac in our midst. It is a peculiarity of kleptomania, as you are no doubt aware, that the subject is unable to differentiate between the intrinsic values of objects. He will purloin an old coat as readily as a diamond ring, or a tobacco pipe costing but a few shillings with the same eagerness as a purse of gold. The fact that this manuscript of mine could be of no possible value to any outside person convinces me that——"

"But, uncle, one moment; I know all about those things that were stolen. It was Meadowes, my man, who pinched them. I caught him snaffling my silk socks. Right in the act, by Jove!"

He was tremendously impressed.

"You amaze me, Bertie! Send for the man at once and question him."

"But he isn't here. You see, directly I found that he was a sock-sneaker I gave him the boot. That's why I went to London—to get a new man."

"Then, if the man Meadowes is no longer in the house it could not be he who purloined my manuscript. The whole thing is inexplicable."

After which we brooded for a bit. Uncle Willoughby pottered about the room, registering baffledness, while I sat sucking at a cigarette, feeling rather like a chappie I'd once read about in a book, who murdered another cove and hid the body under the dining-room table, and then had to be the life and soul of a dinner party, with it there all the time. My guilty secret oppressed me to such an extent that after a while I couldn't stick it any longer. I lit another cigarette and started for a stroll in the grounds, by way of cooling off.

It was one of those still evenings you get in the summer, when you can hear a snail clear its throat a mile away. The sun was sinking over the hills and the gnats were fooling about all over the place, and everything smelled rather topping—what with the falling dew and so on—and I was just beginning to feel a little soothed by the peace of it all when suddenly I heard my name spoken.

"It's about Bertie."

It was the loathsome voice of young blighted Edwin! For a moment I couldn't locate it. Then I realised that it came from the library. My stroll had taken me within a few yards of the open window.

I had often wondered how those Johnnies in books did it—I mean the fellows with whom it was the work of a moment to do about a dozen things that ought to have taken them about ten minutes. But, as a matter of fact, it was the work of a moment with me to chuck away my cigarette, swear a bit, leap about ten yards, dive into a bush that stood near the library window, and stand there with my ears flapping. I was as certain as I've ever been of anything that all sorts of rotten things were in the offing.

"About Bertie?" I heard Uncle Willoughby say.

"About Bertie and your parcel. I heard you talking to him just now. I believe he's got it."

When I tell you that just as I heard these frightful words a fairly substantial beetle of sorts dropped from the bush down the back of my neck, and I couldn't even stir to squash the same, you will understand that I felt pretty rotten. Everything seemed against me.

"What do you mean, boy? I was discussing the disappearance of my manuscript with Bertie only a moment back, and he professed himself as perplexed by the mystery as myself."

"Well, I was in his room yesterday afternoon, doing him an act of kindness, and he came in with a parcel. I could see it, though he tried to keep it behind his back. And then he asked me to go to the smoking-room and snip some cigars for him; and about two minutes afterwards he came down—and he wasn't carrying anything. So it must be in his room."

I understand they deliberately teach these dashed Boy Scouts to cultivate their powers of observation and deduction and what not. Devilish thoughtless and inconsiderate of them, I call it. Look at the trouble it causes.

"It sounds incredible," said Uncle Willoughby, thereby bucking me up a trifle.

"Shall I go and look in his room?" asked young blighted Edwin. "I'm sure the parcel's there."

"But what could be his motive for perpetrating this extraordinary theft?"

"Perhaps he's a—what you said just now."

"A kleptomaniac? Impossible!"

"It might have been Bertie who took all those things from the very start," suggested the little brute hopefully. "He may be like Raffles."

"Raffles?"

"He's a chap in a book who went about pinching things."

"I cannot believe that Bertie would—ah—go about pinching things."

"Well, I'm sure he's got the parcel. I'll tell you what you might do. You might say that Mr. Berkeley wired that he had left something here. He had Bertie's room, you know. You might say you wanted to look for it."

"That would be possible. I——"

I didn't wait to hear any more. Things were getting too hot. I sneaked softly out of my bush and raced for the front door. I sprinted up to my room and made for the drawer where I had put the parcel. And then I found I hadn't the key. It wasn't for the deuce of a time that I recollected I had shifted it to my evening trousers the night before and must have forgotten to take it out again.

Where the dickens were my evening things? I had looked all over the place before I remembered that Jeeves must have taken them away to brush. To leap at the bell and ring it was, with me, the work of a moment. I had just rung it when there was a footstep outside, and in came Uncle Willoughby.

"Oh, Bertie," he said, without a blush, "I have—ah—received a telegram from Berkeley, who occupied this room in your absence, asking me to forward him his—er—his cigarette-case, which, it would appear, he inadvertently omitted to take with him when he left the house. I cannot find it downstairs; and it has, therefore, occurred to me that he may have left it in this room. I will—er—just take a look around."

It was one of the most disgusting spectacles I've ever seen—this white-haired old man, who should have been thinking of the hereafter, standing there lying like an actor.

"I haven't seen it anywhere," I said.

"Nevertheless, I will search. I must—ah—spare no effort."

"I should have seen it if it had been here—what?"

"It may have escaped your notice. It is—er—possibly in one of the drawers."

He began to nose about. He pulled out drawer after drawer, pottering around like an old bloodhound, and babbling from time to time about Berkeley and his cigarette-case in a way that struck me as perfectly ghastly. I just stood there, losing weight every moment.

Then he came to the drawer where the parcel was.

"This appears to be locked," he said, rattling the handle.

"Yes; I shouldn't bother about that one. It—it's—er—locked, and all that sort of thing."

"You have not the key?"

A soft, respectful voice spoke behind me.

"I fancy, sir, that this must be the key you require. It was in the pocket of your evening trousers."

It was Jeeves. He had shimmered in, carrying my evening things, and was standing there holding out the key. I could have massacred the man.

"Thank you," said my uncle.

"Not at all, sir."

The next moment Uncle Willoughby had opened the drawer. I shut my eyes.

"No," said Uncle Willoughby, "there is nothing here. The drawer is empty. Thank you, Bertie. I hope I have not disturbed you. I fancy—er—Berkeley must have taken his case with him after all."

When he had gone I shut the door carefully. Then I turned to Jeeves. The man was putting my evening things out on a chair.

"Er—Jeeves!"

"Sir?"

"Oh, nothing."

It was deuced difficult to know how to begin.

"Er—Jeeves!"

"Sir?"

"Did you—— Was there—— Have you by chance——"

"I removed the parcel this morning, sir."

"Oh—ah—why?"

"I considered it more prudent, sir."

I mused for a while.

"Of course, I suppose all this seems tolerably rummy to you, Jeeves?"

"Not at all, sir. I chanced to overhear you and Lady Florence speaking of the matter the other evening, sir."

"Did you, by Jove?"

"Yes, sir."

"Well — er — Jeeves, I think that, on the whole, if you were to — as it were — freeze on to that parcel until we get back to London ——"

"Exactly, sir."

"And then we might — er — so to speak — chuck it away somewhere — what?"

"Precisely, sir."

"I'll leave it in your hands."

"Entirely, sir."

"You know, Jeeves, you're by way of being rather a topper."

"I endeavour to give satisfaction, sir."

"One in a million, by Jove!"

"It is very kind of you to say so, sir."

"Well, that's about all, then, I think."

"Very good, sir."

Florence came back on Monday. I didn't see her till we were all having tea in the hall. It wasn't till the crowd had cleared away a bit that we got a chance of having a word together.

"Well, Bertie?" she said.

"It's all right."

"You have destroyed the manuscript?"

"Not exactly; but ——"

"What do you mean?"

"I mean I haven't absolutely ——"

"Bertie, your manner is furtive!"

"It's all right. It's this way ——"

And I was just going to explain how things stood when out of the library came leaping Uncle Willoughby looking as braced as a two-year-old. The old boy was a changed man.

"A most remarkable thing, Bertie! I have just been speaking with Mr. Riggs on the telephone, and he tells me he received my manuscript by the first post this morning. I cannot imagine what can have caused the delay. Our postal facilities are extremely inadequate in the rural districts. I shall write to headquarters about it. It is insufferable if valuable parcels are to be delayed in this fashion."

I happened to be looking at Florence's profile at the moment, and at this juncture she swung round and gave me a look that went right through me like a knife. Uncle Willoughby meandered back to the library, and there was a silence that you could have dug bits out of with a spoon.

"I can't understand it," I said at last. "I can't understand it, by Jove!"

"I can. I can understand it perfectly, Bertie. Your heart failed you. Rather than risk offending your uncle you——"

"No, no! Absolutely!"

"You preferred to lose me rather than risk losing the money. Perhaps you did not think I meant what I said. I meant every word. Our engagement is ended."

"But—I say!"

"Not another word!"

"But, Florence, old thing!"

"I do not wish to hear any more. I see now that your Aunt Agatha was perfectly right. I consider that I have had a very lucky escape. There was a time when I thought that, with patience, you might be moulded into something worth while. I see now that you are impossible!"

And she popped off, leaving me to pick up the pieces. When I had collected the *debris* to some extent I went to my room and rang for Jeeves. He came in looking as if nothing had happened or was ever going to happen. He was the calmest thing in captivity.

"Jeeves!" I yelled. "Jeeves, that parcel has arrived in London!"

"Yes, sir?"

"Did you send it?"

"Yes, sir. I acted for the best, sir. I think that both you and Lady Florence overestimated the danger of people being offended at being mentioned in Sir Willoughby's Recollections. It has been my experience, sir, that the normal person enjoys seeing his or her name in print, irrespective of what is said about them. I have an aunt, sir, who a few years ago was a martyr to swollen limbs. She tried Walkinshaw's Supreme Ointment and obtained considerable relief—so much so that she sent them an unsolicited testimonial. Her pride at seeing her photograph in the daily papers in connection with descriptions of her lower limbs before taking, which were nothing less than revolting, was so intense that it led me to believe that publicity, of whatever sort, is what nearly everybody desires. Moreover, if you have ever studied psychology, sir, you will know that respectable old gentlemen are by no means averse to having it advertised that they were extremely wild in their youth. I have an uncle——"

I cursed his aunts and his uncles and him and all the rest of the family.

"Do you know that Lady Florence has broken off her engagement with me?"

"Indeed, sir?"

Not a bit of sympathy! I might have been telling him it was a fine day.

"You're sacked!"

"Very good, sir."

He coughed gently.

"As I am no longer in your employment, sir, I can speak freely without appearing to take a liberty. In my opinion you and Lady Florence were quite unsuitably matched. Her ladyship is of a highly determined and arbitrary temperament, quite opposed to your own. I was in Lord Worplesdon's service for nearly a year, during which time I had ample opportunities of studying her ladyship. The opinion of the servants' hall was far from favourable to her. Her ladyship's temper caused a good deal of adverse comment among us. It was at times quite impossible. You would not have been happy, sir!"

"Get out!"

"I think you would also have found her educational methods a little trying, sir. I have glanced at the book her ladyship gave you — it has been lying on your table since our arrival — and it is, in my opinion, quite unsuitable. You would not have enjoyed it. And I have it from her ladyship's own maid, who happened to overhear a conversation between her ladyship and one of the gentlemen staying here — Mr. Maxwell, who is employed in an editorial capacity by one of the reviews — that it was her intention to start you almost immediately upon Nietzsche. You would not enjoy Nietzsche, sir. He is fundamentally unsound."

"Get out!"

"Very good, sir."

It's rummy how sleeping on a thing often makes you feel quite different about it. It's happened to me over and over again. Somehow or other, when I woke next morning the old heart didn't feel half so broken as it had done. It was a perfectly topping day, and there was something about the way the sun came in at the window and the row the birds were kicking up in the ivy that made me half wonder whether Jeeves wasn't right. After all, though she had a wonderful profile, was it such a catch being engaged to Florence Craye as the casual observer might imagine? Wasn't there something in what Jeeves had said about her character? I began to realise that my ideal wife was something quite different, something a lot more clinging and drooping and prattling, and what not.

I had got as far as this in thinking the thing out when that "Types of

Ethical Theory" caught my eye. I opened it, and I give you my honest word this was what hit me:

> *Of the two antithetic terms in the Greek philosophy one only was real and self-subsisting; and that one was Ideal Thought as opposed to that which it has to penetrate and mould. The other, corresponding to our Nature, was in itself phenomenal, unreal, without any permanent footing, having no predicates that held true for two moments together; in short, redeemed from negation only by including indwelling realities appearing through.*

Well—I mean to say—what? And Nietzsche, from all accounts, a lot worse than that!

"Jeeves," I said, when he came in with my morning tea, "I've been thinking it over. You're engaged again."

"Thank you, sir."

I sucked down a cheerful mouthful. A great respect for this bloke's judgment began to soak through me.

"Oh, Jeeves," I said; "about that check suit."

"Yes, sir?"

"Is it really a frost?"

"A trifle too bizarre, sir, in my opinion."

"But lots of fellows have asked me who my tailor is."

"Doubtless in order to avoid him, sir."

"He's supposed to be one of the best men in London."

"I am saying nothing against his moral character, sir."

I hesitated a bit. I had a feeling that I was passing into this chappie's clutches, and that if I gave in now I should become just like poor old Aubrey Fothergill, unable to call my soul my own. On the other hand, this was obviously a cove of rare intelligence, and it would be a comfort in a lot of ways to have him doing the thinking for me. I made up my mind.

"All right, Jeeves," I said. "You know! Give the bally thing away to somebody!"

He looked down at me like a father gazing tenderly at the wayward child.

"Thank you, sir. I gave it to the under-gardener last night. A little more tea, sir?"

Jeeves and the Unbidden Guest

I'M not absolutely certain of my facts, but I rather fancy it's Shakespeare—or, if not, it's some equally brainy lad—who says that it's always just when a chappie is feeling particularly top-hole and more than usually braced with things in general that Fate sneaks up behind him with the bit of lead piping. There's no doubt the man's right. It's absolutely that way with me. Take, for instance, the fairly rummy matter of Lady Malvern and her son Wilmot. A moment before they turned up I was just thinking how thoroughly all right everything was.

It was one of those topping mornings, and I had just climbed out from under the cold shower, feeling like a two-year-old. As a matter of fact, I was especially bucked just then because the day before I had asserted myself with Jeeves—absolutely asserted myself, don't you know. You see, the way things had been going on I was rapidly becoming a dashed serf. The man had jolly well oppressed me. I didn't so much mind when he made me give up one of my new suits, because Jeeves's judgment about suits is sound. But I as near as a toucher rebelled when he wouldn't let me wear a pair of cloth-topped boots which I loved like a couple of brothers. And when he tried to tread on me like a worm in the matter of a hat, I jolly well put my foot down and showed him who was who. It's a long story, and I haven't time to tell you now, but the point is that he wanted me to wear the Longacre—as worn by John Drew—when I had set my heart on the Country Gentleman—as worn by another famous actor chappie—and the end of the matter was that, after a rather painful scene, I bought the Country Gentleman. So that's how things stood on this particular morning, and I was feeling kind of manly and independent.

Well, I was in the bathroom, wondering what there was going to be for breakfast while I massaged the good old spine with a rough towel and sang slightly, when there was a tap at the door. I stopped singing and opened the door an inch.

"What ho without there!"

"Lady Malvern wishes to see you, sir," said Jeeves.

"Eh?"

"Lady Malvern, sir. She is waiting in the sitting-room."

"Pull yourself together, Jeeves, my man," I said, rather severely, for I bar practical jokes before breakfast. "You know perfectly well there's no one waiting for me in the sitting-room. How could there be when it's barely ten o'clock yet?"

"I gathered from her ladyship, sir, that she had landed from an ocean liner at an early hour this morning."

This made the thing a bit more plausible. I remembered that when I had arrived in America about a year before, the proceedings had begun at some ghastly hour like six, and that I had been shot out on to a foreign shore considerably before eight.

"Who the deuce is Lady Malvern, Jeeves?"

"Her ladyship did not confide in me, sir."

"Is she alone?"

"Her ladyship is accompanied by a Lord Pershore, sir. I fancy that his lordship would be her ladyship's son."

"Oh, well, put out rich raiment of sorts, and I'll be dressing."

"Our heather-mixture lounge is in readiness, sir."

"Then lead me to it."

While I was dressing I kept trying to think who on earth Lady Malvern could be. It wasn't till I had climbed through the top of my shirt and was reaching out for the studs that I remembered.

"I've placed her, Jeeves. She's a pal of my Aunt Agatha."

"Indeed, sir?"

"Yes. I met her at lunch one Sunday before I left London. A very vicious specimen. Writes books. She wrote a book on social conditions in India when she came back from the Durbar."

"Yes, sir? Pardon me, sir, but not that tie!"

"Eh?"

"Not that tie with the heather-mixture lounge, sir!"

It was a shock to me. I thought I had quelled the fellow. It was rather a solemn moment. What I mean is, if I weakened now, all my good work the night before would be thrown away. I braced myself.

"What's wrong with this tie? I've seen you give it a nasty look before. Speak out like a man! What's the matter with it?"

"Too ornate, sir."

"Nonsense! A cheerful pink. Nothing more."

"Unsuitable, sir."

"Jeeves, this is the tie I wear!"

"Very good, sir."

Dashed unpleasant. I could see that the man was wounded. But I was firm. I tied the tie, got into the coat and waistcoat, and went into the sitting-room.

"Halloa! Halloa! Halloa!" I said. "What?"

"Ah! How do you do, Mr. Wooster? You have never met my son Wilmot, I think? Motty, darling, this is Mr. Wooster."

Lady Malvern was a hearty, happy, healthy, overpowering sort of dashed female, not so very tall but making up for it by measuring about six feet from the O. P. to the Prompt Side. She fitted into my biggest arm-chair as if it had been built round her by some one who knew they were wearing arm-chairs tight about the hips that season. She had bright, bulging eyes and a lot of yellow hair, and when she spoke she showed about fifty-seven front teeth. She was one of those women who kind of numb a fellow's faculties. She made me feel as if I were ten years old and had been brought into the drawing-room in my Sunday clothes to say how-d'you-do. Altogether by no means the sort of thing a chappie would wish to find in his sitting-room before breakfast.

Motty, the son, was about twenty-three, tall and thin and meek-looking. He had the same yellow hair as his mother, but he wore it plastered down and parted in the middle. His eyes bulged, too, but they weren't bright. They were a dull grey with pink rims. His chin gave up the struggle about half-way down, and he didn't appear to have any eyelashes. A mild, furtive, sheepish sort of blighter, in short.

"Awfully glad to see you," I said. "So you've popped over, eh? Making a long stay in America?"

"About a month. Your aunt gave me your address and told me to be sure and call on you."

I was glad to hear this, as it showed that Aunt Agatha was beginning to come round a bit. There had been some unpleasantness a year before, when she had sent me over to New York to disentangle my Cousin Gussie from the clutches of a girl on the music-hall stage. When I tell you that by the time I had finished my operations Gussie had not only married the girl but had gone on the stage himself and was doing well, you'll understand that Aunt Agatha was upset to no small extent. I simply hadn't dared go back and face her, and it was a relief to find that time had healed the wound and all that sort of thing enough to make her tell her pals to look me up. What I mean is, much as I liked America, I didn't want to have England barred to me for the rest of my natural; and, believe me, England is a jolly sight too small for any one to live in with Aunt Agatha, if she's really on the warpath. So I was braced on hearing these kind words and smiled genially on the assemblage.

"Your aunt said that you would do anything that was in your power to be of assistance to us."

"Rather! Oh, rather! Absolutely!"

"Thank you so much. I want you to put dear Motty up for a little while."

I didn't get this for a moment.

"Put him up? For my clubs?"

"No, no! Darling Motty is essentially a home bird. Aren't you, Motty, darling?"

Motty, who was sucking the knob of his stick, uncorked himself.

"Yes, mother," he said, and corked himself up again.

"I should not like him to belong to clubs. I mean put him up here. Have him to live with you while I am away."

These frightful words trickled out of her like honey. The woman simply didn't seem to understand the ghastly nature of her proposal. I gave Motty the swift east-to-west. He was sitting with his mouth nuzzling the stick, blinking at the wall. The thought of having this planted on me for an indefinite period appalled me. Absolutely appalled me, don't you know. I was just starting to say that the shot wasn't on the board at any price, and that the first sign Motty gave of trying to nestle into my little home I would yell for the police, when she went on, rolling placidly over me, as it were.

There was something about this woman that sapped a chappie's will-power.

"I am leaving New York by the midday train, as I have to pay a visit to Sing-Sing prison. I am extremely interested in prison conditions in America. After that I work my way gradually across to the coast, visiting the points of interest on the journey. You see, Mr. Wooster, I am in America principally on business. No doubt you read my book, *India and the Indians*? My publishers are anxious for me to write a companion volume on the United States. I shall not be able to spend more than a month in the country, as I have to get back for the season, but a month should be ample. I was less than a month in India, and my dear friend Sir Roger Cremorne wrote his *America from Within* after a stay of only two weeks. I should love to take dear Motty with me, but the poor boy gets so sick when he travels by train. I shall have to pick him up on my return."

From where I sat I could see Jeeves in the dining-room, laying the breakfast-table. I wished I could have had a minute with him alone. I felt certain that he would have been able to think of some way of putting a stop to this woman.

"It will be such a relief to know that Motty is safe with you, Mr. Wooster. I know what the temptations of a great city are. Hitherto dear Motty has been sheltered from them. He has lived quietly with me in the country. I know that you will look after him carefully, Mr. Wooster. He will give very little trouble." She talked about the poor blighter as if he wasn't there. Not that Motty seemed to mind. He had stopped chewing his walking-stick and was sitting there with his mouth open. "He is a vegetarian and a teetotaller and is devoted to reading. Give him a nice book and he will be quite contented." She got up. "Thank you so much, Mr. Wooster! I don't know what I should have done without your help. Come, Motty! We have just time to see a few of the sights before my train goes. But I shall have to rely on you for most of my information about New York, darling. Be sure to keep your eyes open and take notes of your impressions! It will be such a help. Good-bye, Mr. Wooster. I will send Motty back early in the afternoon."

They went out, and I howled for Jeeves.

"Jeeves! What about it?"

"Sir?"

"What's to be done? You heard it all, didn't you? You were in the dining-room most of the time. That pill is coming to stay here."

"Pill, sir?"

"The excrescence."

"I beg your pardon, sir?"

I looked at Jeeves sharply. This sort of thing wasn't like him. It was as if he were deliberately trying to give me the pip. Then I understood. The man was really upset about that tie. He was trying to get his own back.

"Lord Pershore will be staying here from to-night, Jeeves," I said, coldly.

"Very good, sir. Breakfast is ready, sir."

I could have sobbed into the bacon and eggs. That there wasn't any sympathy to be got out of Jeeves was what put the lid on it. For a moment I almost weakened and told him to destroy the hat and tie if he didn't like them, but I pulled myself together again. I was dashed if I was going to let Jeeves treat me like a bally one-man chain-gang!

But, what with brooding on Jeeves and brooding on Motty, I was in a pretty reduced sort of state. The more I examined the situation, the more blighted it became. There was nothing I could do. If I slung Motty out, he would report to his mother, and she would pass it on to Aunt Agatha, and I didn't like to think what would happen then. Sooner or later, I should be wanting to go back to England, and I didn't want to get there and find Aunt Agatha waiting on the quay for me with a stuffed eelskin. There was absolutely nothing for it but to put the fellow up and make the best of it.

About midday Motty's luggage arrived, and soon afterward a large parcel of what I took to be nice books. I brightened up a little when I saw it. It was one of those massive parcels and looked as if it had enough in it to keep the chappie busy for a year. I felt a trifle more cheerful, and I got my Country Gentleman hat and stuck it on my head, and gave the pink tie a twist, and reeled out to take a bite of lunch with one or two of the lads at a neighbouring hostelry; and what with excellent browsing and sluicing and cheery conversation and what-not, the afternoon passed quite happily. By dinner-time I had almost forgotten blighted Motty's existence.

I dined at the club and looked in at a show afterward, and it wasn't till fairly late that I got back to the flat. There were no signs of Motty, and I took it that he had gone to bed.

It seemed rummy to me, though, that the parcel of nice books was still there with the string and paper on it. It looked as if Motty, after seeing mother off at the station, had decided to call it a day.

Jeeves came in with the nightly whisky-and-soda. I could tell by the chappie's manner that he was still upset.

"Lord Pershore gone to bed, Jeeves?" I asked, with reserved hauteur and what-not.

"No, sir. His lordship has not yet returned."

"Not returned? What do you mean?"

"His lordship came in shortly after six-thirty, and, having dressed, went out again."

At this moment there was a noise outside the front door, a sort of scrabbling noise, as if somebody were trying to paw his way through the woodwork. Then a sort of thud.

"Better go and see what that is, Jeeves."

"Very good, sir."

He went out and came back again.

"If you would not mind stepping this way, sir, I think we might be able to carry him in."

"Carry him in?"

"His lordship is lying on the mat, sir."

I went to the front door. The man was right. There was Motty huddled up outside on the floor. He was moaning a bit.

"He's had some sort of dashed fit," I said. I took another look. "Jeeves! Some one's been feeding him meat!"

"Sir?"

"He's a vegetarian, you know. He must have been digging into a steak or something. Call up a doctor!"

"I hardly think it will be necessary, sir. If you would take his lordship's legs, while I——"

"Great Scot, Jeeves! You don't think—he can't be——"

"I am inclined to think so, sir."

And, by Jove, he was right! Once on the right track, you couldn't mistake it. Motty was under the surface.

It was the deuce of a shock.

"You never can tell, Jeeves!"

"Very seldom, sir."

"Remove the eye of authority and where are you?"

"Precisely, sir."

"Where is my wandering boy to-night and all that sort of thing, what?"

"It would seem so, sir."

"Well, we had better bring him in, eh?"

"Yes, sir."

So we lugged him in, and Jeeves put him to bed, and I lit a cigarette and sat down to think the thing over. I had a kind of foreboding. It seemed to me that I had let myself in for something pretty rocky.

Next morning, after I had sucked down a thoughtful cup of tea, I went into Motty's room to investigate. I expected to find the fellow a wreck, but there he was, sitting up in bed, quite chirpy, reading Gingery stories.

"What ho!" I said.

"What ho!" said Motty.

"What ho! What ho!"

"What ho! What ho! What ho!"

After that it seemed rather difficult to go on with the conversation.

"How are you feeling this morning?" I asked.

"Topping!" replied Motty, blithely and with abandon. "I say, you know, that fellow of yours—Jeeves, you know—is a corker. I had a most frightful headache when I woke up, and he brought me a sort of rummy dark drink, and it put me right again at once. Said it was his own invention. I must see more of that lad. He seems to me distinctly one of the ones!"

I couldn't believe that this was the same blighter who had sat and sucked his stick the day before.

"You ate something that disagreed with you last night, didn't you?" I said, by way of giving him a chance to slide out of it if he wanted to. But he wouldn't have it at any price.

"No!" he replied, firmly. "I didn't do anything of the kind. I drank too much! Much too much! Lots and lots too much! And, what's more, I'm going to do it again! I'm going to do it every night. If ever you see me sober, old top," he said, with a kind of holy exaltation, "tap me on the shoulder and say, 'Tut! Tut!' and I'll apologize and remedy the defect."

"But I say, you know, what about me?"

"What about you?"

"Well, I'm, so to speak, as it were, kind of responsible for you. What I mean to say is, if you go doing this sort of thing I'm apt to get in the soup somewhat."

"I can't help your troubles," said Motty, firmly. "Listen to me, old thing: this is the first time in my life that I've had a real chance to yield to the temptations of a great city. What's the use of a great city having temptations if fellows don't yield to them! Makes it so bally discouraging for a great city. Besides, mother told me to keep my eyes open and collect impressions."

I sat on the edge of the bed. I felt dizzy.

"I know just how you feel, old dear," said Motty, consolingly. "And, if my principles would permit it, I would simmer down for your sake. But duty first! This is the first time I've been let out alone, and I mean to make the most of it. We're only young once. Why interfere with life's morning? Young man, rejoice in thy youth! Tra-la! What ho!"

Put like that, it did seem reasonable.

"All my bally life, dear boy," Motty went on, "I've been cooped up in the ancestral home at Much Middlefold, in Shropshire, and till you've been cooped up in Much Middlefold you don't know what cooping is! The only time we get any excitement is when one of the choir-boys is caught sucking chocolate during the sermon. When that happens, we talk about it for days. I've got about a month of New York, and I mean to store up a few happy memories for the long winter evenings. This is my only chance to collect a past, and I'm going to do it. Now tell me, old sport, as man to man, how does one get in touch with that very decent chappie Jeeves? Does one ring a bell or shout a bit? I should like to discuss the subject of a good stiff b.-and-s. with him!"

I had had a sort of vague idea, don't you know, that if I stuck close to Motty and went about the place with him, I might act as a bit of a damper on the gaiety. What I mean is, I thought that if, when he was being the life and soul of the party, he were to catch my reproving eye he might ease up a trifle on the revelry. So the next night I took him along to supper with me. It was the last time. I'm a quiet, peaceful sort of chappie who has lived all his life in London, and I can't stand the pace these swift sportsmen from the rural districts set. What I mean to say is, I'm all for rational enjoyment and so forth, but I think a chappie makes himself conspicuous when he throws soft-boiled eggs at the electric fan. And decent mirth and all that sort of thing are all right, but I do bar dancing on tables and having to dash all over the place dodging waiters, managers, and chuckers-out, just when you want to sit still and digest.

Directly I managed to tear myself away that night and get home, I made up my mind that this was jolly well the last time that I went about with Motty. The only time I met him late at night after that was once when I passed the door of a fairly low-down sort of restaurant and had to step aside to dodge him as he sailed through the air *en route* for the opposite pavement, with a muscular sort of looking chappie peering out after him with a kind of gloomy satisfaction.

In a way, I couldn't help sympathizing with the fellow. He had about four weeks to have the good time that ought to have been spread over about ten years, and I didn't wonder at his wanting to be pretty busy. I should have been just the same in his place. Still, there was no denying that it was a bit thick. If it hadn't been for the thought of Lady Malvern and Aunt Agatha in the background, I should have regarded Motty's rapid work with an indulgent smile. But I couldn't get rid of the feeling that, sooner or later, I was the lad who was scheduled to get it behind the ear. And what with brooding on this prospect, and sitting up in the old flat waiting for the familiar footstep, and putting it to bed when it got there, and stealing into the sick-chamber next morning to contemplate the wreckage, I was beginning to lose weight. Absolutely becoming the good old shadow, I give you my honest word. Starting at sudden noises and what-not.

And no sympathy from Jeeves. That was what cut me to the quick.

The man was still thoroughly pipped about the hat and tie, and simply wouldn't rally round. One morning I wanted comforting so much that I sank the pride of the Woosters and appealed to the fellow direct.

"Jeeves," I said, "this is getting a bit thick!"

"Sir?" Business and cold respectfulness.

"You know what I mean. This lad seems to have chucked all the principles of a well-spent boyhood. He has got it up his nose!"

"Yes, sir."

"Well, I shall get blamed, don't you know. You know what my Aunt Agatha is!"

"Yes, sir."

"Very well, then."

I waited a moment, but he wouldn't unbend.

"Jeeves," I said, "haven't you any scheme up your sleeve for coping with this blighter?"

"No, sir."

And he shimmered off to his lair. Obstinate devil! So dashed absurd, don't you know. It wasn't as if there was anything wrong with that Country Gentleman hat. It was a remarkably priceless effort, and much admired by the lads. But, just because he preferred the Longacre, he left me flat.

It was shortly after this that young Motty got the idea of bringing pals back in the small hours to continue the gay revels in the home. This was where I began to crack under the strain. You see, the part of town where I was living wasn't the right place for that sort of thing. I knew lots of chappies down Washington Square way who started the evening at about two a.m.—artists and writers and what-not, who frolicked considerably till checked by the arrival of the morning milk. That was all right. They like that sort of thing down there. The neighbours can't get to sleep unless there's some one dancing Hawaiian dances over their heads. But on Fifty-seventh Street the atmosphere wasn't right, and when Motty turned up at three in the morning with a collection of hearty lads, who only stopped singing their college song when they started singing "The Old Oaken Bucket," there was a marked peevishness among the old settlers in the flats. The management was extremely terse over the telephone at breakfast-time, and took a lot of soothing.

The next night I came home early, after a lonely dinner at a place which I'd chosen because there didn't seem any chance of meeting Motty there. The sitting-room was quite dark, and I was just moving to switch on the light, when there was a sort of explosion and something collared hold of my trouser-leg. Living with Motty had reduced me to such an extent that I was simply unable to cope with this thing. I jumped backward with a loud yell of anguish, and tumbled out into the hall just as Jeeves came out of his den to see what the matter was.

"Did you call, sir?"

"Jeeves! There's something in there that grabs you by the leg!"

"That would be Rollo, sir."

"Eh?"

"I would have warned you of his presence, but I did not hear you come in. His temper is a little uncertain at present, as he has not yet settled down."

"Who the deuce is Rollo?"

"His lordship's bull-terrier, sir. His lordship won him in a raffle, and tied him to the leg of the table. If you will allow me, sir, I will go in and switch on the light."

There really is nobody like Jeeves. He walked straight into the sitting-room, the biggest feat since Daniel and the lions' den, without a quiver. What's more, his magnetism or whatever they call it was such that the dashed animal, instead of pinning him by the leg, calmed down as if he had had a bromide, and rolled over on his back with all his paws in the air. If Jeeves had been his rich uncle he couldn't have been more chummy. Yet directly he caught sight of me again, he got all worked up and seemed to have only one idea in life — to start chewing me where he had left off.

"Rollo is not used to you yet, sir," said Jeeves, regarding the bally quadruped in an admiring sort of way. "He is an excellent watchdog."

"I don't want a watchdog to keep me out of my rooms."

"No, sir."

"Well, what am I to do?"

"No doubt in time the animal will learn to discriminate, sir. He will learn to distinguish your peculiar scent."

"What do you mean — my peculiar scent? Correct the impression that I intend to hang about in the hall while life slips by, in the hope that one of these days that dashed animal will decide that I smell all right." I thought for a bit. "Jeeves!"

"Sir?"

"I'm going away — to-morrow morning by the first train. I shall go and stop with Mr. Todd in the country."

"Do you wish me to accompany you, sir?"

"No."

"Very good, sir."

"I don't know when I shall be back. Forward my letters."

"Yes, sir."

As a matter-of-fact, I was back within the week. Rocky Todd, the pal I went to stay with, is a rummy sort of a chap who lives all alone in the wilds of Long Island, and likes it; but a little of that sort of thing goes a long way with me. Dear old Rocky is one of the best, but after a few days in his cottage in the woods, miles away from anywhere, New York, even with Motty on the premises, began to look pretty good to me. The days down on Long Island have forty-eight hours in them; you can't get to sleep at night because of the bellowing of the crickets; and you have to walk two miles for a drink and six for an evening paper. I thanked Rocky for his kind hospitality, and caught the only train they have down in those parts. It landed me in New York about dinner-time. I went straight to the old flat. Jeeves came out of his lair. I looked round cautiously for Rollo.

"Where's that dog, Jeeves? Have you got him tied up?"

"The animal is no longer here, sir. His lordship gave him to the porter, who sold him. His lordship took a prejudice against the animal on account of being bitten by him in the calf of the leg."

I don't think I've ever been so bucked by a bit of news. I felt I had misjudged Rollo. Evidently, when you got to know him better, he had a lot of intelligence in him.

"Ripping!" I said. "Is Lord Pershore in, Jeeves?"

"No, sir."

"Do you expect him back to dinner?"

"No, sir."

"Where is he?"

"In prison, sir."

Have you ever trodden on a rake and had the handle jump up and hit you? That's how I felt then.

"In prison!"

"Yes, sir."

"You don't mean — in prison?"

"Yes, sir."

I lowered myself into a chair.

"Why?" I said.

"He assaulted a constable, sir."

"Lord Pershore assaulted a constable!"

"Yes, sir."

I digested this.

"But, Jeeves, I say! This is frightful!"

"Sir?"

"What will Lady Malvern say when she finds out?"

"I do not fancy that her ladyship will find out, sir."

"But she'll come back and want to know where he is."

"I rather fancy, sir, that his lordship's bit of time will have run out by then."

"But supposing it hasn't?"

"In that event, sir, it may be judicious to prevaricate a little."

"How?"

"If I might make the suggestion, sir, I should inform her ladyship that his lordship has left for a short visit to Boston."

"Why Boston?"

"Very interesting and respectable centre, sir."

"Jeeves, I believe you've hit it."

"I fancy so, sir."

"Why, this is really the best thing that could have happened. If this hadn't turned up to prevent him, young Motty would have been in a sanatorium by the time Lady Malvern got back."

"Exactly, sir."

The more I looked at it in that way, the sounder this prison wheeze seemed to me. There was no doubt in the world that prison was just what the doctor ordered for Motty. It was the only thing that could have pulled him up. I was sorry for the poor blighter, but after all, I reflected, a chappie who had lived all his life with Lady Malvern, in a small village in the interior of Shropshire, wouldn't have much to kick at in a prison. Altogether, I began to feel absolutely braced again. Life became like what the poet Johnnie says — one grand, sweet song. Things went on so comfortably and peacefully for a couple of weeks that I give you my word that I'd almost forgotten such a person as Motty existed. The only flaw in the scheme of things was that Jeeves was still pained and distant. It wasn't anything he said, or did, mind you, but there was a rummy something about him all the time. Once when I was tying the pink tie I caught sight of him in the looking-glass. There was a kind of grieved look in his eye.

And then Lady Malvern came back, a good bit ahead of schedule. I hadn't been expecting her for days. I'd forgotten how time had been slipping along. She turned up one morning while I was still in bed sipping tea and thinking of this and that. Jeeves flowed in with the announcement that he had just loosed her into the sitting-room. I draped a few garments round me and went in.

There she was, sitting in the same arm-chair, looking as massive as ever. The only difference was that she didn't uncover the teeth as she had done the first time.

"Good morning," I said. "So you've got back, what?"

"I have got back."

There was something sort of bleak about her tone, rather as if she had swallowed an east wind. This I took to be due to the fact that she probably hadn't breakfasted. It's only after a bit of breakfast that I'm able to regard the world with that sunny cheeriness which makes a fellow the universal favourite. I'm never much of a lad till I've engulfed an egg or two and a beaker of coffee.

"I suppose you haven't breakfasted?"

"I have not yet breakfasted."

"Won't you have an egg or something? Or a sausage or something? Or something?"

"No, thank you."

She spoke as if she belonged to an anti-sausage society or a league for the suppression of eggs. There was a bit of a silence.

"I called on you last night," she said, "but you were out."

"Awfully sorry! Had a pleasant trip?"

"Extremely, thank you."

"See everything? Niag'ra Falls, Yellowstone Park, and the jolly old Grand Canyon, and what-not?"

"I saw a great deal."

There was another slightly *frappé* silence. Jeeves floated silently into the dining-room and began to lay the breakfast-table.

"I hope Wilmot was not in your way, Mr. Wooster?"

I had been wondering when she was going to mention Motty.

"Rather not! Great pals! Hit it off splendidly."

"You were his constant companion, then?"

"Absolutely! We were always together. Saw all the sights, don't you know. We'd take in the Museum of Art in the morning, and have a bit of lunch at some good vegetarian place, and then toddle along to a sacred concert in the afternoon, and home to an early dinner. We usually played dominoes after dinner. And then the early bed and the refreshing sleep. We had a great time. I was awfully sorry when he went away to Boston."

"Oh! Wilmot is in Boston?"

"Yes. I ought to have let you know, but of course we didn't know where you were. You were dodging all over the place like a snipe—I mean, don't you know, dodging all over the place, and we couldn't get at you. Yes, Motty went off to Boston."

"You're sure he went to Boston?"

"Oh, absolutely." I called out to Jeeves, who was now messing about in the next room with forks and so forth: "Jeeves, Lord Pershore didn't change his mind about going to Boston, did he?"

"No, sir."

"I thought I was right. Yes, Motty went to Boston."

"Then how do you account, Mr. Wooster, for the fact that when I went yesterday afternoon to Blackwell's Island prison, to secure material for my book, I saw poor, dear Wilmot there, dressed in a striped suit, seated beside a pile of stones with a hammer in his hands?"

I tried to think of something to say, but nothing came. A chappie has to be a lot broader about the forehead than I am to handle a jolt like this. I strained the old bean till it creaked, but between the collar and the hair parting nothing stirred. I was dumb. Which was lucky, because I wouldn't have had a chance to get any persiflage out of my system. Lady Malvern collared the conversation. She had been bottling it up, and now it came out with a rush:—

"So this is how you have looked after my poor, dear boy, Mr. Wooster! So this is how you have abused my trust! I left him in your charge, thinking that I could rely on you to shield him from evil. He came to you innocent, unversed in the ways of the world, confiding, unused to the temptations of a large city, and you led him astray!"

I hadn't any remarks to make. All I could think of was the picture of Aunt Agatha drinking all this in and reaching out to sharpen the hatchet against my return.

"You deliberately——"

Far away in the misty distance a soft voice spoke:—

"If I might explain, your ladyship."

Jeeves had projected himself in from the dining-room and materialized on the rug. Lady Malvern tried to freeze him with a look, but you can't do that sort of thing to Jeeves. He is look-proof.

"I fancy, your ladyship, that you may have misunderstood Mr. Wooster, and that he may have given you the impression that he was in New York when his lordship was—removed. When Mr. Wooster informed your ladyship that his lordship had gone to Boston, he was relying on the version I had given him of his lordship's movements. Mr. Wooster was away, visiting a friend in the country, at the time, and knew nothing of the matter till your ladyship informed him."

Lady Malvern gave a kind of grunt. It didn't rattle Jeeves.

"I feared Mr. Wooster might be disturbed if he knew the truth, as he is so attached to his lordship and has taken such pains to look after him, so I took the liberty of telling him that his lordship had gone away for a visit. It might have been hard for Mr. Wooster to believe that his lordship had gone to prison voluntarily and from the best motives, but your ladyship, knowing him better, will readily understand."

"What!" Lady Malvern goggled at him. "Did you say that Lord Pershore went to prison voluntarily?"

"If I might explain, your ladyship. I think that your ladyship's parting words made a deep impression on his lordship. I have frequently heard him speak to Mr. Wooster of his desire to do something to follow your ladyship's instructions and collect material for your ladyship's book on America. Mr. Wooster will bear me out when I say that his lordship was frequently extremely depressed at the thought that he was doing so little to help."

"Absolutely, by Jove! Quite pipped about it!" I said.

"The idea of making a personal examination into the prison system of the country—from within—occurred to his lordship very suddenly one night. He embraced it eagerly. There was no restraining him."

Lady Malvern looked at Jeeves, then at me, then at Jeeves again. I could see her struggling with the thing.

"Surely, your ladyship," said Jeeves, "it is more reasonable to suppose that a gentleman of his lordship's character went to prison of his own volition than that he committed some breach of the law which necessitated his arrest?"

Lady Malvern blinked. Then she got up.

"Mr. Wooster," she said, "I apologize. I have done you an injustice. I should have known Wilmot better. I should have had more faith in his pure, fine spirit."

"Absolutely!" I said.

"Your breakfast is ready, sir," said Jeeves.

I sat down and dallied in a dazed sort of way with a poached egg.

"Jeeves," I said, "you are certainly a life-saver!"

"Thank you, sir."

"Nothing would have convinced my Aunt Agatha that I hadn't lured that blighter into riotous living."

"I fancy you are right, sir."

I champed my egg for a bit. I was most awfully moved, don't you know, by the way Jeeves had rallied round. Something seemed to tell me that this was an occasion that called for rich rewards. For a moment I hesitated. Then I made up my mind.

"Jeeves!"

"Sir?"

"That pink tie!"

"Yes, sir?"

"Burn it!"

"Thank you, sir."

"And, Jeeves!"

"Yes, sir?"

"Take a taxi and get me that Longacre hat, as worn by John Drew!"

"Thank you very much, sir."

I felt most awfully braced. I felt as if the clouds had rolled away and all was as it used to be. I felt like one of those chappies in the novels who calls off the fight with his wife in the last chapter and decides to forget and forgive. I felt I wanted to do all sorts of other things to show Jeeves that I appreciated him.

"Jeeves," I said, "it isn't enough. Is there anything else you would like?"

"Yes, sir. If I may make the suggestion—fifty dollars."

"Fifty dollars?"

"It will enable me to pay a debt of honour, sir. I owe it to his lordship."

"You owe Lord Pershore fifty dollars?"

"Yes, sir. I happened to meet him in the street the night his lordship was arrested. I had been thinking a good deal about the most suitable method of inducing him to abandon his mode of living, sir. His lordship was a little over-excited at the time, and I fancy that he mistook me for a friend of his. At any rate, when I took the liberty of wagering him fifty dollars that he would not punch a passing policeman in the eye, he accepted the bet very cordially and won it."

I produced my pocket-book and counted out a hundred.

"Take this, Jeeves," I said; "fifty isn't enough. Do you know, Jeeves, you're—well, you absolutely stand alone!"

"I endeavour to give satisfaction, sir," said Jeeves.

Jeeves and the Hard-boiled Egg

SOMETIMES of a morning, as I've sat in bed sucking down the early cup of tea and watched my man Jeeves flitting about the room and putting out the raiment for the day, I've wondered what the deuce I should do if the fellow ever took it into his head to leave me. It's not so bad now I'm in New York, but in London the anxiety was frightful. There used to be all sorts of attempts on the part of low blighters to sneak him away from me. Young Reggie Foljambe to my certain knowledge offered him double what I was giving him, and Alistair Bingham-Reeves, who's got a valet who had been known to press his trousers sideways, used to look at him, when he came to see me, with a kind of glittering, hungry eye which disturbed me deucedly. Bally pirates!

The thing, you see, is that Jeeves is so dashed competent. You can spot it even in the way he shoves studs into a shirt.

I rely on him absolutely in every crisis, and he never lets me down. And, what's more, he can always be counted on to extend himself on behalf of any pal of mine who happens to be to all appearances knee-deep in the bouillon. Take the rather rummy case, for instance, of dear old Bicky and his uncle, the hard-boiled egg.

It happened after I had been in America for a few months. I got back to the flat latish one night, and when Jeeves brought me the final drink he said: —

"Mr. Bickersteth called to see you this evening, sir, while you were out."

"Oh?" I said.

"Twice, sir. He appeared a trifle agitated."

"What, pipped?"

"He gave that impression, sir."

I sipped the whisky. I was sorry if Bicky was in trouble, but, as a matter of fact, I was rather glad to have something I could discuss freely with Jeeves just then, because things had been a bit strained between us for some time, and it had been rather difficult to hit on anything to talk about that wasn't apt to take a personal turn. You see, I had decided — rightly or wrongly — to grow a moustache, and this had cut Jeeves to the quick. He couldn't stick the thing at any price, and I had been living ever since in an atmosphere of bally disapproval till I was getting jolly well fed up with it. What I mean is, while there's no doubt that in certain matters of dress Jeeves's judgment is absolutely sound and should be followed, it seemed to me that it was getting a bit too thick if he was going to edit my face as well as my costume. No one can call me an unreasonable chappie, and many's the time I've given in like a lamb when Jeeves has voted against one of my pet suits or ties; but when it comes to a valet's staking out a claim on your upper lip you've simply got to have a bit of the good old bulldog pluck and defy the blighter.

"He said that he would call again later, sir."

"Something must be up, Jeeves."

"Yes, sir."

I gave the moustache a thoughtful twirl. It seemed to hurt Jeeves a good deal, so I chucked it.

"I see by the paper, sir, that Mr. Bickersteth's uncle is arriving on the *Carmantic*."

"Yes?"

"His Grace the Duke of Chiswick, sir."

This was news to me, that Bicky's uncle was a duke. Rum, how little one knows about one's pals! I had met Bicky for the first time at a species of beano or jamboree down in Washington Square, not long after my arrival in New York. I suppose I was a bit homesick at the time, and I rather took to Bicky when I found that he was an Englishman and had, in fact, been up at Oxford with me. Besides, he was a frightful chump, so we naturally drifted together; and while we were taking a quiet snort in a corner that wasn't all cluttered up with artists and sculptors and what not, he furthermore endeared himself to me by a most extraordinarily gifted imitation of a bull-terrier chasing a cat up a tree. But, though we had subsequently become extremely pally, all I really knew about him was that he was generally hard up, and had an uncle who relieved the strain a bit from time to time by sending him monthly remittances.

"If the Duke of Chiswick is his uncle," I said, "why hasn't he a title? Why isn't he Lord What-Not?"

"Mr. Bickersteth is the son of his grace's late sister, sir, who married Captain Rollo Bickersteth of the Coldstream Guards."

Jeeves knows everything.

"Is Mr. Bickersteth's father dead too?"

"Yes, sir."

"Leave any money?"

"No, sir."

I began to understand why poor old Bicky was always more or less on the rocks. To the casual and irreflective observer, if you know what I mean, it may sound a pretty good wheeze having a duke for an uncle, but the trouble about old Chiswick was that, though an extremely wealthy old buster, owning half London and about five counties up north, he was notoriously the most prudent spender in England. He was what American chappies would call a hard-boiled egg. If Bicky's people hadn't left him anything and he depended on what he could prise out of the old duke, he was in a pretty bad way. Not that that explained why he was hunting me like this, because he was a chap who never borrowed money. He said he wanted to keep his pals, so never bit any one's ear on principle.

At this juncture the door-bell rang. Jeeves floated out to answer it.

"Yes, sir. Mr. Wooster has just returned," I heard him say. And Bicky came trickling in, looking pretty sorry for himself.

"Halloa, Bicky!" I said. "Jeeves told me you had been trying to get me. Jeeves, bring another glass, and let the revels commence. What's the trouble, Bicky?"

"I'm in a hole, Bertie. I want your advice."

"Say on, old lad!"

"My uncle's turning up to-morrow, Bertie."

"So Jeeves told me."

"The Duke of Chiswick, you know."

"So Jeeves told me."

Bicky seemed a bit surprised.

"Jeeves seems to know everything."

"Rather rummily, that's exactly what I was thinking just now myself."

"Well, I wish," said Bicky, gloomily, "that he knew a way to get me out of the hole I'm in."

Jeeves shimmered in with the glass, and stuck it competently on the table.

"Mr. Bickersteth is in a bit of a hole, Jeeves," I said, "and wants you to rally round."

"Very good, sir."

Bicky looked a bit doubtful.

"Well, of course, you know, Bertie, this thing is by way of being a bit private and all that."

"I shouldn't worry about that, old top. I bet Jeeves knows all about it already. Don't you, Jeeves?"

"Yes, sir."

"Eh?" said Bicky, rattled.

"I am open to correction, sir, but is not your dilemma due to the fact that you are at a loss to explain to his grace why you are in New York instead of in Colorado?"

Bicky rocked like a jelly in a high wind.

"How the deuce do you know anything about it?"

"I chanced to meet his grace's butler before we left England. He informed me that he happened to overhear his grace speaking to you on the matter, sir, as he passed the library-door."

Bicky gave a hollow sort of laugh.

"Well, as everybody seems to know all about it, there's no need to try to keep it dark. The old boy turfed me out, Bertie, because he said I was a brainless nincompoop. The idea was that he would give me a remittance on condition that I dashed out to some blighted locality of the name of Colorado and learned farming or ranching, or whatever they call it, at some bally ranch or farm or whatever it's called. I didn't fancy the idea a bit. I should have had to ride horses and pursue cows, and so forth. I hate horses. They bite at you. I was all against the scheme. At the same time, don't you know, I had to have that remittance."

"I get you absolutely, dear boy."

"Well, when I got to New York it looked a decent sort of place to me, so I thought it would be a pretty sound notion to stop here. So I cabled to my uncle telling him that I had dropped into a good business wheeze in the city and wanted to chuck the ranch idea. He wrote back that it was all right, and here I've been ever since. He thinks I'm doing well at something or other over here. I never dreamed, don't you know, that he would ever come out here. What on earth am I to do?"

"Jeeves," I said, "what on earth is Mr. Bickersteth to do?"

"You see," said Bicky, "I had a wireless from him to say that he was coming to stay with me—to save hotel bills, I suppose. I've always given him the impression that I was living in pretty good style. I can't have him to stay at my boarding-house."

"Thought of anything, Jeeves?" I said.

"To what extent, sir, if the question is not a delicate one, are you prepared to assist Mr. Bickersteth?"

"I'll do anything I can for you, of course, Bicky, old man."

"Then, if I might make the suggestion, sir, you might lend Mr. Bickersteth——"

"No, by Jove!" said Bicky, firmly. "I never have touched you, Bertie, and I'm not going to start now. I may be a chump, but it's my boast that I don't owe a penny to a single soul — not counting tradesmen, of course."

"I was about to suggest, sir, that you might lend Mr. Bickersteth this flat. Mr. Bickersteth could give his grace the impression that he was the owner of it. With your permission I could convey the notion that I was in Mr. Bickersteth's employment and not in yours. You would be residing here temporarily as Mr. Bickersteth's guest. His grace would occupy the second spare bedroom. I fancy that you would find this answer satisfactorily, sir."

Bicky had stopped rocking himself and was staring at Jeeves in an awed sort of way.

"I would advocate the dispatching of a wireless message to his grace on board the vessel, notifying him of the change of address. Mr. Bickersteth could meet his grace at the dock and proceed directly here. Will that meet the situation, sir?"

"Absolutely."

"Thank you, sir."

Bicky followed him with his eye till the door closed.

"How does he do it, Bertie?" he said. "I'll tell you what I think it is. I believe it's something to do with the shape of his head. Have you ever noticed his head, Bertie, old man? It sort of sticks out at the back!"

I hopped out of bed pretty early next morning, so as to be among those present when the old boy should arrive. I knew from experience that these ocean liners fetch up at the dock at a deucedly ungodly hour. It wasn't much after nine by the time I'd dressed and had my morning tea and was leaning out of the window, watching the street for Bicky and his uncle. It was one of those jolly, peaceful mornings that make a chappie wish he'd got a soul or something, and I was just brooding on life in general when I became aware of the dickens of a spat in progress down below. A taxi had driven up, and an old boy in a top hat had got out and was kicking up a frightful row about the fare. As far as I could make out, he was trying to get the cab chappie to switch from New York to London prices, and the cab chappie had apparently never heard of London before, and didn't seem to think a lot of it now. The old boy said that in London the trip would have set him back eightpence; and the cabby said he should worry. I called to Jeeves.

"The duke has arrived, Jeeves."

"Yes, sir?"

"That'll be him at the door now."

Jeeves made a long arm and opened the front door, and the old boy crawled in, looking licked to a splinter.

"How do you do, sir?" I said, bustling up and being the ray of sunshine. "Your nephew went down to the dock to meet you, but you must have missed him. My name's Wooster, don't you know. Great pal of Bicky's, and all that sort of thing. I'm staying with him, you know. Would you like a cup of tea? Jeeves, bring a cup of tea."

Old Chiswick had sunk into an armchair and was looking about the room.

"Does this luxurious flat belong to my nephew Francis?"

"Absolutely."

"It must be terribly expensive."

"Pretty well, of course. Everything costs a lot over here, you know."

He moaned. Jeeves filtered in with the tea. Old Chiswick took a stab at it to restore his tissues, and nodded.

"A terrible country, Mr. Wooster! A terrible country! Nearly eight shillings for a short cab-drive! Iniquitous!" He took another look round the room. It seemed to fascinate him. "Have you any idea how much my nephew pays for this flat, Mr. Wooster?"

"About two hundred dollars a month, I believe."

"What! Forty pounds a month!"

I began to see that, unless I made the thing a bit more plausible, the scheme might turn out a frost. I could guess what the old boy was thinking. He was trying to square all this prosperity with what he knew of poor old Bicky. And one had to admit that it took a lot of squaring, for dear old Bicky, though a stout fellow and absolutely unrivalled as an imitator of bull-terriers and cats, was in many ways one of the most pronounced fatheads that ever pulled on a suit of gents' underwear.

"I suppose it seems rummy to you," I said, "but the fact is New York often bucks chappies up and makes them show a flash of speed that you wouldn't have imagined them capable of. It sort of develops them. Something in the air, don't you know. I imagine that Bicky in the past, when you knew him, may have been something of a chump, but it's quite different now. Devilish efficient sort of chappie, and looked on in commercial circles as quite the nib!"

"I am amazed! What is the nature of my nephew's business, Mr. Wooster?"

"Oh, just business, don't you know. The same sort of thing Carnegie and Rockefeller and all these coves do, you know." I slid for the door. "Awfully sorry to leave you, but I've got to meet some of the lads elsewhere."

Coming out of the lift I met Bicky bustling in from the street.

"Halloa, Bertie! I missed him. Has he turned up?"

"He's upstairs now, having some tea."

"What does he think of it all?"

"He's absolutely rattled."

"Ripping! I'll be toddling up, then. Toodle-oo, Bertie, old man. See you later."

"Pip-pip, Bicky, dear boy."

He trotted off, full of merriment and good cheer, and I went off to the club to sit in the window and watch the traffic coming up one way and going down the other.

It was latish in the evening when I looked in at the flat to dress for dinner.

"Where's everybody, Jeeves?" I said, finding no little feet pattering about the place. "Gone out?"

"His grace desired to see some of the sights of the city, sir. Mr. Bickersteth is acting as his escort. I fancy their immediate objective was Grant's Tomb."

"I suppose Mr. Bickersteth is a bit braced at the way things are going—what?"

"Sir?"

"I say, I take it that Mr. Bickersteth is tolerably full of beans."

"Not altogether, sir."

"What's his trouble now?"

"The scheme which I took the liberty of suggesting to Mr. Bickersteth and yourself has, unfortunately, not answered entirely satisfactorily, sir."

"Surely the duke believes that Mr. Bickersteth is doing well in business, and all that sort of thing?"

"Exactly, sir. With the result that he has decided to cancel Mr. Bickersteth's monthly allowance, on the ground that, as Mr. Bickersteth is doing so well on his own account, he no longer requires pecuniary assistance."

"Great Scot, Jeeves! This is awful!"

"Somewhat disturbing, sir."

"I never expected anything like this!"

"I confess I scarcely anticipated the contingency myself, sir."

"I suppose it bowled the poor blighter over absolutely?"

"Mr. Bickersteth appeared somewhat taken aback, sir."

My heart bled for Bicky.

"We must do something, Jeeves."

"Yes, sir."

"Can you think of anything?"

"Not at the moment, sir."

"There must be something we can do."

"It was a maxim of one of my former employers, sir—as I believe I mentioned to you once before—the present Lord Bridgnorth, that there is always a way. I remember his lordship using the expression on the occasion—he was then a business gentleman and had not yet received his title—when a patent hair-restorer which he chanced to be promoting failed to attract the public. He put it on the market under another name as a depilatory, and amassed a substantial fortune. I have generally found his lordship's aphorism based on sound foundations. No doubt we shall be able to discover some solution of Mr. Bickersteth's difficulty, sir."

"Well, have a stab at it, Jeeves!"

"I will spare no pains, sir."

I went and dressed sadly. It will show you pretty well how pipped I was when I tell you that I as near as a toucher put on a white tie with a dinner-jacket. I sallied out for a bit of food more to pass the time than because I wanted it. It seemed brutal to be wading into the bill of fare with poor old Bicky headed for the breadline.

When I got back old Chiswick had gone to bed, but Bicky was there, hunched up in an arm-chair, brooding pretty tensely, with a cigarette hanging out of the corner of his mouth and a more or less glassy stare in his eyes. He had the aspect of one who had been soaked with what the newspaper chappies call "some blunt instrument."

"This is a bit thick, old thing—what!" I said.

He picked up his glass and drained it feverishly, overlooking the fact that it hadn't anything in it.

"I'm done, Bertie!" he said.

He had another go at the glass. It didn't seem to do him any good.

"If only this had happened a week later, Bertie! My next month's money was due to roll in on Saturday. I could have worked a wheeze I've been reading about in the magazine advertisements. It seems that you can make a dashed amount of money if you can only collect a few dollars and start a chicken-farm. Jolly sound scheme, Bertie! Say you buy a hen — call it one hen for the sake of argument. It lays an egg every day of the week. You sell the eggs seven for twenty-five cents. Keep of hen costs nothing. Profit practically twenty-five cents on every seven eggs. Or look at it in another way: Suppose you have a dozen hens. Each of the hens has a dozen chickens. The chickens grow up and have more chickens. Why, in no time you'd have the place covered knee-deep in hens, all laying eggs, at twenty-five cents for every seven. You'd make a fortune. Jolly life, too, keeping hens!" He had begun to get quite worked up at the thought of it, but he slopped back in his chair at this juncture with a good deal of gloom. "But, of course, it's no good," he said, "because I haven't the cash."

"You've only to say the word, you know, Bicky, old top."

"Thanks awfully, Bertie, but I'm not going to sponge on you."

That's always the way in this world. The chappies you'd like to lend money to won't let you, whereas the chappies you don't want to lend it to will do everything except actually stand you on your head and lift the specie out of your pockets. As a lad who has always rolled tolerably freely in the right stuff, I've had lots of experience of the second class. Many's the time, back in London, I've hurried along Piccadilly and felt the hot breath of the toucher on the back of my neck and heard his sharp, excited yapping as he closed in on me. I've simply spent my life scattering largesse to blighters I didn't care a hang for; yet here was I now, dripping doubloons and pieces of eight and longing to hand them over, and Bicky, poor fish, absolutely on his uppers, not taking any at any price.

"Well, there's only one hope, then."

"What's that?"

"Jeeves."

"Sir?"

There was Jeeves, standing behind me, full of zeal. In this matter of shimmering into rooms the chappie is rummy to a degree. You're sitting in the old arm-chair, thinking of this and that, and then suddenly you look up, and there he is. He moves from point to point with as little uproar as a jelly-fish. The thing startled poor old Bicky considerably. He rose from his seat like a rocketing pheasant. I'm used to Jeeves now, but often in the days when he first came to me I've bitten my tongue freely on finding him unexpectedly in my midst.

"Did you call, sir?"

"Oh, there you are, Jeeves!"

"Precisely, sir."

"Jeeves, Mr. Bickersteth is still up the pole. Any ideas?"

"Why, yes, sir. Since we had our recent conversation I fancy I have found what may prove a solution. I do not wish to appear to be taking a liberty, sir, but I think that we have overlooked his grace's potentialities as a source of revenue."

Bicky laughed what I have sometimes seen described as a hollow, mocking laugh, a sort of bitter cackle from the back of the throat, rather like a gargle.

"I do not allude, sir," explained Jeeves, "to the possibility of inducing his grace to part with money. I am taking the liberty of regarding his grace in the light of an at present—if I may say so—useless property, which is capable of being developed."

Bicky looked at me in a helpless kind of way. I'm bound to say I didn't get it myself.

"Couldn't you make it a bit easier, Jeeves?"

"In a nutshell, sir, what I mean is this: His grace is, in a sense, a prominent personage. The inhabitants of this country, as no doubt you are aware, sir, are peculiarly addicted to shaking hands with prominent personages. It occurred to me that Mr. Bickersteth or yourself might know of persons who would be willing to pay a small fee—let us say two dollars or three—for the privilege of an introduction, including handshake, to his grace."

Bicky didn't seem to think much of it.

"Do you mean to say that any one would be mug enough to part with solid cash just to shake hands with my uncle?"

"I have an aunt, sir, who paid five shillings to a young fellow for bringing a moving-picture actor to tea at her house one Sunday. It gave her social standing among the neighbours."

Bicky wavered.

"If you think it could be done——"

"I feel convinced of it, sir."

"What do you think, Bertie?"

"I'm for it, old boy, absolutely. A very brainy wheeze."

"Thank you, sir. Will there be anything further? Good night, sir."

And he floated out, leaving us to discuss details.

Until we started this business of floating old Chiswick as a money-making proposition I had never realized what a perfectly foul time those

Stock Exchange chappies must have when the public isn't biting freely. Nowadays I read that bit they put in the financial reports about "The market opened quietly" with a sympathetic eye, for, by Jove, it certainly opened quietly for us! You'd hardly believe how difficult it was to interest the public and make them take a flutter on the old boy. By the end of a week the only name we had on our list was a delicatessen-store keeper down in Bicky's part of the town, and as he wanted us to take it out in sliced ham instead of cash that didn't help much. There was a gleam of light when the brother of Bicky's pawnbroker offered ten dollars, money down, for an introduction to old Chiswick, but the deal fell through, owing to its turning out that the chap was an anarchist and intended to kick the old boy instead of shaking hands with him. At that, it took me the deuce of a time to persuade Bicky not to grab the cash and let things take their course. He seemed to regard the pawnbroker's brother rather as a sportsman and benefactor of his species than otherwise.

The whole thing, I'm inclined to think, would have been off if it hadn't been for Jeeves. There is no doubt that Jeeves is in a class of his own. In the matter of brain and resource I don't think I have ever met a chappie so supremely like mother made. He trickled into my room one morning with the good old cup of tea, and intimated that there was something doing.

"Might I speak to you with regard to that matter of his grace, sir?"

"It's all off. We've decided to chuck it."

"Sir?"

"It won't work. We can't get anybody to come."

"I fancy I can arrange that aspect of the matter, sir."

"Do you mean to say you've managed to get anybody?"

"Yes, sir. Eighty-seven gentlemen from Birdsburg, sir."

I sat up in bed and spilt the tea.

"Birdsburg?"

"Birdsburg, Missouri, sir."

"How did you get them?"

"I happened last night, sir, as you had intimated that you would be absent from home, to attend a theatrical performance, and entered into conversation between the acts with the occupant of the adjoining seat. I had observed that he was wearing a somewhat ornate decoration in his buttonhole, sir—a large blue button with the words 'Boost for Birdsburg' upon it in red letters, scarcely a judicious addition to a gentleman's evening costume. To my surprise I noticed that the auditorium was full of persons similarly decorated. I ventured to inquire the explanation, and was informed that these gentlemen, forming a party of eighty-seven, are a convention from a town of the name of Birdsburg in the State of Missouri. Their visit, I gathered, was purely of a social and pleasurable nature, and my informant spoke at some length of the entertainments arranged for their stay in the city. It was when he related with a considerable amount of satisfaction and pride that a deputation of their number had been introduced to and had shaken hands with a well-known prize-fighter that it occurred to me to broach the subject of his grace. To make a long story short, sir, I have arranged, subject to your approval, that the entire convention shall be presented to his grace to-morrow afternoon."

I was amazed. This chappie was a Napoleon.

"Eighty-seven, Jeeves! At how much a head?"

"I was obliged to agree to a reduction for quantity, sir. The terms finally arrived at were one hundred and fifty dollars for the party."

I thought a bit.

"Payable in advance?"

"No, sir. I endeavoured to obtain payment in advance, but was not successful."

"Well, anyway, when we get it I'll make it up to five hundred. Bicky'll never know. Do you suppose Mr. Bickersteth would suspect anything, Jeeves, if I made it up to five hundred?"

"I fancy not, sir. Mr. Bickersteth is an agreeable gentleman, but not bright."

"All right, then. After breakfast run down to the bank and get me some money."

"Yes, sir."

"You know, you're a bit of a marvel, Jeeves."

"Thank you, sir."

"Right-o!"

"Very good, sir."

When I took dear old Bicky aside in the course of the morning and told him what had happened he nearly broke down. He tottered into the sitting-room and buttonholed old Chiswick, who was reading the comic section of the morning paper with a kind of grim resolution.

"Uncle," he said, "are you doing anything special to-morrow afternoon? I mean to say, I've asked a few of my pals in to meet you, don't you know."

The old boy cocked a speculative eye at him.

"There will be no reporters among them?"

"Reporters? Rather not! Why?"

"I refuse to be badgered by reporters. There were a number of adhesive young men who endeavoured to elicit from me my views on America while the boat was approaching the dock. I will not be subjected to this persecution again."

"That'll be absolutely all right, uncle. There won't be a newspaperman in the place."

"In that case I shall be glad to make the acquaintance of your friends."

"You'll shake hands with them, and so forth?"

"I shall naturally order my behaviour according to the accepted rules of civilized intercourse."

Bicky thanked him heartily and came off to lunch with me at the club, where he babbled freely of hens, incubators, and other rotten things.

After mature consideration we had decided to unleash the Birdsburg contingent on the old boy ten at a time. Jeeves brought his theatre-pal round to see us, and we arranged the whole thing with him. A very decent chappie, but rather inclined to collar the conversation and turn it in the direction of his home-town's new water-supply system. We settled that, as an hour was about all he would be likely to stand, each gang should consider itself entitled to seven minutes of the duke's society by Jeeves's stop-watch, and that when their time was up Jeeves should slide into the room and cough meaningly. Then we parted with what I believe are called mutual expressions of good-will, the Birdsburg chappie extending a cordial invitation to us all to pop out some day and take a look at the new water-supply system, for which we thanked him.

Next day the deputation rolled in. The first shift consisted of the cove we had met and nine others almost exactly like him in every respect. They all looked deuced keen and businesslike, as if from youth up they had been working in the office and catching the boss's eye and what not. They shook hands with the old boy with a good deal of apparent satisfaction — all except one chappie, who seemed to be brooding about something — and then they stood off and became chatty.

"What message have you for Birdsburg, duke?" asked our pal.

The old boy seemed a bit rattled.

"I have never been to Birdsburg."

The chappie seemed pained.

"You should pay it a visit," he said. "The most rapidly-growing city in the country. Boost for Birdsburg!"

"Boost for Birdsburg!" said the other chappies reverently.

The chappie who had been brooding suddenly gave tongue.

"Say!"

He was a stout sort of well-fed cove with one of those determined chins and a cold eye.

The assemblage looked at him.

"As a matter of business," said the chappie—"mind you, I'm not questioning anybody's good faith, but, as a matter of strict business—I think this gentleman here ought to put himself on record before witnesses as stating that he really is a duke."

"What do you mean, sir?" cried the old boy, getting purple.

"No offence, simply business. I'm not saying anything, mind you, but there's one thing that seems kind of funny to me. This gentleman here says his name's Mr. Bickersteth, as I understand it. Well, if you're the Duke of Chiswick, why isn't he Lord Percy Something? I've read English novels, and I know all about it."

"This is monstrous!"

"Now don't get hot under the collar. I'm only asking. I've a right to know. You're going to take our money, so it's only fair that we should see that we get our money's worth."

The water-supply cove chipped in:—

"You're quite right, Simms. I overlooked that when making the agreement. You see, gentlemen, as business men we've a right to reasonable guarantees of good faith. We are paying Mr. Bickersteth here a hundred and fifty dollars for this reception, and we naturally want to know——"

Old Chiswick gave Bicky a searching look; then he turned to the water-supply chappie. He was frightfully calm.

"I can assure you that I know nothing of this," he said, quite politely. "I should be grateful if you would explain."

"Well, we arranged with Mr. Bickersteth that eighty-seven citizens of Birdsburg should have the privilege of meeting and shaking hands with you for a financial consideration mutually arranged, and what my friend Simms here means—and I'm with him—is that we have only Mr. Bickersteth's word for it—and he is a stranger to us—that you are the Duke of Chiswick at all."

Old Chiswick gulped.

"Allow me to assure you, sir," he said, in a rummy kind of voice, "that I am the Duke of Chiswick."

"Then that's all right," said the chappie, heartily. "That was all we wanted to know. Let the thing go on."

"I am sorry to say," said old Chiswick, "that it cannot go on. I am feeling a little tired. I fear I must ask to be excused."

"But there are seventy-seven of the boys waiting round the corner at this moment, duke, to be introduced to you."

"I fear I must disappoint them."

"But in that case the deal would have to be off."

"That is a matter for you and my nephew to discuss."

The chappie seemed troubled.

"You really won't meet the rest of them?"

"No!"

"Well, then, I guess we'll be going."

They went out, and there was a pretty solid silence. Then old Chiswick turned to Bicky: —

"Well?"

Bicky didn't seem to have anything to say.

"Was it true what that man said?"

"Yes, uncle."

"What do you mean by playing this trick?"

Bicky seemed pretty well knocked out, so I put in a word: —

"I think you'd better explain the whole thing, Bicky, old top."

Bicky's Adam's-apple jumped about a bit; then he started: —

"You see, you had cut off my allowance, uncle, and I wanted a bit of money to start a chicken farm. I mean to say it's an absolute cert if you once get a bit of capital. You buy a hen, and it lays an egg every day of the week, and you sell the eggs, say, seven for twenty-five cents.

"Keep of hen costs nothing. Profit practically ——"

"What is all this nonsense about hens? You led me to suppose you were a substantial business man."

"Old Bicky rather exaggerated, sir," I said, helping the chappie out. "The fact is, the poor old lad is absolutely dependent on that remittance of yours, and when you cut it off, don't you know, he was pretty solidly in the soup, and had to think of some way of closing in on a bit of the ready pretty quick. That's why we thought of this hand-shaking scheme."

Old Chiswick foamed at the mouth.

"So you have lied to me! You have deliberately deceived me as to your financial status!"

"Poor old Bicky didn't want to go to that ranch," I explained. "He doesn't like cows and horses, but he rather thinks he would be hot stuff among the hens. All he wants is a bit of capital. Don't you think it would be rather a wheeze if you were to——"

"After what has happened? After this—this deceit and foolery? Not a penny!"

"But——"

"Not a penny!"

There was a respectful cough in the background.

"If I might make a suggestion, sir?"

Jeeves was standing on the horizon, looking devilish brainy.

"Go ahead, Jeeves!" I said.

"I would merely suggest, sir, that if Mr. Bickersteth is in need of a little ready money, and is at a loss to obtain it elsewhere, he might secure the sum he requires by describing the occurrences of this afternoon for the Sunday issue of one of the more spirited and enterprising newspapers."

"By Jove!" I said.

"By George!" said Bicky.

"Great heavens!" said old Chiswick.

"Very good, sir," said Jeeves.

Bicky turned to old Chiswick with a gleaming eye.

"Jeeves is right! I'll do it! The *Chronicle* would jump at it. They eat that sort of stuff."

Old Chiswick gave a kind of moaning howl.

"I absolutely forbid you, Francis, to do this thing!"

"That's all very well," said Bicky, wonderfully braced, "but if I can't get the money any other way——"

"Wait! Er—wait, my boy! you are so impetuous! We might arrange something."

"I won't go to that bally ranch."

"No, no! No, no, my boy! I would not suggest it. I would not for a moment suggest it. I—I think——" He seemed to have a bit of a struggle with himself. "I—I think that, on the whole, it would be best if you returned with me to England. I—I might—in fact, I think I see my way to doing—to—I might be able to utilize your services in some secretarial position."

"I shouldn't mind that."

"I should not be able to offer you a salary, but, as you know, in English political life the unpaid secretary is a recognized figure——"

"The only figure I'll recognize," said Bicky, firmly, "is five hundred quid a year, paid quarterly."

"My dear boy!"

"Absolutely!"

"But your recompense, my dear Francis, would consist in the unrivalled opportunities you would have, as my secretary, to gain experience, to accustom yourself to the intricacies of political life, to—in fact, you would be in an exceedingly advantageous position."

"Five hundred a year!" said Bicky, rolling it round his tongue. "Why, that would be nothing to what I could make if I started a chicken farm. It stands to reason. Suppose you have a dozen hens. Each of the hens has a dozen chickens. After a bit the chickens grow up and have a dozen chickens each themselves, and then they all start laying eggs! There's a fortune in it. You can get anything you like for eggs in America. Chappies keep them on ice for years and years, and don't sell them till they fetch about a dollar a whirl. You don't think I'm going to chuck a future like this for anything under five hundred o' goblins a year—what?"

A look of anguish passed over old Chiswick's face, then he seemed to be resigned to it. "Very well, my boy," he said.

"What-o!" said Bicky. "All right, then."

"Jeeves," I said. Bicky had taken the old boy off to dinner to celebrate, and we were alone. "Jeeves, this has been one of your best efforts."

"Thank you, sir."

"It beats me how you do it."

"Yes, sir."

"The only trouble is you haven't got much out of it—what!"

"I fancy Mr. Bickersteth intends—I judge from his remarks—to signify his appreciation of anything I have been fortunate enough to do to assist him, at some later date when he is in a more favourable position to do so."

"It isn't enough, Jeeves!"

"Sir?"

It was a wrench, but I felt it was the only possible thing to be done. "Bring my shaving things."

A gleam of hope shone in the chappie's eye, mixed with doubt.

"You mean, sir?"

"And shave off my moustache."

There was a moment's silence. I could see the fellow was deeply moved.

"Thank you very much indeed, sir," he said, in a low voice, and popped off.

Jeeves and the Chump Cyril

YOU know, the longer I live, the more clearly I see that half the trouble in this bally world is caused by the light-hearted and thoughtless way in which chappies dash off letters of introduction and hand them to other chappies to deliver to chappies of the third part. It's one of those things that make you wish you were living in the Stone Age. What I mean to say is, if a fellow in those days wanted to give anyone a letter of introduction, he had to spend a month or so carving it on a large-sized boulder, and the chances were that the other chappie got so sick of lugging the thing round in the hot sun that he dropped it after the first mile. But nowadays it's so easy to write letters of introduction that everybody does it without a second thought, with the result that some perfectly harmless cove like myself gets in the soup.

Mark you, all the above is what you might call the result of my riper experience. I don't mind admitting that in the first flush of the thing, so to speak, when Jeeves told me—this would be about three weeks after I'd landed in America—that a blighter called Cyril Bassington-Bassington had arrived and I found that he had brought a letter of introduction to me from Aunt Agatha . . . where was I? Oh, yes . . . I don't mind admitting, I was saying, that just at first I was rather bucked. You see, after the painful events which had resulted in my leaving England I hadn't expected to get any sort of letter from Aunt Agatha which would pass the censor, so to speak. And it was a pleasant surprise to open this one and find it almost civil. Chilly, perhaps, in parts, but on the whole quite tolerably polite. I looked on the thing as a hopeful sign. Sort of olive-branch, you know. Or do I mean orange blossom? What

I'm getting at is that the fact that Aunt Agatha was writing to me without calling me names seemed, more or less, like a step in the direction of peace.

And I was all for peace, and that right speedily. I'm not saying a word against New York, mind you. I liked the place, and was having quite a ripe time there. But the fact remains that a fellow who's been used to London all his life does get a trifle homesick on a foreign strand, and I wanted to pop back to the cosy old flat in Berkeley Street—which could only be done when Aunt Agatha had simmered down and got over the Glossop episode. I know that London is a biggish city, but, believe me, it isn't half big enough for any fellow to live in with Aunt Agatha when she's after him with the old hatchet. And so I'm bound to say I looked on this chump Bassington-Bassington, when he arrived, more or less as a Dove of Peace, and was all for him.

He would seem from contemporary accounts to have blown in one morning at seven-forty-five, that being the ghastly sort of hour they shoot you off the liner in New York. He was given the respectful raspberry by Jeeves, and told to try again about three hours later, when there would be a sporting chance of my having sprung from my bed with a glad cry to welcome another day and all that sort of thing. Which was rather decent of Jeeves, by the way, for it so happened that there was a slight estrangement, a touch of coldness, a bit of a row in other words, between us at the moment because of some rather priceless purple socks which I was wearing against his wishes: and a lesser man might easily have snatched at the chance of getting back at me a bit by loosing Cyril into my bedchamber at a moment when I couldn't have stood a two-minutes' conversation with my dearest pal. For until I have had my early cup of tea and have brooded on life for a bit absolutely undisturbed, I'm not much of a lad for the merry chit-chat.

So Jeeves very sportingly shot Cyril out into the crisp morning air, and didn't let me know of his existence till he brought his card in with the Bohea.

"And what might all this be, Jeeves?" I said, giving the thing the glassy gaze.

"The gentleman has arrived from England, I understand, sir. He called to see you earlier in the day."

"Good Lord, Jeeves! You don't mean to say the day starts earlier than this?"

"He desired me to say he would return later, sir."

"I've never heard of him. Have *you* ever heard of him, Jeeves?"

"I am familiar with the name Bassington-Bassington, sir. There are three branches of the Bassington-Bassington family—the Shropshire Bassington-Bassingtons, the Hampshire Bassington-Bassingtons, and the Kent Bassington-Bassingtons."

"England seems pretty well stocked up with Bassington-Bassingtons."

"Tolerably so, sir."

"No chance of a sudden shortage, I mean, what?"

"Presumably not, sir."

"And what sort of a specimen is this one?"

"I could not say, sir, on such short acquaintance."

"Will you give me a sporting two to one, Jeeves, judging from what you have seen of him, that this chappie is not a blighter or an excrescence?"

"No, sir. I should not care to venture such liberal odds."

"I knew it. Well, the only thing that remains to be discovered is what kind of a blighter he is."

"Time will tell, sir. The gentleman brought a letter for you, sir."

"Oh, he did, did he?" I said, and grasped the communication. And then I recognised the handwriting. "I say, Jeeves, this is from my Aunt Agatha!"

"Indeed, sir?"

"Don't dismiss it in that light way. Don't you see what this means? She says she wants me to look after this excrescence while he's in New York. By Jove, Jeeves, if I only fawn on him a bit, so that he sends back a favourable report to head-quarters, I may yet be able to get back to England in time for Goodwood. Now is certainly the time for all good men to come to the aid of the party, Jeeves. We must rally round and cosset this cove in no uncertain manner."

"Yes, sir."

"He isn't going to stay in New York long," I said, taking another look at the letter. "He's headed for Washington. Going to give the nibs there the once-over, apparently, before taking a whirl at the Diplomatic Service. I should say that we can win this lad's esteem and affection with a lunch and a couple of dinners, what?"

"I fancy that should be entirely adequate, sir."

"This is the jolliest thing that's happened since we left England. It looks to me as if the sun were breaking through the clouds."

"Very possibly, sir."

He started to put out my things, and there was an awkward sort of silence.

"Not those socks, Jeeves," I said, gulping a bit but having a dash at the careless, off-hand tone. "Give me the purple ones."

"I beg your pardon, sir?"

"Those jolly purple ones."

"Very good, sir."

He lugged them out of the drawer as if he were a vegetarian fishing a caterpillar out of the salad. You could see he was feeling deeply. Deuced painful and all that, this sort of thing, but a chappie has got to assert himself every now and then. Absolutely.

I was looking for Cyril to show up again any time after breakfast, but he didn't appear: so towards one o'clock I trickled out to the Lambs Club, where I had an appointment to feed the Wooster face with a cove of the name of Caffyn I'd got pally with since my arrival—George Caffyn, a fellow who wrote plays and what not. I'd made a lot of friends during my stay in New York, the city being crammed with bonhomous lads who one and all extended a welcoming hand to the stranger in their midst.

Caffyn was a bit late, but bobbed up finally, saying that he had been kept at a rehearsal of his new musical comedy, "Ask Dad"; and we started in. We had just reached the coffee, when the waiter came up and said that Jeeves wanted to see me.

Jeeves was in the waiting-room. He gave the socks one pained look as I came in, then averted his eyes.

"Mr. Bassington-Bassington has just telephoned, sir."

"Oh?"

"Yes, sir."

"Where is he?"

"In prison, sir."

I reeled against the wallpaper. A nice thing to happen to Aunt Agatha's nominee on his first morning under my wing, I did *not* think!

"In prison!"

"Yes, sir. He said on the telephone that he had been arrested and would be glad if you could step round and bail him out."

"Arrested! What for?"

"He did not favour me with his confidence in that respect, sir."

"This is a bit thick, Jeeves."

"Precisely, sir."

I collected old George, who very decently volunteered to stagger along with me, and we hopped into a taxi. We sat around at the police-station for a bit on a wooden bench in a sort of ante-room, and presently a policeman appeared, leading in Cyril.

"Halloa! Halloa! Halloa!" I said. "What?"

My experience is that a fellow never really looks his best just after he's come out of a cell. When I was up at Oxford, I used to have a regular job bailing out a pal of mine who never failed to get pinched every Boat-Race night, and he always looked like something that had been dug up by the roots. Cyril was in pretty much the same sort of shape. He had a black eye and a torn collar, and altogether was nothing to write home about—especially if one was writing to Aunt Agatha. He was a thin, tall chappie with a lot of light hair and pale-blue goggly eyes which made him look like one of the rarer kinds of fish.

"I got your message," I said.

"Oh, are you Bertie Wooster?"

"Absolutely. And this is my pal George Caffyn. Writes plays and what not, don't you know."

We all shook hands, and the policeman, having retrieved a piece of chewing-gum from the underside of a chair, where he had parked it against a rainy day, went off into a corner and began to contemplate the infinite.

"This is a rotten country," said Cyril.

"Oh, I don't know, you know, don't you know!" I said.

"We do our best," said George.

"Old George is an American," I explained. "Writes plays, don't you know, and what not."

"Of course, I didn't invent the country," said George. "That was Columbus. But I shall be delighted to consider any improvements you may suggest and lay them before the proper authorities."

"Well, why don't the policemen in New York dress properly?"

George took a look at the chewing officer across the room.

"I don't see anything missing," he said

"I mean to say, why don't they wear helmets like they do in London? Why do they look like postmen? It isn't fair on a fellow. Makes it dashed confusing. I was simply standing on the pavement, looking at things, when a fellow who looked like a postman prodded me in the ribs with a club. I didn't see why I should have postmen prodding me. Why the dickens should a fellow come three thousand miles to be prodded by postmen?"

"The point is well taken," said George. "What did you do?"

"I gave him a shove, you know. I've got a frightfully hasty temper, you know. All the Bassington-Bassingtons have got frightfully hasty tempers, don't you know! And then he biffed me in the eye and lugged me off to this beastly place."

"I'll fix it, old son," I said. And I hauled out the bank-roll and went off to open negotiations, leaving Cyril to talk to George. I don't mind admitting that I was a bit perturbed. There were furrows in the old brow, and I had a kind of foreboding feeling. As long as this chump stayed in New York, I was responsible for him: and he didn't give me the impression of being the species of cove a reasonable chappie would care to be responsible for for more than about three minutes.

I mused with a considerable amount of tensity over Cyril that night, when I had got home and Jeeves had brought me the final whisky. I couldn't help feeling that this visit of his to America was going to be one of those times that try men's souls and what not. I hauled out Aunt Agatha's letter of introduction and re-read it, and there was no getting away from the fact that she undoubtedly appeared to be somewhat wrapped up in this blighter and to consider it my mission in life to shield him from harm while on the premises. I was deuced thankful that he had taken such a liking for George Caffyn, old George being a steady sort of cove. After I had got him out of his dungeon-cell, he and old George had gone off together, as chummy as brothers, to watch the afternoon rehearsal of "Ask Dad." There was some talk, I gathered, of their dining together. I felt pretty easy in my mind while George had his eye on him.

I had got about as far as this in my meditations, when Jeeves came in with a telegram. At least, it wasn't a telegram: it was a cable — from Aunt Agatha — and this is what it said: —

> Has Cyril Bassington-Bassington called yet? On no account introduce him into theatrical circles. Vitally important. Letter follows.

I read it a couple of times.

"This is rummy, Jeeves!"

"Yes, sir."

"Very rummy and dashed disturbing!"

"Will there be anything further to-night, sir?"

Of course, if he was going to be as bally unsympathetic as that there was nothing to be done. My idea had been to show him the cable and ask his advice. But if he was letting those purple socks rankle to that extent, the good old *noblesse oblige* of the Woosters couldn't lower itself to the extent of pleading with the man. Absolutely not. So I gave it a miss.

"Nothing more, thanks."

"Good night, sir."

"Good night."

He floated away, and I sat down to think the thing over. I had been directing the best efforts of the old bean to the problem for a matter of half an hour, when there was a ring at the bell. I went to the door, and there was Cyril, looking pretty festive.

"I'll come in for a bit if I may," he said. "Got something rather priceless to tell you."

He curveted past me into the sitting-room, and when I got there after shutting the front door I found him reading Aunt Agatha's cable and giggling in a rummy sort of manner. "Oughtn't to have looked at this, I suppose. Caught sight of my name and read it without thinking. I say, Wooster, old friend of my youth, this is rather funny. Do you mind if I have a drink? Thanks awfully and all that sort of rot. Yes, it's rather funny, considering what I came to tell you. Jolly old Caffyn has given me a small part in that musical comedy of his, 'Ask Dad.' Only a bit, you know, but quite tolerably ripe. I'm feeling frightfully braced, don't you know!"

He drank his drink, and went on. He didn't seem to notice that I wasn't jumping about the room, yapping with joy.

"You know, I've always wanted to go on the stage, you know," he said. "But my jolly old guv'nor wouldn't stick it at any price. Put the old Waukeesi down with a bang, and turned bright purple whenever the subject was mentioned. That's the real reason why I came over here, if you want to know. I knew there wasn't a chance of my being able to work this stage wheeze in London without somebody getting on to it and tipping off the guv'nor, so I rather brainily sprang the scheme of popping over to Washington to broaden my mind. There's nobody to interfere on this side, you see, so I can go right ahead!"

I tried to reason with the poor chump.

"But your guv'nor will have to know some time."

"That'll be all right. I shall be the jolly old star by then, and he won't have a leg to stand on."

"It seems to me he'll have one leg to stand on while he kicks me with the other."

"Why, where do you come in? What have you got to do with it?"

"I introduced you to George Caffyn."

"So you did, old top, so you did. I'd quite forgotten. I ought to have thanked you before. Well, so long. There's an early rehearsal of 'Ask Dad' to-morrow morning, and I must be toddling. Rummy the thing should be called 'Ask Dad,' when that's just what I'm not going to do. See what I mean, what, what? Well, pip-pip!"

"Toodle-oo!" I said sadly, and the blighter scudded off. I dived for the phone and called up George Caffyn.

"I say, George, what's all this about Cyril Bassington-Bassington?"

"What about him?"

"He tells me you've given him a part in your show."

"Oh, yes. Just a few lines."

"But I've just had fifty-seven cables from home telling me on no account to let him go on the stage."

"I'm sorry. But Cyril is just the type I need for that part. He's simply got to be himself."

"It's pretty tough on me, George, old man. My Aunt Agatha sent this blighter over with a letter of introduction to me, and she will hold me responsible."

"She'll cut you out of her will?"

"It isn't a question of money. But—of course, you've never met my Aunt Agatha, so it's rather hard to explain. But she's a sort of human vampire-bat, and she'll make things most fearfully unpleasant for me when I go back to England. She's the kind of woman who comes and rags you before breakfast, don't you know."

"Well, don't go back to England, then. Stick here and become President."

"But, George, old top——!"

"Good night!"

"But, I say, George, old man!"

"You didn't get my last remark. It was 'Good night!' You Idle Rich may not need any sleep, but I've got to be bright and fresh in the morning. God bless you!"

I felt as if I hadn't a friend in the world. I was so jolly well worked up that I went and banged on Jeeves's door. It wasn't a thing I'd have cared to do as a rule, but it seemed to me that now was the time for all good men to come to the aid of the party, so to speak, and that it was up to Jeeves to rally round the young master, even if it broke up his beauty-sleep.

Jeeves emerged in a brown dressing-gown.

"Sir?"

"Deuced sorry to wake you up, Jeeves, and what not, but all sorts of dashed disturbing things have been happening."

"I was not asleep. It is my practice, on retiring, to read a few pages of some instructive book."

"That's good! What I mean to say is, if you've just finished exercising the old bean, it's probably in mid-season form for tackling problems. Jeeves, Mr. Bassington-Bassington is going on the stage!"

"Indeed, sir?"

"Ah! The thing doesn't hit you! You don't get it properly! Here's the point. All his family are most fearfully dead against his going on the stage. There's going to be no end of trouble if he isn't headed off. And, what's worse, my Aunt Agatha will blame *me*, you see."

"I see, sir."

"Well, can't you think of some way of stopping him?"

"Not, I confess, at the moment, sir."

"Well, have a stab at it."

"I will give the matter my best consideration, sir. Will there be anything further to-night?"

"I hope not! I've had all I can stand already."

"Very good, sir."

He popped off.

The part which old George had written for the chump Cyril took up about two pages of typescript; but it might have been Hamlet, the way that poor, misguided pinhead worked himself to the bone over it. I suppose, if I heard him his lines once, I did it a dozen times in the first couple of days. He seemed to think that my only feeling about the whole affair was one of enthusiastic admiration, and that he could rely on my support and sympathy. What with trying to imagine how Aunt Agatha was going to take this thing, and being woken up out of the dreamless in the small hours every other night to give my opinion of some new bit of business which Cyril had invented, I became more or less the good old shadow. And all the time Jeeves remained still pretty cold and distant about the purple socks. It's this sort of thing that ages a chappie, don't you know, and makes his youthful *joie-de-vivre* go a bit groggy at the knees.

In the middle of it Aunt Agatha's letter arrived. It took her about six pages to do justice to Cyril's father's feelings in regard to his going on the stage and about six more to give me a kind of sketch of what she would say, think, and do if I didn't keep him clear of injurious influences while he was in America. The letter came by the afternoon mail, and left me with a pretty firm conviction that it wasn't a thing I ought to keep to myself. I didn't even wait to ring the bell: I whizzed for the kitchen, bleating for Jeeves, and butted into the middle of a regular tea-party of sorts. Seated at the table were a depressed-looking cove who might have been a valet or something, and a boy in a Norfolk suit. The valet-chappie was drinking a whisky and soda, and the boy was being tolerably rough with some jam and cake.

"Oh, I say, Jeeves!" I said. "Sorry to interrupt the feast of reason and flow of soul and so forth, but——"

At this juncture the small boy's eye hit me like a bullet and stopped me in my tracks. It was one of those cold, clammy, accusing sort of eyes—the kind that makes you reach up to see if your tie is straight: and he looked at me as if I were some sort of unnecessary product which Cuthbert the Cat had brought in after a ramble among the local ash-cans. He was a stoutish infant with a lot of freckles and a good deal of jam on his face.

"Hallo! Hallo! Hallo!" I said. "What?" There didn't seem much else to say.

The stripling stared at me in a nasty sort of way through the jam. He may have loved me at first sight, but the impression he gave me was that he didn't think a lot of me and wasn't betting much that I would improve a great deal on acquaintance. I had a kind of feeling that I was about as popular with him as a cold Welsh rabbit.

"What's your name?" he asked.

"My name? Oh, Wooster, don't you know, and what not."

"My pop's richer than you are!"

That seemed to be all about me. The child having said his say, started in on the jam again. I turned to Jeeves.

"I say, Jeeves, can you spare a moment? I want to show you something."

"Very good, sir." We toddled into the sitting-room.

"Who is your little friend, Sidney the Sunbeam, Jeeves?"

"The young gentleman, sir?"

"It's a loose way of describing him, but I know what you mean."

"I trust I was not taking a liberty in entertaining him, sir?"

"Not a bit. If that's your idea of a large afternoon, go ahead."

"I happened to meet the young gentleman taking a walk with his father's valet, sir, whom I used to know somewhat intimately in London, and I ventured to invite them both to join me here."

"Well, never mind about him, Jeeves. Read this letter."

He gave it the up-and-down.

"Very disturbing, sir!" was all he could find to say.

"What are we going to do about it?"

"Time may provide a solution, sir."

"On the other hand, it mayn't, what?"

"Extremely true, sir."

We'd got as far as this, when there was a ring at the door. Jeeves shimmered off, and Cyril blew in, full of good cheer and blitheringness.

"I say, Wooster, old thing," he said, "I want your advice. You know this jolly old part of mine. How ought I to dress it? What I mean is, the first act scene is laid in an hotel of sorts, at about three in the afternoon. What ought I to wear, do you think?"

I wasn't feeling fit for a discussion of gent's suitings.

"You'd better consult Jeeves," I said.

"A hot and by no means unripe idea! Where is he?"

"Gone back to the kitchen, I suppose."

"I'll smite the good old bell, shall I? Yes? No?"

"Right-o!"

Jeeves poured silently in.

"Oh, I say, Jeeves," began Cyril, "I just wanted to have a syllable or two with you. It's this way—Hallo, who's this?"

I then perceived that the stout stripling had trickled into the room after Jeeves. He was standing near the door looking at Cyril as if his worst fears had been realised. There was a bit of a silence. The child remained there, drinking Cyril in for about half a minute; then he gave his verdict:

"Fish-face!"

"Eh? What?" said Cyril.

The child, who had evidently been taught at his mother's knee to speak the truth, made his meaning a trifle clearer.

"You've a face like a fish!"

He spoke as if Cyril was more to be pitied than censured, which I am bound to say I thought rather decent and broad-minded of him. I don't mind admitting that, whenever I looked at Cyril's face, I always had a feeling that he couldn't have got that way without its being mostly his own fault. I found myself warming to this child. Absolutely, don't you know. I liked his conversation.

It seemed to take Cyril a moment or two really to grasp the thing, and then you could hear the blood of the Bassington-Bassingtons begin to sizzle.

"Well, I'm dashed!" he said. "I'm dashed if I'm not!"

"I wouldn't have a face like that," proceeded the child, with a good deal of earnestness, "not if you gave me a million dollars." He thought for a moment, then corrected himself. "Two million dollars!" he added.

Just what occurred then I couldn't exactly say, but the next few minutes were a bit exciting. I take it that Cyril must have made a dive for the infant. Anyway, the air seemed pretty well congested with arms and legs and things. Something bumped into the Wooster waistcoat just around the third button, and I collapsed on to the settee and rather lost interest in things for the moment. When I had unscrambled myself, I found that Jeeves and the child had retired and Cyril was standing in the middle of the room snorting a bit.

"Who's that frightful little brute, Wooster?"

"I don't know. I never saw him before to-day."

"I gave him a couple of tolerably juicy buffets before he legged it. I say, Wooster, that kid said a dashed odd thing. He yelled out something about Jeeves promising him a dollar if he called me—er—what he said."

It sounded pretty unlikely to me.

"What would Jeeves do that for?"

"It struck me as rummy, too."

"Where would be the sense of it?"

"That's what I can't see."

"I mean to say, it's nothing to Jeeves what sort of a face you have!"

"No!" said Cyril. He spoke a little coldly, I fancied. I don't know why. "Well, I'll be popping. Toodle-oo!"

"Pip-pip!"

It must have been about a week after this rummy little episode that George Caffyn called me up and asked me if I would care to go and see a run-through of his show. "Ask Dad," it seemed, was to open out of town in Schenectady on the following Monday, and this was to be a sort of preliminary dress-rehearsal. A preliminary dress-rehearsal, old George explained, was the same as a regular dress-rehearsal inasmuch as it was apt to look like nothing on earth and last into the small hours, but more exciting because they wouldn't be timing the piece and consequently all the blighters who on these occasions let their angry passions rise would have plenty of scope for interruptions, with the result that a pleasant time would be had by all.

The thing was billed to start at eight o'clock, so I rolled up at ten-fifteen, so as not to have too long to wait before they began. The dress-parade was still going on. George was on the stage, talking to a cove in shirt-sleeves and an absolutely round chappie with big spectacles and a practically hairless dome. I had seen George with the latter merchant once or twice at the club, and I knew that he was Blumenfield, the manager. I waved to George, and slid into a seat at the back of the house, so as to be out of the way when the fighting started. Presently George hopped down off the stage and came and joined me, and fairly soon after that the curtain went down. The chappie at the piano whacked out a well-meant bar or two, and the curtain went up again.

I can't quite recall what the plot of "Ask Dad" was about, but I do know that it seemed able to jog along all right without much help from Cyril. I was rather puzzled at first. What I mean is, through brooding on Cyril and hearing him in his part and listening to his views on what ought and what ought not to be done, I suppose I had got a sort of impression rooted in the old bean that he was pretty well the backbone of the show, and that the rest of the company didn't do much except go on and fill in when he happened to be off the stage. I sat there for nearly half an hour, waiting for him to make his entrance, until I suddenly discovered he had been on from the start. He was, in fact, the rummy-looking plug-ugly who was now leaning against a potted palm a couple of feet from the O.P. side, trying to appear intelligent while the heroine sang a song about Love being like something which for the moment has slipped my memory. After the second refrain he began to dance in company with a dozen other equally weird birds. A painful spectacle for one who could see a vision of Aunt Agatha reaching for the hatchet and old Bassington-Bassington senior putting on his strongest pair of hob-nailed boots. Absolutely!

The dance had just finished, and Cyril and his pals had shuffled off into the wings when a voice spoke from the darkness on my right.

"Pop!"

Old Blumenfield clapped his hands, and the hero, who had just been about to get the next line off his diaphragm, cheesed it. I peered into the shadows. Who should it be but Jeeves's little playmate with the freckles! He was now strolling down the aisle with his hands in his pockets as if the place belonged to him. An air of respectful attention seemed to pervade the building.

"Pop," said the stripling, "that number's no good." Old Blumenfield beamed over his shoulder.

"Don't you like it, darling?"

"It gives me a pain."

"You're dead right."

"You want something zippy there. Something with a bit of jazz to it!"

"Quite right, my boy. I'll make a note of it. All right. Go on!"

I turned to George, who was muttering to himself in rather an overwrought way.

"I say, George, old man, who the dickens is that kid?"

Old George groaned a bit hollowly, as if things were a trifle thick.

"I didn't know he had crawled in! It's Blumenfield's son. Now we're going to have a Hades of a time!"

"Does he always run things like this?"

"Always!"

"But why does old Blumenfield listen to him?"

"Nobody seems to know. It may be pure fatherly love, or he may regard him as a mascot. My own idea is that he thinks the kid has exactly the amount of intelligence of the average member of the audience, and that what makes a hit with him will please the general public. While, conversely, what he doesn't like will be too rotten for anyone. The kid is a pest, a wart, and a pot of poison, and should be strangled!"

The rehearsal went on. The hero got off his line. There was a slight outburst of frightfulness between the stage-manager and a Voice named Bill that came from somewhere near the roof, the subject under discussion being where the devil Bill's "ambers" were at that particular juncture. Then things went on again until the moment arrived for Cyril's big scene.

I was still a trifle hazy about the plot, but I had got on to the fact that Cyril was some sort of an English peer who had come over to America doubtless for the best reasons. So far he had only had two lines to say. One was "Oh, I say!" and the other was "Yes, by Jove!"; but I seemed to recollect, from hearing him read his part, that pretty soon he was due rather to spread himself. I sat back in my chair and waited for him to bob up.

He bobbed up about five minutes later. Things had got a bit stormy by that time. The Voice and the stage-director had had another of their love-feasts — this time something to do with why Bill's "blues" weren't on the job or something. And, almost as soon as that was over, there was a bit of unpleasantness because a flower-pot fell off a window-ledge and nearly brained the hero. The atmosphere was consequently more or less hotted up when Cyril, who had been hanging about at the back of the stage, breezed down centre and toed the mark for his most substantial chunk of entertainment. The heroine had been saying something — I forget what — and all the chorus, with Cyril at their head, had begun to surge round her in the restless sort of way those chappies always do when there's a number coming along.

Cyril's first line was, "Oh, I say, you know, you mustn't say that, really!" and it seemed to me he passed it over the larynx with a goodish deal of vim and *je-ne-sais-quoi*. But, by Jove, before the heroine had time for the come-back, our little friend with the freckles had risen to lodge a protest.

"Pop!"

"Yes, darling?"

"That one's no good!"

"Which one, darling?"

"The one with a face like a fish."

"But they all have faces like fish, darling."

The child seemed to see the justice of this objection. He became more definite.

"The ugly one."

"Which ugly one? That one?" said old Blumenfield, pointing to Cyril.

"Yep! He's rotten!"

"I thought so myself."

"He's a pill!"

"You're dead right, my boy. I've noticed it for some time."

Cyril had been gaping a bit while these few remarks were in progress. He now shot down to the footlights. Even from where I was sitting, I could see that these harsh words had hit the old Bassington-Bassington family pride a frightful wallop. He started to get pink in the ears, and then in the nose, and then in the cheeks, till in about a quarter of a minute he looked pretty much like an explosion in a tomato cannery on a sunset evening.

"What the deuce do you mean?"

"What the deuce do *you* mean?" shouted old Blumenfield. "Don't yell at me across the footlights!"

"I've a dashed good mind to come down and spank that little brute!"

"What!"

"A dashed good mind!"

Old Blumenfield swelled like a pumped-up tyre. He got rounder than ever.

"See here, mister—I don't know your darn name——!"

"My name's Bassington-Bassington, and the jolly old Bassington-Bassingtons—I mean the Bassington-Bassingtons aren't accustomed——"

Old Blumenfield told him in a few brief words pretty much what he thought of the Bassington-Bassingtons and what they weren't accustomed to. The whole strength of the company rallied round to enjoy his remarks. You could see them jutting out from the wings and protruding from behind trees.

"You got to work good for my pop!" said the stout child, waggling his head reprovingly at Cyril.

"I don't want any bally cheek from you!" said Cyril, gurgling a bit.

"What's that?" barked old Blumenfield. "Do you understand that this boy is my son?"

"Yes, I do," said Cyril. "And you both have my sympathy!"

"You're fired!" bellowed old Blumenfield, swelling a good bit more. "Get out of my theatre!"

About half-past ten next morning, just after I had finished lubricating the good old interior with a soothing cup of Oolong, Jeeves filtered into my bedroom, and said that Cyril was waiting to see me in the sitting-room.

"How does he look, Jeeves?"

"Sir?"

"What does Mr. Bassington-Bassington look like?"

"It is hardly my place, sir, to criticise the facial peculiarities of your friends."

"I don't mean that. I mean, does he appear peeved and what not?"

"Not noticeably, sir. His manner is tranquil."

"That's rum!"

"Sir?"

"Nothing. Show him in, will you?"

I'm bound to say I had expected to see Cyril showing a few more traces of last night's battle. I was looking for a bit of the overwrought soul and the quivering ganglions, if you know what I mean. He seemed pretty ordinary and quite fairly cheerful.

"Hallo, Wooster, old thing!"

"Cheero!"

"I just looked in to say good-bye."

"Good-bye?"

"Yes. I'm off to Washington in an hour." He sat down on the bed. "You know, Wooster, old top," he went on, "I've been thinking it all over, and really it doesn't seem quite fair to the jolly old guv'nor, my going on the stage and so forth. What do you think?"

"I see what you mean."

"I mean to say, he sent me over here to broaden my jolly old mind and words to that effect, don't you know, and I can't help thinking it would be a bit of a jar for the old boy if I gave him the bird and went on the stage instead. I don't know if you understand me, but what I mean to say is, it's a sort of question of conscience."

"Can you leave the show without upsetting everything?"

"Oh, that's all right. I've explained everything to old Blumenfield, and he quite sees my position. Of course, he's sorry to lose me—said he didn't see how he could fill my place and all that sort of thing—but, after all, even if it does land him in a bit of a hole, I think I'm right in resigning my part, don't you?"

"Oh, absolutely."

"I thought you'd agree with me. Well, I ought to be shifting. Awfully glad to have seen something of you, and all that sort of rot. Pip-pip!"

"Toodle-oo!"

He sallied forth, having told all those bally lies with the clear, blue, pop-eyed gaze of a young child. I rang for Jeeves. You know, ever since last night I had been exercising the old bean to some extent, and a good deal of light had dawned upon me.

"Jeeves!"

"Sir?"

"Did you put that pie-faced infant up to bally-ragging Mr. Bassington-Bassington?"

"Sir?"

"Oh, you know what I mean. Did you tell him to get Mr. Bassington-Bassington sacked from the 'Ask Dad' company?"

"I would not take such a liberty, sir." He started to put out my clothes. "It is possible that young Master Blumenfield may have gathered from casual remarks of mine that I did not consider the stage altogether a suitable sphere for Mr. Bassington-Bassington."

"I say, Jeeves, you know, you're a bit of a marvel."

"I endeavour to give satisfaction, sir."

"And I'm frightfully obliged, if you know what I mean. Aunt Agatha would have had sixteen or seventeen fits if you hadn't headed him off."

"I fancy there might have been some little friction and unpleasantness, sir. I am laying out the blue suit with the thin red stripe, sir. I fancy the effect will be pleasing."

It's a rummy thing, but I had finished breakfast and gone out and got as far as the lift before I remembered what it was that I had meant to do to reward Jeeves for his really sporting behaviour in this matter of the chump Cyril. It cut me to the heart to do it, but I had decided to give him his way and let those purple socks pass out of my life. After all, there are times when a cove must make sacrifices. I was just going to nip back and break the glad news to him, when the lift came up, so I thought I would leave it till I got home.

The coloured chappie in charge of the lift looked at me, as I hopped in, with a good deal of quiet devotion and what not.

"I wish to thank yo', suh," he said, "for yo' kindness."

"Eh? What?"

"Misto' Jeeves done give me them purple socks, as you told him. Thank yo' very much, suh!"

I looked down. The blighter was a blaze of mauve from the ankle-bone southward. I don't know when I've seen anything so dressy.

"Oh, ah! Not at all! Right-o! Glad you like them!" I said.

Well, I mean to say, what? Absolutely!

Jeeves in the Springtime

"'MORNING, Jeeves," I said.

"Good morning, sir," said Jeeves.

He put the good old cup of tea softly on the table by my bed, and I took a refreshing sip. Just right, as usual. Not too hot, not too sweet, not too weak, not too strong, not too much milk, and not a drop spilled in the saucer. A most amazing cove, Jeeves. So dashed competent in every respect. I've said it before, and I'll say it again. I mean to say, take just one small instance. Every other valet I've ever had used to barge into my room in the morning while I was still asleep, causing much misery: but Jeeves seems to know when I'm awake by a sort of telepathy. He always floats in with the cup exactly two minutes after I come to life. Makes a deuce of a lot of difference to a fellow's day.

"How's the weather, Jeeves?"

"Exceptionally clement, sir."

"Anything in the papers?"

"Some slight friction threatening in the Balkans, sir. Otherwise, nothing."

"I say, Jeeves, a man I met at the club last night told me to put my shirt on Privateer for the two o'clock race this afternoon. How about it?"

"I should not advocate it, sir. The stable is not sanguine."

That was enough for me. Jeeves knows. How, I couldn't say, but he knows. There was a time when I would laugh lightly, and go ahead, and lose my little all against his advice, but not now.

"Talking of shirts," I said, "have those mauve ones I ordered arrived yet?"

"Yes, sir. I sent them back."

"Sent them back?"

"Yes, sir. They would not have become you."

Well, I must say I'd thought fairly highly of those shirtings, but I bowed to superior knowledge. Weak? I don't know. Most fellows, no doubt, are all for having their valets confine their activities to creasing trousers and what not without trying to run the home; but it's different with Jeeves. Right from the first day he came to me, I have looked on him as a sort of guide, philosopher, and friend.

"Mr. Little rang up on the telephone a few moments ago, sir. I informed him that you were not yet awake."

"Did he leave a message?"

"No, sir. He mentioned that he had a matter of importance to discuss with you, but confided no details."

"Oh, well, I expect I shall be seeing him at the club."

"No doubt, sir."

I wasn't what you might call in a fever of impatience. Bingo Little is a chap I was at school with, and we see a lot of each other still. He's the nephew of old Mortimer Little, who retired from business recently with a goodish pile. (You've probably heard of Little's Liniment—It Limbers Up the Legs.) Bingo biffs about London on a pretty comfortable allowance given him by his uncle, and leads on the whole a fairly unclouded life. It wasn't likely that anything which he described as a matter of importance would turn out to be really so frightfully important. I took it that he had discovered some new brand of cigarette which he wanted me to try, or something like that, and didn't spoil my breakfast by worrying.

After breakfast I lit a cigarette and went to the open window to inspect the day. It certainly was one of the best and brightest.

"Jeeves," I said.

"Sir?" said Jeeves. He had been clearing away the breakfast things, but at the sound of the young master's voice cheesed it courteously.

"You were absolutely right about the weather. It is a juicy morning."

"Decidedly, sir."

"Spring and all that."

"Yes, sir."

"In the spring, Jeeves, a livelier iris gleams upon the burnished dove."

"So I have been informed, sir."

"Right ho! Then bring me my whangee, my yellowest shoes, and the old green Homburg. I'm going into the Park to do pastoral dances."

I don't know if you know that sort of feeling you get on these days round about the end of April and the beginning of May, when the sky's a light blue, with cotton-wool clouds, and there's a bit of a breeze blowing from the west? Kind of uplifted feeling. Romantic, if you know what I mean. I'm not much of a ladies' man, but on this particular morning it seemed to me that what I really wanted was some charming girl to buzz up and ask me to save her from assassins or something. So that it was a bit of an anti-climax when I merely ran into young Bingo Little, looking perfectly foul in a crimson satin tie decorated with horseshoes.

"Hallo, Bertie," said Bingo.

"My God, man!" I gargled. "The cravat! The gent's neckwear! Why? For what reason?"

"Oh, the tie?" He blushed. "I—er—I was given it."

He seemed embarrassed, so I dropped the subject. We toddled along a bit, and sat down on a couple of chairs by the Serpentine.

"Jeeves tells me you want to talk to me about something," I said.

"Eh?" said Bingo, with a start. "Oh yes, yes. Yes."

I waited for him to unleash the topic of the day, but he didn't seem to want to get going. Conversation languished. He stared straight ahead of him in a glassy sort of manner.

"I say, Bertie," he said, after a pause of about an hour and a quarter.

"Hallo!"

"Do you like the name Mabel?"

"No."

"No?"

"No."

"You don't think there's a kind of music in the word, like the wind rustling gently through the tree-tops?"

"No."

He seemed disappointed for a moment; then cheered up.

"Of course, you wouldn't. You always were a fatheaded worm without any soul, weren't you?"

"Just as you say. Who is she? Tell me all."

For I realised now that poor old Bingo was going through it once again. Ever since I have known him—and we were at school together—he has been perpetually falling in love with someone, generally in the spring, which seems to act on him like magic. At school he had the finest collection of actresses' photographs of anyone of his time; and at Oxford his romantic nature was a byword.

"You'd better come along and meet her at lunch," he said, looking at his watch.

"A ripe suggestion," I said. "Where are you meeting her? At the Ritz?"

"Near the Ritz."

He was geographically accurate. About fifty yards east of the Ritz there is one of those blighted tea-and-bun shops you see dotted about all over London, and into this, if you'll believe me, young Bingo dived like a homing rabbit; and before I had time to say a word we were wedged in at a table, on the brink of a silent pool of coffee left there by an early luncher.

I'm bound to say I couldn't quite follow the development of the scenario. Bingo, while not absolutely rolling in the stuff, has always had a fair amount of the ready. Apart from what he got from his uncle, I knew that he had finished up the jumping season well on the right side of the ledger. Why, then, was he lunching the girl at this God-forsaken eatery? It couldn't be because he was hard up.

Just then the waitress arrived. Rather a pretty girl.

"Aren't we going to wait——?" I started to say to Bingo, thinking it somewhat thick that, in addition to asking a girl to lunch with him in a place like this, he should fling himself on the foodstuffs before she turned up, when I caught sight of his face, and stopped.

The man was goggling. His entire map was suffused with a rich blush. He looked like the Soul's Awakening done in pink.

"Hallo, Mabel!" he said, with a sort of gulp.

"Hallo!" said the girl.

"Mabel," said Bingo, "this is Bertie Wooster, a pal of mine."

"Pleased to meet you," she said. "Nice morning."

"Fine," I said.

"You see I'm wearing the tie," said Bingo.

"It suits you beautiful," said the girl.

Personally, if anyone had told me that a tie like that suited me, I should have risen and struck them on the mazzard, regardless of their age and sex; but poor old Bingo simply got all flustered with gratification, and smirked in the most gruesome manner.

"Well, what's it going to be to-day?" asked the girl, introducing the business touch into the conversation.

Bingo studied the menu devoutly.

"I'll have a cup of cocoa, cold veal and ham pie, slice of fruit cake, and a macaroon. Same for you, Bertie?"

I gazed at the man, revolted. That he could have been a pal of mine all these years and think me capable of insulting the old tum with this sort of stuff cut me to the quick.

"Or how about a bit of hot steak-pudding, with a sparkling limado to wash it down?" said Bingo.

You know, the way love can change a fellow is really frightful to contemplate. This chappie before me, who spoke in that absolutely careless way of macaroons and limado, was the man I had seen in happier days telling the head-waiter at Claridge's exactly how he wanted the *chef* to prepare the *sole frite au gourmet aux champignons,* and saying he would jolly well sling it back if it wasn't just right. Ghastly! Ghastly!

A roll and butter and a small coffee seemed the only things on the list that hadn't been specially prepared by the nastier-minded members of the Borgia family for people they had a particular grudge against, so I chose them, and Mabel hopped it.

"Well?" said Bingo rapturously.

I took it that he wanted my opinion of the female poisoner who had just left us.

"Very nice," I said.

He seemed dissatisfied.

"You don't think she's the most wonderful girl you ever saw?" he said wistfully.

"Oh, absolutely!" I said, to appease the blighter. "Where did you meet her?"

"At a subscription dance at Camberwell."

"What on earth were you doing at a subscription dance at Camberwell?"

"Your man Jeeves asked me if I would buy a couple of tickets. It was in aid of some charity or other."

"Jeeves? I didn't know he went in for that sort of thing."

"Well, I suppose he has to relax a bit every now and then. Anyway, he was there, swinging a dashed efficient shoe. I hadn't meant to go at first, but I turned up for a lark. Oh, Bertie, think what I might have missed!"

"What might you have missed?" I asked, the old lemon being slightly clouded.

"Mabel, you chump. If I hadn't gone I shouldn't have met Mabel."

"Oh, ah!"

At this point Bingo fell into a species of trance, and only came out of it to wrap himself round the pie and macaroon.

"Bertie," he said, "I want your advice."

"Carry on."

"At least, not your advice, because that wouldn't be much good to anybody. I mean, you're a pretty consummate old ass, aren't you? Not that I want to hurt your feelings, of course."

"No, no, I see that."

"What I wish you would do is to put the whole thing to that fellow Jeeves of yours, and see what he suggests. You've often told me that he has helped other pals of yours out of messes. From what you tell me, he's by way of being the brains of the family."

"He's never let me down yet."

"Then put my case to him."

"What case?"

"My problem."

"What problem?"

"Why, you poor fish, my uncle, of course. What do you think my uncle's going to say to all this? If I sprang it on him cold, he'd tie himself in knots on the hearthrug."

"One of these emotional Johnnies, eh?"

"Somehow or other his mind has got to be prepared to receive the news. But how?"

"Ah!"

"That's a lot of help, that 'ah'! You see, I'm pretty well dependent on the old boy. If he cut off my allowance, I should be very much in the soup. So you put the whole binge to Jeeves and see if he can't scare up a happy ending somehow. Tell him my future is in his hands, and that, if the wedding bells ring out, he can rely on me, even unto half my kingdom. Well, call it ten quid. Jeeves would exert himself with ten quid on the horizon, what?"

"Undoubtedly," I said.

I wasn't in the least surprised at Bingo wanting to lug Jeeves into his private affairs like this. It was the first thing I would have thought of doing myself if I had been in any hole of any description. As I have frequently had occasion to observe, he is a bird of the ripest intellect, full of bright ideas. If anybody could fix things for poor old Bingo, he could.

I stated the case to him that night after dinner.

"Jeeves."

"Sir?"

"Are you busy just now?"

"No, sir."

"I mean, not doing anything in particular?"

"No, sir. It is my practice at this hour to read some improving book; but, if you desire my services, this can easily be postponed, or, indeed, abandoned altogether."

"Well, I want your advice. It's about Mr. Little."

"Young Mr. Little, sir, or the elder Mr. Little, his uncle, who lives in Pounceby Gardens?"

Jeeves seemed to know everything. Most amazing thing. I'd been pally with Bingo practically all my life, and yet I didn't remember ever having heard that his uncle lived anywhere in particular.

"How did you know he lived in Pounceby Gardens?" I said.

"I am on terms of some intimacy with the elder Mr. Little's cook, sir. In fact, there is an understanding."

I'm bound to say that this gave me a bit of a start. Somehow I'd never thought of Jeeves going in for that sort of thing.

"Do you mean you're engaged?"

"It may be said to amount to that, sir."

"Well, well!"

"She is a remarkably excellent cook, sir," said Jeeves, as though he felt called on to give some explanation. "What was it you wished to ask me about Mr. Little?"

I sprang the details on him.

"And that's how the matter stands, Jeeves," I said. "I think we ought to rally round a trifle and help poor old Bingo put the thing through. Tell me about old Mr. Little. What sort of a chap is he?"

"A somewhat curious character, sir. Since retiring from business he has become a great recluse, and now devotes himself almost entirely to the pleasures of the table."

"Greedy hog, you mean?"

"I would not, perhaps, take the liberty of describing him in precisely those terms, sir. He is what is usually called a gourmet. Very particular about what he eats, and for that reason sets a high value on Miss Watson's services."

"The cook?"

"Yes, sir."

"Well, it looks to me as though our best plan would be to shoot young Bingo in on him after dinner one night. Melting mood, I mean to say, and all that."

"The difficulty is, sir, that at the moment Mr. Little is on a diet, owing to an attack of gout."

"Things begin to look wobbly."

"No, sir, I fancy that the elder Mr. Little's misfortune may be turned to the younger Mr. Little's advantage. I was speaking only the other day to Mr. Little's valet, and he was telling me that it has become his principal duty to read to Mr. Little in the evenings. If I were in your place, sir, I should send young Mr. Little to read to his uncle."

"Nephew's devotion, you mean? Old man touched by kindly action, what?"

"Partly that, sir. But I would rely more on young Mr. Little's choice of literature."

"That's no good. Jolly old Bingo has a kind face, but when it comes to literature he stops at the *Sporting Times.*"

"That difficulty may be overcome. I would be happy to select books for Mr. Little to read. Perhaps I might explain my idea further?"

"I can't say I quite grasp it yet."

"The method which I advocate is what, I believe, the advertisers call Direct Suggestion, sir, consisting as it does of driving an idea home by constant repetition. You may have had experience of the system?"

"You mean they keep on telling you that some soap or other is the best, and after a bit you come under the influence and charge round the corner and buy a cake?"

"Exactly, sir. The same method was the basis of all the most valuable propaganda during the recent war. I see no reason why it should not be adopted to bring about the desired result with regard to the subject's views on class distinctions. If young Mr. Little were to read day after day to his uncle a series of narratives in which marriage with young persons of an inferior social status was held up as both feasible and admirable, I fancy it would prepare the elder Mr. Little's mind for the reception of the information that his nephew wishes to marry a waitress in a tea-shop."

"*Are* there any books of that sort nowadays? The only ones I ever see mentioned in the papers are about married couples who find life grey, and can't stick each other at any price."

"Yes, sir, there are a great many, neglected by the reviewers but widely read. You have never encountered 'All for Love," by Rosie M. Banks?"

"No."

"Nor 'A Red, Red Summer Rose,' by the same author?"

"No."

"I have an aunt, sir, who owns an almost complete set of Rosie M. Banks'. I could easily borrow as many volumes as young Mr. Little might require. They make very light, attractive reading."

"Well, it's worth trying."

"I should certainly recommend the scheme, sir."

"All right, then. Toddle round to your aunt's to-morrow and grab a couple of the fruitiest. We can but have a dash at it."

"Precisely, sir."

Bingo reported three days later that Rosie M. Banks was the goods and beyond a question the stuff to give the troops. Old Little had jibbed somewhat at first at the proposed change of literary diet, he not being much of a lad for fiction and having stuck hitherto exclusively to the heavier monthly reviews; but Bingo had got chapter one of "All for Love" past his guard before he knew what was happening, and after that there was nothing to it. Since then they had finished "A Red, Red Summer Rose," "Madcap Myrtle" and "Only a Factory Girl," and were halfway through "The Courtship of Lord Strathmorlick."

Bingo told me all this in a husky voice over an egg beaten up in sherry. The only blot on the thing from his point of view was that it wasn't doing a bit of good to the old vocal cords, which were beginning to show signs of cracking under the strain. He had been looking his symptoms up in a medical dictionary, and he thought he had got "clergyman's throat." But against this you had to set the fact that he was making an undoubted hit in the right quarter, and also that after the evening's reading he always stayed on to dinner; and, from what he told me, the dinners turned out by old Little's cook had to be tasted to be believed. There were tears in the old blighter's eyes as he got on the subject of the clear soup. I suppose to a fellow who for weeks had been tackling macaroons and limado it must have been like Heaven.

Old Little wasn't able to give any practical assistance at these banquets, but Bingo said that he came to the table and had his whack of arrowroot, and sniffed the dishes, and told stories of *entrées* he had had in the past, and sketched out scenarios of what he was going to do to the bill of fare in the future, when the doctor put him in shape; so I suppose he enjoyed himself, too, in a way. Anyhow, things seemed to be buzzing along quite satisfactorily, and Bingo said he had got an idea which, he thought, was going to clinch the thing. He wouldn't tell me what it was, but he said it was a pippin.

"We make progress, Jeeves," I said.

"That is very satisfactory, sir."

"Mr. Little tells me that when he came to the big scene in 'Only a Factory Girl,' his uncle gulped like a stricken bull-pup."

"Indeed, sir?"

"Where Lord Claude takes the girl in his arms, you know, and says——"

"I am familiar with the passage, sir. It is distinctly moving. It was a great favourite of my aunt's."

"I think we're on the right track."

"It would seem so, sir."

"In fact, this looks like being another of your successes. I've always said, and I always shall say, that for sheer brain, Jeeves, you stand alone. All the other great thinkers of the age are simply in the crowd, watching you go by."

"Thank you very much, sir. I endeavour to give satisfaction."

About a week after this, Bingo blew in with the news that his uncle's gout had ceased to trouble him, and that on the morrow he would be back at the old stand working away with knife and fork as before.

"And, by the way," said Bingo, "he wants you to lunch with him to-morrow."

"Me? Why me? He doesn't know I exist."

"Oh, yes, he does. I've told him about you."

"What have you told him?"

"Oh, various things. Anyhow, he wants to meet you. And take my tip, laddie—you go! I should think lunch to-morrow would be something special."

I don't know why it was, but even then it struck me that there was something dashed odd—almost sinister, if you know what I mean—about young Bingo's manner. The old egg had the air of one who has something up his sleeve.

"There is more in this than meets the eye," I said. "Why should your uncle ask a fellow to lunch whom he's never seen?"

"My dear old fathead, haven't I just said that I've been telling him all about you—that you're my best pal—at school together, and all that sort of thing?"

"But even then—and another thing. Why are you so dashed keen on my going?"

Bingo hesitated for a moment.

"Well, I told you I'd got an idea. This is it. I want you to spring the news on him. I haven't the nerve myself."

"What! I'm hanged if I do!"

"And you call yourself a pal of mine!"

"Yes, I know; but there are limits."

"Bertie," said Bingo reproachfully, "I saved your life once."

"When?"

"Didn't I? It must have been some other fellow, then. Well, anyway, we were boys together and all that. You can't let me down."

"Oh, all right," I said. "But, when you say you haven't nerve enough for any dashed thing in the world, you misjudge yourself. A fellow who —— "

"Cheerio!" said young Bingo. "One-thirty to-morrow. Don't be late."

I'm bound to say that the more I contemplated the binge, the less I liked it. It was all very well for Bingo to say that I was slated for a magnificent lunch; but what good is the best possible lunch to a fellow if he is slung out into the street on his ear during the soup course? However, the word of a Wooster is his bond and all that sort of rot, so at one-thirty next day I tottered up the steps of No. 16, Pounceby Gardens, and punched the bell. And half a minute later I was up in the drawing-room, shaking hands with the fattest man I have ever seen in my life.

The motto of the Little family was evidently "variety." Young Bingo is long and thin and hasn't had a superfluous ounce on him since we first met; but the uncle restored the average and a bit over. The hand which grasped mine wrapped it round and enfolded it till I began to wonder if I'd ever get it out without excavating machinery.

"Mr. Wooster, I am gratified—I am proud—I am honoured."

It seemed to me that young Bingo must have boosted me to some purpose.

"Oh, ah!" I said.

He stepped back a bit, still hanging on to the good right hand.

"You are very young to have accomplished so much!"

I couldn't follow the train of thought. The family, especially my Aunt Agatha, who has savaged me incessantly from childhood up, have always rather made a point of the fact that mine is a wasted life, and that, since I won the prize at my first school for the best collection of wild flowers made during the summer holidays, I haven't done a dam' thing to land me on the nation's scroll of fame. I was wondering if he couldn't have got me mixed up with someone else, when the telephone-bell rang outside in the hall, and the maid came in to say that I was wanted. I buzzed down, and found it was young Bingo.

"Hallo!" said young Bingo. "So you've got there? Good man! I knew I could rely on you. I say, old crumpet, did my uncle seem pleased to see you?"

"Absolutely all over me. I can't make it out."

"Oh, that's all right. I just rang up to explain. The fact is, old man, I know you won't mind, but I told him that you were the author of those books I've been reading to him."

"What!"

"Yes, I said that 'Rosie M. Banks' was your pen-name, and you didn't want it generally known, because you were a modest, retiring sort of chap. He'll listen to you now. Absolutely hang on your words. A brightish idea, what? I doubt if Jeeves in person could have thought up a better one than that. Well, pitch it strong, old lad, and keep steadily before you the fact that I must have my allowance raised. I can't possibly marry on what I've got now. If this film is to end with the slow fade-out on the embrace, at least double is indicated. Well, that's that. Cheerio!"

And he rang off. At that moment the gong sounded, and the genial host came tumbling downstairs like the delivery of a ton of coals.

I always look back to that lunch with a sort of aching regret. It was the lunch of a lifetime, and I wasn't in a fit state to appreciate it. Subconsciously, if you know what I mean, I could see it was pretty special, but I had got the wind up to such a frightful extent over the ghastly situation in which young Bingo had landed me that its deeper meaning never really penetrated. Most of the time I might have been eating sawdust for all the good it did me.

Old Little struck the literary note right from the start.

"My nephew has probably told you that I have been making a close study of your books of late?" he began.

"Yes. He did mention it. How—er—how did you like the bally things?"

He gazed reverently at me.

"Mr. Wooster, I am not ashamed to say that the tears came into my eyes as I listened to them. It amazes me that a man as young as you can have been able to plumb human nature so surely to its depths; to play with so unerring a hand on the quivering heart-strings of your reader; to write novels so true, so human, so moving, so vital!"

"Oh, it's just a knack," I said.

The good old persp. was bedewing my forehead by this time in a pretty lavish manner. I don't know when I've been so rattled.

"Do you find the room a trifle warm?"

"Oh, no, no, rather not. Just right."

"Then it's the pepper. If my cook has a fault—which I am not prepared to admit—it is that she is inclined to stress the pepper a trifle in her made dishes. By the way, do you like her cooking?"

I was so relieved that we had got off the subject of my literary output that I shouted approval in a ringing baritone.

"I am delighted to hear it, Mr. Wooster. I may be prejudiced, but to my mind that woman is a genius."

"Absolutely!" I said.

"She has been with me seven years, and in all that time I have not known her guilty of a single lapse from the highest standard. Except once, in the winter of 1917, when a purist might have condemned a certain mayonnaise of hers as lacking in creaminess. But one must make allowances. There had been several air-raids about that time, and no doubt the poor woman was shaken. But nothing is perfect in this world, Mr. Wooster, and I have had my cross to bear. For seven years I have lived in constant apprehension lest some evilly-disposed person might lure her from my employment. To my certain knowledge she has received offers, lucrative offers, to accept service elsewhere. You may judge of my dismay, Mr. Wooster, when only this morning the bolt fell. She gave notice!"

"Good Lord!"

"Your consternation does credit, if I may say so, to the heart of the author of 'A Red, Red Summer Rose.' But I am thankful to say the worst has not happened. The matter has been adjusted. Jane is not leaving me."

"Good egg!"

"Good egg, indeed—though the expression is not familiar to me. I do not remember having come across it in your books. And, speaking of your books, may I say that what has impressed me about them even more than the moving poignancy of the actual narrative, is your philosophy of life. If there were more men like you, Mr. Wooster, London would be a better place."

This was dead opposite to my Aunt Agatha's philosophy of life, she having always rather given me to understand that it is the presence in it of chappies like me that makes London more or less of a plague spot; but I let it go.

"Let me tell you, Mr. Wooster, that I appreciate your splendid defiance of the outworn fetishes of a purblind social system. I appreciate it! *You* are big enough to see that rank is but the guinea stamp and that, in the magnificent words of Lord Bletchmore in 'Only a Factory Girl,' 'Be her origin ne'er so humble, a good woman is the equal of the finest lady on earth!' "

I sat up.

"I say! Do you think that?"

"I do, Mr. Wooster. I am ashamed to say that there was a time when I was like other men, a slave to the idiotic convention which we call Class Distinction. But, since I read your books——"

I might have known it. Jeeves had done it again.

"You think it's all right for a chappie in what you might call a certain social position to marry a girl of what you might describe as the lower classes?"

"Most assuredly I do, Mr. Wooster."

I took a deep breath, and slipped him the good news.

"Young Bingo—your nephew, you know—wants to marry a waitress," I said.

"I honour him for it," said old Little.

"You don't object?"

"On the contrary."

I took another deep breath and shifted to the sordid side of the business.

"I hope you won't think I'm butting in, don't you know," I said, "but—er—well, how about it?"

"I fear I do not quite follow you."

"Well, I mean to say, his allowance and all that. The money you're good enough to give him. He was rather hoping that you might see your way to jerking up the total a bit."

Old Little shook his head regretfully.

"I fear that can hardly be managed. You see, a man in my position is compelled to save every penny. I will gladly continue my nephew's existing allowance, but beyond that I cannot go. It would not be fair to my wife."

"What! But you're not married?"

"Not yet. But I propose to enter upon that holy state almost immediately. The lady who for years has cooked so well for me honoured me by accepting my hand this very morning." A cold gleam of triumph came into his eye. "Now let 'em try to get her away from me!" he muttered, defiantly.

"Young Mr. Little has been trying frequently during the afternoon to reach you on the telephone, sir," said Jeeves that night, when I got home.

"I'll bet he has," I said. I had sent poor old Bingo an outline of the situation by messenger-boy shortly after lunch.

"He seemed a trifle agitated."

"I don't wonder. Jeeves," I said, "so brace up and bite the bullet. I'm afraid I've bad news for you.

"That scheme of yours — reading those books to old Mr. Little and all that — has blown out a fuse."

"They did not soften him?"

"They did. That's the whole bally trouble. Jeeves, I'm sorry to say that *fiancée* of yours — Miss Watson, you know — the cook, you know — well, the long and the short of it is that she's chosen riches instead of honest worth, if you know what I mean."

"Sir?"

"She's handed you the mitten and gone and got engaged to old Mr. Little!"

"Indeed, sir?"

"You don't seem much upset."

"That fact is, sir, I had anticipated some such outcome."

I stared at him. "Then what on earth did you suggest the scheme for?"

"To tell you the truth, sir, I was not wholly averse from a severance of my relations with Miss Watson. In fact, I greatly desired it. I respect Miss Watson exceedingly, but I have seen for a long time that we were not suited. Now, the *other* young person with whom I have an understanding ——"

"Great Scott, Jeeves! There isn't another?"

"Yes, sir."

"How long has this been going on?"

"For some weeks, sir. I was greatly attracted by her when I first met her at a subscription dance at Camberwell."

"My sainted aunt! Not—"

Jeeves inclined his head gravely.

"Yes, sir. By an odd coincidence it is the same young person that young Mr. Little— I have placed the cigarettes on the small table. Good night, sir."

Absent Treatment

I WANT to tell you all about dear old Bobbie Cardew. It's a most interesting story. I can't put in any literary style and all that; but I don't have to, don't you know, because it goes on its Moral Lesson. If you're a man you mustn't miss it, because it'll be a warning to you; and if you're a woman you won't want to, because it's all about how a girl made a man feel pretty well fed up with things.

If you're a recent acquaintance of Bobbie's, you'll probably be surprised to hear that there was a time when he was more remarkable for the weakness of his memory than anything else. Dozens of fellows, who have only met Bobbie since the change took place, have been surprised when I told them that. Yet it's true. Believe *me*.

In the days when I first knew him Bobbie Cardew was about the most pronounced young rotter inside the four-mile radius. People have called me a silly ass, but I was never in the same class with Bobbie. When it came to being a silly ass, he was a plus four man, while my handicap was about six. Why, if I wanted him to dine with me, I used to post him a letter at the beginning of the week, and then the day before send him a telegram and a 'phone-call on the day itself, and—half an hour before the time we'd fixed—a messenger in a taxi, whose business it was to see that he got in and that the chauffeur had the address all correct. By doing that I generally managed to get him, unless he had left town before my messenger arrived.

The funny thing was that he wasn't altogether a fool in other ways. Deep down in him there was a kind of stratum of sense. I had known him, once or twice, show an almost human intelligence. But to reach that stratum, mind you, you needed dynamite.

At least, that's what I thought. But there was another way which hadn't occurred to me. Marriage, I mean. Marriage, the dynamite of the soul; that was what hit Bobbie. He married. Have you ever seen a bull-pup chasing a bee? The pup sees the bee. It looks good to him. But he doesn't know what's at the end of it till he gets there. It was like that with Bobbie. He fell in love, got married—with a sort of whoop, as if it were the greatest fun in the world—and then began to find out things.

She wasn't the sort of girl you would have expected Bobbie to rave about. And yet, I don't know. What I mean is, she worked for her living; and to a fellow who has never done a hand's turn in his life there's undoubtedly a sort of fascination, a kind of romance, about a girl who works for her living.

Her name was Anthony. Mary Anthony. She was about five feet six; she had a ton and a half of red-gold hair, grey eyes, and one of those determined chins. She was a hospital nurse. When Bobbie smashed himself up at polo, she was told off by the authorities to smooth his brow and rally round with cooling unguents and all that; and the old boy hadn't been up and about again for more than a week before they popped off to the registrar's and fixed it up. Quite the romance.

Bobbie broke the news to me at the club one evening, and next day he introduced me to her. I admired her. I've never worked myself—my name's Pepper, by the way. Almost forgot to mention it. Reggie Pepper. My uncle Edward was Pepper, Wells, and Co., the colliery people. He left me a sizable chunk of bullion—I say I've never worked myself, but I admire any one who earns a living under difficulties, especially a girl. And this girl had had a rather unusually tough time of it, being an orphan and all that, and having had to do everything off her own bat for years.

Mary and I got along together splendidly. We don't now, but we'll come to that later. I'm speaking of the past. She seemed to think Bobbie the greatest thing on earth, judging by the way she looked at him when she thought I wasn't noticing. And Bobbie seemed to think the same about her. So that I came to the conclusion that, if only dear old Bobbie didn't forget to go to the wedding, they had a sporting chance of being quite happy.

Well, let's brisk up a bit here, and jump a year. The story doesn't really start till then.

They took a flat and settled down. I was in and out of the place quite a good deal. I kept my eyes open, and everything seemed to me to be running along as smoothly as you could want. If this was marriage, I thought, I couldn't see why fellows were so frightened of it. There were a lot of worse things that could happen to a man.

But we now come to the incident of the Quiet Dinner, and it's just here that love's young dream hits a snag, and things begin to occur.

I happened to meet Bobbie in Piccadilly, and he asked me to come back to dinner at the flat. And, like a fool, instead of bolting and putting myself under police protection, I went.

When we got to the flat, there was Mrs. Bobbie looking—well, I tell you, it staggered me. Her gold hair was all piled up in waves and crinkles and things, with a what-d'-you-call-it of diamonds in it. And she was wearing the most perfectly ripping dress. I couldn't begin to describe it. I can only say it was the limit. It struck me that if this was how she was in the habit of looking every night when they were dining quietly at home together, it was no wonder that Bobbie liked domesticity.

"Here's old Reggie, dear," said Bobbie. "I've brought him home to have a bit of dinner. I'll 'phone down to the kitchen and ask them to send it up now—what?"

She stared at him as if she had never seen him before. Then she turned scarlet. Then she turned as white as a sheet. Then she gave a little laugh. It was most interesting to watch. Made me wish I was up a tree about eight hundred miles away. Then she recovered herself.

"I am so glad you were able to come, Mr. Pepper," she said, smiling at me.

And after that she was all right. At least, you would have said so. She talked a lot at dinner, and chaffed Bobbie, and played us ragtime on the piano afterwards, as if she hadn't a care in the world. Quite a jolly little party it was—not. I'm no lynx-eyed sleuth, and all that sort of thing, but I had seen her face at the beginning, and I knew that she was working the whole time, and working hard, to keep herself in hand, and that she would have given that diamond what's-its-name in her hair and everything else she possessed to have one good scream—just one. I've sat through some pretty thick evenings in my time, but that one had the rest beaten in a canter. At the very earliest moment I grabbed my hat and got away.

Having seen what I did, I wasn't particularly surprised to meet Bobbie at the club next day looking about as merry and bright as a lonely gum-drop at an Eskimo tea-party.

He started in straightaway. He seemed glad to have some one to talk to about it.

"Do you know how long I've been married?" he said.

I didn't exactly.

"About a year, isn't it?"

"Not *about* a year," he said, sadly. "Exactly a year—yesterday!"

Then I understood. I saw light—a regular flash of light.

"Yesterday was——?"

"The anniversary of the wedding. I'd arranged to take Mary to the Savoy, and on to Covent Garden. She particularly wanted to hear Caruso. I had the ticket for the box in my pocket. Do you know, all through dinner I had a kind of rummy idea that there was something I'd forgotten, but I couldn't think what?"

"Till your wife mentioned it?"

He nodded.

"She—mentioned it," he said, thoughtfully.

I didn't ask for details. Women with hair and chins like Mary's may be angels most of the time, but, when they take off their wings for a bit, they aren't half-hearted about it.

"To be absolutely frank, old top," said poor old Bobbie, in a broken sort of way, "my stock's pretty low at home."

There didn't seem much to be done. I just lit a cigarette and sat there. He didn't want to talk. Presently he went out. I stood at the window of our upper smoking-room, which looks out on to Piccadilly, and watched him. He walked slowly along for a few yards, stopped, then walked on again, and finally turned into a jeweller's. Which was an instance of what I meant when I said that deep down in him there was a certain stratum of sense.

It was from now on that I began to be really interested in this problem of Bobbie's married life. Of course, one's always mildly interested in one's friends' marriages, hoping they'll turn out well and all that; but this was different. The average man isn't like Bobbie, and the average girl isn't like Mary. It was that old business of the immovable mass and the irresistible force. There was Bobbie, ambling gently through life, a dear old chap in a hundred ways, but undoubtedly a chump of the first water.

And there was Mary, determined that he shouldn't be a chump. And Nature, mind you, on Bobbie's side. When Nature makes a chump like dear old Bobbie, she's proud of him, and doesn't want her handiwork disturbed. She gives him a sort of natural armour to protect him against outside interference. And that armour is shortness of memory. Shortness of memory keeps a man a chump, when, but for it, he might cease to be one. Take my case, for instance. I'm a chump. Well, if I had remembered half the things people have tried to teach me during my life, my size in hats would be about number nine. But I didn't. I forgot them. And it was just the same with Bobbie.

For about a week, perhaps a bit more, the recollection of that quiet little domestic evening bucked him up like a tonic. Elephants, I read somewhere, are champions at the memory business, but they were fools to Bobbie during that week. But, bless you, the shock wasn't nearly big enough. It had dinted the armour, but it hadn't made a hole in it. Pretty soon he was back at the old game.

It was pathetic, don't you know. The poor girl loved him, and she was frightened. It was the thin end of the wedge, you see, and she knew it. A man who forgets what day he was married when he's been married one year, will forget, at about the end of the fourth, that he's married at all. If she meant to get him in hand at all, she had got to do it now, before he began to drift away.

I saw that clearly enough, and I tried to make Bobbie see it, when he was by way of pouring out his troubles to me one afternoon. I can't remember what it was that he had forgotten the day before, but it was something she had asked him to bring home for her — it may have been a book.

"It's such a little thing to make a fuss about," said Bobbie. "And she knows that it's simply because I've got such an infernal memory about everything. I can't remember anything. Never could."

He talked on for a while, and, just as he was going, he pulled out a couple of sovereigns.

"Oh, by the way," he said.

"What's this for?" I asked, though I knew.

"I owe it you."

"How's that?" I said.

"Why, that bet on Tuesday. In the billiard-room. Murray and Brown were playing a hundred up, and I gave you two to one that Brown would win, and Murray beat him by twenty odd."

"So you do remember some things?" I said.

He got quite excited. Said that if I thought he was the sort of rotter who forgot to pay when he lost a bet, it was pretty rotten of me after knowing him all these years, and a lot more like that.

"Subside, laddie," I said.

Then I spoke to him like a father.

"What you've got to do, my old college chum," I said, "is to pull yourself together, and jolly quick, too. As things are shaping, you're due for a nasty knock before you know what's hit you. You've got to make an effort. Don't say you can't. This two quid business shows that, even if your memory is rocky, you can remember some things. What you've got to do is to see that wedding anniversaries and so on are included in the list. It may be a brain-strain, but you can't get out of it."

"I suppose you're right," said Bobbie. "But it beats me why she thinks such a lot of these rotten little dates. What's it matter if I forget what day we were married on or what day she was born on or what day the cat had the measles? She knows I love her just as much as if I were a memorizing freak at the halls."

"That's not enough for a woman," I said. "They want to be shown. Bear that in mind, and you're all right. Forget it, and there'll be trouble."

He chewed the knob of his stick.

"Women are frightfully rummy," he said, gloomily.

"You should have thought of that before you married one," I said.

I don't see that I could have done any more. I had put the whole thing in a nutshell for him. You would have thought he'd have seen the point, and that it would have made him brace up and get a hold on himself. But, no. Off he went again in the same old way. I gave up arguing with him. I had a good deal of time on my hands, but not enough to amount to anything when it was a question of reforming dear old Bobbie by argument. If you see a man asking for trouble, and insisting on getting it, the only thing to do is to stand by and wait till it comes to him. After that you may get a chance. But till then there's nothing to be done. But I thought a lot about him.

Bobbie didn't get into the soup all at once. Weeks went by, and months, and still nothing happened. Now and then he'd come into the club with a kind of cloud on his shining morning face, and I'd know that there had been doings in the home; but it wasn't till well on in the spring that he got the thunderbolt just where he had been asking for it — in the thorax.

I was smoking a quiet cigarette one morning in the window looking out over Piccadilly, and watching the buses and motors going up one way and down the other — most interesting it is; I often do it — when in rushed Bobbie, with his eyes bulging and his face the colour of an oyster, waving a piece of paper in his hand.

"Reggie," he said. "Reggie, old top, she's gone!"

"Gone!" I said. "Who?"

"Mary, of course! Gone! Left me! Gone!"

"Where?" I said.

Silly question? Perhaps you're right. Anyhow, dear old Bobbie nearly foamed at the mouth.

"Where? How should I know where? Here, read this."

He pushed the paper into my hand. It was a letter.

"Go on," said Bobbie. "Read it."

So I did. It certainly was quite a letter. There was not much of it, but it was all to the point.

This is what it said: —

"My dear Bobbie, — I am going away. When you care enough about me to remember to wish me many happy returns on my birthday, I will come back. My address will be Box 341, *London Morning News*."

I read it twice, then I said, "Well, why don't you?"

"Why don't I what?"

"Why don't you wish her many happy returns? It doesn't seem much to ask."

"But she says on her birthday."

"Well, when is her birthday?"

"Can't you understand?" said Bobbie. "I've forgotten."

"Forgotten!" I said.

"Yes," said Bobbie. "Forgotten."

"How do you mean, forgotten?" I said. "Forgotten whether it's the twentieth or the twenty-first, or what? How near do you get to it?"

"I know it came somewhere between the first of January and the thirty-first of December. That's how near I get to it."

"Think."

"Think? What's the use of saying 'Think'? Think I haven't thought? I've been knocking sparks out of my brain ever since I opened that letter."

"And you can't remember?"

"No."

I rang the bell and ordered restoratives.

"Well, Bobbie," I said, "it's a pretty hard case to spring on an untrained amateur like me. Suppose some one had come to Sherlock Holmes and said, 'Mr. Holmes, here's a case for you. When is my wife's birthday?' Wouldn't that have given Sherlock a jolt? However, I know enough about the game to understand that a fellow can't shoot off his deductive theories unless you start him with a clue, so rouse yourself out of that pop-eyed trance and come across with two or three. For instance, can't you remember the last time she had a birthday? What sort of weather was it? That might fix the month."

Bobbie shook his head.

"It was just ordinary weather, as near as I can recollect."

"Warm?"

"Warmish."

"Or cold?"

"Well, fairly cold, perhaps. I can't remember."

I ordered two more of the same. They seemed indicated in the Young Detective's Manual. "You're a great help, Bobbie," I said. "An invaluable assistant. One of those indispensable adjuncts without which no home is complete."

Bobbie seemed to be thinking.

"I've got it," he said suddenly. "Look here. I gave her a present on her last birthday. All we have to do is to go to the shop, hunt up the date when it was bought, and the thing's done."

"Absolutely. What did you give her?"

He sagged.

"I can't remember," he said.

Getting ideas is like golf. Some days you're right off it, others it's as easy as falling off a log. I don't suppose dear old Bobbie had ever had two ideas in the same morning before in his life; but now he did it without an effort. He just loosed another dry Martini into the undergrowth, and before you could turn round it had flushed quite a brain-wave.

Do you know those little books called "When were you born?" There's one for each month. They tell you your character, your talents, your strong points, and your weak points at fourpence-halfpenny a go. Bobbie's idea was to buy the whole twelve, and go through them till we found out which month hit off Mary's character. That would give us the month, and narrow it down a whole lot.

A pretty hot idea for a non-thinker like dear old Bobbie. We sallied out at once. He took half and I took half, and we settled down to work. As I say, it sounded good. But when we came to go into the thing, we saw that there was a flaw. There was plenty of information all right, but there wasn't a single month that didn't have something that exactly hit off Mary. For instance, in the December book it said, "December people are apt to keep their own secrets. They are extensive travellers." Well, Mary had certainly kept her secret, and she had travelled quite extensively enough for Bobbie's needs. Then, October people were "born with original ideas" and "loved moving." You couldn't have summed up Mary's little jaunt more neatly. February people had "wonderful memories"—Mary's speciality.

We took a bit of a rest, then had another go at the thing.

Bobbie was all for May, because the book said that women born in that month were "inclined to be capricious, which is always a barrier to a happy married life"; but I plumped for February, because February women "are unusually determined to have their own way, are very earnest, and expect a full return in their companions or mates." Which he owned was about as like Mary as anything could be.

In the end he tore the books up, stamped on them, burnt them, and went home.

It was wonderful what a change the next few days made in dear old Bobbie. Have you ever seen that picture, "The Soul's Awakening"? It represents a flapper of sorts gazing in a startled sort of way into the middle distance with a look in her eyes that seems to say, "Surely that is George's step I hear on the mat! Can this be love?" Well, Bobbie had a soul's awakening too. I don't suppose he had ever troubled to think in his life before—not really *think*. But now he was wearing his brain to the bone. It was painful in a way, of course, to see a fellow human being so thoroughly in the soup, but I felt strongly that it was all for the best. I could see as plainly as possible that all these brain-storms were improving Bobbie out of knowledge. When it was all over he might possibly become a rotter again of a sort, but it would only be a pale reflection of the rotter he had been. It bore out the idea I had always had that what he needed was a real good jolt.

I saw a great deal of him these days. I was his best friend, and he came to me for sympathy. I gave it him, too, with both hands, but I never failed to hand him the Moral Lesson when I had him weak.

One day he came to me as I was sitting in the club, and I could see that he had had an idea. He looked happier than he had done in weeks.

"Reggie," he said, "I'm on the trail. This time I'm convinced that I shall pull it off. I've remembered something of vital importance."

"Yes?" I said.

"I remember distinctly," he said, "that on Mary's last birthday we went together to the Coliseum. How does that hit you?"

"It's a fine bit of memorizing," I said; "but how does it help?"

"Why, they change the programme every week there."

"Ah!" I said. "Now you are talking."

"And the week we went one of the turns was Professor Some One's Terpsichorean Cats. I recollect them distinctly. Now, are we narrowing it down, or aren't we? Reggie, I'm going round to the Coliseum this minute, and I'm going to dig the date of those Terpsichorean Cats out of them, if I have to use a crowbar."

So that got him within six days; for the management treated us like brothers; brought out the archives, and ran agile fingers over the pages till they treed the cats in the middle of May.

"I told you it was May," said Bobbie. "Maybe you'll listen to me another time."

"If you've any sense," I said, "there won't be another time."

And Bobbie said that there wouldn't.

Once you get your memory on the run, it parts as if it enjoyed doing it. I had just got off to sleep that night when my telephone-bell rang. It was Bobbie, of course. He didn't apologize.

"Reggie," he said, "I've got it now for certain. It's just come to me. We saw those Terpsichorean Cats at a *matinée*, old man."

"Yes?" I said.

"Well, don't you see that that brings it down to two days? It must have been either Wednesday the seventh or Saturday the tenth."

"Yes," I said, "if they didn't have daily *matinées* at the Coliseum."

I heard him give a sort of howl.

"Bobbie," I said. My feet were freezing, but I was fond of him.

"Well?"

"I've remembered something too. It's this. The day you went to the Coliseum I lunched with you both at the Ritz. You had forgotten to bring any money with you, so you wrote a cheque."

"But I'm always writing cheques."

"You are. But this was for a tenner, and made out to the hotel. Hunt up your cheque-book and see how many cheques for ten pounds payable to the Ritz Hotel you wrote out between May the fifth and May the tenth."

He gave a kind of gulp.

"Reggie," he said, "you're a genius. I've always said so. I believe you've got it. Hold the line."

Presently he came back again.

"Halloa!" he said.

"I'm here," I said.

"It was the eighth. Reggie, old man, I——"

"Topping," I said. "Good night."

It was working along into the small hours now, but I thought I might as well make a night of it and finish the thing up, so I rang up an hotel near the Strand.

"Put me through to Mrs. Cardew," I said.

"It's late," said the man at the other end.

"And getting later every minute," I said. "Buck along, laddie."

I waited patiently. I had missed my beauty-sleep, and my feet had frozen hard, but I was past regrets.

"What is the matter?" said Mary's voice.

"My feet are cold," I said. "But I didn't call you up to tell you that particularly. I've just been chatting with Bobbie, Mrs. Cardew."

"Oh! is that Mr. Pepper?"

"Yes. He's remembered it, Mrs. Cardew."

She gave a sort of scream. I've often thought how interesting it must be to be one of those Exchange girls. The things they must hear, don't you know. Bobbie's howl and gulp and Mrs. Bobbie's scream and all about my feet and all that. Most interesting it must be.

"He's remembered it!" she gasped. "Did you tell him?"

"No."

Well, I hadn't.

"Mr. Pepper."

"Yes?"

"Was he—has he been—was he very worried?"

I chuckled. This was where I was billed to be the life and soul of the party.

"Worried! He was about the most worried man between here and Edinburgh. He has been worrying as if he was paid to do it by the nation. He has started out to worry after breakfast, and——"

Oh, well, you can never tell with women. My idea was that we should pass the rest of the night slapping each other on the back across the wire, and telling each other what bally brainy conspirators we were, don't you know, and all that. But I'd got just as far as this, when she bit at me. Absolutely! I heard the snap. And then she said "Oh!" in that choked kind of way. And when a woman says "Oh!" like that, it means all the bad words she'd love to say if she only knew them.

And then she began.

"What brutes men are! What horrid brutes! How you could stand by and see poor dear Bobbie worrying himself into a fever, when a word from you would have put everything right, I can't——"

"But——"

"And you call yourself his friend! His friend!" (Metallic laugh, most unpleasant.) "It shows how one can be deceived. I used to think you a kind-hearted man."

"But, I say, when I suggested the thing, you thought it perfectly——"

"I thought it hateful, abominable."

"But you said it was absolutely top——"

"I said nothing of the kind. And if I did, I didn't mean it. I don't wish to be unjust, Mr. Pepper, but I must say that to me there seems to be something positively fiendish in a man who can go out of his way to separate a husband from his wife, simply in order to amuse himself by gloating over his agony——"

"But——!"

"When one single word would have——"

"But you made me promise not to——" I bleated.

"And if I did, do you suppose I didn't expect you to have the sense to break your promise?"

I had finished. I had no further observations to make. I hung up the receiver, and crawled into bed.

I still see Bobbie when he comes to the club, but I do not visit the old homestead. He is friendly, but he stops short of issuing invitations. I ran across Mary at the Academy last week, and her eyes went through me like a couple of bullets through a pat of butter. And as they came out the other side, and I limped off to piece myself together again, there occurred to me the simple epitaph which, when I am no more, I intend to have inscribed on my tombstone. It was this: "He was a man who acted from the best motives. There is one born every minute."

Lines and Business

I DON'T want to bore you, don't you know, and all that sort of rot, but I must tell you about dear old Freddie Meadowes. I'm not a flier at literary style, and all that, but I'll get some writer chappie to give the thing a wash and brush up when I've finished, so that'll be all right.

Dear old Freddie, don't you know, has been a dear old pal of mine for years and years; so when I went into the club one morning and found him sitting alone in a dark corner, staring glassily at nothing, and generally looking like the last rose of summer, you can understand I was quite disturbed about it. As a rule, the old rotter is the life and soul of our set. Quite the little lump of fun, and all that sort of thing.

Jimmy Pinkerton was with me at the time. Jimmy's a fellow who writes plays — a deuced brainy sort of fellow — and between us we set to work to question the poor pop-eyed chappie, until finally we got at what the matter was.

As we might have guessed, it was a girl. He had had a quarrel with Angela West, the girl he was engaged to, and she had broken off the engagement. What the row had been about he didn't say, but apparently she was pretty well fed up. She wouldn't let him come near her, refused to talk on the 'phone, and sent back his letters unopened.

I was sorry for poor old Freddie. I knew what it felt like. I was once in love myself with a girl called Elizabeth Shoolbred, and the fact that she couldn't stand me at any price will be recorded in my autobiography. I knew the thing for Freddie.

"Change of scene is what you want, old scout," I said. "Come with me to Marvis Bay. I've taken a cottage there. Jimmy's coming down on the twenty-fourth. We'll be a cosy party."

"He's absolutely right," said Jimmy. "Change of scene's the thing. I knew a man. Girl refused him. Man went abroad. Two months later girl wired him, 'Come back. Muriel.' Man started to write out a reply; suddenly found that he couldn't remember girl's surname; so never answered at all."

But Freddie wouldn't be comforted. He just went on looking as if he had swallowed his last sixpence. However, I got him to promise to come to Marvis Bay with me. He said he might as well be there as anywhere.

Do you know Marvis Bay? It's in Dorsetshire. It isn't what you'd call a fiercely-exciting spot, but it has its good points. You spend the day there bathing and sitting on the sands, and in the evening you stroll out on the shore with the gnats. At nine o'clock you rub ointment on the wounds and go to bed.

It seemed to suit poor old Freddie. Once the moon was up and the breeze sighing in the trees, you couldn't drag him from that beach with a rope. He became quite a popular pet with the gnats. They'd hang round waiting for him to come out, and would give perfectly good strollers the miss-in-baulk just so as to be in good condition for him.

Yes, it was a peaceful sort of life, but by the end of the first week I began to wish that Jimmy Pinkerton had arranged to come down earlier; for as a companion Freddie, poor old chap, wasn't anything to write home to mother about. When he wasn't chewing a pipe and scowling at the carpet, he was sitting at the piano, playing "The Rosary" with one finger. He couldn't play anything except "The Rosary," and he couldn't play much of that. Somewhere round about the third bar a fuse would blow out, and he'd have to start all over again.

He was playing it as usual one morning when I came in from bathing.

"Reggie," he said, in a hollow voice, looking up, "I've seen her."

"Seen her?" I said. "What, Miss West?"

"I was down at the post-office, getting the letters, and we met in the doorway. She cut me!"

He started "The Rosary" again, and side-slipped in the second bar.

"Reggie," he said, "you ought never to have brought me here. I must go away."

"Go away?" I said. "Don't talk such rot. This is the best thing that could have happened. This is where you come out strong."

"She cut me."

"Never mind. Be a sportsman. Have another dash at her."

"She looked clean through me!"

"Of course she did. But don't mind that. Put this thing in my hands. I'll see you through. Now, what you want," I said, "is to place her under some obligation to you. What you want is to get her timidly thanking you. What you want—— "

"But what's she going to thank me timidly for?"

I thought for a moment.

"Look out for a chance and save her from drowning," I said.

"I can't swim," said Freddie.

That was Freddie all over, don't you know. A dear old chap in a thousand ways, but no help to a fellow, if you know what I mean.

He cranked up the piano once more and I sprinted for the open.

I strolled out on to the sands and began to think this thing over. There was no doubt that the brain-work had got to be done by me. Dear old Freddie had his strong qualities. He was top-hole at polo, and in happier days I've heard him give an imitation of cats fighting in a back-yard that would have surprised you. But apart from that he wasn't a man of enterprise.

Well, don't you know, I was rounding some rocks, with my brain whirring like a dynamo, when I caught sight of a blue dress, and, by Jove, it was the girl. I had never met her, but Freddie had sixteen photographs of her sprinkled round his bedroom, and I knew I couldn't be mistaken. She was sitting on the sand, helping a small, fat child build a castle. On a chair close by was an elderly lady reading a novel. I heard the girl call her "aunt." So, doing the Sherlock Holmes business, I deduced that the fat child was her cousin. It struck me that if Freddie had been there he would probably have tried to work up some sentiment about the kid on the strength of it. Personally I couldn't manage it. I don't think I ever saw a child who made me feel less sentimental. He was one of those round, bulging kids.

After he had finished the castle he seemed to get bored with life, and began to whimper. The girl took him off to where a fellow was selling sweets at a stall. And I walked on.

Now, fellows, if you ask them, will tell you that I'm a chump. Well, I don't mind. I admit it. I *am* a chump. All the Peppers have been chumps. But what I do say is that every now and then, when you'd least expect it, I get a pretty hot brain-wave: and that's what happened now. I doubt if the idea that came to me then would have occurred to a single one of any dozen of the brainiest chappies you care to name.

It came to me on my return journey. I was walking back along the shore, when I saw the fat kid meditatively smacking a jelly-fish with a spade. The girl wasn't with him. In fact, there didn't seem to be any one in sight. I was just going to pass on when I got the brain-wave. I thought the whole thing out in a flash, don't you know. From what I had seen of the two, the girl was evidently fond of this kid, and, anyhow, he was her cousin, so what I said to myself was this: If I kidnap this young heavyweight for the moment, and if, when the girl has got frightfully anxious about where he can have got to, dear old Freddie suddenly appears leading the infant by the hand and telling a story to the effect that he has found him wandering at large about the country and practically saved his life, why, the girl's gratitude is bound to make her chuck hostilities and be friends again. So I gathered in the kid and made off with him. All the way home I pictured that scene of reconciliation. I could see it so vividly, don't you know, that, by George, it gave me quite a choky feeling in my throat.

Freddie, dear old chap, was rather slow at getting on to the fine points of the idea. When I appeared, carrying the kid, and dumped him down in our sitting-room, he didn't absolutely effervesce with joy, if you know what I mean. The kid had started to bellow by this time, and poor old Freddie seemed to find it rather trying.

"Stop it!" he said. "Do you think nobody's got any troubles except you? What the deuce is all this, Reggie?"

The kid came back at him with a yell that made the window rattle. I raced to the kitchen and fetched a jar of honey. It was the right stuff. The kid stopped bellowing and began to smear his face with the stuff.

"Well?" said Freddie, when silence had set in.

I explained the idea. After a while it began to strike him.

"You're not such a fool as you look, sometimes, Reggie," he said, handsomely. "I'm bound to say this seems pretty good."

And he disentangled the kid from the honey-jar and took him out, to scour the beach for Angela.

I don't know when I've felt so happy. I was so fond of dear old Freddie that to know that he was so soon going to be his old bright self again made me feel as if somebody had left me about a million pounds. I was leaning back in a chair on the veranda, smoking peacefully, when down the road I saw the old boy returning, and, by George, the kid was still with him. And Freddie looked as if he hadn't a friend in the world.

"Hello!" I said. "Couldn't you find her?"

"Yes, I found her," he replied, with one of those bitter, hollow laughs.

"Well, then —?"

Freddie sank into a chair and groaned.

"This isn't her cousin, you idiot!" he said. "He's no relation at all. He's just a kid she happened to meet on the beach. She had never seen him before in her life."

"What! Who is he, then?"

"I don't know. Oh, Lord, I've had a time! Thank goodness you'll probably spend the next few years of your life in Dartmoor for kidnapping. That's my only consolation. I'll come and jeer at you through the bars."

"Tell me all, old boy," I said.

It took him a good long time to tell the story, for he broke off in the middle of nearly every sentence to call me names, but I gathered gradually what had happened. She had listened like an iceberg while he told the story he had prepared, and then—well, she didn't actually call him a liar, but she gave him to understand in a general sort of way that if he and Dr. Cook ever happened to meet, and started swapping stories, it would be about the biggest duel on record. And then he had crawled away with the kid, licked to a splinter.

"And mind, this is your affair," he concluded. "I'm not mixed up in it at all. If you want to escape your sentence, you'd better go and find the kid's parents and return him before the police come for you."

By Jove, you know, till I started to tramp the place with this infernal kid, I never had a notion it would have been so deuced difficult to restore a child to its anxious parents. It's a mystery to me how kidnappers ever get caught. I searched Marvis Bay like a bloodhound, but nobody came forward to claim the infant. You'd have thought, from the lack of interest in him, that he was stopping there all by himself in a cottage of his own. It wasn't till, by an inspiration, I thought to ask the sweet-stall man that I found out that his name was Medwin, and that his parents lived at a place called Ocean Rest, in Beach Road.

I shot off there like an arrow and knocked at the door. Nobody answered. I knocked again. I could hear movements inside, but nobody came. I was just going to get to work on that knocker in such a way that the idea would filter through into these people's heads that I wasn't standing there just for the fun of the thing, when a voice from somewhere above shouted, "Hi!"

I looked up and saw a round, pink face, with grey whiskers east and west of it, staring down from an upper window.

"Hi!" it shouted again.

"What the deuce do you mean by 'Hi'?" I said.

"You can't come in," said the face. "Hello, is that Tootles?"

"My name is not Tootles, and I don't want to come in," I said. "Are you Mr. Medwin? I've brought back your son."

"I see him. Peep-bo, Tootles! Dadda can see 'oo!"

The face disappeared with a jerk. I could hear voices. The face reappeared.

"Hi!"

I churned the gravel madly.

"Do you live here?" said the face.

"I'm staying here for a few weeks."

"What's your name?"

"Pepper. But——"

"Pepper? Any relation to Edward Pepper, the colliery owner?"

"My uncle. But——"

"I used to know him well. Dear old Edward Pepper! I wish I was with him now."

"I wish you were," I said.

He beamed down at me.

"This is most fortunate," he said. "We were wondering what we were to do with Tootles. You see, we have the mumps here. My daughter Bootles has just developed mumps. Tootles must not be exposed to the risk of infection. We could not think what we were to do with him. It was most fortunate your finding him. He strayed from his nurse. I would hesitate to trust him to the care of a stranger, but you are different. Any nephew of Edward Pepper's has my implicit confidence. You must take Tootles to your house. It will be an ideal arrangement. I have written to my brother in London to come and fetch him. He may be here in a few days."

"May!"

"He is a busy man, of course; but he should certainly be here within a week. Till then Tootles can stop with you. It is an excellent plan. Very much obliged to you. Your wife will like Tootles."

"I haven't got a wife," I yelled; but the window had closed with a bang, as if the man with the whiskers had found a germ trying to escape, don't you know, and had headed it off just in time.

I breathed a deep breath and wiped my forehead.

The window flew up again.

"Hi!"

A package weighing about a ton hit me on the head and burst like a bomb.

"Did you catch it?" said the face, reappearing. "Dear me, you missed it! Never mind. You can get it at the grocer's. Ask for Bailey's Granulated

Breakfast Chips. Tootles takes them for breakfast with a little milk. Be certain to get Bailey's."

My spirit was broken, if you know what I mean. I accepted the situation. Taking Tootles by the hand, I walked slowly away. Napoleon's retreat from Moscow was a picnic by the side of it.

As we turned up the road we met Freddie's Angela.

The sight of her had a marked effect on the kid Tootles. He pointed at her and said, "Wah!"

The girl stopped and smiled. I loosed the kid, and he ran to her.

"Well, baby?" she said, bending down to him. "So father found you again, did he? Your little son and I made friends on the beach this morning," she said to me.

This was the limit. Coming on top of that interview with the whiskered lunatic it so utterly unnerved me, don't you know, that she had nodded good-bye and was half-way down the road before I caught up with my breath enough to deny the charge of being the infant's father.

I hadn't expected dear old Freddie to sing with joy when he found out what had happened, but I did think he might have showed a little more manly fortitude. He leaped up, glared at the kid and clutched his head. He didn't speak for a long time, but, on the other hand, when he began he did not leave off for a long time. He was quite emotional, dear old boy. It beat me where he could have picked up such expressions.

"Well," he said, when he had finished, "say something! Heavens! man, why don't you say something?"

"You don't give me a chance, old top," I said, soothingly.

"What are you going to do about it?"

"What *can* we do about it?"

"We can't spend our time acting as nurses to this—this exhibit."

He got up.

"I'm going back to London," he said.

"Freddie!" I cried. "Freddie, old man!" My voice shook. "Would you desert a pal at a time like this?"

"I would. This is your business, and you've got to manage it."

"Freddie," I said, "you've got to stand by me. You must. Do you realize that this child has to be undressed, and bathed, and dressed again? You wouldn't leave me to do all that single-handed? Freddie, old scout, we were at school together. Your mother likes me. You owe me a tenner."

He sat down again.

"Oh, well," he said, resignedly.

"Besides, old top," I said, "I did it all for your sake, don't you know?"

He looked at me in a curious way.

"Reggie," he said, in a strained voice, "one moment. I'll stand a good deal, but I won't stand for being expected to be grateful."

Looking back at it, I see that what saved me from Colney Hatch in that crisis was my bright idea of buying up most of the contents of the local sweet-shop. By serving out sweets to the kid practically incessantly we managed to get through the rest of that day pretty satisfactorily. At eight o'clock he fell asleep in a chair, and, having undressed him by unbuttoning every button in sight and, where there were no buttons, pulling till something gave, we carried him up to bed.

Freddie stood looking at the pile of clothes on the floor, and I knew what he was thinking. To get the kid undressed had been simple—a mere matter of muscle. But how were we to get him into his clothes again? I stirred the pile with my foot. There was a long linen arrangement which might have been anything. Also a strip of pink flannel which was like nothing on earth. We looked at each other and smiled wanly.

But in the morning I remembered that there were children at the next bungalow but one. We went there before breakfast and borrowed their nurse. Women are wonderful, by George they are! She had that kid dressed and looking fit for anything in about eight minutes. I showered wealth on her, and she promised to come in morning and evening. I sat down to breakfast almost cheerful again. It was the first bit of silver lining there had been to the cloud up to date.

"And after all," I said, "there's lots to be said for having a child about the house, if you know what I mean. Kind of cosy and domestic—what?"

Just then the kid upset the milk over Freddie's trousers, and when he had come back after changing his clothes he began to talk about what a much-maligned man King Herod was. The more he saw of Tootles, he said, the less he wondered at those impulsive views of his on infanticide.

Two days later Jimmy Pinkerton came down. Jimmy took one look at the kid, who happened to be howling at the moment, and picked up his portmanteau.

"For me," he said, "the hotel. I can't write dialogue with that sort of thing going on. Whose work is this? Which of you adopted this little treasure?"

I told him about Mr. Medwin and the mumps. Jimmy seemed interested.

"I might work this up for the stage," he said "It wouldn't make a bad situation for act two of a farce."

"Farce!" snarled poor old Freddie.

"Rather. Curtain of act one on hero, a well-meaning, half-baked sort of idiot just like — that is to say, a well-meaning, half-baked sort of idiot, kidnapping the child. Second act, his adventures with it. I'll rough it out to-night. Come along and show me the hotel, Reggie."

As we went I told him the rest of the story, the Angela part. He laid down his portmanteau and looked at me like an owl through his glasses.

"What!" he said. "Why, hang it, this *is* a play, ready-made. It's the old 'Tiny Hand' business. Always safe stuff. Parted lovers. Lisping child. Reconciliation over the little cradle. It's big. Child, centre. Girl, L.C.; Freddie, up stage, by the piano. Can Freddie play the piano?"

"He can play a little of 'The Rosary' with one finger."

Jimmy shook his head.

"No; we shall have to cut out the soft music. But the rest's all right. Look here." He squatted in the sand. "This stone is the girl. This bit of seaweed's the child. This nutshell is Freddie. Dialogue leading up to child's line. Child speaks like, 'Boofer lady, does 'oo love dadda?' Business of outstretched hands. Hold picture for a moment. Freddie crosses L., takes girl's hand. Business of swallowing lump in throat. Then big speech. 'Ah, Marie,' or whatever her name is — Jane — Agnes — Angela? Very well. 'Ah, Angela, has not this gone on too long? A little child rebukes us! Angela!' And so on. Freddie must work up his own part. I'm just giving you the general outline. And we must get a good line for the child. 'Boofer lady, does 'oo love dadda?' isn't definite enough. We want something more — ah! 'Kiss Freddie,' that's it. Short, crisp, and has the punch."

"But, Jimmy, old top," I said, "the only objection is, don't you know, that there's no way of getting the girl to the cottage. She cuts Freddie. She wouldn't come within a mile of him."

Jimmy frowned.

"That's awkward," he said. "Well, we shall have to make it an exterior set instead of an interior. We can easily corner her on the beach somewhere, when we're ready. Meanwhile, we must get the kid letter-perfect. First rehearsal for lines and business eleven sharp to-morrow."

Poor old Freddie was in such a gloomy state of mind that we decided not to tell him the idea till we had finished coaching the kid. He wasn't in the mood to have a thing like that hanging over him. So we concentrated on Tootles. And pretty early in the proceedings we saw that the only way to get Tootles worked up to the spirit of the thing was to introduce sweets of some sort as a submotive, so to speak.

"The chief difficulty," said Jimmy Pinkerton, at the end of the first rehearsal, "is to establish a connexion in the kid's mind between his line and the sweets. Once he has grasped the basic fact that those two words, clearly spoken, result automatically in acid-drops, we have got a success."

I've often thought, don't you know, how interesting it must be to be one of those animal-trainer Johnnies: to stimulate the dawning intelligence, and that sort of thing. Well, this was every bit as exciting. Some days success seemed to be staring us in the eye, and the kid got the line out as if he'd been an old professional. And then he'd go all to pieces again. And time was flying.

"We must hurry up, Jimmy," I said. "The kid's uncle may arrive any day now and take him away."

"And we haven't an understudy," said Jimmy. "There's something in that. We must work! My goodness, that kid's a bad study. I've known deaf-mutes who would have learned the part quicker."

I will say this for the kid, though: he was a trier. Failure didn't discourage him. Whenever there was any kind of sweet near he had a dash at his line, and kept on saying something till he got what he was after. His only fault was his uncertainty. Personally, I would have been prepared to risk it, and start the performance at the first opportunity, but Jimmy said no.

"We're not nearly ready," said Jimmy. "To-day, for instance, he said 'Kick Freddie.' That's not going to win any girl's heart. And she might do it, too. No; we must postpone production awhile yet."

But, by George, we didn't. The curtain went up the very next afternoon.

It was nobody's fault—certainly not mine. It was just Fate. Freddie had settled down at the piano, and I was leading the kid out of the house to exercise it, when, just as we'd got out on to the veranda, along came the girl Angela on her way to the beach. The kid set up his usual yell at the sight of her, and she stopped at the foot of the steps.

"Hello, baby!" she said. "Good morning," she said to me. "May I come up?"

She didn't wait for an answer. She just came. She seemed to be that sort of girl. She came up on the veranda and started fussing over the kid. And six feet away, mind you, Freddie smiting the piano in the sitting-room. It was a dashed disturbing situation, don't you know. At any minute Freddie might take it into his head to come out on to the veranda, and we hadn't even begun to rehearse him in his part.

I tried to break up the scene.

"We were just going down to the beach," I said.

"Yes?" said the girl. She listened for a moment. "So you're having your piano tuned?" she said. "My aunt has been trying to find a tuner for ours. Do you mind if I go in and tell this man to come on to us when he's finished here?"

"Er—not yet," I said. "Not yet, if you don't mind. He can't bear to be disturbed when he's working. It's the artistic temperament. I'll tell him later."

"Very well," she said, getting up to go. "Ask him to call at Pine Bungalow. West is the name. Oh, he seems to have stopped. I suppose he will be out in a minute now. I'll wait."

"Don't you think—shouldn't we be going on to the beach?" I said.

She had started talking to the kid and didn't hear. She was feeling in her pocket for something.

"The beach," I babbled.

"See what I've brought for you, baby," she said. And, by George, don't you know, she held up in front of the kid's bulging eyes a chunk of toffee about the size of the Automobile Club.

That finished it. We had just been having a long rehearsal, and the kid was all worked up in his part. He got it right first time.

"Kiss Fweddie!" he shouted.

And the front door opened, and Freddie came out on to the veranda, for all the world as if he had been taking a cue.

He looked at the girl, and the girl looked at him. I looked at the ground, and the kid looked at the toffee.

"Kiss Fweddie!" he yelled. "Kiss Fweddie!"

The girl was still holding up the toffee, and the kid did what Jimmy Pinkerton would have called "business of outstretched hands" towards it.

"Kiss Fweddie!" he shrieked.

"What does this mean?" said the girl, turning to me.

"You'd better give it him, don't you know," I said. "He'll go on till you do."

She gave the kid his toffee, and he subsided. Poor old Freddie still stood there gaping, without a word.

"What does it mean?" said the girl again. Her face was pink, and her eyes were sparkling in the sort of way, don't you know, that makes a fellow feel as if he hadn't any bones in him, if you know what I mean. Did you ever tread on your partner's dress at a dance and tear it, and see her smile at you like an angel and say: "*Please* don't apologize. It's nothing," and then suddenly meet her clear blue eyes and feel as if you had stepped on the teeth of a rake and had the handle jump up and hit you in the face? Well, that's how Freddie's Angela looked.

"*Well?*" she said, and her teeth gave a little click.

I gulped. Then I said it was nothing. Then I said it was nothing much. Then I said, "Oh, well, it was this way." And, after a few brief remarks about Jimmy Pinkerton, I told her all about it. And all the while Idiot Freddie stood there gaping, without a word.

And the girl didn't speak, either. She just stood listening.

And then she began to laugh. I never heard a girl laugh so much. She leaned against the side of the veranda and shrieked. And all the while Freddie, the World's Champion Chump, stood there, saying nothing.

Well, I sidled towards the steps. I had said all I had to say, and it seemed to me that about here the stage-direction "exit" was written in my part. I gave poor old Freddie up in despair. If only he had said a word, it might have been all right. But there he stood, speechless. What can a fellow do with a fellow like that?

Just out of sight of the house I met Jimmy Pinkerton.

"Hello, Reggie!" he said. "I was just coming to you. Where's the kid? We must have a big rehearsal to-day."

"No good," I said, sadly. "It's all over. The thing's finished. Poor dear old Freddie has made an ass of himself and killed the whole show."

"Tell me," said Jimmy.

I told him.

"Fluffed in his lines, did he?" said Jimmy, nodding thoughtfully. "It's always the way with these amateurs. We must go back at once. Things look bad, but it may not be too late," he said, as we started. "Even now a few well-chosen words from a man of the world, and——"

"Great Scot!" I cried. "Look!"

In front of the cottage stood six children, a nurse, and the fellow from the grocer's staring. From the windows of the houses opposite projected about four hundred heads of both sexes, staring. Down the road came galloping five more children, a dog, three men, and a boy, about to stare. And on our porch, as unconscious of the spectators as if they had been alone in the Sahara, stood Freddie and Angela, clasped in each other's arms.

Dear old Freddie may have been fluffy in his lines, but, by George, his business had certainly gone with a bang!

Disentangling Old Duggie

DOESN'T some poet or philosopher fellow say that it's when our intentions are best that we always make the worst breaks? I can't put my hand on the passage, but you'll find it in Shakespeare or somewhere, I'm pretty certain.

At any rate, it's always that way with me. And the affair of Douglas Craye is a case in point.

I had dined with Duggie (a dear old pal of mine) one night at his club, and as he was seeing me out he said: "Reggie, old top"—my name's Reggie Pepper—"Reggie, old top, I'm rather worried."

"Are you, Duggie, old pal?" I said.

"Yes, Reggie, old fellow," he said, "I am. It's like this. The Booles have asked me down to their place for the week-end, and I don't know whether to go or not. You see, they have early breakfast, and besides that there's a frightful risk of music after dinner. On the other hand, young Roderick Boole thinks he can play piquet."

"I should go," I said.

"But I'm not sure Roderick's going to be there this time."

It was a problem, and I didn't wonder poor old Dug had looked pale and tired at dinner.

Then I had the idea which really started all the trouble.

"Why don't you consult a palmist?" I said.

"That sounds a good idea," said Duggie.

"Go and see Dorothea in Forty-second Street. She's a wonder. She'll settle it for you in a second. She'll see from your lines that you are thinking of making a journey, and she'll either tell you to get a move on, which will mean that Roderick will be there, or else to keep away because she sees disaster."

"You seem to be next to the game all right."

"I've been to a good many of them. You'll like Dorothea."

"What did you say her name was — Dorothea? What do I do? Do I just walk in? Shan't I feel a fearful chump? How much do I give her?"

"Five bucks. You'd better write and make a date."

"All right," said Duggie. "But I know I shall look a frightful fool."

About a week later I ran into him between the acts at the Knickerbocker. The old boy was beaming.

"Reggie," he said, "you did me the best turn anyone's ever done me, sending me to Mrs. Darrell."

"Mrs. Darrell?"

"You know. Dorothea. Her real name's Darrell. She's a widow. Her husband was in some regiment, and left her without a penny. It's a frightfully pathetic story. Haven't time to tell you now. My boy, she's a marvel. She had hardly looked at my hand, when she said: 'You will prosper in any venture you undertake.' And next day, by George, I went down to the Booles' and separated young Roderick from seventy dollars. She's a wonderful woman. Did you ever see just that shade of hair?"

"I didn't notice her hair."

He gaped at me in a sort of petrified astonishment.

"You — didn't — notice — her — hair!" he gasped.

I can't fix the dates exactly, but it must have been about three weeks after this that I got a telegram: "Call Madison Avenue immediately — Florence Craye."

She needn't have signed her name. I should have known who it was from by the wording. Ever since I was a kid, Duggie's sister Florence has oppressed me to the most fearful extent. Not that I'm the only one. Her brothers live in terror of her, I know. Especially Edwin. He's never been able to get away from her and it's absolutely broken his spirit. He's a mild, hopeless sort of chump who spends all his time at home — they live near Philadelphia — and has never been known to come to New York. He's writing a history of the family, or something, I believe.

You see, events have conspired, so to speak, to let Florence do pretty much as she likes with them. Originally there was old man Craye, Duggie's father, who made a fortune out of the Soup Trust; Duggie's elder brother Edwin; Florence; and Duggie. Mrs. Craye has been dead some years. Then came the smash. It happened through the old man.

Most people, if you ask them, will tell you that he ought to be in Bloomingdale; and I'm not sure they're not right. At any rate, one morning he came down to breakfast, lifted the first cover on the sideboard, said in a sort of despairing way, "Eggs! Eggs! Eggs! Curse all eggs!" and walked out of the room. Nobody thought much of it till about an hour afterward, when they found that he had packed a grip, left the house, and caught the train to New York. Next day they got a letter from him, saying that he was off to Europe, never to return, and that all communications were to be addressed to his lawyers. And from that day none of them had seen him. He wrote occasionally, generally from Paris; and that was all.

Well, directly news of this got about, down swooped a series of aunts to grab the helm. They didn't stay long. Florence had them out, one after the other, in no time. If any lingering doubt remained in their minds, don't you know, as to who was going to be boss at home, it wasn't her fault. Since then she has run the show.

I went to Madison Avenue. It was one of the aunts' houses. There was no sign of the aunt when I called—she had probably climbed a tree and pulled it up after her—but Florence was there.

She is a tall woman with what, I believe, is called "a presence." Her eyes are bright and black, and have a way of getting right inside you, don't you know, and running up and down your spine. She has a deep voice. She is about ten years older than Duggie's brother Edwin, who is six years older than Duggie.

"Good afternoon," she said. "Sit down."

I poured myself into a chair.

"Reginald," she said, "what is this I hear about Douglas?"

I said I didn't know.

"He says that you introduced him."

"Eh?"

"To this woman—this Mrs. Darrell."

"Mrs. Darrell?"

My memory's pretty rocky, and the name conveyed nothing to me. She pulled out a letter.

"Yes," she said, "Mrs. Dorothy Darrell."

"Great Scott! Dorothea!"

Her eyes resumed their spine drill.

"Who is she?"

"Only a palmist."

"Only a palmist!" Her voice absolutely boomed. "Well, my brother Douglas is engaged to be married to her."

"Many happy returns of the day," I said.

I don't know why I said it. It wasn't what I meant to say. I'm not sure I meant to say anything.

She glared at me. By this time I was pure jelly. I simply flowed about the chair.

"You are facetious, Reginald," she said.

"No, no, no," I shouted. "It slipped out. I wouldn't be facetious for worlds."

"I am glad. It is no laughing matter. Have you any suggestions?"

"Suggestions?"

"You don't imagine it can be allowed to go on? The engagement must be broken, of course. But how?"

"Why don't you tell him he mustn't?"

"I shall naturally express my strong disapproval, but it may not be effective. When out of the reach of my personal influence, my wretched brother is self-willed to a degree."

I saw what she meant. Good old Duggie wasn't going to have those eyes patrolling his spine if he knew it. He meant to keep away and conduct this business by letter. There was going to be no personal interview with sister, if he had to dodge about America like a snipe.

We sat for a long time without speaking. Then I became rather subtle. I had a brain-wave and saw my way to making things right for Dug and at the same time squaring myself with Florence. After all, I thought, the old boy couldn't keep away from home for the rest of his life. He would have to go there sooner or later. And my scheme made it pleasant and easy for him.

"I'll tell you what I should do if I were you," I said. "I'm not sure I didn't read some book or see some play somewhere or other where they tried it on, and it worked all right. Fellow got engaged to a girl, and the family didn't like it, but, instead of kicking, they pretended to be tickled to pieces, and had the fellow and the girl down to visit them. And then, after the fellow had seen the girl with the home circle as a background, don't you know, he came to the conclusion that it wouldn't do, and broke off the engagement."

It seemed to strike her.

"I hardly expected so sensible a suggestion from you, Reginald," she said. "It is a very good plan. It shows that you really have a definite substratum of intelligence; and it is all the more deplorable that you should idle your way through the world as you do, when you might be performing some really useful work."

That was Florence all over. Even when she patted you on the head, she had to do it with her knuckles.

"I will invite them down next week," she went on. "You had better come, too."

"It's awfully kind of you, but the fact is——"

"Next Wednesday. Take the three-forty-seven."

I met Duggie next day. He was looking happy, but puzzled, like a man who has found a dime on the street and is wondering if there's a string tied to it. I congratulated him on his engagement.

"Reggie," he said, "a queer thing has happened. I feel as if I'd trodden on the last step when it wasn't there. I've just had a letter from my sister Florence asking me to bring Dorothy home on Wednesday. Florence doesn't seem to object to the idea of the engagement at all; and I'd expected that I'd have to call out the police reserves when she heard of it. I believe there's a catch somewhere."

I tapped him on the breastbone.

"There is, Dug," I said, "and I'll tell you what it is. I saw her yesterday, and I can put you next to the game. She thinks that if you see Mrs. Darrell mingling with the home circle, you'll see flaws in her which you don't see when you don't see her mingling with the home circle, don't you see? Do you see now?"

He laughed—heroically, don't you know.

"I'm afraid she'll be disappointed. Love like mine is not dependent on environment."

Which wasn't bad, I thought, if it was his own.

I said good-by to him, and toddled along rather pleased with myself. It seemed to me that I had handled his affairs in a pretty masterly manner for a chap who's supposed to be one of the biggest chumps in New York.

Well, of course, the thing was an absolute fliver, as I ought to have guessed it would be. Whatever could have induced me to think that a fellow like poor old Dug stood a dog's chance against a determined female like his sister Florence, I can't imagine. It was like expecting a rabbit to put up a show with a python. From the very start there was only one possible end to the thing. To a woman like Florence, who had trained herself as tough as whalebone by years of scrapping with her father and occasional by-battles with aunts, it was as easy as killing rats with a stick.

I was sorry for Mrs. Darrell. She was a really good sort and, as a matter of fact, just the kind of wife who would have done old Duggie a bit of good. And on her own ground I shouldn't wonder if she might not have made a fight for it. But now she hadn't a chance. Poor old Duggie was just like so much putty in Florence's hands when he couldn't get away from her. You could see the sawdust trickling out of Love's Young Dream in a steady flow.

I took Mrs. Darrell for a walk one afternoon, to see if I couldn't cheer her up a bit, but it wasn't much good. She hardly spoke a word till we were on our way home. Then she said with a sort of jerk: "I'm going back to New York tomorrow, Mr. Pepper."

I suppose I ought to have pretended to be surprised, but I couldn't work it.

"I'm afraid you've had a bad time," I said. "I'm very sorry."

She laughed.

"Thank you," she said. "It's nice of you to be sympathetic instead of tactful. You're rather a dear, Mr. Pepper."

I hadn't any remarks to make. I whacked at a nettle with my stick.

"I shall break off my engagement after dinner, so that Douglas can have a good night's rest. I'm afraid he has been brooding on the future a good deal. It will be a great relief to him."

"Oh, no," I said.

"Oh, yes. I know exactly how he feels. He thought he could carry me off, but he finds he overestimated his powers. He has remembered that he is a Craye. I imagine that the fact has been pointed out to him."

"If you ask my opinion," I said—I was feeling pretty sore about it—"that woman Florence is an absolute cat."

"My dear Mr. Pepper, I wouldn't have dreamed of asking your opinion on such a delicate subject. But I'm glad to have it. Thank you very much. Do I strike you as a vindictive woman, Mr. Pepper?"

"I don't think you do," I said.

"By nature I don't think I am. But I'm feeling a little vindictive just at present."

She stopped suddenly.

"I don't know why I'm boring you like this, Mr. Pepper," she said. "For goodness' sake let's be cheerful. Say something bright."

I was going to take a whirl at it, but she started in to talk, and talked all the rest of the way. She seemed to have cheered up a whole lot.

She left next day. I gather she fired Duggie as per schedule, for the old boy looked distinctly brighter, and Florence wore an off-duty expression and was quite decently civil. Mrs. Darrell bore up all right. She avoided Duggie, of course, and put in most of the time talking to Edwin. He evidently appreciated it, for I had never seen him look so nearly happy before.

I went back to New York directly afterward, and I hadn't been there much more than a week when a most remarkably queer thing happened. Turning in at Hammerstein's for half an hour one evening, whom should I meet but brother Edwin, quite fairly festive, with a fat cigar in his mouth. "Hello, Reggie," he said.

"What are you doing here?" I said.

"I had to come up to New York to look up a life of Hilary de Craye at the library. I believe Mister Man was a sort of ancestor."

"This isn't the library."

"I was beginning to guess as much. The difference is subtle but well marked."

It struck me that there was another difference that was subtle but well marked, and that was the difference between the Edwin I'd left messing about over his family history a week before and the jovial rounder who was blowing smoke in my face now.

"As a matter of fact," he said, "the library would be all the better for a little of this sort of thing. It's too conservative. That's what's the trouble with the library. What's the matter with having a cross-talk team and a few performing dogs there? It would brighten the place up and attract custom. Reggie, you're looking fatigued. I've heard there's a place somewhere in this city, if you can only find it, expressly designed for supplying first-aid to the fatigued. Let's go and look for it."

I'm not given to thinking much as a rule, but I couldn't help pondering over this meeting with Edwin. It's hard to make you see the remarkableness of the whole thing, for, of course, if you look at it, in one way, there's nothing so record-breaking in smoking a cigar and drinking a highball. But then you have never seen Edwin. There are degrees in everything, don't you know. For Edwin to behave as he did with me that night was simply nothing more nor less than a frightful outburst, and it disturbed me. Not that I cared what Edwin did, as a rule, but I couldn't help feeling a sort of what-d'you-call-it — a presentiment, that somehow, in some way I didn't understand, I was mixed up in it, or was soon going to be. I think the whole fearful family had got on my nerves to such an extent that the mere sight of any of them made me jumpy.

And, by George, I was perfectly right, don't you know. In a day or two along came the usual telegram from Florence, telling me to come to Madison Avenue.

The mere idea of Madison Avenue was beginning to give me that tired feeling, and I made up my mind I wouldn't go near the place. But of course I did. When it came to the point, I simply hadn't the common manly courage to keep away.

Florence was there as before.

"Reginald," she said, "I think I shall go raving mad."

This struck me as a mighty happy solution of everybody's troubles, but I felt it was too good to be true.

"Over a week ago," she went on, "my brother Edwin came up to New York to consult a book at the library. I anticipated that this would occupy perhaps an afternoon, and was expecting him back by an early train next day. He did not arrive. He sent an incoherent telegram. But even then I suspected nothing." She paused. "Yesterday morning," she said, "I had a letter from my aunt Augusta."

She paused again. She seemed to think I ought to be impressed.

Her eyes tied a bowknot in my spine.

"Let me read you her letter. No, I will tell you its contents. Aunt Augusta had seen Edwin lunching at the Waldorf with a creature."

"A what?"

"My aunt described her. Her hair was of a curious dull bronze tint."

"Your aunt's?"

"The woman's. It was then that I began to suspect. How many women with dull bronze hair does Edwin know?"

"Great Scott! Why ask me?"

I had got used to being treated as a sort of "Hey, Bill!" by Florence, but I was darned if I was going to be expected to be an encyclopedia as well.

"One," she said. "That appalling Darrell woman."

She drew a deep breath.

"Yesterday evening," she said, "I saw them together in a taximeter cab. They were obviously on their way to some theatre."

She fixed me with her eye.

"Reginald," she said, "you must go and see her the first thing to-morrow."

"What!" I cried. "Me? Why? Why me?"

"Because you are responsible for the whole affair. You introduced Douglas to her. You suggested that he should bring her home. Go to her to-morrow and ascertain her intentions."

"But——"

"The very first thing."

"But wouldn't it be better to have a talk with Edwin?"

"I have made every endeavour to see Edwin, but he deliberately avoids me. His answers to my telegrams are willfully evasive."

There was no doubt that Edwin had effected a thorough bolt. He was having quite a pleasant little vacation: Two Weeks in Sunny New York. And from what I'd seen of him, he seemed to be thriving on it. I didn't wonder Florence had got rather anxious. She'd have been more anxious if she had seen him when I did. He'd got a sort of "New-York-is-so-bracing" look about him, which meant a whole heap of trouble before he trotted back to the fold.

Well, I started off to interview Mrs. Darrell, and, believe me, I didn't like the prospect. I think they ought to train A. D. T. messengers to do this sort of thing. I found her alone. The rush hour of clients hadn't begun.

"How do you do, Mr. Pepper?" she said. "How nice of you to call."

Very friendly, and all that. It made the situation darned difficult for a fellow, if you see what I mean.

"Say," I said. "What about it, don't you know?"

"I certainly don't," she said. "What ought I to know about what?"

"Well, about Edwin—Edwin Craye," I said.

She smiled.

"Oh! So you're an ambassador, Mr. Pepper?"

"Well, as a matter of fact, I did come to see if I could find out how things were running. What's going to happen?"

"Are you consulting me professionally? If so, you must show me your hand. Or perhaps you would rather I showed you mine?"

It was subtle, but I got on to it after a bit.

"Yes," I said, "I wish you would."

"Very well. Do you remember a conversation we had, Mr. Pepper, my last afternoon at the Crayes'? We came to the conclusion that I was rather a vindictive woman."

"By George! You're stringing old Edwin so as to put one over on Florence?"

She flushed a little.

"How very direct you are, Mr. Pepper! How do you know I'm not very fond of Mr. Craye? At any rate, I'm very sorry for him."

"He's such a chump."

"But he's improving every day. Have you seen him? You must notice the difference?"

"There is a difference."

"He only wanted taking out of himself. I think he found his sister Florence's influence a little oppressive sometimes."

"No, but see here," I said, "are you going to marry him?"

"I'm only a palmist. I don't pretend to be a clairvoyant. A marriage may be indicated in Mr. Craye's hand, but I couldn't say without looking at it."

"But I shall have to tell her something definite, or she won't give me a moment's peace."

"Tell her her brother is of age. Surely that's definite enough?"

And I couldn't get any more out of her. I went back to Florence and reported. She got pretty excited about it.

"Oh, if I were a man!" she said.

I didn't see how that would have helped. I said so.

"I'd go straight to Edwin and *drag* him away. He is staying at his club. If I were a man I could go in and find him——"

"Not if you weren't a member," I said.

"—And tell him what I thought of his conduct. As I'm only a woman, I have to wait in the hall while a deceitful small boy pretends to go and look for him."

It had never struck me before what a spendid institution a club was. Only a few days back I'd been thinking that the subscription to mine was a bit steep. But now I saw that the place earned every cent of the money.

"Have you no influence with him, Reginald?"

I said I didn't think I had. She called me something. Invertebrate, or something. I didn't catch it.

"Then there's only one thing to do. You must find my father and tell him all. Perhaps you may rouse him to a sense of what is right. You may make him remember that he has duties as a parent."

I thought it far more likely that I should make him remember that he had a foot. I hadn't a very vivid recollection of old man Craye. I was quite a kid when he made his great speech on the Egg Question and beat it for Europe—but what I did recollect didn't encourage me to go and chat with him about the duties of a parent.

As I remember him, he was a rather large man with elephantiasis of the temper. I distinctly recalled one occasion when I was spending a school vacation at his home, and he found me trying to shave old Duggie, then a kid of fourteen, with his razor.

"I shouldn't be able to find him," I said.

"You can get his address from his lawyers."

"He may be at the North Pole."

"Then you must go to the North Pole."

"But say—!"

"Reginald!"

"Oh, all right."

I knew just what would happen. Parbury and Stevens, the lawyers, simply looked at me as if I had been caught snatching bags. At least, Stevens did. And Parbury would have done it, too, only he had been dead a good time. Finally, after drinking me in for about a quarter of an hour, Stevens said that if I desired to address a communication to his client, care of this office, it would be duly forwarded. Good morning. Good morning. Anything further? No, thanks. Good morning, *Good* morning.

I handed the glad news on to Florence and left her to do what she liked about it. She went down and interviewed Stevens. I suppose he'd had experience of her. At any rate, he didn't argue. He yielded up the address in level time. Old man Craye was living in Paris, but was to arrive in New York that night, and would doubtless be at his club.

It was the same club where Edwin was hiding from Florence. I pointed this out to her.

"There's no need for me to butt in after all," I said. "He'll meet Edwin there, and they can fight it out in the smoking room. You've only to drop him a line explaining the facts."

"I shall certainly communicate with him in writing, but, nevertheless, you must see him. I cannot explain everything in a letter."

"But doesn't it strike you that he may think it pretty bad gall-impertinence, don't you know, for a comparative stranger like me to be tackling a delicate family affair like this?"

"You will explain that you are acting for me."

"It wouldn't be better if old Duggie went along instead?"

"I *wish* you to go, Reginald."

Well, of course, it was all right, don't you know, but I was losing several pounds a day over the business. I was getting so light that I felt that, when the old man kicked me, I should just soar up to the ceiling like an air balloon.

The club was one of those large clubs that look like prisons. I used to go there to lunch with my uncle, the one who left me his money, and I always hated the place. It was one of those clubs that are all red leather and hushed whispers.

I'm bound to say, though, there wasn't much hushed whispering when I started my interview with old man Craye. His voice was one of my childhood's recollections.

He was most extraordinarily like Florence. He had just the same eyes. I felt boneless from the start.

"Good morning," I said.

"What?" he said. "Speak up. Don't mumble."

I hadn't known he was deaf. The last time we'd had any conversation—on the subject of razors—he had done all the talking. This seemed to me to put the lid on it.

"I only said 'Good morning,' " I shouted.

"Good what? Speak up. I believe you're sucking candy. Oh, good morning? I remember you now. You're the boy who spoiled my razor."

I didn't half like this reopening of old wounds. I hurried on.

"I came about Edwin," I said.

"Who?"

"Edwin. Your son."

"What about him?"

"Florence told me to see you."

"Who?"

"Florence. Your daughter."

"What about her?"

All this vaudeville team business, mind you, as if we were bellowing at each other across the street. All round the room you could see old gentlemen shooting out of their chairs like rockets and dashing off at a gallop to write to the governing board about it. Thousands of waiters had appeared from nowhere, and were hanging about, dusting table legs. If ever a business wanted to be discussed privately, this seemed to me to be it. And it was just about as private as a conversation through megaphones in Longacre Square.

"Didn't she write to you?"

"I got a letter from her. I tore it up. I didn't read it."

Pleasant, was it not? It was not. I began to understand what a shipwrecked sailor must feel when he finds there's something gone wrong with the life belt.

I thought I might as well get to the point and get it over.

"Edwin's going to marry a palmist," I said.

"Who the devil's Harry?"

"Not Harry. Marry. He's going to marry a palmist."

About four hundred waiters noticed a speck of dust on an ash tray at the table next to ours, and swooped down on it.

"Edwin is going to marry a palmist?"

"Yes."

"She must be mad. Hasn't she seen Edwin?"

And just then who should stroll in but Edwin himself. I sighted him and gave him a hail.

He curveted up to us. It was amazing the way the fellow had altered. He looked like a two-year-old. Flower in his button-hole and a six-inch grin, and all that. The old man seemed surprised, too. I didn't wonder. The Edwin he remembered was a pretty different kind of a fellow.

"Hullo, dad," he said. "Fancy meeting you here. Have a cigarette?"

He shoved out his case. Old man Craye helped himself in a sort of dazed way.

"You *are* Edwin?" he said slowly.

I began to sidle out. They didn't notice me. They had moved to a settee, and Edwin seemed to be telling his father a funny story.

At least, he was talking and grinning, and the old man was making a noise like distant thunder, which I supposed was his way of chuckling. I slid out and left them.

Some days later Duggie called on me. The old boy was looking scared.

"Reggie," he said, "what do doctors call it when you think you see things when you don't? Hal-something. I've got it, whatever it is. It's sometimes caused by overwork. But it can't be that with me, because I've not been doing any work. You don't think my brain's going or anything like that, do you?"

"What do you mean? What's been happening?"

"It's like being haunted. I read a story somewhere of a fellow who kept thinking he saw a battleship bearing down on him. I've got it, too. Four times in the last three days I could have sworn I saw my father and Edwin. I saw them as plainly as I see you. And, of course, Edwin's at home and father's in Europe somewhere. Do you think it's some sort of a warning? Do you think I'm going to die?"

"It's all right, old top," I said. "As a matter of fact, they are both in New York just now."

"You don't mean that? Great Scot, what a relief! But, Reggie, old fox, it couldn't have been them really. The last time was at Louis Martin's, and the fellow I mistook for Edwin was dancing all by himself in the middle of the floor."

I admitted it was pretty queer.

I was away for a few days after that in the country. When I got back I found a pile of telegrams waiting for me. They were all from Florence, and they all wanted me to go to Madison Avenue. The last of the batch, which had arrived that morning, was so peremptory that I felt as if something had bitten me when I read it.

For a moment I admit I hung back. Then I rallied. There are times in a man's life when he has got to show a flash of the old bulldog pluck, don't you know, if he wants to preserve his self-respect. I did then. My grip was still unpacked. I told my man to put it on a cab. And in about two ticks I was bowling off to the club. I left for England next day by the *Lusitania*.

About three weeks later I fetched up at Nice. You can't walk far at Nice without bumping into a casino. The one I hit my first evening was the Casino Municipale in the Place Masséna. It looked more or less of a Home From Home, so I strolled in.

There was quite a crowd round the boule tables, and I squashed in. And when I'd worked through into the front rank I happened to look down the table, and there was Edwin, with a green Tyrolese hat hanging over one ear, clutching out for a lot of five-franc pieces which the croupier was steering toward him at the end of a rake.

I was feeling lonesome, for I knew no one in the place, so I edged round in his direction.

Halfway there I heard my name called, and there was Mrs. Darrell.

I saw the whole thing in a flash. Old man Craye hadn't done a thing to prevent it—apart from being eccentric, he was probably glad that Edwin had had the sense to pick out anybody half as good a sort—and the marriage had taken place. And here they were on their honeymoon.

I wondered what Florence was thinking of it.

"Well, well, well, here we all are," I said. "I've just seen Edwin. He seems to be winning."

"Dear boy!" she said. "He does enjoy it so. I think he gets so much more out of life than he used to, don't you?"

"Sure thing. May I wish you happiness? Why didn't you let me know and collect the silver fish-slice?"

"Thank you so much, Mr. Pepper. I did write to you, but I suppose you never got the letter."

"Mr. Craye didn't make any objections, then?"

"On the contrary. He was more in favor of the marriage than anyone."

"And I'll tell you why," I said. "I'm rather a chump, you know, but I observe things. I bet he was most frightfully grateful to you for taking Edwin in hand and making him human."

"Why, you're wonderful, Mr. Pepper. That is exactly what he said himself. It was that that first made us friends."

"And—er—Florence?"

She sighed.

"I'm afraid Florence has taken the thing a little badly. But I hope to win her over in time. I want all my children to love me."

"All your what?"

"I think of them as my children, you see, Mr. Pepper. I adopted them as my own when I married their father. Did you think I had married Edwin? What a funny mistake. I am very fond of Edwin, but not in that way. No, I married Mr. Craye. We left him at our villa tonight, as he had some letters to get off. You must come and see us, Mr. Pepper. I always feel that it was you who brought us together, you know. I wonder if you will be seeing Florence when you get back? Will you give her my very best love?"

Brother Alfred

I THINK one of the rummiest affairs I was ever mixed up with in the course of a lifetime devoted to butting into other people's business was that affair of George Lattaker at Monte Carlo. I wouldn't bore you, don't you know, for the world, but I think you ought to hear about it.

We had come to Monte Carlo on the yacht *Circe*, belonging to an old sportsman of the name of Marshall. Among those present were myself, my man Voules, a Mrs. Vanderley, her daughter Stella, Mrs. Vanderley's maid Pilbeam, and George.

George was a dear old pal of mine. In fact, it was I who had worked him into the party. You see, George was due to meet his Uncle Augustus, who was scheduled, George having just reached his twenty-fifth birthday, to hand over to him a legacy left by one of George's aunts, for which he had been trustee. The aunt had died when George was quite a kid. It was a date that George had been looking forward to; for, though he had a sort of income, an income, after all, is only an income, whereas a chunk of o'goblins is a pile. George's uncle was in Monte Carlo, and had written George that he would come to London and unbelt; but it struck me that a far better plan was for George to go to his uncle at Monte Carlo instead. Kill two birds with one stone, don't you know. Fix up his affairs and have a pleasant holiday simultaneously. So George had tagged along, and at the time when the trouble started we were anchored in Monaco Harbour, and Uncle Augustus was due next day.

Looking back, I may say that, so far as I was mixed up in it, the thing began at seven o'clock in the morning, when I was aroused from a dreamless sleep by the dickens of a scrap in progress outside my stateroom door. The chief ingredients were a female voice that sobbed and said, "Oh, Harold!" and a male voice "raised in anger," as they say, which, after considerable difficulty, I identified as Voules's. I hardly recognized it. In his official capacity Voules talks exactly like you'd expect a statue to talk, if it could. In private, however, he evidently relaxed to some extent, and to have that sort of thing going on in my midst at that hour was too much for me.

"Voules!" I yelled.

Spion Kop ceased with a jerk. There was silence, then sobs diminishing in the distance, and finally a tap at the door. Voules entered with that impassive, my-lord-the-carriage-waits look which is what I pay him for. You wouldn't have believed he had a drop of any sort of emotion in him.

"Voules," I said, "are you under the delusion that I'm going to be Queen of the May? You've called me early all right. It's only just seven."

"I understood you to summon me, sir."

"I summoned you to find out why you were making that infernal noise outside."

"I owe you an apology, sir. I am afraid that in the 'eat of the moment I raised my voice."

"It's a wonder you didn't raise the roof. Who was that with you?"

"Miss Pilbeam, sir; Mrs. Vanderley's maid."

"What was all the trouble about?"

"I was breaking our engagement, sir."

I couldn't help gaping. Somehow one didn't associate Voules with engagements. Then it struck me that I'd no right to butt in on his secret sorrows, so I switched the conversation.

"I think I'll get up," I said.

"Yes, sir."

"I can't wait to breakfast with the rest. Can you get me some right away?"

"Yes, sir."

So I had a solitary breakfast and went up on deck to smoke. It was a lovely morning. Blue sea, gleaming Casino, cloudless sky, and all the rest of the hippodrome. Presently the others began to trickle up. Stella Vanderley was one of the first. I thought she looked a bit pale and tired. She said she hadn't slept well. That accounted for it. Unless you get your eight hours, where are you?

"Seen George?" I asked.

I couldn't help thinking the name seemed to freeze her a bit. Which was queer, because all the voyage she and George had been particularly close pals. In fact, at any moment I expected George to come to me and slip his little hand in mine and whisper, "I've done it, old scout; she loves muh!"

"I have not seen Mr. Lattaker," she said.

I didn't pursue the subject. George's stock was apparently low that a.m.

The next item in the day's programme occurred a few minutes later, when the morning papers arrived.

Mrs. Vanderley opened hers and gave a scream.

"The poor, dear Prince!" she said.

"What a shocking thing!" said old Marshall.

"I knew him in Vienna," said Mrs. Vanderley. "He waltzed divinely."

Then I got at mine and saw what they were talking about. The paper was full of it. It seemed that late the night before His Serene Highness the Prince of Saxburg-Liegnitz (I always wonder why they call these chaps "Serene") had been murderously assaulted in a dark street on his way back from the Casino to his yacht. Apparently he had developed the habit of going about without an escort, and some rough-neck, taking advantage of this, had laid for him and slugged him with considerable vim. The Prince had been found lying pretty well beaten up and insensible in the street by a passing pedestrian, and had been taken back to his yacht, where he still lay unconscious.

"This is going to do somebody no good," I said. "What do you get for slugging a Serene Highness? I wonder if they'll catch the fellow?"

" 'Later,' " read old Marshal. " 'The pedestrian who discovered His Serene Highness proves to have been Mr. Denman Sturgis, the eminent private investigator. Mr. Sturgis has offered his services to the police, and is understood to be in possession of a most important clue.' That's the fellow who had charge of that kidnapping case in Chicago. If any one can catch the man, he can."

About five minutes later, just as the rest of them were going to move off to breakfast, a boat hailed us and came alongside. A tall, thin man came up the gangway. He looked round the group, and fixed on old Marshall as the probable owner of the yacht.

"Good morning," he said. "I believe you have a Mr. Lattaker on board—Mr. George Lattaker?"

"Yes," said Marshall. "He's down below. Want to see him? Whom shall I say?"

"He would not know my name. I should like to see him for a moment on somewhat urgent business."

"Take a seat. He'll be up in a moment. Reggie, my boy, go and hurry him up."

I went down to George's state-room.

"George, old man!" I shouted.

No answer. I opened the door and went in. The room was empty. What's more, the bunk hadn't been slept in. I don't know when I've been more surprised. I went on deck.

"He isn't there," I said.

"Not there!" said old Marshall. "Where is he, then? Perhaps he's gone for a stroll ashore. But he'll be back soon for breakfast. You'd better wait for him. Have you breakfasted? No? Then will you join us?"

The man said he would, and just then the gong went and they trooped down, leaving me alone on deck.

I sat smoking and thinking, and then smoking a bit more, when I thought I heard somebody call my name in a sort of hoarse whisper. I looked over my shoulder, and, by Jove, there at the top of the gangway, in evening dress, dusty to the eyebrows and without a hat, was dear old George.

"Great Scot!" I cried.

" 'Sh!" he whispered. "Any one about?"

"They're all down at breakfast."

He gave a sigh of relief, sank into my chair, and closed his eyes. I regarded him with pity. The poor old boy looked a wreck.

"I say!" I said, touching him on the shoulder.

He leaped out of the chair with a smothered yell.

"Did you do that? What did you do it for? What's the sense of it? How do you suppose you can ever make yourself popular if you go about touching people on the shoulder? My nerves are sticking a yard out of my body this morning. Reggie!"

"Yes, old boy?"

"I did a murder last night."

"What?"

"It's the sort of thing that might happen to anybody. Directly Stella Vanderley broke off our engagement I——"

"Broke off your engagement? How long were you engaged?"

"About two minutes. It may have been less. I hadn't a stop-watch. I proposed to her at ten last night in the saloon. She accepted me. I was just going to kiss her when we heard some one coming. I went out. Coming along the corridor was that infernal what's-her-name—Mrs. Vanderley's maid—Pilbeam. Have you ever been accepted by the girl you love, Reggie?"

"Never. I've been refused dozens——"

"Then you won't understand how I felt. I was off my head with joy. I hardly knew what I was doing. I just felt I had to kiss the nearest thing handy. I couldn't wait. It might have been the ship's cat. It wasn't. It was Pilbeam."

"You kissed her?"

"I kissed her. And just at that moment the door of the saloon opened and out came Stella."

"Great Scot!"

"Exactly what I said. It flashed across me that to Stella, dear girl, not knowing the circumstances, the thing might seem a little odd. It did. She broke off the engagement, and I got out the dinghy and rowed off. I was mad. I didn't care what became of me. I simply wanted to forget. I went ashore. I—— It's just on the cards that I may have drowned my sorrows a bit. Anyhow, I don't remember a thing, except that I can recollect having the deuce of a scrap with somebody in a dark street and somebody falling, and myself legging it for all I was worth. I woke up this morning in the Casino gardens. I've lost my hat."

I dived for the paper.

"Read," I said. "It's all there."

He read.

"Good heavens!" he said.

"You didn't do a thing to His Serene Nibs, did you?"

"Reggie, this is awful."

"Cheer up. They say he'll recover."

"That doesn't matter."

"It does to him."

He read the paper again.

"It says they've a clue."

"They always say that."

"But— My hat!"

"Eh?"

"My hat. I must have dropped it during the scrap. This man, Denman Sturgis, must have found it. It had my name in it!"

"George," I said, "you mustn't waste time. Oh!"

He jumped a foot in the air.

"Don't do it!" he said, irritably. "Don't bark like that. What's the matter?"

"The man!"

"What man?"

"A tall, thin man with an eye like a gimlet. He arrived just before you did. He's down in the saloon now, having breakfast. He said he wanted to see you on business, and wouldn't give his name. I didn't like the look of him from the first. It's this fellow Sturgis. It must be."

"No!"

"I feel it. I'm sure of it."

"Had he a hat?"

"Of course he had a hat."

"Fool! I mean mine. Was he carrying a hat?"

"By Jove, he *was* carrying a parcel. George, old scout, you must get a move on. You must light out if you want to spend the rest of your life out of prison. Slugging a Serene Highness is *lèse-majesté*. It's worse than hitting a policeman. You haven't got a moment to waste."

"But I haven't any money. Reggie, old man, lend me a tenner or something. I must get over the frontier into Italy at once. I'll wire my uncle to meet me in—"

"Look out," I cried; "there's some one coming!"

He dived out of sight just as Voules came up the companion-way, carrying a letter on a tray.

"What's the matter?" I said. "What do you want?"

"I beg your pardon, sir. I thought I heard Mr. Lattaker's voice. A letter has arrived for him."

"He isn't here."

"No, sir. Shall I remove the letter?"

"No; give it to me. I'll give it to him when he comes."

"Very good, sir."

"Oh, Voules! Are they all still at breakfast? The gentleman who came to see Mr. Lattaker? Still hard at it?"

"He is at present occupied with a kippered herring, sir."

"Ah! That's all, Voules."

"Thank you, sir."

He retired. I called to George, and he came out.

"Who was it?"

"Only Voules. He brought a letter for you. They're all at breakfast still. The sleuth's eating kippers."

"That'll hold him for a bit. Full of bones."

He began to read his letter. He gave a kind of grunt of surprise at the first paragraph.

"Well, I'm hanged!" he said, as he finished. "Reggie, this is a queer thing."

"What's that?"

He handed me the letter, and directly I started in on it I saw why he had grunted. This is how it ran: —

MY DEAR GEORGE, —

I shall be seeing you to-morrow, I hope; but I think it is better, before we meet, to prepare you for a curious situation that has arisen in connexion with the legacy which your father inherited from your Aunt Emily, and which you are expecting me, as trustee, to hand over to you, now that you have reached your twenty-fifth birthday. You have doubtless heard your father speak of your twin-brother Alfred, who was lost or kidnapped — which, was never ascertained — when you were both babies. When no news was received of him for so many years, it was supposed that he was dead. Yesterday, however, I received a letter purporting to come from him, in which it was stated that he had been living all this time in Buenos Ayres as the adopted son of a wealthy South American, and has only recently discovered his identity. He states that he is on his way to meet me, and will arrive any day now. Of course, like other claimants, he may prove to be an impostor, but meanwhile his intervention will, I fear, cause a certain delay before I can hand over your money to you. It will be necessary to go into a thorough examination of credentials, etc., and this will take some time. But I will go fully into the matter with you when we meet.

Your affectionate uncle,
AUGUSTUS ARBUTT.

I read it through twice, and the second time I had one of those ideas I do sometimes get, though admittedly a chump of the premier class. I have seldom had such a thoroughly corking brain-wave.

"Why, old top," I said, "this lets you out."

"Lets me out of half the darned money, if that's what you mean. If this chap's not an impostor—and there's no earthly reason to suppose he is, though I've never heard my father say a word about him—we shall have to split the money. Aunt Emily's will left the money to my father, or, failing him, his 'offspring.' I thought that meant me, but apparently there are a crowd of us. I call it rotten work, springing unexpected offspring on a fellow at the eleventh hour like this."

"Why, you chump," I said, "it's going to save you. This lets you out of your spectacular dash across the frontier. All you've got to do is to stay here and be your brother Alfred. It came to me in a flash."

He looked at me in a kind of dazed way.

"You ought to be in some sort of a home, Reggie."

"Ass!" I cried. "Don't you understand? Have you ever heard of twin-brothers who weren't exactly alike? Who's to say you aren't Alfred if you swear you are? Your uncle will be there to back you up that you have a brother Alfred."

"And Alfred will be there to call me a liar."

"He won't. It's not as if you had to keep it up for the rest of your life. It's only for an hour or two, till we can get this detective off the yacht. We sail for England to-morrow morning."

At last the thing seemed to sink into him. His face brightened.

"Why, I really do believe it would work," he said.

"Of course it would work. If they want proof, show them your mole. I'll swear George hadn't one."

"And as Alfred I should get a chance of talking to Stella and making things all right for George. Reggie, old top, you're a genius."

"No, no."

"You *are*."

"Well, it's only sometimes. I can't keep it up."

And just then there was a gentle cough behind us. We spun round.

"What the devil are you doing here, Voules?" I said.

"I beg your pardon, sir. I have heard all."

I looked at George. George looked at me.

"Voules is all right," I said. "Decent Voules! Voules wouldn't give us away, would you, Voules?"

"Yes, sir."

"You would?"

"Yes, sir."

"But, Voules, old man," I said, "be sensible. What would you gain by it?"

"Financially, sir, nothing."

"Whereas, by keeping quiet"—I tapped him on the chest—"by holding your tongue, Voules, by saying nothing about it to anybody, Voules, old fellow, you might gain a considerable sum."

"Am I to understand, sir, that, because you are rich and I am poor, you think that you can buy my self-respect?"

"Oh, come!" I said.

"How much?" said Voules.

So we switched to terms. You wouldn't believe the way the man haggled. You'd have thought a decent, faithful servant would have been delighted to oblige one in a little matter like that for a fiver. But not Voules. By no means. It was a hundred down, and the promise of another hundred when we had got safely away, before he was satisfied. But we fixed it up at last, and poor old George got down to his state-room and changed his clothes.

He'd hardly gone when the breakfast-party came on deck.

"Did you meet him?" I asked.

"Meet whom?" said old Marshall.

"George's twin-brother Alfred."

"I didn't know George had a brother."

"Nor did he till yesterday. It's a long story. He was kidnapped in infancy, and every one thought he was dead. George had a letter from his uncle about him yesterday. I shouldn't wonder if that's where George has gone, to see his uncle and find out about it. In the meantime, Alfred has arrived. He's down in George's state-room now, having a brush-up. It'll amaze you, the likeness between them. You'll think it *is* George at first. Look! Here he comes."

And up came George, brushed and clean, in an ordinary yachting suit.

They were rattled. There was no doubt about that. They stood looking at him, as if they thought there was a catch somewhere, but weren't quite certain where it was. I introduced him, and still they looked doubtful.

"Mr. Pepper tells me my brother is not on board," said George.

"It's an amazing likeness," said old Marshall.

"Is my brother like me?" asked George, amiably.

"No one could tell you apart," I said.

"I suppose twins always are alike," said George. "But if it ever came to a question of identification, there would be one way of distinguishing us. Do you know George well, Mr. Pepper?"

"He's a dear old pal of mine."

"You've been swimming with him, perhaps?"

"Every day last August."

"Well, then, you would have noticed it if he had had a mole like this on the back of his neck, wouldn't you?"

He turned his back and stooped and showed the mole. His collar hid it at ordinary times. I had seen it often when we were bathing together.

"Has George a mole like that?" he asked.

"No," I said. "Oh, no."

"You would have noticed it if he had?"

"Yes," I said. "Oh, yes."

"I'm glad of that," said George. "It would be a nuisance not to be able to prove one's own identity."

That seemed to satisfy them all. They couldn't get away from it. It seemed to me that from now on the thing was a walk-over. And I think George felt the same, for, when old Marshall asked him if he had had breakfast, he said he had not, went below, and pitched in as if he hadn't a care in the world.

Everything went right till lunch-time. George sat in the shade on the fore-deck talking to Stella most of the time. When the gong went and the rest had started to go below, he drew me back. He was beaming.

"It's all right," he said. "What did I tell you?"

"What did you tell me?"

"Why, about Stella. Didn't I say that Alfred would fix things for George? I told her she looked worried, and got her to tell me what the trouble was. And then——"

"You must have shown a flash of speed if you got her to confide in you after knowing you for about two hours."

"Perhaps I did," said George, modestly. "I had no notion, till I became him, what a persuasive sort of chap my brother Alfred was. Anyway, she told me all about it, and I started in to show her that George was a pretty good sort of fellow on the whole, who oughtn't to be turned down for what was evidently merely temporary insanity. She saw my point."

"And it's all right?"

"Absolutely, if only we can produce George. How much longer does that infernal sleuth intend to stay here? He seems to have taken root."

"I fancy he thinks that you're bound to come back sooner or later, and is waiting for you."

"He's an absolute nuisance," said George.

We were moving towards the companion-way, to go below for lunch, when a boat hailed us. We went to the side and looked over.

"It's my uncle," said George.

A stout man came up the gangway.

"Halloa, George!" he said. "Get my letter?"

"I think you are mistaking me for my brother," said George. "My name is Alfred Lattaker."

"What's that?"

"I am George's brother Alfred. Are you my Uncle Augustus?"

The stout man stared at him.

"You're very like George," he said.

"So every one tells me."

"And you're really Alfred?"

"I am."

"I'd like to talk business with you for a moment."

He cocked his eye at me. I sidled off and went below.

At the foot of the companion-steps I met Voules.

"I beg your pardon, sir," said Voules. "If it would be convenient, I should be glad to have the afternoon off."

I'm bound to say I rather liked his manner. Absolutely normal. Not a trace of the fellow-conspirator about it. I gave him the afternoon off.

I had lunch — George didn't show up — and as I was going out I was waylaid by the girl Pilbeam. She had been crying.

"I beg your pardon, sir, but did Mr. Voules ask you for the afternoon?"

I didn't see what business it was of hers, but she seemed all worked up about it, so I told her.

"Yes, I have given him the afternoon off."

She broke down — absolutely collapsed. Devilish unpleasant it was.

I'm hopeless in a situation like this. After I'd said, "There, there!" which didn't seem to help much, I hadn't any remarks to make.

"He s-said he was going to the tables to gamble away all his savings and then shoot himself, because he had nothing left to live for."

I suddenly remembered the scrap in the small hours outside my stateroom door. I hate mysteries. I meant to get to the bottom of this. I couldn't have a really first-class valet like Voules going about the place shooting himself up. Evidently the girl Pilbeam was at the bottom of the thing. I questioned her. She sobbed.

I questioned her more. I was firm. And eventually she yielded up the facts. Voules had seen George kiss her the night before; that was the trouble.

Things began to piece themselves together. I went up to interview George. There was going to be another job for persuasive Alfred. Voules's mind had got to be eased as Stella's had been. I couldn't afford to lose a fellow with his genius for preserving a trouser-crease.

I found George on the fore-deck. What is it Shakespeare or somebody says about some fellow's face being sicklied o'er with the pale cast of care? George's was like that. He looked green.

"Finished with your uncle?" I said.

He grinned a ghostly grin.

"There isn't any uncle," he said. "There isn't any Alfred. And there isn't any money."

"Explain yourself, old top," I said.

"It won't take long. The old crook has spent every penny of the trust money. He's been at it for years, ever since I was a kid. When the time came to cough up, and I was due to see that he did it, he went to the tables in the hope of a run of luck, and lost the last remnant of the stuff. He had to find a way of holding me for a while and postponing the squaring of accounts while he got away, and he invented this twin-brother business. He knew I should find out sooner or later, but meanwhile he would be able to get off to South America, which he has done. He's on his way now."

"You let him go?"

"What could I do? I can't afford to make a fuss with that man Sturgis around. I can't prove there's no Alfred, when my only chance of avoiding prison is to be Alfred."

"Well, you've made things right for yourself with Stella Vanderley, anyway," I said, to cheer him up.

"What's the good of that now? I've hardly any money and no prospects. How can I marry her?"

I pondered.

"It looks to me, old top," I said at last, "as if things were in a bit of a mess."

"You've guessed it," said poor old George.

I spent the afternoon musing on Life. If you come to think of it, what a queer thing Life is! So unlike anything else, don't you know, if you see what I mean. At any moment you may be strolling peacefully along, and all the time Life's waiting around the corner to fetch you one. You can't tell when you may be going to get it. It's all dashed puzzling. Here was poor old George, as well-meaning a fellow as ever stepped, getting swatted all over the ring by the hand of Fate. Why? That's what I asked myself. Just Life, don't you know. That's all there was about it.

It was close on six o'clock when our third visitor of the day arrived. We were sitting on the after-deck in the cool of the evening—old Marshall, Denman Sturgis, Mrs. Vanderley, Stella, George and I—when he came up. We had been talking of George, and old Marshall was suggesting the advisability of sending out search-parties. He was worried. So was Stella Vanderley. So, for that matter, were George and I, only not for the same reason.

We were just arguing the thing out when the visitor appeared. He was a well-built, stiff sort of fellow. He spoke with a German accent.

"Mr. Marshall?" he said. "I am Count Fritz von Cöslin, equerry to His Serene Highness"—he clicked his heels together and saluted—"the Prince of Saxburg-Liegnitz."

Mrs. Vanderley jumped up.

"Why, Count," she said, "what ages since we met in Vienna! You remember?"

"Could I ever forget? And the charming Miss Stella, she is well, I suppose not?"

"Stella, you remember Count Fritz?"

Stella shook hands with him.

"And how is the poor, dear Prince?" asked Mrs. Vanderley. "What a terrible thing to have happened!"

"I rejoice to say that my high-born master is better. He has regained consciousness and is sitting up and taking nourishment."

"That's good," said old Marshall.

"In a spoon only," sighed the Count. "Mr. Marshall, with your permission I should like a word with Mr. Sturgis."

"Mr. Who?"

The gimlet-eyed sportsman came forward.

"I am Denman Sturgis, at your service."

"The deuce you are! What are you doing here?"

"Mr. Sturgis," explained the Count, "graciously volunteered his services —"

"I know. But what's he doing here?"

"I am waiting for Mr. George Lattaker, Mr. Marshall."

"Eh?"

"You have not found him?" asked the Count, anxiously.

"Not yet, Count; but I hope to do so shortly. I know what he looks like now. This gentleman is his twin-brother. They are doubles."

"You are sure this gentleman is not Mr. George Lattaker?"

George put his foot down firmly on the suggestion.

"Don't go mixing me up with my brother," he said. "I am Alfred. You can tell me by my mole."

He exhibited the mole. He was taking no risks.

The Count clicked his tongue regretfully.

"I am sorry," he said.

George didn't offer to console him.

"Don't worry," said Sturgis. "He won't escape me. I shall find him."

"Do, Mr. Sturgis, do. And quickly. Find swiftly that noble young man."

"What?" shouted George.

"That noble young man, George Lattaker, who, at the risk of his life, saved my high-born master from the assassin."

George sat down suddenly.

"I don't understand," he said, feebly.

"We were wrong, Mr. Sturgis," went on the Count. "We leaped to the conclusion — was it not so? — that the owner of the hat you found was also the assailant of my high-born master. We were wrong. I have heard the story from His Serene Highness's own lips. He was passing down a dark street when a ruffian in a mask sprang out upon him. Doubtless he had been followed from the Casino, where he had been winning heavily. My high-born master was taken by surprise. He was felled. But before he lost consciousness he perceived a young man in evening dress, wearing the hat you found, running swiftly towards him. The hero engaged the assassin in combat, and my high-born master remembers no more. His Serene Highness asks repeatedly, 'Where is my brave preserver?' His gratitude is princely. He seeks for this young man to reward him. Ah, you should be proud of your brother, sir!"

"Thanks," said George, limply.

"And you, Mr. Sturgis, you must redouble your efforts. You must search the land; you must scour the sea to find George Lattaker."

"He needn't take all that trouble," said a voice from the gangway.

It was Voules. His face was flushed, his hat was on the back of his head, and he was smoking a fat cigar.

"I'll tell you where to find George Lattaker!" he shouted.

He glared at George, who was staring at him.

"Yes, look at me," he yelled. "Look at me. You won't be the first this afternoon who's stared at the mysterious stranger who won for two hours without a break. I'll be even with you now, Mr. Blooming Lattaker. I'll learn you to break a poor man's heart. Mr. Marshall and gents, this morning I was on deck, and I over'eard 'im plotting to put up a game on you. They'd spotted that gent there as a detective, and they arranged that blooming Lattaker was to pass himself off as his own twin-brother. And if you wanted proof, blooming Pepper tells him to show them his mole and he'd swear George hadn't one. Those were his very words. That man there is George Lattaker, Hesquire, and let him deny it if he can."

George got up.

"I haven't the least desire to deny it, Voules."

"Mr. Voules, if *you* please."

"It's true," said George, turning to the Count. "The fact is, I had rather a foggy recollection of what happened last night. I only remembered knocking some one down, and, like you, I jumped to the conclusion that I must have assaulted His Serene Highness."

"Then you are really George Lattaker?" asked the Count.

"I am."

" 'Ere, what does all this mean?" demanded Voules.

"Merely that I saved the life of His Serene Highness the Prince of Saxburg-Liegnitz, Mr. Voules."

"It's a swindle!" began Voules, when there was a sudden rush and the girl Pilbeam cannoned into the crowd, sending me into old Marshall's chair, and flung herself into the arms of Voules.

"Oh, Harold!" she cried. "I thought you were dead. I thought you'd shot yourself."

He sort of braced himself together to fling her off, and then he seemed to think better of it and fell into the clinch.

It was all dashed romantic, don't you know, but there *are* limits.

"Voules, you're sacked," I said.

"Who cares?" he said. "Think I was going to stop on now I'm a gentleman of property? Come along, Emma, my dear. Give a month's notice and get your 'at, and I'll take you to dinner at Ciro's."

"And you, Mr. Lattaker," said the Count, "may I conduct you to the presence of my high-born master? He wishes to show his gratitude to his preserver."

"You may," said George. "May I have my hat, Mr. Sturgis?"

There's just one bit more. After dinner that night I came up for a smoke, and, strolling on to the fore-deck, almost bumped into George and Stella. They seemed to be having an argument.

"I'm not sure," she was saying, "that I believe that a man can be so happy that he wants to kiss the nearest thing in sight, as you put it."

"Don't you?" said George. "Well, as it happens, I'm feeling just that way now."

I coughed, and he turned round.

"Halloa, Reggie!" he said.

"Halloa, George!" I said. "Lovely night."

"Beautiful," said Stella.

"The moon," I said.

"Ripping," said George.

"Lovely," said Stella.

"And look at the reflection of the stars on the—"

George caught my eye.

"Pop off," he said.

I popped.

Rallying Round Clarence

HAVE you ever thought about—and, when I say thought about, I mean really carefully considered the question of—the coolness, the cheek, or, if you prefer it, the gall with which Woman, as a sex, fairly bursts? *I* have, by Jove! But then I've had it thrust on my notice, by George, in a way I should imagine has happened to pretty few fellows. And the limit was reached by that business of the Yeardsley "Venus."

To make you understand the full what-d'you-call-it of the situation, I shall have to explain just how matters stood between Mrs. Yeardsley and myself.

When I first knew her she was Elizabeth Shoolbred. Old Worcestershire family; pots of money; pretty as a picture. Her brother Bill was at Oxford with me.

I loved Elizabeth Shoolbred. I loved her, don't you know. And there was a time, for about a week, when we were engaged to be married. But just as I was beginning to take a serious view of life and study furniture catalogues and feel pretty solemn when the restaurant orchestra played "The Wedding Glide," I'm hanged if she didn't break it off, and a month later she was married to a fellow of the name of Yeardsley—Clarence Yeardsley, an artist.

What with golf, and billiards, and a bit of racing, and fellows at the club rallying round and kind of taking me out of myself, as it were, I got over it, and came to look on the affair as a closed page in the book of my life, if you know what I mean. It didn't seem likely to me that we should meet again, as she and Clarence had settled down in the country somewhere and never came to London, and I'm bound to own that, by the time I got her letter, the wound had pretty well healed, and I was to a certain extent sitting up and taking nourishment. In fact, to be absolutely honest, I was jolly thankful the thing had ended as it had done.

This letter I'm telling you about arrived one morning out of a blue sky, as it were. It ran like this:—

MY DEAR OLD REGGIE,—

What ages it seems since I saw anything of you. How are you? We have settled down here in the most perfect old house, with a lovely garden, in the middle of delightful country. Couldn't you run down here for a few days? Clarence and I would be so glad to see you. Bill is here, and is most anxious to meet you again. He was speaking of you only this morning. *Do* come. Wire your train, and I will send the car to meet you.

Yours most sincerely,
ELIZABETH YEARDSLEY.

P.S. — We can give you new milk and fresh eggs. Think of that!

P.P.S. — Bill says our billard-table is one of the best he has ever played on.

P.P.S.S. — We are only half a mile from a golf course. Bill says it is better than St. Andrews.

P.P.S.S.S. — You *must* come!

Well, a fellow comes down to breakfast one morning, with a bit of a head on, and finds a letter like that from a girl who might quite easily have blighted his life! It rattled me rather, I must confess.

However, that bit about the golf settled me. I knew Bill knew what he was talking about, and, if he said the course was so topping, it must be something special. So I went.

Old Bill met me at the station with the car. I hadn't come across him for some months, and I was glad to see him again. And he apparently was glad to see me.

"Thank goodness you've come," he said, as we drove off. "I was just about at my last grip."

"What's the trouble, old scout?" I asked.

"If I had the artistic what's-its-name," he went on, "if the mere mention of pictures didn't give me the pip, I dare say it wouldn't be so bad. As it is, it's rotten!"

"Pictures?"

"Pictures. Nothing else is mentioned in this household. Clarence is an artist. So is his father. And you know yourself what Elizabeth is like when one gives her her head?"

I remembered then — it hadn't come back to me before — that most of my time with Elizabeth had been spent in picture-galleries. During the period when I had let her do just what she wanted to do with me, I had had to follow her like a dog through gallery after gallery, though pictures are poison to me, just as they are to old Bill. Somehow it had never struck me that she would still be going on in this way after marrying an artist. I should have thought that by this time the mere sight of a picture would have fed her up. Not so, however, according to old Bill.

"They talk pictures at every meal," he said. "I tell you, it makes a chap feel out of it. How long are you down for?"

"A few days."

"Take my tip, and let me send you a wire from London. I go there to-morrow. I promised to play against the Scottish. The idea was that I was to come back after the match. But you couldn't get me back with a lasso."

I tried to point out the silver lining.

"But, Bill, old scout, your sister says there's a most corking links near here."

He turned and stared at me, and nearly ran us into the bank.

"You don't mean honestly she said that?"

"She said you said it was better than St. Andrews."

"So I did. Was that all she said I said?"

"Well, wasn't it enough?"

"She didn't happen to mention that I added the words, 'I don't think'?"

"No, she forgot to tell me that."

"It's the worst course in Great Britain."

I felt rather stunned, don't you know. Whether it's a bad habit to have got into or not, I can't say, but I simply can't do without my daily allowance of golf when I'm not in London.

I took another whirl at the silver lining.

"We'll have to take it out in billiards," I said. "I'm glad the table's good."

"It depends what you call good. It's half-size, and there's a seven-inch cut just out of baulk where Clarence's cue slipped. Elizabeth has mended it with pink silk. Very smart and dressy it looks, but it doesn't improve the thing as a billiard-table."

"But she said you said——"

"Must have been pulling your leg."

We turned in at the drive gates of a good-sized house standing well back from the road. It looked black and sinister in the dusk, and I couldn't help feeling, you know, like one of those Johnnies you read about in stories who are lured to lonely houses for rummy purposes and hear a shriek just as they get there. Elizabeth knew me well enough to know that a specially good golf course was a safe draw to me. Not to mention the billiard-table. And she had deliberately played on her knowledge. What was the game? That was what I wanted to know. And then a sudden thought struck me which brought me out in a cold perspiration. She had some girl down here and was going to have a stab at marrying me off. I've often heard that young married women are all over that sort of thing. Certainly she had said there was nobody at the house but Clarence and herself and Bill and Clarence's father, but a woman who could take the name of St. Andrews in vain as she had done wouldn't be likely to stick at a trifle.

"Bill, old scout," I said, "there aren't any frightful girls or any rot of that sort stopping here, are there?"

"Wish there were," he said. "No such luck."

As we pulled up at the front door, it opened, and a woman's figure appeared.

"Have you got him, Bill?" she said, which in my present frame of mind struck me as a jolly creepy way of putting it. The sort of thing Lady Macbeth might have said to Macbeth, don't you know.

"Do you mean me?" I said.

She came down into the light. It was Elizabeth, looking just the same as in the old days.

"Is that you, Reggie? I'm so glad you were able to come. I was afraid you might have forgotten all about it. You know what you are. Come along in and have some tea."

Have you ever been turned down by a girl who afterwards married and then been introduced to her husband? If so, you'll understand how I felt when Clarence burst on me. You know the feeling. First of all, when you hear about the marriage, you say to yourself, "I wonder what he's like." Then you meet him, and think, "There must be some mistake. She can't have preferred *this* to me!" That's what I thought when I set eyes on Clarence.

He was a little thin, nervous-looking chappy of about thirty-five. His hair was getting grey at the temples and straggly on top. He wore pince-nez, and he had a drooping moustache. I'm no Bombardier Wells myself, but in front of Clarence I felt quite a nut. And Elizabeth, mind you, is one of those tall, splendid girls who look like princesses. Honestly, I believe women do it out of pure cussedness.

"How do you do, Mr. Pepper? Hark! Can you hear a mewing cat?" said Clarence. All in one breath, don't you know.

"Eh?" I said.

"A mewing cat. I feel sure I hear a mewing cat. Listen!"

While we were listening the door opened, and a white-haired old gentleman came in. He was built on the same lines as Clarence, but was an earlier model. I took him, correctly, to be Mr. Yeardsley, senior. Elizabeth introduced us.

"Father," said Clarence, "did you meet a mewing cat outside? I feel positive I heard a cat mewing."

"No," said the father, shaking his head; "no mewing cat."

"I can't bear mewing cats," said Clarence. "A mewing cat gets on my nerves!"

"A mewing cat is so trying," said Elizabeth.

"*I* dislike mewing cats," said old Mr. Yeardsley.

That was all about mewing cats for the moment. They seemed to think they had covered the ground satisfactorily, and they went back to pictures.

We talked pictures steadily till it was time to dress for dinner. At least, they did. I just sort of sat around. Presently the subject of picture-robberies came up. Somebody mentioned the "Mona Lisa," and then I happened to remember seeing something in the evening paper, as I was coming down in the train, about some fellow somewhere having had a valuable painting pinched by burglars the night before. It was the first time I had had a chance of breaking into the conversation with any effect, and I meant to make the most of it. The paper was in the pocket of my overcoat in the hall. I went and fetched it.

"Here it is," I said. "A Romney belonging to Sir Bellamy Palmer—"

They all shouted "What!" exactly at the same time, like a chorus. Elizabeth grabbed the paper.

"Let me look! Yes. 'Late last night burglars entered the residence of Sir Bellamy Palmer, Dryden Park, Midford, Hants—' "

"Why, that's near here," I said. "I passed through Midford—"

"Dryden Park is only two miles from this house," said Elizabeth. I noticed her eyes were sparkling.

"Only two miles!" she said. "It might have been us! It might have been the 'Venus'!"

Old Mr. Yeardsley bounded in his chair.

"The 'Venus'!" he cried.

They all seemed wonderfully excited. My little contribution to the evening's chat had made quite a hit.

Why I didn't notice it before I don't know, but it was not till Elizabeth showed it to me after dinner that I had my first look at the Yeardsley

"Venus." When she led me up to it, and switched on the light, it seemed impossible that I could have sat right through dinner without noticing it. But then, at meals, my attention is pretty well riveted on the food-stuffs. Anyway, it was not till Elizabeth showed it to me that I was aware of its existence.

She and I were alone in the drawing-room after dinner. Old Yeardsley was writing letters in the morning-room, while Bill and Clarence were rollicking on the half-size billiard-table with the pink silk tapestry effects. All, in fact, was joy, jollity, and song, so to speak, when Elizabeth, who had been sitting wrapped in thought for a bit, bent towards me and said, "Reggie."

And the moment she said it I knew something was going to happen. You know that pre-what-d'you-call-it you get sometimes? Well, I got it then.

"What o?" I said, nervously.

"Reggie," she said, "I want to ask a great favour of you."

"Yes?"

She stooped down and put a log on the fire, and went on, with her back to me:—

"Do you remember, Reggie, once saying you would do anything in the world for me?"

There! That's what I meant when I said that about the cheek of Woman as a sex. What I mean is, after what had happened, you'd have thought she would have preferred to let the dead past bury its dead, and all that sort of thing, what?

Mind you, I *had* said I would do anything in the world for her. I admit that. But it was a distinctly pre-Clarence remark. He hadn't appeared on the scene then, and it stands to reason that a fellow who may have been a perfect knight-errant to a girl when he was engaged to her doesn't feel nearly so keen on spreading himself in that direction when she has given him the miss-in-baulk and gone and married a man who reason and instinct both tell him is a decided blighter.

I couldn't think of anything to say but "Oh, yes."

"There's something you can do for me now, which will make me everlastingly grateful."

"Yes?" I said.

"Do you know, Reggie," she said, suddenly, "that only a few months ago Clarence was very fond of cats?"

"Eh! Well, he still seems—er—*interested* in them, what?"

"Now they get on his nerves. Everything gets on his nerves."

"Some fellows swear by that stuff you see advertised all over the —"

"No, that wouldn't help him. He doesn't need to take anything. He wants to get rid of something."

"I don't quite follow. Get rid of something?"

"The 'Venus,'" said Elizabeth.

She looked up and caught my bulging eye.

"You saw the 'Venus,'" she said.

"Not that I remember."

"Well, come into the dining-room."

We went into the dining-room, and she switched on the lights.

"There," she said.

On the wall close to the door — that may have been why I hadn't noticed it before; I had sat with my back to it — was a large oil-painting. It was what you'd call a classical picture, I suppose. What I mean is — well, you know what I mean. All I can say is that it's funny I *hadn't* noticed it.

"Is that the 'Venus'?" I said.

She nodded.

"How would you like to have to look at that every time you sat down to a meal?"

"Well, I don't know. I don't think it would affect me much. I'd worry through all right."

She jerked her head impatiently.

"But you're not an artist," she said. "Clarence is."

And then I began to see daylight. What exactly was the trouble I didn't understand, but it was evidently something to do with the good old Artistic Temperament, and I could believe anything about that. It explains everything. It's like the Unwritten Law, don't you know, which you plead in America if you've done anything they want to send you to chokey for and you don't want to go. What I mean is, if you're absolutely off your rocker, but don't find it convenient to be scooped into the luny-bin, you simply explain that, when you said you were a tea-pot, it was just your Artistic Temperament, and they apologize and go away. So I stood by to hear just how the A. T. had affected Clarence, the Cat's Friend, ready for anything.

And, believe me, it had hit Clarence badly.

It was this way. It seemed that old Yeardsley was an amateur artist and that this "Venus" was his masterpiece. He said so, and he ought to have known. Well, when Clarence married, he had given it to him as a wedding-present, and had hung it where it stood with his own hands. All right so far, what? But mark the sequel. Temperamental Clarence, being a professional artist and consequently some streets ahead of the dad at the game, saw flaws in the "Venus." He couldn't stand it at any price. He didn't like the drawing. He didn't like the expression of the face. He didn't like the colouring. In fact, it made him feel quite ill to look at it. Yet, being devoted to his father and wanting to do anything rather than give him pain, he had not been able to bring himself to store the thing in the cellar, and the strain of confronting the picture three times a day had begun to tell on him to such an extent that Elizabeth felt something had to be done.

"Now you see," she said.

"In a way," I said. "But don't you think it's making rather heavy weather over a trifle?"

"Oh, can't you understand? Look!" Her voice dropped as if she was in church, and she switched on another light. It shone on the picture next to old Yeardsley's. "There!" she said. "Clarence painted *that!*"

She looked at me expectantly, as if she were waiting for me to swoon, or yell, or something. I took a steady look at Clarence's effort. It was another Classical picture. It seemed to me very much like the other one.

Some sort of art criticism was evidently expected of me, so I made a dash at it.

"Er—'Venus'?" I said.

Mark you, Sherlock Holmes would have made the same mistake. On the evidence, I mean.

"No. 'Jocund Spring,' " she snapped. She switched off the light. "I see you don't understand even now. You never had any taste about pictures. When we used to go to the galleries together, you would far rather have been at your club."

This was so absolutely true that I had no remark to make. She came up to me, and put her hand on my arm.

"I'm sorry, Reggie. I didn't mean to be cross. Only I do want to make you understand that Clarence is *suffering*. Suppose—suppose—well, let us take the case of a great musician. Suppose a great musician had to sit and listen to a cheap, vulgar tune—the same tune—day after day, day after day, wouldn't you expect his nerves to break? Well, it's just like that with Clarence. Now you see?"

"Yes, but——"

"But what? Surely I've put it plainly enough?"

"Yes. But what I mean is, where do I come in? What do you want me to do?"

"I want you to steal the 'Venus.' "

I looked at her.

"You want me to —— ?"

"Steal it. Reggie!" Her eyes were shining with excitement. "Don't you see? It's Providence. When I asked you to come here, I had just got the idea. I knew I could rely on you. And then by a miracle this robbery of the Romney takes place at a house not two miles away. It removes the last chance of the poor old man suspecting anything and having his feelings hurt. Why, it's the most wonderful compliment to him. Think! One night thieves steal a splendid Romney; the next the same gang take his 'Venus.' It will be the proudest moment of his life. Do it to-night, Reggie. I'll give you a sharp knife. You simply cut the canvas out of the frame, and it's done."

"But one moment," I said. "I'd be delighted to be of any use to you, but in a purely family affair like this, wouldn't it be better — in fact, how about tackling old Bill on the subject?"

"I have asked Bill already. Yesterday. He refused."

"But if I'm caught?"

"You can't be. All you have to do is to take the picture, open one of the windows, leave it open, and go back to your room."

It sounded simple enough.

"And as to the picture itself — when I've got it?"

"Burn it. I'll see that you have a good fire in your room."

"But —— "

She looked at me. She always did have the most wonderful eyes.

"Reggie," she said; nothing more. Just "Reggie."

She looked at me.

Well, after all, if you see what I mean —— The days that are no more, don't you know. Auld Lang Syne, and all that sort of thing. You follow me?

"All right," I said. "I'll do it."

I don't know if you happen to be one of those Johnnies who are steeped in crime, and so forth, and think nothing of pinching diamond necklaces. If you're not, you'll understand that I felt a lot less keen on the job I'd taken on when I sat in my room, waiting to get busy, than I had done when I promised to tackle it in the dining-room. On paper it all seemed easy enough, but I couldn't help feeling there was a catch somewhere, and I've never known time pass slower. The kick-off was scheduled for one o'clock in the morning, when the household might be expected to be pretty sound asleep, but at a quarter to I couldn't stand it any longer. I lit the lantern I had taken from Bill's bicycle, took a grip of my knife, and slunk downstairs.

The first thing I did on getting to the dining-room was to open the window. I had half a mind to smash it, so as to give an extra bit of local colour to the affair, but decided not to on account of the noise. I had put my lantern on the table, and was just reaching out for it, when something happened. What it was for the moment I couldn't have said. It might have been an explosion of some sort or an earthquake. Some solid object caught me a frightful whack on the chin. Sparks and things occurred inside my head, and the next thing I remember is feeling something wet and cold splash into my face, and hearing a voice that sounded like old Bill's say, "Feeling better now?"

I sat up. The lights were on, and I was on the floor, with old Bill kneeling beside me with a soda siphon.

"What happened?" I said.

"I'm awfully sorry, old man," he said. "I hadn't a notion it was you. I came in here, and saw a lantern on the table and the window open and a chap with a knife in his hand, so I didn't stop to make inquiries. I just let go at his jaw for all I was worth. What on earth do you think you're doing? Were you walking in your sleep?"

"It was Elizabeth," I said. "Why, you know all about it. She said she had told you."

"You don't mean —— "

"The picture. You refused to take it on, so she asked me."

"Reggie, old man," he said, "I'll never believe what they say about repentance again. It's a fool's trick and upsets everything. If I hadn't repented, and thought it was rather rough on Elizabeth not to do a little thing like that for her, and come down here to do it after all, you wouldn't have stopped that sleep-producer with your chin. I'm sorry."

"Me, too," I said, giving my head another shake to make certain it was still on.

"Are you feeling better now?"

"Better than I was. But that's not saying much."

"Would you like some more soda-water? No? Well, how about getting this job finished and going to bed? And let's be quick about it too. You made a noise like a ton of bricks when you went down just now, and it's on the cards some of the servants may have heard. Toss you who carves."

"Heads."

"Tails it is," he said, uncovering the coin. "Up you get. I'll hold the light. Don't spike yourself on that sword of yours."

It was as easy a job as Elizabeth had said. Just four quick cuts, and the thing came out of its frame like an oyster. I rolled it up. Old Bill had put the lantern on the floor and was at the sideboard, collecting whisky, soda, and glasses.

"We've got a long evening before us," he said. "You can't burn a picture of that size in one chunk. You'd set the chimney on fire. Let's do the thing comfortably. Clarence can't grudge us the stuff. We've done him a bit of good this trip. To-morrow'll be the maddest, merriest day of Clarence's glad New Year. On we go."

We went up to my room, and sat smoking and yarning away and sipping our drinks, and every now and then cutting a slice off the picture and shoving it in the fire till it was all gone. And what with the cosiness of it, and the cheerful blaze, and the comfortable feeling of doing good by stealth, I don't know when I've had a jollier time since the days when we used to brew in my study at school.

We had just put the last slice on when Bill sat up suddenly, and gripped my arm.

"I heard something," he said.

I listened, and, by Jove, I heard something, too. My room was just over the dining-room, and the sound came up to us quite distinctly. Stealthy footsteps, by George! And then a chair falling over.

"There's somebody in the dining-room," I whispered.

There's a certain type of chap who takes a pleasure in positively chivvying trouble. Old Bill's like that. If I had been along, it would have taken me about three seconds to persuade myself that I hadn't really heard anything after all. I'm a peaceful sort of cove, and believe in living and letting live, and so forth. To old Bill, however, a visit from burglars was pure jam. He was out of his chair in one jump.

"Come on," he said. "Bring the poker."

I brought the tongs as well. I felt like it. Old Bill collared the knife. We crept downstairs.

"We'll fling the door open and make a rush," said Bill.

"Supposing they shoot, old scout?"

"Burglars never shoot," said Bill.

Which was comforting provided the burglars knew it.

Old Bill took a grip of the handle, turned it quickly, and in he went. And then we pulled up sharp, staring.

The room was in darkness except for a feeble splash of light at the near end. Standing on a chair in front of Clarence's "Jocund Spring," holding a candle in one hand and reaching up with a knife in the other, was old Mr. Yeardsley, in bedroom slippers and a grey dressing-gown. He had made a final cut just as we rushed in. Turning at the sound, he stopped, and he and the chair and the candle and the picture came down in a heap together. The candle went out.

"What on earth?" said Bill.

I felt the same. I picked up the candle and lit it, and then a most fearful thing happened. The old man picked himself up, and suddenly collapsed into a chair and began to cry like a child. Of course, I could see it was only the Artistic Temperament, but still, believe me, it was devilish unpleasant. I looked at old Bill. Old Bill looked at me. We shut the door quick, and after that we didn't know what to do. I saw Bill look at the sideboard, and I knew what he was looking for. But we had taken the siphon upstairs, and his ideas of first aid stopped short at squirting soda-water. We just waited, and presently old Yeardsley switched off, sat up, and began talking with a rush.

"Clarence, my boy, I was tempted. It was that burglary at Dryden Park. It tempted me. It made it all so simple. I knew you would put it down to the same gang, Clarence, my boy. I——"

It seemed to dawn upon him at this point that Clarence was not among those present.

"Clarence?" he said, hesitatingly.

"He's in bed," I said.

"In bed! Then he doesn't know? Even now—— Young men, I throw myself on your mercy. Don't be hard on me. Listen." He grabbed at Bill, who side-stepped. "I can explain everything—everything."

He gave a gulp.

"You are not artists, you two young men, but I will try to make you understand, make you realize what this picture means to me. I was two years painting it. It is my child. I watched it grow. I loved it. It was part of my life. Nothing would have induced me to sell it. And then Clarence married, and in a mad moment I gave my treasure to him. You cannot understand, you two young men, what agonies I suffered. The thing was done. It was irrevocable. I saw how Clarence valued the picture. I knew that I could never bring myself to ask him for it back. And yet I was lost without it. What could I do? Till this evening I could see no hope. Then came this story of the theft of the Romney from a house quite close to this, and I saw my way. Clarence would never suspect. He would put the robbery down to the same band of criminals who stole the Romney. Once the idea had come, I could not drive it out. I fought against it, but to no avail. At last I yielded, and crept down here to carry out my plan. You found me." He grabbed again, at me this time, and got me by the arm. He had a grip like a lobster. "Young man," he said, "you would not betray me? You would not tell Clarence?"

I was feeling most frightfully sorry for the poor old chap by this time, don't you know, but I thought it would be kindest to give it him straight instead of breaking it by degrees.

"I won't say a word to Clarence, Mr. Yeardsley," I said. "I quite understand your feelings. The Artistic Temperament, and all that sort of thing, I mean—what? *I* know. But I'm afraid—— Well, look!"

I went to the door and switched on the electric light, and there, staring him in the face, were the two empty frames. He stood goggling at them in silence. Then he gave a sort of wheezy grunt.

"The gang! The burglars! They *have* been here, and they have taken Clarence's picture!" He paused. "It might have been mine! My Venus!" he whispered.

It was getting most fearfully painful, you know, but he had to know the truth.

"I'm awfully sorry, you know," I said. "But it *was*."

He started, poor old chap.

"Eh? What do you mean?"

"They *did* take your Venus."

"But I have it here."

I shook my head.

"That's Clarence's 'Jocund Spring,' " I said.

He jumped at it and straightened it out.

"What! What are you talking about? Do you think I don't know my own picture—my child—my Venus? See! My own signature in the corner. Can you read, boy? Look: 'Matthew Yeardsley.' This is *my* picture!"

And—well, by Jove! it *was*, don't you know.

Well, we got him off to bed, him and his infernal Venus, and we settled down to take a steady look at the position of affairs. Bill said it was my fault for getting hold of the wrong picture, and I said it was Bill's fault for fetching me such a crack on the jaw that I couldn't be expected to see what I was getting hold of, and then there was a pretty massive silence for a bit.

"Reggie," said Bill, at last, "how exactly do you feel about facing Clarence and Elizabeth at breakfast?"

"Old scout," I said, "I was thinking much the same myself."

"Reggie," said Bill, "I happen to know there's a milk-train leaving Midford at three-fifteen. It isn't what you'd call a flier. It gets to London at about half-past nine. Well — er — in the circumstances, how about it?"

Concealed Art

IF a fellow has lots of money and lots of time and lots of curiosity about other fellows' business, it is astonishing, don't you know, what a lot of strange affairs he can get mixed up in. Now, I have money and curiosity and all the time there is. My name's Pepper — Reggie Pepper. My uncle was the colliery-owner chappie, and he left me the dickens of a pile. And ever since the lawyer slipped the stuff into my hand, whispering "It's yours!" life seems to have been one thing after another.

For instance, the dashed rummy case of dear old Archie. I first ran into old Archie when he was studying in Paris, and when he came back to London he looked me up, and we celebrated. He always liked me because I didn't mind listening to his theories of Art. For Archie, you must know, was an artist. Not an ordinary artist either, but one of those fellows you read about who are several years ahead of the times, and paint the sort of thing that people will be educated up to by about 1999 or thereabouts.

Well, one day as I was sitting in the club watching the traffic coming up one way and going down the other, and thinking nothing in particular, in blew the old boy. He was looking rather worried.

"Reggie, I want your advice."

"You shall have it," I said. "State your point, old top."

"It's like this — I'm engaged to be married."

"My dear old scout, a million con——"

"Yes, I know. Thanks very much, and all that, but listen."

"What's the trouble? Don't you like her?"

A kind of rapt expression came over his face.

"Like her! Why, she's the only——"

He gibbered for a spell. When he had calmed down, I said, "Well then, what's your trouble?"

"Reggie," he said, "do you think a man is bound to tell his wife all about his past life?"

"Oh, well," I said, "of course, I suppose she's prepared to find that a man has—er—sowed his wild oats, don't you know, and all that sort of thing, and——"

He seemed quite irritated.

"Don't be a chump. It's nothing like that. Listen. When I came back to London and started to try and make a living by painting, I found that people simply wouldn't buy the sort of work I did at any price. Do you know, Reggie, I've been at it three years now, and I haven't sold a single picture."

I whooped in a sort of amazed way, but I should have been far more startled if he'd told me he *had* sold a picture. I've seen his pictures, and they are like nothing on earth. So far as I can make out what he says, they aren't supposed to be. There's one in particular, called "The Coming of Summer," which I sometimes dream about when I've been hitting it up a shade too vigorously. It's all dots and splashes, with a great eye staring out of the middle of the mess. It looks as if summer, just as it was on the way, had stubbed its toe on a bomb. He tells me it's his masterpiece, and that he will never do anything like it again. I should like to have that in writing.

"Well, artists eat, just the same as other people," he went on, "and personally I like mine often and well cooked. Besides which, my sojourn in Paris gave me a rather nice taste in light wines. The consequence was that I came to the conclusion, after I had been back a few months, that something had to be done. Reggie, do you by any remote chance read a paper called *Funny Slices*?"

"Every week."

He gazed at me with a kind of wistful admiration.

"I envy you, Reggie. Fancy being able to make a statement like that openly and without fear. Then I take it you know the Doughnut family?"

"I should say I did."

His voice sank almost to a whisper, and he looked over his shoulder nervously.

"Reggie, I do them."

"You what?"

"I do them — draw them — paint them. I am the creator of the Doughnut family."

I stared at him, absolutely astounded. I was simply dumb. It was the biggest surprise of my life. Why, dash it, the Doughnut family was the best thing in its line in London. There is Pa Doughnut, Ma Doughnut, Aunt Bella, Cousin Joe, and Mabel, the daughter, and they have all sorts of slapstick adventures. Pa, Ma and Aunt Bella are pure gargoyles; Cousin Joe is a little more nearly semi-human, and Mabel is a perfect darling. I had often wondered who did them, for they were unsigned, and I had often thought what a deuced brainy fellow the chap must be. And all the time it was old Archie. I stammered as I tried to congratulate him.

He winced.

"Don't gargle, Reggie, there's a good fellow," he said. "My nerves are all on edge. Well, as I say, I do the Doughnuts. It was that or starvation. I got the idea one night when I had a toothache, and next day I took some specimens round to an editor. He rolled in his chair, and told me to start in and go on till further notice. Since then I have done them without a break. Well, there's the position. I must go on drawing these infernal things, or I shall be penniless. The question is, am I to tell her?"

"Tell her? Of course you must tell her."

"Ah, but you don't know her, Reggie. Have you ever heard of Eunice Nugent?"

"Not to my knowledge."

"As she doesn't sprint up and down the joyway at the Hippodrome, I didn't suppose you would."

I thought this rather uncalled-for, seeing that, as a matter of fact, I scarcely know a dozen of the Hippodrome chorus, but I made allowances for his state of mind.

"She's a poetess," he went on, "and her work has appeared in lots of good magazines. My idea is that she would be utterly horrified if she knew, and could never be quite the same to me again. But I want you to meet her and judge for yourself. It's just possible that I am taking too morbid a view of the matter, and I want an unprejudiced outside opinion. Come and lunch with us at the Piccadilly tomorrow, will you?"

He was absolutely right. One glance at Miss Nugent told me that the poor old boy had got the correct idea. I hardly know how to describe the impression she made on me. On the way to the Pic, Archie had told me that what first attracted him to her was the fact that she was so utterly unlike Mabel Doughnut; but that had not prepared me for what she really was. She was kind of intense, if you know what I mean—kind of spiritual. She was perfectly pleasant, and drew me out about golf and all that sort of thing; but all the time I felt that she considered me an earthy worm whose loftier soul-essence had been carelessly left out of his composition at birth. She made me wish that I had never seen a musical comedy or danced on a supper table on New Year's Eve. And if that was the impression she made on me, you can understand why poor old Archie jibbed at the idea of bringing her *Funny Slices*, and pointing at the Doughnuts and saying, "Me—I did it!" The notion was absolutely out of the question. The shot wasn't on the board. I told Archie so directly we were alone.

"Old top," I said, "you must keep it dark."

"I'm afraid so. But I hate the thought of deceiving her."

"You must get used to that now you're going to be a married man," I said.

"The trouble is, how am I going to account for the fact that I can do myself pretty well?"

"Why, tell her you have private means, of course. What's your money invested in?"

"Practically all of it in B. and O. P. Rails. It is a devilish good thing. A pal of mine put me onto it."

"Tell her that you have a pile of money in B. and O. P., then. She'll take it for granted it's a legacy. A spiritual girl like Miss Nugent isn't likely to inquire further."

"Reggie, I believe you're right. It cuts both ways, that spiritual gag. I'll do it."

They were married quietly. I held the towel for Archie, and a spectacled girl with a mouth like a rat-trap, who was something to do with the Woman's Movement, saw fair play for Eunice. And then they went off to Scotland for their honeymoon. I wondered how the Doughnuts were going to get on in old Archie's absence, but it seemed that he had buckled down to it and turned out three months' supply in advance. He told me that long practice had enabled him to Doughnut almost without conscious effort. When he came back to London he would give an hour a week to them and do them on his head. Pretty soft! It seemed to me that the marriage was going to be a success.

One gets out of touch with people when they marry. I am not much on the social-call game, and for nearly six months I don't suppose I saw Archie more than twice or three times. When I did, he appeared sound in wind and limb, and reported that married life was all to the velvet, and that he regarded bachelors like myself as so many excrescences on the social system. He compared me, if I remember rightly, to a wart, and advocated drastic treatment.

It was perhaps seven months after he had told Eunice that he endowed her with all his worldly goods—she not suspecting what the parcel contained—that he came to me unexpectedly one afternoon with a face so long and sick-looking that my finger was on the button and I was ordering brandy and soda before he had time to speak.

"Reggie," he said, "an awful thing has happened. Have you seen the paper today?"

"Yes. Why?"

"Did you read the Stock Exchange news? Did you see that some lunatic has been jumping around with a club and hammering the stuffing out of B. and O. P.? This afternoon they are worth practically nothing."

"By jove! And all your money was in it. What rotten luck!" Then I spotted the silver lining. "But, after all, it doesn't matter so very much. What I mean is, bang go your little savings and all that sort of thing; but, after all, you're making quite a good income, so why worry?"

"I might have known you would miss the point," he said. "Can't you understand the situation? This morning at breakfast Eunice got hold of the paper first. 'Archie,' she said, 'didn't you tell me all your money was in B. and O. P.?' 'Yes,' I said. 'Why?' 'Then we're ruined.' Now do you see? If I had had time to think, I could have said that I had another chunk in something else, but I had committed myself, I have either got to tell her about those infernal Doughnuts, or else conceal the fact that I had money coming in."

"Great Scot! What on earth are you going to do?"

"I can't think. We can struggle along in a sort of way, for it appears that she has small private means of her own. The idea at present is that we shall live on them. We're selling the car, and trying to get out of the rest of our lease up at the flat, and then we're going to look about for a cheaper place, probably down Chelsea way, so as to be near my studio.

What was that stuff I've been drinking? Ring for another of the same, there's a good fellow. In fact, I think you had better keep your finger permanently on the bell. I shall want all they've got."

The spectacle of a fellow human being up to his neck in the consommé is painful, of course, but there's certainly what the advertisements at the top of magazine stories call a "tense human interest" about it, and I'm bound to say that I saw as much as possible of poor old Archie from now on. His sad case fascinated me. It was rather thrilling to see him wrestling with New Zealand mutton-hash and draught beer down at his Chelsea flat, with all the suppressed anguish of a man who has let himself get accustomed to delicate food and vintage wines, and think that a word from him could send him whizzing back to the old life again whenever he wished. But at what a cost, as they say in the novels. That was the catch. He might hate this new order of things, but his lips were sealed.

I personally came in for a good deal of quiet esteem for the way in which I stuck to him in his adversity. I don't think Eunice had thought much of me before, but now she seemed to feel that I had formed a corner in golden hearts. I took advantage of this to try and pave the way for a confession on poor old Archie's part.

"I wonder, Archie, old top," I said one evening after we had dined on mutton-hash and were sitting round trying to forget it, "I wonder you don't try another line in painting. I've heard that some of these fellows who draw for the comic papers——"

Mrs. Archie nipped me in the bud.

"How can you suggest such a thing, Mr. Pepper? A man with Archie's genius! I know the public is not educated up to his work, but it is only a question of time. Archie suffers, like all pioneers, from being ahead of his generation. But, thank Heaven, he need not sully his genius by stooping——"

"No, no," I said. "Sorry. I only suggested it."

After that I gave more time than ever to trying to think of a solution. Sometimes I would lie awake at night, and my manner towards Wilberforce, my man, became so distrait that it almost caused a rift. He asked me one morning which suit I would wear that day, and, by Jove, I said, "Oh, any of them. I don't mind." There was a most frightful silence, and I woke up to find him looking at me with such a dashed wounded expression in his eyes that I had to tip him a couple of quid to bring him round again.

Well, you can't go on straining your brain like that forever without something breaking loose, and one night, just after I had gone to bed, I got it. Yes, by gad, absolutely got it. And I was so excited that I hopped out from under the blankets there and then, and rang up old Archie on the phone.

"Archie, old scout," I said, "can the misses hear what I'm saying? Well then, don't say anything to give the show away. Keep on saying, 'Yes? Halloa?' so that you can tell her it was someone on the wrong wire. I've got it, my boy. All you've got to do to solve the whole problem is to tell her you've sold one of your pictures. Make the price as big as you like. Come and lunch with me tomorrow at the club, and we'll settle the details."

There was a pause, and then Archie's voice said, "Halloa, halloa?" It might have been a bit disappointing, only there was a tremble in it which made me understand how happy I had made the old boy. I went back to bed and slept like a king.

Next day we lunched together, and fixed the thing up. I have never seen anyone so supremely braced. We examined the scheme from every angle and there wasn't a flaw in it. The only difficulty was to hit on a plausible purchaser. Archie suggested me, but I couldn't see it. I said it would sound fishy. Eventually I had a brain wave, and suggested J. Bellingwood Brackett, the American millionaire. He lives in London, and you see his name in the papers everyday as having bought some painting or statue or something, so why shouldn't he buy Archie's "Coming of Summer?" And Archie said, "Exactly — why shouldn't he? And if he had had any sense in his fat head, he would have done it long ago, dash him!" Which shows you that dear old Archie was bracing up, for I've heard him use much the same language in happier days about a referee.

He went off, crammed to the eyebrows with good food and happiness, to tell Mrs. Archie that all was well, and that the old home was saved, and that Canterbury mutton might now be definitely considered as off the bill of fare.

He told me on the phone that night that he had made the price two thousand pounds, because he needed the money, and what was two thousand to a man who had been fleecing the widow and the orphan for forty odd years without a break? I thought the price was a bit high, but I agreed that J. Bellingwood could afford it. And happiness, you might say, reigned supreme.

I don't know when I've had such a nasty jar as I got when Wilberforce brought me the paper in bed, and I languidly opened it and this jumped out and bit at me:

BELLINGWOOD BRACKETT DISCOVERS
ENGLISH GENIUS

PAYS STUPENDOUS PRICE FOR YOUNG ARTIST'S PICTURE

HITHERTO UNKNOWN FUTURIST RECEIVED £2,000

Underneath there was a column, some of it about Archie, the rest about the picture; and scattered over the page were two photographs of old Archie, looking more like Pa Doughnut than anything human, and a smudged reproduction of "The Coming of Summer"; and, believe me, frightful as the original of that weird exhibit looked, the reproduction had it licked to a whisper. It was one of the ghastliest things I have ever seen.

Well, after the first shock I recovered a bit. After all, it was fame for dear old Archie. As soon as I had had lunch I went down to the flat to congratulate him.

He was sitting there with Mrs. Archie. He was looking a bit dazed, but she was simmering with joy. She welcomed me as the faithful friend.

"Isn't it perfectly splendid, Mr. Pepper, to think that Archie's genius has at last been recognized? How quiet he kept it. I had no idea that Mr. Brackett was even interested in his work. I wonder how he heard of it?"

"Oh, these things get about," I said. "You can't keep a good man down."

"Think of two thousand pounds for one picture — and the first he has ever sold!"

"What beats me," I said, "is how the papers got hold of it."

"Oh, I sent it to the papers," said Mrs. Archie, in an offhand way.

"I wonder who did the writing up," I said.

"They would do that in the office, wouldn't they?" said Mrs. Archie.

"I suppose they would," I said. "They are wonders at that sort of thing."

I couldn't help wishing that Archie would enter into the spirit of the thing a little more and perk up, instead of sitting there looking like a codfish. The thing seemed to have stunned the poor chappie.

"After this, Archie," I said, "all you have to do is to sit in your studio, while the police see that the waiting line of millionaires doesn't straggle over the pavement. They'll fight —— "

"What's that?" said Archie, starting as if someone had dug a red-hot needle into his calf.

It was only a ring at the bell, followed by a voice asking if Mr. Ferguson was at home.

"Probably an interviewer," said Mrs. Archie. "I suppose we shall get no peace for a long time to come."

The door opened, and the cook came in with a card. " 'Renshaw Liggett,' " said Mrs. Archie. "I don't know him. Do you, Archie? It must be an interviewer. Ask him to come in, Julia."

And in he came.

My knowledge of chappies in general, after a fairly wide experience, is that some chappies seem to kind of convey an atmosphere of unpleasantness the moment you come into contact with them. Renshaw Liggett gave me this feeling directly he came in; and when he fixed me with a sinister glance and said, "Mr. Ferguson?" I felt inclined to say "Not guilty." I backed a step or two and jerked my head towards Archie, and Renshaw turned the searchlight off me and switched it onto him.

"You are Mr. Archibald Ferguson, the artist?"

Archie nodded pallidly, and Renshaw nodded, as much as to say that you couldn't deceive him. He produced a sheet of paper. It was the middle page of the *Mail*.

"You authorized the publication of this?"

Archie nodded again.

"I represent Mr. Brackett. The publication of this most impudent fiction has caused Mr. Brackett extreme annoyance, and, as it might also lead to other and more serious consequences, I must insist that a full denial be published without a moment's delay."

"What do you mean?" cried Mrs. Archie. "Are you mad?"

She had been standing, listening to the conversation in a sort of trance. Now she jumped into the fight with a vim that turned Renshaw's attention to her in a second.

"No, madam, I am not mad. Nor, despite the interested assertions of certain parties whom I need not specify by name, is Mr. Brackett. It may be news to you, Mrs. Ferguson, that an action is even now pending in New York, whereby certain parties are attempting to show that my client, Mr. Brackett, is non compos and should be legally restrained from exercising control over his property. Their case is extremely weak, for even if we admit their contention that our client did, on the eighteenth of June last, attempt to walk up Fifth Avenue in his pyjamas, we shall be able to show that his action was the result of an election bet. But as the parties to whom I have alluded will undoubtedly snatch at every straw in their efforts to prove that Mr. Brackett is mentally infirm, the prejudicial effect of this publication cannot be over-estimated. Unless Mr. Brackett can clear himself of the stigma of having given two thousand pounds for this extraordinary production of an absolutely unknown artist, the strength of his case must be seriously shaken. I may add that my client's lavish patronage of Art is already one of the main planks in the platform of the parties already referred to. They adduce his extremely generous expenditure in this direction as evidence that he is incapable of a proper handling of his money. I need scarcely point out with what sinister pleasure, therefore, they must have contemplated—this."

And he looked at "The Coming of Summer" as if it were a black beetle.

I must say, much as I disliked the blighter, I couldn't help feeling that he had right on his side. It hadn't occurred to me in quite that light before, but, considering it calmly now, I could see that a man who would disgorge two thousand of the best for Archie's Futurist masterpiece might very well step straight into the nut factory, and no questions asked.

Mrs. Archie came right back at him, as game as you please.

"I am sorry for Mr. Brackett's domestic troubles, but my husband can prove without difficulty that he did buy the picture. Can't you, dear?"

Archie, extremely white about the gills, looked at the ceiling and at the floor and at me and Renshaw Liggett.

"No," he said finally. "I can't. Because he didn't."

"Exactly," said Renshaw, "and I must ask you to publish that statement in tomorrow's papers without fail." He rose, and made for the door. "My client has no objection to young artists advertising themselves, realizing that this is an age of strenuous competition, but he firmly refuses to permit them to do it at his expense. Good afternoon."

And he legged it, leaving behind him one of the most chunky silences I have ever been mixed up in. For the life of me, I couldn't see who was to make the next remark. I was jolly certain that it wasn't going to be me.

Eventually Mrs. Archie opened the proceedings.

"What does it mean?"

Archie turned to me with a sort of frozen calm.

"Reggie, would you mind stepping into the kitchen and asking Julia for this week's *Funny Slices*? I know she has it."

He was right. She unearthed it from a cupboard. I trotted back with it to the sitting room. Archie took the paper from me, and held it out to his wife, Doughnuts uppermost.

"Look!" he said.

She looked.

"I do them. I have done them every week for three years. No, don't speak yet. Listen. This is where all my money came from, all the money I lost when B. and O. P. Rails went smash. And this is where the money came from to buy 'The Coming of Summer.' It wasn't Brackett who bought it; it was myself."

Mrs. Archie was devouring the Doughnuts with wide-open eyes. I caught a glimpse of them myself, and only just managed not to laugh, for it was the set of pictures where Pa Doughnut tries to fix the electric light, one of the very finest things dear old Archie had ever done.

"I don't understand," she said.

"I draw these things. I have sold my soul."

"Archie!"

He winced, but stuck to it bravely.

"Yes, I knew how you would feel about it, and that was why I didn't dare to tell you, and why we fixed up this story about old Brackett. I couldn't bear to live on you any longer, and to see you roughing it here, when we might be having all the money we wanted."

Suddenly, like a boiler exploding, she began to laugh.

"They're the funniest things I ever saw in my life," she gurgled. "Mr. Pepper, do look! He's trying to cut the electric wire with the scissors, and everything blazes up. And you've been hiding this from me all that time!"

Archie goggled dumbly. She dived at a table, and picked up a magazine, pointing to one of the advertisement pages.

"Read!" she cried. "Read it aloud."

And in a shaking voice Archie read:

> You think you are perfectly well, don't you? You wake up in the morning and spring out of bed and say to yourself that you have never been better in your life. You're wrong! Unless you are avoiding coffee as you would avoid the man who always tells you the smart things his little boy said yesterday, and drinking
>
> SAFETY FIRST MOLASSINE
>
> for breakfast, you cannot be
>
> Perfectly Well.

It is a physical impossibility. Coffee contains an appreciable quantity of the deadly drug caffeine, and therefore —

"I wrote *that,*" she said. "And I wrote the advertisement of the Spiller Baby Food on page ninety-four, and the one about the Preeminent Breakfast Sausage on page eighty-six. Oh, Archie, dear, the torments I have been through, fearing that you would some day find me out and despise me. I couldn't help it. I had no private means, and I didn't make enough out of my poetry to keep me in hats. I learned to write advertisements four years ago at a correspondence school, and I've been doing them ever since. And now I don't mind your knowing, now that you have told me this perfectly splendid news. Archie!"

She rushed into his arms like someone charging in for a bowl of soup at a railway station buffet. And I drifted out. It seemed to me that this was a scene in which I was not on. I sidled to the door, and slid forth. They didn't notice me. My experience is that nobody ever does — much.

The Test Case

WELL-MEANING chappies at the club sometimes amble up to me and tap me on the wishbone, and say "Reggie, old top," — my name's Reggie Pepper — "you ought to get married, old man." Well, what I mean to say is, it's all very well, and I see their point and all that sort of thing; but it takes two to make a marriage, and to date I haven't met a girl who didn't seem to think the contract was too big to be taken on.

Looking back, it seems to me that I came nearer to getting over the home-plate with Ann Selby than with most of the others. In fact, but for circumstances over which I had no dashed control, I am inclined to think that we should have brought it off. I'm bound to say that, now that what the poet chappie calls the first fine frenzy has been on the ice for awhile and I am able to consider the thing calmly, I am deuced glad we didn't. She was one of those strong-minded girls, and I hate to think of what she would have done to me.

At the time, though, I was frightfully in love, and, for quite a while after she definitely gave me the mitten, I lost my stroke at golf so completely that a child could have given me a stroke a hole and got away with it. I was all broken up, and I contend to this day that I was dashed badly treated.

Let me give you what they call the data.

One day I was lunching with Ann, and was just proposing to her as usual, when, instead of simply refusing me, as she generally did, she fixed me with a thoughtful eye and kind of opened her heart.

"Do you know, Reggie, I am in doubt."

"Give me the benefit of it," I said. Which I maintain was pretty good on the spur of the moment, but didn't get a hand. She simply ignored it, and went on.

"Sometimes," she said, "you seem to me entirely vapid and brainless; at other times you say or do things which suggest that there are possibilities in you; that, properly stimulated and encouraged, you might overcome the handicap of large private means and do something worthwhile. I wonder if that is simply my imagination?" She watched me very closely as she spoke.

"Rather not. You've absolutely summed me up. With you beside me, stimulating and all that sort of rot, don't you know, I should show a flash of speed which would astonish you."

"I wish I could be certain."

"Take a chance on it."

She shook her head.

"I must be certain. Marriage is such a gamble. I have just been staying with my sister Hilda and her husband——"

"Dear old Harold Bodkin. I know him well. In fact, I've a standing invitation to go down there and stay as long as I like. Harold is one of my best pals. Harold is a corker. Good old Harold is——"

"I would rather you didn't eulogize him, Reggie. I am extremely angry with Harold. He is making Hilda perfectly miserable."

"What on earth do you mean? Harold wouldn't dream of hurting a fly. He's one of those dreamy, sentimental chumps who——"

"It is precisely his sentimentality which is at the bottom of the whole trouble. You know, of course, that Hilda is not his first wife?"

"That's right. His first wife died about five years ago."

"He still cherishes her memory."

"Very sporting of him."

"Is it! If you were a girl, how would you like to be married to a man who was always making you bear in mind that you were only number two in his affections; a man whose idea of a pleasant conversation was a string of anecdotes illustrating what a dear woman his first wife was. A man who expected you to upset all your plans if they clashed with some anniversary connected with his other marriage?"

"That does sound pretty rotten. Does Harold do all that?"

"That's only a small part of what he does. Why, if you will believe me, every evening at seven o'clock he goes and shuts himself up in a little room at the top of the house, and meditates."

"What on earth does he do that for?"

"Apparently his first wife died at seven in the evening. There is a portrait of her in the room. I believe he lays flowers in front of it. And Hilda is expected to greet him on his return with a happy smile."

"Why doesn't she kick?"

"I have been trying to persuade her to, but she won't. She just pretends she doesn't mind. She has a nervous, sensitive temperament, and the thing is slowly crushing her. Don't talk to me of Harold."

Considering that she had started him as a topic, I thought this pretty unjust. I didn't want to talk of Harold. I wanted to talk about myself.

"Well, what has all this got to do with your not wanting to marry me?" I said.

"Nothing, except that it is an illustration of the risks a woman runs when she marries a man of a certain type."

"Great Scot! You surely don't class me with Harold?"

"Yes, in a way you are very much alike. You have both always had large private means, and have never had the wholesome discipline of work."

"But, dash it, Harold, on your showing, is an absolute nut. Why should you think that I would be anything like that?"

"There's always the risk."

A hot idea came to me.

"Look here, Ann," I said, "Suppose I pull off some stunt which only a deuced brainy chappie could get away with? Would you marry me then?"

"Certainly. What do you propose to do?"

"Do! What do I propose to do! Well, er, to be absolutely frank, at the moment I don't quite know."

"You never will know, Reggie. You're one of the idle rich, and your brain, if you ever had one, has atrophied."

Well, that seemed to me to put the lid on it. I didn't mind a heart-to-heart talk, but this was mere abuse. I changed the subject.

"What would you like after that fish?" I said coldly.

You know how it is when you get an idea. For awhile it sort of simmers inside you, and then suddenly it sizzles up like a rocket, and there you are, right up against it. That's what happened now. I went away from that luncheon, vaguely determined to pull off some stunt which would prove that I was right there with the gray matter, but without any clear notion of what I was going to do. Side by side with this in my mind was the case of dear old Harold. When I wasn't brooding on the stunt, I was brooding on Harold. I was fond of the good old lad, and I hated the idea of his slowly wrecking the home purely by being a chump. And all of a sudden the two things clicked together like a couple of chemicals, and there I was with a corking plan for killing two birds with one stone—putting one across that would startle and impress Ann, and at the same time healing the breach between Harold and Hilda.

My idea was that, in a case like this, it's no good trying opposition. What you want is to work it so that the chappie quits of his own accord. You want to egg him on to overdoing the thing till he gets so that he says to himself, "Enough! Never again!" That was what was going to happen to Harold.

When you're going to do a thing, there's nothing like making a quick start. I wrote to Harold straight away, proposing myself for a visit. And Harold wrote back telling me to come right along.

Harold and Hilda lived alone in a large house. I believe they did a good deal of entertaining at times, but on this occasion I was the only guest. The only other person of note in the place was Ponsonby, the butler.

Of course, if Harold had been an ordinary sort of chappie, what I had come to do would have been a pretty big order. I don't mind many things, but I do hesitate to dig into my host's intimate private affairs. But Harold was such a simple-minded Johnnie, so grateful for a little sympathy and advice, that my job wasn't so very difficult.

It wasn't as if he minded talking about Amelia, which was his first wife's name. The difficulty was to get him to talk of anything else. I began to understand what Ann meant by saying it was tough on Hilda.

I'm bound to say the old boy was clay in my hands. People call me a chump, but Harold was a super-chump, and I did what I liked with him. The second morning of my visit, after breakfast, he grabbed me by the arm.

"This way, Reggie. I'm just going to show old Reggie Amelia's portrait, dear."

There was a little room all by itself on the top floor. He explained to me that it had been his studio. At one time Harold used to do a bit of painting in an amateur way.

"There!" he said, pointing at the portrait. "I did that myself, Reggie. It was away being cleaned when you were here last. It's like dear Amelia, isn't it?"

I suppose it was, in a way. At any rate, you could recognize the likeness when you were told who it was supposed to be.

He sat down in front of it, and gave it the thoughtful once-over.

"Do you know, Reggie, old top, sometimes when I sit here, I feel as if Amelia were back again."

"It would be a bit awkward for you if she was."

"How do you mean?"

"Well, old lad, you happen to be married to someone else."

A look of childlike enthusiasm came over his face.

"Reggie, I want to tell you how splendid Hilda is. Lots of other women might object to my still cherishing Amelia's memory, but Hilda has been so nice about it from the beginning. She understands so thoroughly."

I hadn't much breath left after that, but I used what I had to say: "She doesn't object?"

"Not a bit," said Harold. "It makes everything so pleasant."

When I had recovered a bit, I said, "What do you mean by everything?"

"Well," he said, "for instance, I come up here every evening at seven and—er—think for a few minutes."

"A few minutes?!"

"What do you mean?"

"Well, a few minutes isn't long."

"But I always have my cocktail at a quarter past."

"You could postpone it."

"And Ponsonby likes us to start dinner at seven-thirty."

"What on earth has Ponsonby to do with it?"

"Well, he likes to get off by nine, you know. I think he goes off and plays bowls at the roadhouse. You see, Reggie, old man, we have to study Ponsonby a little. He's always on the verge of giving notice — in fact, it was only by coaxing him on one or two occasions that we got him to stay on — and he's such a treasure that I don't know what we should do if we lost him. But, if you think that I ought to stay longer —— ?"

"Certainly I do. You ought to do a thing like this properly, or not at all."

He sighed.

"It's a frightful risk, but in future we'll dine at eight."

It seemed to me that there was a suspicion of a cloud on Ponsonby's shining morning face, when the news was broken to him that for the future he couldn't unleash himself on the local bowling talent as early as usual, but he made no kick, and the new order of things began.

My next offensive movement I attribute to a flash of absolute genius. I was glancing through a photograph album in the drawing-room before lunch, when I came upon a face which I vaguely remembered. It was one of those wide, flabby faces, with bulging eyes, and something about it struck me as familiar. I consulted Harold, who came in at that moment.

"That?" said Harold. "That's Percy." He gave a slight shudder. "Amelia's brother, you know. An awful fellow. I haven't seen him for years."

Then I placed Percy. I had met him once or twice in the old days, and I had a brainwave. Percy was everything that poor old Harold disliked most. He was hearty at breakfast, a confirmed back-slapper, and a man who prodded you in the chest when he spoke to you.

"You haven't seen him for years!" I said in a shocked voice.

"Thank heaven!" said Harold devoutly.

I put down the photograph album, and looked at him in a deuced serious way. "Then it's high time you asked him to come here."

Harold blanched. "Reggie, old man, you don't know what you are saying. You can't remember Percy. I wish you wouldn't say these things, even in fun."

"I'm not saying it in fun. Of course, it's none of my business, but you have paid me the compliment of confiding in me about Amelia, and I feel justified in speaking. All I can say is that, if you cherish her memory as you say you do, you show it in a very strange way. How you can square your neglect of Percy with your alleged devotion to Amelia's memory, beats me. It seems to me that you have no choice. You must either drop the whole thing and admit that your love for her is dead, or else you must stop this infernal treatment of her favourite brother. You can't have it both ways."

He looked at me like a hunted stag. "But, Reggie, old man! Percy! He asks riddles at breakfast."

"I don't care."

"Hilda can't stand him."

"It doesn't matter. You must invite him. It's not a case of what you like or don't like. It's your duty."

He struggled with his feelings for a bit. "Very well," he said in a crushed sort of voice.

At dinner that night he said to Hilda: "I'm going to ask Amelia's brother down to spend a few days. It is so long since we have seen him."

Hilda didn't answer at once. She looked at him in rather a curious sort of way, I thought. "Very well, dear," she said.

I was deuced sorry for the poor girl, but I felt like a surgeon. She would be glad later on, for I was convinced that in a very short while poor old Harold must crack under the strain, especially after I had put across the coup which I was meditating for the very next evening.

It was quite simple. Simple, that is to say, in its working, but a devilish brainy thing for a chappie to have thought out. If Ann had really meant what she had said at lunch that day, and was prepared to stick to her bargain and marry me as soon as I showed a burst of intelligence, she was mine.

What it came to was that, if dear old Harold enjoyed meditating in front of Amelia's portrait, he was jolly well going to have all the meditating he wanted, and a bit over, for my simple scheme was to lurk outside till he had gone into the little room on the top floor, and then, with the aid of one of those jolly little wedges which you use to keep windows from rattling, see to it that the old boy remained there till they sent out search parties.

There wasn't a flaw in my reasoning. When Harold didn't roll in at the sound of the dinner gong, Hilda would take it for granted that he was doing an extra bit of meditating that night, and her pride would stop her sending out a hurry call for him. As for Harold, when he found that all was not well with the door, he would probably yell with considerable vim. But it was odds against anyone hearing him. As for me, you might think that I was going to suffer owing to the probable postponement of dinner. Not so, but far otherwise, for on the night I had selected for the coup I was dining out at the neighbouring inn with my old college chum

Freddy Meadowes. It is true that Freddie wasn't going to be within fifty miles of the place on that particular night, but they weren't to know that.

Did I describe the peculiar isolation of that room on the top floor, where the portrait was? I don't think I did. It was, as a matter of fact, the only room in those parts, for, in the days when he did his amateur painting, old Harold was strong on the artistic seclusion business and hated noise, and his studio was the only room in use on that floor.

In short, to sum up, the thing was a cinch.

Punctually at ten minutes to seven, I was in readiness on the scene. There was a recess with a curtain in front of it a few yards from the door, and there I waited, fondling my little wedge, for Harold to walk up and allow the proceedings to start. It was almost pitch-dark, and that made the time of waiting seem longer. Presently—I seemed to have been there longer than ten minutes—I heard steps approaching. They came past where I stood, and went on into the room. The door closed, and I hopped out and sprinted up to it, and the next moment I had the good old wedge under the wood—as neat a job as you could imagine. And then I strolled downstairs, and toddled off to the inn.

I didn't hurry over my dinner, partly because the browsing and sluicing at the inn was really astonishingly good for a roadhouse and partly because I wanted to give Harold plenty of time for meditation. I suppose it must have been a couple of hours or more when I finally turned in at the front door. Somebody was playing the piano in the drawing room. It could only be Hilda who was playing, and I had doubts as to whether she wanted company just then—mine, at any rate.

Eventually I decided to risk it, for I wanted to hear the latest about dear old Harold, so in I went, and it wasn't Hilda at all; it was Ann Selby.

"Hello," I said. "I didn't know you were coming down here." It seemed so odd, don't you know, as it hadn't been more than ten days or so since her last visit.

"Good evening, Reggie," she said.

"What's been happening?" I asked.

"How do you know anything has been happening?"

"I guessed it."

"Well, you're quite right, as it happens, Reggie. A good deal has been happening." She went to the door, and looked out, listening. Then she shut it, and came back. "Hilda has revolted!"

"Revolted?"

"Yes, put her foot down—made a stand—refused to go on meekly putting up with Harold's insane behaviour."

"I don't understand."

She gave me a look of pity. "You always were so dense, Reggie. I will tell you the whole thing from the beginning. You remember what I spoke to you about, one day when we were lunching together? Well, I don't suppose you have noticed it—I know what you are—but things have been getting steadily worse. For one thing, Harold insisted on lengthening his visits to the top room, and naturally Ponsonby complained. Hilda tells me that she had to plead with him to induce him to stay on. Then the climax came. I don't know if you recollect Amelia's brother Percy? You must have met him when she was alive—a perfectly unspeakable person with a loud voice and overpowering manners. Suddenly, out of a blue sky, Harold announced his intention of inviting him to stay. It was the last straw. This afternoon I received a telegram from poor Hilda, saying that she was leaving Harold and coming to stay with me, and a few hours later the poor child arrived at my apartment."

You mustn't suppose that I stood listening silently to this speech. Every time she seemed to be going to stop for breath I tried to horn in and tell her all these things which had been happening were not mere flukes, as she seemed to think, but parts of a deuced carefully planned scheme of my own. Every time I'd try to interrupt, Ann would wave me down, and carry on without so much as a semicolon.

But at this point I did manage a word in. "I know, I know, I know! I did it all. It was I who suggested to Harold that he should lengthen the meditations, and insisted on his inviting Percy to stay."

I had hardly got the words out, when I saw that they were not making the hit I had anticipated. She looked at me with an expression of absolute scorn, don't you know.

"Well, really, Reggie," she said at last, "I never have had a very high opinion of your intelligence, as you know, but this is a revelation to me. What motive you can have had, unless you did it in a spirit of pure mischief——" She stopped, and there was a glare of undiluted repulsion in her eyes. "Reggie! I can't believe it! Of all the things I loathe most, a practical joker is the worst. Do you mean to tell me you did all this as a practical joke?"

"Great Scot, no! It was like this——"

I paused for a bare second to collect my thoughts, so as to put the thing clearly to her. I might have known what would happen. She dashed right in and collared the conversation.

"Well, never mind. As it happens, there is no harm done. Quite the reverse, in fact. Hilda left a note for Harold telling him what she had done and where she had gone and why she had gone, and Harold found it. The result was that, after Hilda had been with me for some time, in he came in a panic and absolutely grovelled before the dear child. It seems incredible but he had apparently had no notion that his absurd behavior had met with anything but approval from Hilda. He went on as if he were mad. He was beside himself. He clutched his hair and stamped about the room, and then he jumped at the telephone and called this house and got Ponsonby and told him to go straight to the little room on the top floor and take Amelia's portrait down. I thought that a little unnecessary myself, but he was in such a whirl of remorse that it was useless to try and get him to be rational. So Hilda was consoled, and he calmed down, and we all came down here in the automobile. So you see —"

At this moment the door opened, and in came Harold.

"I say — hello, Reggie, old man — I say, it's a funny thing, but we can't find Ponsonby anywhere."

There are moments in a chappie's life, don't you know, when Reason, so to speak, totters, as it were, on its bally throne. This was one of them. The situation seemed somehow to have got out of my grip. I suppose, strictly speaking, I ought, at this juncture, to have cleared my throat and said in an audible tone, "Harold, old top, *I* know where Ponsonby is." But somehow I couldn't. Something seemed to keep the words back. I just stood there and said nothing.

"Nobody seems to have seen anything of him," said Harold. "I wonder where he can have got to."

Hilda came in, looking so happy I hardly recognized her. I remember feeling how strange it was that anybody could be happy just then.

"*I* know," she said. "Of course! Doesn't he always go off to the inn and play bowls at this time?"

"Why, of course," said Harold. "So he does."

And he asked Ann to play something on the piano. And pretty soon we had settled down to a regular jolly musical evening. Ann must have played a matter of two or three thousand tunes, when Harold got up.

"By the way," he said. "I suppose he did what I told him about the picture before he went out. Let's go and see."

"Oh, Harold, what does it matter?" asked Hilda.

"Don't be silly, Harold," said Ann.

I would have said the same thing, only I couldn't say anything.

Harold wasn't to be stopped. He led the way out of the room and upstairs, and we all trailed after him. We had just reached the top floor, when Hilda stopped, and said "Hark!"

It was a voice.

"Hi!" it said. "Hi!"

Harold legged it to the door of the studio. "Ponsonby?"

From within came the voice again, and I have never heard anything to touch the combined pathos, dignity and indignation it managed to condense into two words.

"Yes, sir?"

"What on earth are you doing in there?"

"I came here, sir, in accordance with your instructions on the telephone, and——"

Harold rattled the door. "The darned thing's stuck."

"Yes, sir."

"How on earth did that happen?"

"I could not say, sir."

"How *can* the door have stuck like this?" said Ann.

Somebody—I suppose it was me, though the voice didn't sound familiar—spoke. "Perhaps there's a wedge under it," said this chappie.

"A wedge? What do you mean?"

"One of those little wedges you use to keep windows from rattling, don't you know."

"But why——? You're absolutely right, Reggie, old man, there is!"

He yanked it out, and flung the door open, and out came Ponsonby, looking like Lady Macbeth.

"I wish to give notice, sir," he said, "and I should esteem it a favor if I might go to the pantry and procure some food, as I am extremely hungry."

And he passed from our midst, with Hilda after him, saying: "But, Ponsonby! Be reasonable, Ponsonby!"

Ann Selby turned on me with a swish. "Reggie," she said, "did *you* shut Ponsonby in there?"

"Well, yes, as a matter of fact, I did."

"But why?" asked Harold.

"Well, to be absolutely frank, old top, I thought it was you."

"You thought it was me? But why—what did you want to lock me in for?"

I hesitated. It was a delicate business telling him the idea. And while I was hesitating, Ann jumped in.

"I can tell you why, Harold. It was because Reggie belongs to that sub-species of humanity known as practical jokers. This sort of thing is his idea of humour."

"Humour! Losing us a priceless butler," said Harold. "If that's your idea of——"

Hilda came back, pale and anxious. "Harold, dear, do come and help me reason with Ponsonby. He is in the pantry gnawing a cold chicken, and he only stops to say 'I give notice.' "

"Yes," said Ann. "Go, both of you. I wish to speak to Reggie alone."

That's how I came to lose Ann. At intervals during her remarks I tried to put my side of the case, but it was no good. She wouldn't listen. And presently something seemed to tell me that now was the time to go to my room and pack. Half an hour later I slid silently into the night.

Wasn't it Shakespeare or somebody who said that the road to Hell—or words to that effect—was paved with good intentions? If it was Shakespeare, it just goes to prove what they are always saying about him—that he knew a bit. Take it from one who knows, the old boy was absolutely right.

A CATALOG OF SELECTED

DOVER BOOKS

IN ALL FIELDS OF INTEREST

A CATALOG OF SELECTED DOVER BOOKS IN ALL FIELDS OF INTEREST

THE CLARINET AND CLARINET PLAYING, David Pino. Lively, comprehensive work features suggestions about technique, musicianship, and musical interpretation, as well as guidelines for teaching, making your own reeds, and preparing for public performance. Includes an intriguing look at clarinet history. "A godsend," *The Clarinet*, Journal of the International Clarinet Society. Appendixes. 7 illus. 320pp. 5⅜ x 8½. 40270-3

HOLLYWOOD GLAMOR PORTRAITS, John Kobal (ed.). 145 photos from 1926-49. Harlow, Gable, Bogart, Bacall; 94 stars in all. Full background on photographers, technical aspects. 160pp. 8⅜ x 11¼. 23352-9

THE ANNOTATED CASEY AT THE BAT: A Collection of Ballads about the Mighty Casey/Third, Revised Edition, Martin Gardner (ed.). Amusing sequels and parodies of one of America's best-loved poems: Casey's Revenge, Why Casey Whiffed, Casey's Sister at the Bat, others. 256pp. 5⅜ x 8½. 28598-7

THE RAVEN AND OTHER FAVORITE POEMS, Edgar Allan Poe. Over 40 of the author's most memorable poems: "The Bells," "Ulalume," "Israfel," "To Helen," "The Conqueror Worm," "Eldorado," "Annabel Lee," many more. Alphabetic lists of titles and first lines. 64pp. 5$\frac{3}{16}$ x 8¼. 26685-0

PERSONAL MEMOIRS OF U. S. GRANT, Ulysses Simpson Grant. Intelligent, deeply moving firsthand account of Civil War campaigns, considered by many the finest military memoirs ever written. Includes letters, historic photographs, maps and more. 528pp. 6⅛ x 9¼. 28587-1

ANCIENT EGYPTIAN MATERIALS AND INDUSTRIES, A. Lucas and J. Harris. Fascinating, comprehensive, thoroughly documented text describes this ancient civilization's vast resources and the processes that incorporated them in daily life, including the use of animal products, building materials, cosmetics, perfumes and incense, fibers, glazed ware, glass and its manufacture, materials used in the mummification process, and much more. 544pp. 6⅛ x 9¼. (Available in U.S. only.) 40446-3

RUSSIAN STORIES/RUSSKIE RASSKAZY: A Dual-Language Book, edited by Gleb Struve. Twelve tales by such masters as Chekhov, Tolstoy, Dostoevsky, Pushkin, others. Excellent word-for-word English translations on facing pages, plus teaching and study aids, Russian/English vocabulary, biographical/critical introductions, more. 416pp. 5⅜ x 8½. 26244-8

PHILADELPHIA THEN AND NOW: 60 Sites Photographed in the Past and Present, Kenneth Finkel and Susan Oyama. Rare photographs of City Hall, Logan Square, Independence Hall, Betsy Ross House, other landmarks juxtaposed with contemporary views. Captures changing face of historic city. Introduction. Captions. 128pp. 8¼ x 11. 25790-8

AIA ARCHITECTURAL GUIDE TO NASSAU AND SUFFOLK COUNTIES, LONG ISLAND, The American Institute of Architects, Long Island Chapter, and the Society for the Preservation of Long Island Antiquities. Comprehensive, well-researched and generously illustrated volume brings to life over three centuries of Long Island's great architectural heritage. More than 240 photographs with authoritative, extensively detailed captions. 176pp. 8¼ x 11. 26946-9

NORTH AMERICAN INDIAN LIFE: Customs and Traditions of 23 Tribes, Elsie Clews Parsons (ed.). 27 fictionalized essays by noted anthropologists examine religion, customs, government, additional facets of life among the Winnebago, Crow, Zuni, Eskimo, other tribes. 480pp. 6⅛ x 9¼. 27377-6

FRANK LLOYD WRIGHT'S DANA HOUSE, Donald Hoffmann. Pictorial essay of residential masterpiece with over 160 interior and exterior photos, plans, elevations, sketches and studies. 128pp. 9¼ x 10¾. 29120-0

THE MALE AND FEMALE FIGURE IN MOTION: 60 Classic Photographic Sequences, Eadweard Muybridge. 60 true-action photographs of men and women walking, running, climbing, bending, turning, etc., reproduced from rare 19th-century masterpiece. vi + 121pp. 9 x 12. 24745-7

1001 QUESTIONS ANSWERED ABOUT THE SEASHORE, N. J. Berrill and Jacquelyn Berrill. Queries answered about dolphins, sea snails, sponges, starfish, fishes, shore birds, many others. Covers appearance, breeding, growth, feeding, much more. 305pp. 5¼ x 8¼. 23366-9

ATTRACTING BIRDS TO YOUR YARD, William J. Weber. Easy-to-follow guide offers advice on how to attract the greatest diversity of birds: birdhouses, feeders, water and waterers, much more. 96pp. 5³⁄₁₆ x 8¼. 28927-3

MEDICINAL AND OTHER USES OF NORTH AMERICAN PLANTS: A Historical Survey with Special Reference to the Eastern Indian Tribes, Charlotte Erichsen-Brown. Chronological historical citations document 500 years of usage of plants, trees, shrubs native to eastern Canada, northeastern U.S. Also complete identifying information. 343 illustrations. 544pp. 6½ x 9¼. 25951-X

STORYBOOK MAZES, Dave Phillips. 23 stories and mazes on two-page spreads: Wizard of Oz, Treasure Island, Robin Hood, etc. Solutions. 64pp. 8¼ x 11. 23628-5

AMERICAN NEGRO SONGS: 230 Folk Songs and Spirituals, Religious and Secular, John W. Work. This authoritative study traces the African influences of songs sung and played by black Americans at work, in church, and as entertainment. The author discusses the lyric significance of such songs as "Swing Low, Sweet Chariot," "John Henry," and others and offers the words and music for 230 songs. Bibliography. Index of Song Titles. 272pp. 6½ x 9¼. 40271-1

MOVIE-STAR PORTRAITS OF THE FORTIES, John Kobal (ed.). 163 glamor, studio photos of 106 stars of the 1940s: Rita Hayworth, Ava Gardner, Marlon Brando, Clark Gable, many more. 176pp. 8⅜ x 11¼. 23546-7

BENCHLEY LOST AND FOUND, Robert Benchley. Finest humor from early 30s, about pet peeves, child psychologists, post office and others. Mostly unavailable elsewhere. 73 illustrations by Peter Arno and others. 183pp. 5⅜ x 8½. 22410-4

YEKL and THE IMPORTED BRIDEGROOM AND OTHER STORIES OF YIDDISH NEW YORK, Abraham Cahan. Film Hester Street based on *Yekl* (1896). Novel, other stories among first about Jewish immigrants on N.Y.'s East Side. 240pp. 5⅜ x 8½. 22427-9

SELECTED POEMS, Walt Whitman. Generous sampling from *Leaves of Grass*. Twenty-four poems include "I Hear America Singing," "Song of the Open Road," "I Sing the Body Electric," "When Lilacs Last in the Dooryard Bloom'd," "O Captain! My Captain!"–all reprinted from an authoritative edition. Lists of titles and first lines. 128pp. 5³⁄₁₆ x 8¼. 26878-0

LITTLE BOOK OF EARLY AMERICAN CRAFTS AND TRADES, Peter Stockham (ed.). 1807 children's book explains crafts and trades: baker, hatter, cooper, potter, and many others. 23 copperplate illustrations. 140pp. 4⅝ x 6. 23336-7

VICTORIAN FASHIONS AND COSTUMES FROM HARPER'S BAZAR, 1867–1898, Stella Blum (ed.). Day costumes, evening wear, sports clothes, shoes, hats, other accessories in over 1,000 detailed engravings. 320pp. 9⅜ x 12¼. 22990-4

GUSTAV STICKLEY, THE CRAFTSMAN, Mary Ann Smith. Superb study surveys broad scope of Stickley's achievement, especially in architecture. Design philosophy, rise and fall of the Craftsman empire, descriptions and floor plans for many Craftsman houses, more. 86 black-and-white halftones. 31 line illustrations. Introduction 208pp. 6½ x 9¼. 27210-9

THE LONG ISLAND RAIL ROAD IN EARLY PHOTOGRAPHS, Ron Ziel. Over 220 rare photos, informative text document origin (1844) and development of rail service on Long Island. Vintage views of early trains, locomotives, stations, passengers, crews, much more. Captions. 8⅞ x 11¾. 26301-0

VOYAGE OF THE LIBERDADE, Joshua Slocum. Great 19th-century mariner's thrilling, first-hand account of the wreck of his ship off South America, the 35-foot boat he built from the wreckage, and its remarkable voyage home. 128pp. 5⅜ x 8½. 40022-0

TEN BOOKS ON ARCHITECTURE, Vitruvius. The most important book ever written on architecture. Early Roman aesthetics, technology, classical orders, site selection, all other aspects. Morgan translation. 331pp. 5⅜ x 8½. 20645-9

THE HUMAN FIGURE IN MOTION, Eadweard Muybridge. More than 4,500 stopped-action photos, in action series, showing undraped men, women, children jumping, lying down, throwing, sitting, wrestling, carrying, etc. 390pp. 7⅞ x 10⅝. 20204-6 Clothbd.

TREES OF THE EASTERN AND CENTRAL UNITED STATES AND CANADA, William M. Harlow. Best one-volume guide to 140 trees. Full descriptions, woodlore, range, etc. Over 600 illustrations. Handy size. 288pp. 4½ x 6⅜. 20395-6

SONGS OF WESTERN BIRDS, Dr. Donald J. Borror. Complete song and call repertoire of 60 western species, including flycatchers, juncoes, cactus wrens, many more–includes fully illustrated booklet. Cassette and manual 99913-0

GROWING AND USING HERBS AND SPICES, Milo Miloradovich. Versatile handbook provides all the information needed for cultivation and use of all the herbs and spices available in North America. 4 illustrations. Index. Glossary. 236pp. 5⅜ x 8½. 25058-X

BIG BOOK OF MAZES AND LABYRINTHS, Walter Shepherd. 50 mazes and labyrinths in all–classical, solid, ripple, and more–in one great volume. Perfect inexpensive puzzler for clever youngsters. Full solutions. 112pp. 8⅛ x 11. 22951-3

PIANO TUNING, J. Cree Fischer. Clearest, best book for beginner, amateur. Simple repairs, raising dropped notes, tuning by easy method of flattened fifths. No previous skills needed. 4 illustrations. 201pp. 5⅜ x 8½. 23267-0

HINTS TO SINGERS, Lillian Nordica. Selecting the right teacher, developing confidence, overcoming stage fright, and many other important skills receive thoughtful discussion in this indispensible guide, written by a world-famous diva of four decades' experience. 96pp. 5⅜ x 8½. 40094-8

THE COMPLETE NONSENSE OF EDWARD LEAR, Edward Lear. All nonsense limericks, zany alphabets, Owl and Pussycat, songs, nonsense botany, etc., illustrated by Lear. Total of 320pp. 5⅜ x 8½. (Available in U.S. only.) 20167-8

VICTORIAN PARLOUR POETRY: An Annotated Anthology, Michael R. Turner. 117 gems by Longfellow, Tennyson, Browning, many lesser-known poets. "The Village Blacksmith," "Curfew Must Not Ring Tonight," "Only a Baby Small," dozens more, often difficult to find elsewhere. Index of poets, titles, first lines. xxiii + 325pp. 5⅜ x 8¼. 27044-0

DUBLINERS, James Joyce. Fifteen stories offer vivid, tightly focused observations of the lives of Dublin's poorer classes. At least one, "The Dead," is considered a masterpiece. Reprinted complete and unabridged from standard edition. 160pp. 5$\frac{3}{16}$ x 8¼. 26870-5

GREAT WEIRD TALES: 14 Stories by Lovecraft, Blackwood, Machen and Others, S. T. Joshi (ed.). 14 spellbinding tales, including "The Sin Eater," by Fiona McLeod, "The Eye Above the Mantel," by Frank Belknap Long, as well as renowned works by R. H. Barlow, Lord Dunsany, Arthur Machen, W. C. Morrow and eight other masters of the genre. 256pp. 5⅜ x 8½. (Available in U.S. only.) 40436-6

THE BOOK OF THE SACRED MAGIC OF ABRAMELIN THE MAGE, translated by S. MacGregor Mathers. Medieval manuscript of ceremonial magic. Basic document in Aleister Crowley, Golden Dawn groups. 268pp. 5⅜ x 8½. 23211-5

NEW RUSSIAN-ENGLISH AND ENGLISH-RUSSIAN DICTIONARY, M. A. O'Brien. This is a remarkably handy Russian dictionary, containing a surprising amount of information, including over 70,000 entries. 366pp. 4½ x 6⅛. 20208-9

HISTORIC HOMES OF THE AMERICAN PRESIDENTS, Second, Revised Edition, Irvin Haas. A traveler's guide to American Presidential homes, most open to the public, depicting and describing homes occupied by every American President from George Washington to George Bush. With visiting hours, admission charges, travel routes. 175 photographs. Index. 160pp. 8¼ x 11. 26751-2

NEW YORK IN THE FORTIES, Andreas Feininger. 162 brilliant photographs by the well-known photographer, formerly with *Life* magazine. Commuters, shoppers, Times Square at night, much else from city at its peak. Captions by John von Hartz. 181pp. 9¼ x 10¾. 23585-8

INDIAN SIGN LANGUAGE, William Tomkins. Over 525 signs developed by Sioux and other tribes. Written instructions and diagrams. Also 290 pictographs. 111pp. 6⅛ x 9¼. 22029-X

ANATOMY: A Complete Guide for Artists, Joseph Sheppard. A master of figure drawing shows artists how to render human anatomy convincingly. Over 460 illustrations. 224pp. 8⅜ x 11¼. 27279-6

MEDIEVAL CALLIGRAPHY: Its History and Technique, Marc Drogin. Spirited history, comprehensive instruction manual covers 13 styles (ca. 4th century through 15th). Excellent photographs; directions for duplicating medieval techniques with modern tools. 224pp. 8⅜ x 11¼. 26142-5

DRIED FLOWERS: How to Prepare Them, Sarah Whitlock and Martha Rankin. Complete instructions on how to use silica gel, meal and borax, perlite aggregate, sand and borax, glycerine and water to create attractive permanent flower arrangements. 12 illustrations. 32pp. 5⅜ x 8½. 21802-3

EASY-TO-MAKE BIRD FEEDERS FOR WOODWORKERS, Scott D. Campbell. Detailed, simple-to-use guide for designing, constructing, caring for and using feeders. Text, illustrations for 12 classic and contemporary designs. 96pp. 5⅜ x 8½. 25847-5

SCOTTISH WONDER TALES FROM MYTH AND LEGEND, Donald A. Mackenzie. 16 lively tales tell of giants rumbling down mountainsides, of a magic wand that turns stone pillars into warriors, of gods and goddesses, evil hags, powerful forces and more. 240pp. 5⅜ x 8½. 29677-6

THE HISTORY OF UNDERCLOTHES, C. Willett Cunnington and Phyllis Cunnington. Fascinating, well-documented survey covering six centuries of English undergarments, enhanced with over 100 illustrations: 12th-century laced-up bodice, footed long drawers (1795), 19th-century bustles, 19th-century corsets for men, Victorian "bust improvers," much more. 272pp. 5⅜ x 8¼. 27124-2

ARTS AND CRAFTS FURNITURE: The Complete Brooks Catalog of 1912, Brooks Manufacturing Co. Photos and detailed descriptions of more than 150 now very collectible furniture designs from the Arts and Crafts movement depict davenports, settees, buffets, desks, tables, chairs, bedsteads, dressers and more, all built of solid, quarter-sawed oak. Invaluable for students and enthusiasts of antiques, Americana and the decorative arts. 80pp. 6½ x 9¼. 27471-3

WILBUR AND ORVILLE: A Biography of the Wright Brothers, Fred Howard. Definitive, crisply written study tells the full story of the brothers' lives and work. A vividly written biography, unparalleled in scope and color, that also captures the spirit of an extraordinary era. 560pp. 6⅛ x 9¼. 40297-5

THE ARTS OF THE SAILOR: Knotting, Splicing and Ropework, Hervey Garrett Smith. Indispensable shipboard reference covers tools, basic knots and useful hitches; handsewing and canvas work, more. Over 100 illustrations. Delightful reading for sea lovers. 256pp. 5⅜ x 8½. 26440-8

FRANK LLOYD WRIGHT'S FALLINGWATER: The House and Its History, Second, Revised Edition, Donald Hoffmann. A total revision–both in text and illustrations–of the standard document on Fallingwater, the boldest, most personal architectural statement of Wright's mature years, updated with valuable new material from the recently opened Frank Lloyd Wright Archives. "Fascinating"–*The New York Times.* 116 illustrations. 128pp. 9¼ x 10¾. 27430-6

AUTOBIOGRAPHY: The Story of My Experiments with Truth, Mohandas K. Gandhi. Boyhood, legal studies, purification, the growth of the Satyagraha (nonviolent protest) movement. Critical, inspiring work of the man responsible for the freedom of India. 480pp. 5⅜ x 8½. (Available in U.S. only.) 24593-4

CELTIC MYTHS AND LEGENDS, T. W. Rolleston. Masterful retelling of Irish and Welsh stories and tales. Cuchulain, King Arthur, Deirdre, the Grail, many more. First paperback edition. 58 full-page illustrations. 512pp. 5⅜ x 8½. 26507-2

THE PRINCIPLES OF PSYCHOLOGY, William James. Famous long course complete, unabridged. Stream of thought, time perception, memory, experimental methods; great work decades ahead of its time. 94 figures. 1,391pp. 5⅜ x 8½. 2-vol. set.
Vol. I: 20381-6 Vol. II: 20382-4

THE WORLD AS WILL AND REPRESENTATION, Arthur Schopenhauer. Definitive English translation of Schopenhauer's life work, correcting more than 1,000 errors, omissions in earlier translations. Translated by E. F. J. Payne. Total of 1,269pp. 5⅜ x 8½. 2-vol. set. Vol. 1: 21761-2 Vol. 2: 21762-0

MAGIC AND MYSTERY IN TIBET, Madame Alexandra David-Neel. Experiences among lamas, magicians, sages, sorcerers, Bonpa wizards. A true psychic discovery. 32 illustrations. 321pp. 5⅜ x 8½. (Available in U.S. only.) 22682-4

THE EGYPTIAN BOOK OF THE DEAD, E. A. Wallis Budge. Complete reproduction of Ani's papyrus, finest ever found. Full hieroglyphic text, interlinear transliteration, word-for-word translation, smooth translation. 533pp. 6½ x 9¼. 21866-X

MATHEMATICS FOR THE NONMATHEMATICIAN, Morris Kline. Detailed, college-level treatment of mathematics in cultural and historical context, with numerous exercises. Recommended Reading Lists. Tables. Numerous figures. 641pp. 5⅜ x 8½. 24823-2

PROBABILISTIC METHODS IN THE THEORY OF STRUCTURES, Isaac Elishakoff. Well-written introduction covers the elements of the theory of probability from two or more random variables, the reliability of such multivariable structures, the theory of random function, Monte Carlo methods of treating problems incapable of exact solution, and more. Examples. 502pp. 5⅜ x 8½. 40691-1

THE RIME OF THE ANCIENT MARINER, Gustave Doré, S. T. Coleridge. Doré's finest work; 34 plates capture moods, subtleties of poem. Flawless full-size reproductions printed on facing pages with authoritative text of poem. "Beautiful. Simply beautiful."–*Publisher's Weekly.* 77pp. 9¼ x 12. 22305-1

NORTH AMERICAN INDIAN DESIGNS FOR ARTISTS AND CRAFTSPEOPLE, Eva Wilson. Over 360 authentic copyright-free designs adapted from Navajo blankets, Hopi pottery, Sioux buffalo hides, more. Geometrics, symbolic figures, plant and animal motifs, etc. 128pp. 8⅜ x 11. (Not for sale in the United Kingdom.) 25341-4

SCULPTURE: Principles and Practice, Louis Slobodkin. Step-by-step approach to clay, plaster, metals, stone; classical and modern. 253 drawings, photos. 255pp. 8⅛ x 11. 22960-2

THE INFLUENCE OF SEA POWER UPON HISTORY, 1660–1783, A. T. Mahan. Influential classic of naval history and tactics still used as text in war colleges. First paperback edition. 4 maps. 24 battle plans. 640pp. 5⅜ x 8½. 25509-3

CATALOG OF DOVER BOOKS

THE STORY OF THE TITANIC AS TOLD BY ITS SURVIVORS, Jack Winocour (ed.). What it was really like. Panic, despair, shocking inefficiency, and a little heroism. More thrilling than any fictional account. 26 illustrations. 320pp. 5⅜ x 8½. 20610-6

FAIRY AND FOLK TALES OF THE IRISH PEASANTRY, William Butler Yeats (ed.). Treasury of 64 tales from the twilight world of Celtic myth and legend: "The Soul Cages," "The Kildare Pooka," "King O'Toole and his Goose," many more. Introduction and Notes by W. B. Yeats. 352pp. 5⅜ x 8½. 26941-8

BUDDHIST MAHAYANA TEXTS, E. B. Cowell and others (eds.). Superb, accurate translations of basic documents in Mahayana Buddhism, highly important in history of religions. The Buddha-karita of Asvaghosha, Larger Sukhavativyuha, more. 448pp. 5⅜ x 8½. 25552-2

ONE TWO THREE . . . INFINITY: Facts and Speculations of Science, George Gamow. Great physicist's fascinating, readable overview of contemporary science: number theory, relativity, fourth dimension, entropy, genes, atomic structure, much more. 128 illustrations. Index. 352pp. 5⅜ x 8½. 25664-2

EXPERIMENTATION AND MEASUREMENT, W. J. Youden. Introductory manual explains laws of measurement in simple terms and offers tips for achieving accuracy and minimizing errors. Mathematics of measurement, use of instruments, experimenting with machines. 1994 edition. Foreword. Preface. Introduction. Epilogue. Selected Readings. Glossary. Index. Tables and figures. 128pp. 5⅜ x 8½. 40451-X

DALÍ ON MODERN ART: The Cuckolds of Antiquated Modern Art, Salvador Dalí. Influential painter skewers modern art and its practitioners. Outrageous evaluations of Picasso, Cézanne, Turner, more. 15 renderings of paintings discussed. 44 calligraphic decorations by Dalí. 96pp. 5⅜ x 8½. (Available in U.S. only.) 29220-7

ANTIQUE PLAYING CARDS: A Pictorial History, Henry René D'Allemagne. Over 900 elaborate, decorative images from rare playing cards (14th–20th centuries): Bacchus, death, dancing dogs, hunting scenes, royal coats of arms, players cheating, much more. 96pp. 9¼ x 12¼. 29265-7

MAKING FURNITURE MASTERPIECES: 30 Projects with Measured Drawings, Franklin H. Gottshall. Step-by-step instructions, illustrations for constructing handsome, useful pieces, among them a Sheraton desk, Chippendale chair, Spanish desk, Queen Anne table and a William and Mary dressing mirror. 224pp. 8⅛ x 11¼. 29338-6

THE FOSSIL BOOK: A Record of Prehistoric Life, Patricia V. Rich et al. Profusely illustrated definitive guide covers everything from single-celled organisms and dinosaurs to birds and mammals and the interplay between climate and man. Over 1,500 illustrations. 760pp. 7½ x 10⅛. 29371-8

Paperbound unless otherwise indicated. Available at your book dealer, online at **www.doverpublications.com**, or by writing to Dept. GI, Dover Publications, Inc., 31 East 2nd Street, Mineola, NY 11501. For current price information or for free catalogues (please indicate field of interest), write to Dover Publications or log on to **www.doverpublications.com** and see every Dover book in print. Dover publishes more than 500 books each year on science, elementary and advanced mathematics, biology, music, art, literary history, social sciences, and other areas.